a
Cat Café
Christmas

a Cat Café Christmas

CODI GARY

FOREVER
New York Boston

Forever
Hachette Book Group
1290 Avenue of the Americas, New York, NY 10104
read-forever.com
twitter.com/readforeverpub

First Edition: October 2022

Forever is an imprint of Grand Central Publishing. The Forever name and logo are trademarks of Hachette Book Group, Inc.

Print book interior design by Marie Mundaca

Library of Congress Cataloging-in-Publication Data

Names: Gary, Codi, author.
Title: A Cat Café Christmas / Codi Gary.
Description: First Edition. | New York : Forever, 2022.
Identifiers: LCCN 2022010809 | ISBN 9781538708156 (trade paperback) | ISBN 9781538708170 (ebook)
Subjects: LCGFT: Novels.
Classification: LCC PS3607.A782976 C38 2022 | DDC 813/.6--dc23
LC record available at https://lccn.loc.gov/2022010809

ISBNs: 9781538708156 (trade paperback), 9781538708170 (ebook)

Printed in the United States of America

LSC-C

Printing 3, 2022

This book is for Dr. Carolyn Standen, DVM, who took on a mess of an intern and taught her about veterinary medicine. You did so much for me and all the kitties you cared for. You are an amazing woman and friend. Thank you for everything.

Chapter One

Robin Hood is an orange tabby with gorgeous golden eyes and purrs for days, but watch out! He'll steal your heart and your food!

THE DARK CLOUDS DRIZZLED misty rain as Ben Reese stepped off the curb into a crosswalk and jogged across the street. Downtown Roseville was a suburban paradise that lacked the bumper-to-bumper traffic and tall buildings of neighboring Sacramento. He hated commuting, which is why he'd been excited to take a position at Kilburn Marketing, an up-and-coming marketing firm fifteen minutes from his new home. It was a far cry from his native Boston, but he expected to like the mild winters of Northern California.

Not to mention it took him three thousand miles away from the heartbreak and drama he'd left behind.

As he passed by the window display of the local bank, he chuckled at the falling leaves painted on the glass.

It was mid-November, that time of year when everyone was uploading posts about what they were thankful for to Instagram, just biding time until they could put up their Christmas trees.

He wouldn't be doing any of that this year. In fact, he'd given up social media before making the big move from the East to the West Coast, and it had done wonders for his peace of mind. While he knew it was an essential tool from a marketing standpoint, he didn't feel the need to chronicle his day via stylish pictures and goofy story-time videos. Especially since he didn't have much going on except for work and home improvements on his new place.

His office was a few blocks down on the left, but since it was Saturday, he wasn't heading there today. He'd come downtown to see how his new campaign was doing.

The city had hired Kilburn Marketing to bring more bustle to downtown Roseville this holiday season by drawing attention to the events and unique businesses along the strip. Ben had skimmed through the list of shops on the main stretch and picked out what he hoped was a solid first spotlight, and he wanted to check out the response to this morning's ad.

He rounded the corner onto Second Avenue, and a wave of triumph washed over him. A line of people twenty-five deep stretched out along the sidewalk, waiting for Meow and Furever Cat Café to open. The little pastry shop advertised gourmet coffee drinks, fun merch, and time spent with adoptable cats. His colleague Will Schwartz had dropped in last week to snap a few pictures of the place and its inhabitants for their first downtown feature. Ben had gone to Children of the Horn instead, a store for musical instruments and other kid-friendly creative outlets, to get an interview with the owner for their second feature, which would drop next week in time for Small Business Saturday. Ben thought he'd gotten the better deal. He'd rather listen to children scream and play out of tune than eat a cat-fur pastry and hack up a hair ball.

While he knew pets were a big deal to some people, Ben didn't understand the appeal of a feline companion. Cats were aloof jerks who got into everything and crapped anywhere they wanted. Dogs could be trained at the very least, although he wasn't into owning any animal if he was being honest. He liked his home quiet and orderly, unless he was using a drill. But the café was an unusual business that Kilburn and the city of Roseville thought would be a good start to the series.

Roseville Magazine included the ad this morning and offered the chance to win a fifty-dollar gift card to anyone who visited and snapped a selfie at the café, as long as they tagged Kilburn and the magazine in their post.

Apparently there were a lot of early birds ready to get that worm.

A high-pitched *eep* erupted behind him, and he turned to find a pale woman with copper hair piled high on her head in a messy bun. The collar of a hunter green peacoat was pulled up around her neck, probably to block the sprinkling rain. The thick coat hugged her chest and flared out over her full figure, something Ben could have appreciated if he was in the "interested" frame of mind, but after his last breakup, women were in the same category as Double Stuf Oreos—best avoided, as they did nothing but cause problems for him. He'd devoured packages of the sweet cookie sandwiches in one sitting for several weeks until he couldn't button his pants anymore, and it had taken him twice as long to work off the post-heartbreak weight. He'd always been a big-boned guy, but he'd taken the phrase "eating his feelings" to a whole new level.

Still, she was striking. Women who would blow away if a strong wind came up never appealed to him. The bridge of her nose sported an off-center bump, like she'd taken a good punch to it and never had it set right. A dash of freckles spread out over round cheeks, made darker by the pallor of her face, and wide hazel eyes stared past him at the crowd, lashes fluttering rapidly like the wings of a butterfly.

"What's happening?" she asked quietly.

Ben cocked his head. "Are you asking me or wondering aloud?"

The woman's gaze darted toward him at the same time she reached up with one hand to brush back a strand of damp wayward hair. "A little of both, I suppose."

"It depends on what you're talking about. If you're referring to the crowd of people over there, I'm pretty sure they're waiting for that café to open."

"But where did they come from?" she asked, her voice a touch too high, while gesturing emphatically. Clutched in her left hand was a baby blue leash, and his gaze traveled along the nylon yard, expecting to find a small dog cowering behind her black knee-high boots, but instead, a longhaired black-and-white cat stood next to her, its short, fluffy tail twitching rapidly as the feline regarded him with lemon-yellow eyes.

"Is that a cat... on a leash?"

Her eyes narrowed as she responded, her tone oozing sarcasm. "No, it's a pineapple on a string."

Ben threw up his hands in front of him in peace. "Whoa, it was just a question. I've never seen anyone walking a cat before."

She sighed loudly. "I'm sorry. I've had a rough morning, and this just buttercreams my cake."

Ben coughed, attempting to cover up his amusement at her charming turn of phrase and the way it sounded in her Southern accent. "The people at the café?" He checked his watch. "It doesn't open for another thirty minutes. If you can't stand in line for that long, there's another coffee shop two streets down."

The woman's mouth twisted up in a disgusted pout. "No, thank you. I don't need to spend five dollars on burnt coffee."

It was on the tip of his tongue to ask why cat-fur coffee was more appealing, but considering her companion, he kept that question to himself.

"I really can't deal with this right now." Her Southern accent grew stronger the more she spoke. "I have a gallon's worth of dry shampoo in my hair because my water wasn't working this morning and I couldn't shower, and when I finally got the fifth plumber I called on the phone, he said maybe he could get to me this afternoon for a cost, and I—" She groaned, running a free hand over her face. "I realize I am standing on the sidewalk complaining about my woes to a stranger."

"I'd say it happens all the time, but I think I'm pretty imposing. Most people take one look up at the beard and the resting jerk face and keep moving."

"You are rather tall and impressive. Ironically, I find the bearded look less intimidating than a clean-shaven face in a suit." She clicked her tongue, her gaze returning to the line. "Did you know that one in twenty-five people are sociopaths and many of them work in the corporate world?"

"That's a random factoid. Are you saying I look crazy?"

"No, I was thinking about suits and jobs, and based on how many people are standing over there, at least one of them is one."

"That's a little terrifying."

"Not really. Most sociopaths aren't violent. They get their kicks from firing people and backstabbing."

"Your train of thought is dizzying."

"Adult ADHD. I'll be talking a mile a minute about one thing and suddenly—squirrel!"

Ben didn't hide his amusement this time. "You don't say?"

"Was that you paraphrasing *The Princess Bride*, or do they use *dizzying* a lot where you're from?"

"Where do you think I'm from?" he asked.

"Somewhere back east?"

"Boston."

"Ah, I'm from Alabama. Couple of fishes out of water in the California sun, huh? Well—" She looked up at the gray clouds with a laugh. "California rain I guess is more accurate."

"Maybe. To answer your question, yes, I was paraphrasing.

It's my mother's favorite movie, so I spent a lot of nights watching it with her."

"I totally forgot I asked you a question, to be honest." The woman's lips twitched. "I think that's sweet."

"Funny enough, the guys at my school didn't love my Inigo Montoya impression."

"Oh no. Swirlies or wedgies?"

"Pantsing, actually. Yeah, right there as I walked up the steps of school. When I started wearing a belt, they still tried, but the guy got his finger stuck in my belt and"—Ben made a cracking sound, motioning with his hands like he was splitting a pencil in two—"broke it."

"Now that's karma." She smirked.

"Wow, you've got a mean streak."

"Only for bullies. Can't stand them." A large raindrop splashed against her cheek, and she looked up at the sky. "Drat. Of all the days for Michelle to be gone."

"Pardon?"

She cocked her head to the side, sending waves from her messy bun flying out of their constraints. "The café. I have to be up front today, and that is quite a crowd. I'm afraid I wasn't prepared."

"Oh, you work there?" That made sense, especially with her companion and her animosity toward another coffee house.

"Actually, I run it. Well, my best friend, Charity, and I do. She's the beautiful baker, and I'm the medical brains. Not that she isn't incredibly smart, but I have to have a skill too, right? And being the anxiety-plagued one doesn't have quite the same ring to it. Usually I'm in the back taking care of the cats and cleaning up messes, but we're down a barista." Her face suddenly snapped back into a scowl. "I wish I knew why these people were here."

"You sound upset about it. Doesn't more people mean more money and adoptions?"

"Technically, yes," she said, although her expression still read like she wasn't convinced. "But crowds are different than a steady stream of customers. I get anxious when there are too many people around me—and yes, I realize I am oversharing again, but you asked."

"I did." Ben watched the rapid rise and fall of her chest and grimaced. "Are you going to have an anxiety attack?"

"I'm not sure. I guess if I curl up in the fetal position and start rocking back and forth, you'll have your answer."

"I only ask because I'll feel responsible if you pass out on me."

Her dark eyebrows knitted together. "Why is that?"

Ben waved his hand toward the crowd. "I work for Kilburn Marketing, and the city is doing features on the downtown shops. Your café was our first story this morning in *Roseville Magazine*, and behold, it was a success."

"This is all because of an article?" she asked, her voice eerily calm.

"And a contest. The magazine is giving away a fifty-dollar gift card for sharing your café on social media."

"This..."

Ben rushed ahead, like he was pitching a sales point to a client. "I know it's a bit overwhelming, but your café has a unique concept that appeals to...a certain type of person."

Her scowl deepened. "I wasn't going to call this overwhelming. I was going to say *disastrous*."

"Disastrous?" The woman was off her rocker. Other shops would kill for this kind of exposure, especially with small businesses going under left and right.

"Yes! You basically bribed people who have no interest in our business to show up and attract more people. Who is to say they buy anything? They're going to be thundering through our lobby to take a picture and then leave without it benefiting us at all."

"Whoa, wait a second. I'm betting every single one of them grabs at least a coffee, and if ten people see their post online, statistically, at least one should check your rescue out in the future. Given, of course, that they're a..."

"A what? Someone with good taste?"

Taken aback by her suspicious tone, he spluttered, "You know. A cat person."

"Which you aren't, I take it?"

"To be honest, I'm not much for animals in general, but cats..." He had a feeling he was wandering into dangerous territory and caught himself.

"Cats are what? Awesome? Empathetic? Cuddle bugs? Entertaining?"

A high-pitched growl revved by her feet, and Ben looked down at her cat, who watched him with a similar expression as his mistress—ears pinned back, eyes narrowed, and that rumbling chain-saw noise erupting from its body.

"I don't need you or your company's help. Our nonprofit is doing fine."

Irritation sliced through Ben's gut. He couldn't believe

how ungrateful she was being, and he let his emotions get the better of him. "Yeah, if you expect the *non* to be literal," he sniped.

Her eyes widened, and he silently cursed himself. He didn't know this woman or her business, and here he was, standing on the sidewalk having a bickering match over something that wasn't even his idea. He was just the unlucky messenger.

"How do you know we aren't doing well?"

"I don't for sure, but my colleague came back after checking out your place and he said it was dead inside." *Why are you still talking? Just tell her to have a nice day and scram!*

Maybe because he'd been feeling so good about the campaign before she'd walked into his day and stomped on it like his job was a roach under her boot heel. Or that before she'd flipped the switch on him, he'd found her entertaining. Interesting.

Just another reason he couldn't trust his judgment when it came to women. She'd gone from a bundle of energy to a downer in three seconds flat. All because he'd steered more business her way.

"Look—" He started to apologize, but she cut him off with a sweep of her hand.

"I don't know what your *colleague*"—she sneered at the word like it tasted awful—"thinks he saw, but we do just fine! He probably came in at an off hour!"

Yep, it was definitely time to move on before the claws came out, and he wasn't talking about the cat. "Fine, my mistake. I'll be sure to pass on your displeasure to the city."

"Great!" she snapped, spinning away from him and

stomping around the crowd, her peacoat swishing to and fro with the same rhythm as her cat's tail.

What the heck just happened? He'd experienced irate clients when they didn't get enough exposure and return on investment, but too much?

Ben didn't like to entertain stereotypes, but maybe the crazy cat lady wasn't a myth after all.

Chapter Two

Fluffernutter McFluff is a white domestic longhair waiting for his special person to walk through the door. He doesn't do much, but he looks cute doing it!

Kara Ingalls muttered to herself as she scooped litter boxes, still peeved over the morning she'd had. She'd hit the snooze button a few times, trying to catch up on some much-needed sleep, but when Kara got up to brush her teeth, she realized her water wasn't working. Leaving the house without a shower, Kara spent the majority of her drive to work calling plumbers, finally finding one who could come out this afternoon to fix it—with a hundred-dollar premium attached to it since it was a Saturday. While the blow to her account was painful, she'd sell a kidney to get her water back.

That setback was bad enough, but she'd come into work expecting a slow day up front. It was just over a month before Christmas, and Kara knew the minute Thanksgiving hit, the holidays would rush by like a gust of wind. With the limited shopping time, she'd assumed most people would spend this weekend shopping for their Thanksgiving meals and prepping for Christmas, so being up front wouldn't be as stressful.

Instead, she'd pulled around and found the parking lot behind the café full, and she'd cursed the entire time she circled back to the parking garage at the end of Main Street. When Kara finally parked on the second level and released Theo from his crate, he'd simply twitched his little stub tail and trotted along while Kara stomped angrily to work, ready to have whoever parked in her spot towed.

Then she'd seen the line wrapped around the front of the building and slipped into a swirling vortex of panic.

Any other morning, Kara hung out in the back during rushes while Michelle and Charity served, but Michelle was visiting her parents in the Bay Area this weekend, so it was just the two of them. Staring into a large group of people waving cell phones around and snapping pictures brought on a host of bad memories she'd rather leave buried. And while maybe she shouldn't have dumped her upcoming anxiety attack on Mr. Bearded Marketing Guy, his holier-than-thou attitude rubbed her wrong.

Plus, you could never trust someone who didn't like animals. *Any animals!* A dog person was one thing, but someone who liked living alone without any kind of companionship?

Yep, definitely a sociopath.

He probably has a girlfriend to keep him company.

Kara hated the fact that, before she knew he was the catalyst to the cherry on top of her atrocious day, she'd checked out his ring finger, noting the lack of band. Not that she was looking for romantic entanglements, but he had lovely brown eyes and his smile was wide and warm. For a split second, a zing of attraction had sparked to life, and she'd almost asked him to join her for a coffee sometime.

Of course, the conversation took a downward spiral off a cliff after she'd found out that mess of people out front was his fault, talking about how their rescue was going to fail. He had no idea if that was true, no matter what his coworker saw.

What really stung was that the colleague hadn't been far off with his assessment. If they didn't figure out some way to attract more customers—*the right customers*—to come in and keep coming, they wouldn't last past January. They were already so deep in the red that Kara wasn't sure if they could dig themselves out without some kind of hefty donation. That didn't mean they needed to do big crowd-drawing events that wouldn't do anything more than sell "a cup of coffee," as he'd put it.

Kara scrubbed harder at the crusted wet food at the bottom of Matilda's cage, ignoring the cries of displeasure whenever Kara came too close to the moody calico's new dwelling in the row above. She had no idea what happened last night, but every cage looked like a bomb went off, and with only one empty, she couldn't just move the cats to a new clean cage and take care of the cleanup later.

When they'd built Meow and Furever, she'd included plans for a full veterinary clinic, open to the public for extra revenue to keep the café going, but they'd run out of funding before they could complete it. They'd managed to install a large wall of cages for cats to recover and quarantine before they were allowed into the social room, but the potential surgery prep room and suite were being used as storage at the moment. Kara had thought they'd be able to launch the clinic in the new year, but they were taking in more cats than they were adopting out, and at this rate, she'd been considering taking a job at a veterinary hospital on nights and weekends to help keep the café afloat.

Charity kept prodding Kara to establish a better social-media presence, but Kara knew the repercussions of going viral, and the last thing she wanted was the café to get drowned in negative attention because of her past.

"All right, Peanut," she murmured as she pulled the fat marbled tabby out of his dirty cage to move him into the clean one. "You made quite a mess, didn't you?"

The chunky cat purred in delight, twisting in her arms so he could make biscuits against her upper shoulder. When he headbutted her under the chin, her doldrums nearly melted under his sweet affections. Ironically named, the five-year-old domestic shorthair became her ward when his father moved out of state to marry a woman he met on social media who was allergic to cats.

For Kara, that would have been a dealbreaker, but she'd simply smiled and handed him paperwork. She didn't open Meow and Furever to counsel people on why they should keep their pets. It wasn't about them. It was about advocating for the cats who deserved better than to be dumped because they were no longer convenient.

Kara lifted Peanut into his new cage, rubbing his ears lightly before she closed the door. All the cats they fostered had their own personality quirks that would attract the right owner. It was just a matter of getting them in the door without having to put herself out there on social media.

Maybe we'll buy a coffee-cup costume and I can dance out front to lure people inside.

That would be better than having to suffer through the trolls and indignities of the online world. She grabbed a new rag and the disinfectant spray, going to work on Peanut's dirty cage. Kara was done with stupid people, crappy water pumps, and her black cloud of a mood. She was going to scrub the cranky away.

"Whew, you'll bust right through that steel cage if you keep attacking it like that."

Kara jumped and swung around to face Charity Simmons. "Good lord, you scared me! Where were you?"

Charity held up her hands and the two tote bags hanging from her fists, her long black hair swinging off her shoulders with the motion. "We needed more milk, so I ran down to the store after I got done filling the case. I called your name, but you were off in your own little world." Charity leaned against the side of the exam table, studying her with dark eyes. "You seem more wound up than usual. Is it the army of cat lovers outside or has something else got you in a tizzy?"

"They're not cat lovers," she grumbled. "They've been bribed to come here."

"I know. I read the ad and figured we'd be busy this morning. Are you okay with it?"

"Not really, but I'm willing to admit we need the exposure. I just wish I didn't have to be front and center for it while a bunch of people snap pictures of the place to win a gift card."

"Come on, Kar. You are so paranoid someone is going to recognize your name or your face, but even if they do, you didn't do anything wrong. You were cleared of all charges."

Kara winced, closing the door on the newly cleaned cage with a snap. "Maybe in court, but the media crucified me, and now that he's being released in a few weeks, it's going to stir everything up again."

"I still can't believe he only got two years. Where is the justice in that? Ferris Worthington used you to get close to people and destroyed all the good you did by being a greedy, loathsome, disgusting—"

"I remember what he did," Kara interrupted, immediately regretting her curt response. It wasn't Charity's fault that a cold rush of panic still seized her heart every time a camera flashed. Going viral for being the "Grinch's Bride" was a definite low point in her life. It wasn't even a good nickname. Worthy—she almost snorted aloud at the ironic nickname—had swept her off her feet with his charm. They'd been dating two months when he suddenly proposed, down on one knee the day after Halloween, and she'd shouted yes three times before falling into his arms and knocking him to the ground. Six weeks later, her world came crashing down when the police stormed her office Christmas party, taking Worthy and her to the police station in handcuffs. She'd spent hours being interrogated until Charity and her father, Royce Simmons, saved the day.

While Kara appreciated Royce acting as her lawyer, it wrecked her that Worthy had put her in the position to even need one. He'd gotten close to her so he could steal hundreds of thousands of dollars in donations and people's personal information. Everyone now knew she wasn't involved in Worthy's dealings, but the damage was done. She'd lost her job as the head of fundraising for Half-a-Million Lives, a national free spay-and-neuter program for cats, because she'd let Worthy borrow her laptop and hadn't pass code–protected the files.

Kara worked at a high-kill shelter for years as a veterinarian after college, and, burned out over the emotional toll shelter medicine took, she'd taken the job at Half-a-Million Lives because she wanted to make a difference for pets before they got to shelters. Only she'd trusted the wrong man with her heart *and* her computer.

Because the company's donations came from people nationwide, the story of Worthy's crimes went viral. People recognized her from memes, fake news articles, and conspiracy TikToks. There was no way to escape the public's persecution, especially when some people seemed to only get their news from social media.

She closed her eyes, taking a deep, trembling breath as she beat back the painful memories. If Kara let herself fall down that rabbit hole, she'd never make it out front, and Charity needed her. Just another reason she hated every social platform. Social media was a bane of society that she'd managed to avoid at all costs the last few years but, unfortunately, not something that could be ignored when you ran a business.

When she'd lost her job, Kara took a position as the

overnight veterinarian at a twenty-four-hour emergency veterinary hospital. The fast-paced atmosphere kept her busy, but like in shelter medicine, she was the last hope for an animal. When Charity came to her with the idea of opening a cat café, she'd rejected it outright. She couldn't imagine working for another nonprofit, let alone being a partner in one after the fiasco with Worthy, but Charity kept after her until she'd finally convinced her that they could do it. With Charity's baking skills and Kara's knowledge of veterinary medicine and nonprofits, they could make it a success. Kara even tried pointing out the irony of Charity opening a *charity*, but she wouldn't be swayed.

Charity had a bachelor's degree in business, but her passion was baking. They'd spent weeks fine-tuning the business plan and emptied all of their savings into the building, the renovations, and the equipment, plus a loan they were struggling to pay back. It became clear after the first few weeks that they needed an online presence, and Kara reluctantly opened an Instagram for the café. But she kept her social media posts focused on the cats, adorable foam art that their barista, Michelle, created, and styled photos featuring Charity's amazing baked goods. Without Charity's delicious treats, Meow and Furever would be just another rescue in a sea of nonprofits.

Not a single photo of Kara graced the Instagram feed and she'd like to keep it that way. Having a crowd of people snapping pictures in the small lobby of the café would make that hard to manage.

Before she could open her eyes, Charity hugged her. "I am so sorry for bringing it up."

Kara hugged her back with a soft smile. "It's okay. I'm just in a crap mood, and I shouldn't be. I need to focus on the positive."

"Positive, smositive. Tell me about your woes. We've got—" Charity paused and pulled away to look at her smart watch. "Ten minutes. Lay it on me, babe."

The two of them met at UC Davis and clicked instantly, despite Kara being a trailer park–raised white girl from Alabama and Charity being an upper-middle-class Black girl from California. Kara didn't know what she'd have done without Charity the last fifteen years and never wanted to discover a future where her bestie wasn't right by her side.

"Been a morning."

Charity shook her playfully. "Hurry up and give me all the gory details. We'll have to let the horde in soon, and before we do, I want all your demons exorcised so you're once again my hyper, happy friend who makes my day better just because she exists."

"Well, jeez, now you're going to make me cry."

"No, none of that. Unless you're crying because you are just as grateful for me."

"I am."

"Good." Charity patted her back and released her. "Now spill!"

"I woke up to no water this morning, and I was ready to take out a couple of plumbers' kneecaps on the way to work."

"Oh, sweetie, that sucks. On the plus side, you smell good for skipping a shower this morning."

"Thank goodness for that!"

"That's not all, is it?"

"No, there's more. I met the guy who created the magazine ad outside this morning, and I wasn't exactly cordial."

"What did you say?"

"Nothing . . . much."

Charity sighed. "Which means you stuck your foot all the way down your throat."

"I wouldn't feel too bad for him. He's not an animal person."

"Well, in that case, to heck with him," Charity said, shooting Kara a reassuring wink, and relief rushed through Kara. "Although, maybe from now on, we thank people who do us a solid and not upset them. Even if they aren't our cup of tea."

"I will, if there is a next time. But he was irritating."

Charity laughed. "Then forget about him! I'm calling a cease and desist on the negativity! You finish up back here and take that piss-poor mood out on the cages until they sparkle, and I will race through the front once more and make sure it is picture perfect. Love you, and"—Charity picked up the totes she'd set down and softly tapped them together—"break!"

Charity disappeared through the swinging door like a whirlwind, and, alone again, Kara worked fast, moving, cleaning, and feeding the rest of the kitties in her care. Once she finished with the clinic cleanup, she scrubbed her hands at the sink and pushed through the door, holding it for Theo as he trotted past her to his spot on a large cat tree shaped like a castle by the front door. To the left were glass walls encasing a large room, decorated with chairs, couches, and tables. Robin Hood, a sleek orange tabby, followed along on the other side of the clear wall, meowing belligerently.

"Hey, you got breakfast. It's my turn."

Robin Hood huffed as she hung a right to join Charity behind the counter. The cat sat down, his tail swishing behind him as he tracked her every move with his amber-brown eyes.

"Stop staring at me, creeper," she said, but the cat simply pawed at the glass, the rush of his pads making squeaky sounds.

Charity handed her a plate with a cheese Danish and clicked the tongs in her other hand at Kara. "You know, talking to animals is the first step toward crazy town. Or becoming Dr. Dolittle."

"Welp, I sure as heck ain't Dolittle," she said, ducking behind the counter to take a big bite of the sweet, cheesy goodness. The warm, buttery crust disintegrated in her mouth, and it was heaven. Kara made little moans in the back of her throat as she devoured her Danish, but Robin Hood kept stroking the wall, and she finally paused to point her finger at him with no real heat. "Hey! Knock it off, troublemaker."

Charity thumped her gently on the top of her hand with a spatula. "Stop picking on my boy!"

"Your boy, humph. If you like him so much, why don't you adopt him?"

"You know my landlord hates cats."

"So, move. You're always complaining about the place because he's cheap and takes forever to fix things."

"Have you looked at the price of rentals lately?

Astronomical! My place is close to work, and he hasn't jacked the rent up yet, so I'm still able to save money."

Kara shrugged. "You could save more money if you moved into my house, where you would only need to split utilities and you could adopt that cat."

Charity blew Robin Hood a kiss. "I do love him."

"A pesky food-thieving cat—what's not to love?"

"Exactly. You love him too or you wouldn't have taken him in."

"I hate when you're right." Kara took another bite and used the napkin Charity handed her to wipe some pastry glaze from her face. "Do I have time to chug a latte before we open the doors?"

Charity checked her smart watch with a noncommittal hum. "We have five minutes, so it would have to be a tepid latte chugged at lightning speed."

"So you're saying I've got time." Kara shoved the last of her Danish into her mouth and hopped up to steam the milk for her drink, quirking a brow at Charity's gorgeous yellow dress as she chewed. "You are awfully spruced up for a day of serving. And I love your boots."

"These old things?" Charity cocked one foot, showing off the cuffed brown knee-high boots with nary a scuff on them.

Kara scoffed. "Uh-uh. Don't give me that. Spill the tea while this espresso drips."

Charity leaned her hip against the counter, facing Kara. "I've got a date after we close. Just a guy I met swiping on an app, but he seems promising."

Although her first inclination was to interrogate Charity

about her mystery date, she knew better. Charity hated to be fussed over. She'd come from a home with two helicopter parents and seemed to still be rebelling against them as an adult.

"I hope you have a wonderful time." Kara dumped the espresso shots and milk into her travel cup, finishing it off with a dash of syrup and whipped cream. She took a sip and smacked her lips. "Perfect. Snapping a lid on this baby and going to open the floodgates."

"Oh, and don't forget, we need to talk about Friendsgiving, since it's next week! There is a lot to plan for, and I'm not spending all day in the kitchen alone."

"You mean I can't just show up and eat?"

"No!"

"That's rude." Kara took her time crossing the lobby floor, wishing her heart wasn't fluttering so violently. With her hand on the lock, she glanced at Charity. "You ready?"

"You got this, babe."

I'm not so sure, she thought, a second before she pulled the doors wide.

"Welcome to Meow and Furever! Come on in!"

Chapter Three

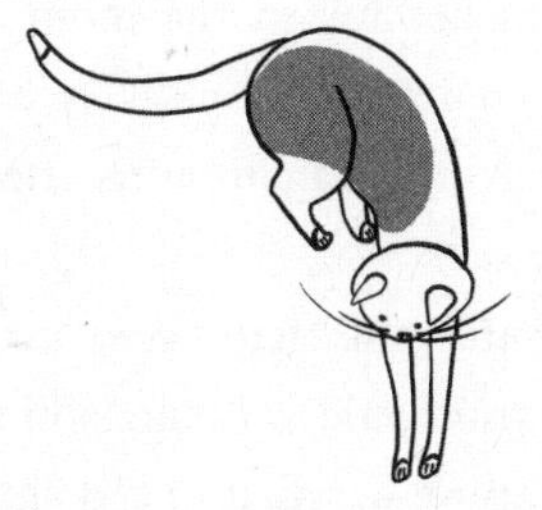

Come meet Peanut, a marbled-tabby domestic shorthair with a little extra junk in the trunk. Need a cat who will cuddle you on these cool winter nights? He's got you, boo!

"WHEW!" WILL SCHWARTZ HOLLERED, flexing his arms in front of him. "We are *men*!"

Ben laughed, setting his level down on the newly installed granite countertops in his kitchen. After his encounter with the cat woman this morning, he'd met Schwartz back here with breakfast burritos and coffees, and several hours later, Ben was ready to call it a day. "It looks good in here. Want a tonic?"

Schwartz hesitated for a half a second before he laughed. "Yeah, Coke if you have it. It still takes me a minute to decipher your lingo. When I think tonic, it's that nasty water my dad uses in his mixed drinks to get through Christmas with my grandma Elsie."

"I can't help that you Californians don't speak proper English."

"Up yours, Boston!"

Ben chuckled as he crossed the room and grabbed two Cokes out of the cooler. Ben handed a bottle to Schwartz and tapped the top of his against his friend's drink before twisting the top off.

"Thanks for doing this with me, man. I know there are better things you could be doing on a Saturday, but I appreciate you jumping in when I need you."

"Hey, what are friends for? Besides, I think all this lifting and moving is giving me muscles." Schwartz rolled up the arm of his T-shirt and flexed. "What do you think? Could I be Captain America?"

Ben cocked his head to the side, studying the small bulge in Schwartz's arm. "Maybe in a few more weeks."

"It better be doing something! My entire body has creaked and cracked since I started helping you, and I'm only thirty-five!"

Ben had to agree with Schwartz. His own muscles hadn't stopped aching since he'd closed on the house. Of course, when he'd started, he'd been incredibly out of shape with about six weeks of depression weight on top of it.

Sweat soaked the back and front of his T-shirt, and he couldn't wait to clean up in a cool shower. They'd started with the master bed and bath since it was the place he'd be spending the most time, and had been working their way out from there. Today they'd been in the kitchen, installing cabinets and countertops. With the cabinets in, Ben just needed to pick out new appliances. The 1976 ranch home hadn't been updated in any way, shape, or form until now, but Ben could envision what it would look like when he had everything moved in. Leather couches in the living room with a curved high-definition TV. Maybe a coffee table, if he found one he liked. He planned on installing wood blinds on the windows, and the other two bedrooms would be fully furnished for guests.

His phone buzzed in his pocket, and he pulled it out to check the caller ID. His mother's face flashed across the screen, and he hit the button on the side to silence the vibrations.

"Solicitor?" Schwartz asked.

"My mom."

"Oof, if I ignored my mother's calls, she'd think I was dead and send police around to do a wellness check."

If he didn't stop avoiding his mother's calls, Ben wouldn't be surprised if she did the same. But he knew what she wanted to talk about, and he couldn't have that conversation again. There was no way he could go home for the holidays, especially if his brother and former fiancée would be in attendance. If he took his mother's call, she'd beg him to forgive the happy couple, and he wouldn't do that. Not even for her.

"I take it you aren't going home for Thanksgiving?"

"Not this year."

"You can come with me to my folks', but fair warning, they might try to set you up with my sister."

Ben paused mid-drink to study Schwartz. "Why?"

"Because she's single and you're single."

"I'm emotionally unavailable," Ben said.

Schwartz shrugged. "My mother doesn't care about that. The minute we hit thirty, she started throwing potential spouses at us like baseballs."

"That's terrifying."

"No, that's mom; so, if you do decide to tag along, remember I did warn you."

"I think I'll stick around here and work on the house. Maybe order one of those precooked meals and have leftovers for days."

Schwartz finished off his bottle of soda and got up, launching it into the recycling bin. "I don't know, man. That sounds really lonely. I'm not sure what kind of drama you have going on with your family, but I couldn't hold a grudge for long."

If you knew the whole story, you could. Ben didn't want to explain to Schwartz that it wasn't just drama keeping him from heading back to Boston. He'd avoided divulging the details of his last relationship because he didn't want to see that expression of surprise before pity settled into its place. Nothing sadder than a man getting dumped by his fiancée for his younger, more successful, and—even Ben could admit—better-looking brother. Up until the moment she'd returned his ring and told him why she couldn't marry him, he'd been proud of Boone's success. But now, he kept waiting for karma to throat-punch his brother.

Meow.

Ben frowned, his head swinging toward the distant cry. "Did you hear that?"

"What?" Schwartz asked, cocking his head to the side.

"It sounded like a cat."

"It's probably outside," Schwartz said, stretching his arms over his head. "You do live in a residential neighborhood. Bound to be some free-roaming critters around."

"Maybe." Ben tossed his empty bottle in the recycling and considered Schwartz's assessment of his holiday plans. Maybe it looked sad from the outside, but it was better to be lonely by choice than because the person you were supposed to spend the rest of your life with changed their mind.

Although he was getting a little tired of his own company. "You still need a wingman sometimes?"

Surprise streaked across Schwartz's face. "Seriously? I thought you weren't available?"

"I've been thinking that maybe I don't have to be ready to date in order to go out and have fun."

Schwartz whooped and grabbed Ben around the waist, lifting the bigger man off his feet. "Fantastic! Ow!" Schwartz hollered the word, dropping Ben and clutching at his back. "Big mistake."

"You're the idiot who picked me up."

"How about a little sympathy for the guy with the aching back?"

Meow!

Ben twirled to the right, narrowing his eyes. "That sounds like it's coming from inside."

Schwartz groaned as he rubbed his back and Ben shushed him. Another muffled cry broke the quiet, and Schwartz stilled. "You're right."

Ben headed toward the noise, weaving down the hall. When he opened the door to one of the guest rooms, the animal's call echoed in the empty space. Ben's gaze scanned the dark carpet, white walls, and closed window. He hadn't started this room yet, planning to tackle both guest bedrooms next and finish up in the guest bathroom.

Schwartz came in behind him, hovering in the doorway. "Pop open the air vent on the floor. Could be in the system."

Ben did as he suggested, kneeling down onto his hands and knees next to the rectangular grate hidden within the old shag carpet. The bitter scent of stale cigarettes and dust flew up his nose, lingering inside. Ben sneezed as he shifted onto his stomach, lifting the grate up with one hand while the thumb of his other scrolled for the flashlight app on his phone.

Light erupted from the back of his phone, and Ben slipped it down into the dark vent, whistling. "Come here. Here boy. Or girl."

"It's not a dog, dude. Try 'here kitty,'" Schwartz called in a high voice.

Ben grunted. "Maybe you should be down here." He waited a second, listening, then he clicked his tongue. "Here kitty, kitty."

Soft taps echoed through the vent, getting louder. "I'll be damned."

"I told you. Something about 'here kitty, kitty' always works."

Ben spotted the small dirty kitten as it poked its head into view, ears first, followed by a slender, triangular face. It caught sight of Ben and opened its mouth, releasing another pitiful whine. Ben lifted himself up off his stomach and sat back on his haunches. "How the heck did it get down there?"

"Why you asking me?" Schwartz looked over Ben's shoulder and down the hole. "Cute little bugger."

"If you say so. Here." Ben scooted back, trying to make room for Schwartz. "I'll move out of the way so you can grab it."

"Sorry, my dude, but there is no way I can get down on my hands and knees with my back spasming like this." As if to emphasize his pain, Schwartz's hand flew to his lower back with a whimper. "I may not be able to get up. You'll have to grab it."

"What if it attacks me?" The cat didn't look vicious, but he'd heard stories about how unpredictable animals were.

"It's a kitten, dude. They barely have teeth. Besides, he seems friendly."

Ben stared at the dirt-streaked face and slowly lowered his hand down into the hole. Did cats carry rabies? He had no idea, and sweat broke out on his forehead.

Get a grip, man. You've seen rats bigger than this thing.

His palm connected with a furry back, and his fingers wrapped around the slight body, noting that it seemed to be vibrating in his hand.

"Are they supposed to tremble like this?"

"He's probably cold from living in the air vents."

Ben lifted the grimy creature out of the hole and sat back against the wall, holding the animal away from him. It didn't try to squirm away like he'd anticipated. Instead, it dangled in his hand limply, its small blue-gray eyes staring back at him as though it didn't know quite what to make of him.

"Doesn't look very old," Schwartz said. "You probably have a crack in your system somewhere, and it wandered in by accident. If you notice a mama cat in the neighborhood going nuts, it's most likely hers, although giving it back probably wouldn't do it any favors."

"Why do you say that?" Ben studied the kitten from an arm's length away. Beneath the patches of grime were short tufts of orange fur, covering a bony body lighter than a handful of cotton.

"If the mom's feral, she'll be struggling to feed herself. And with the busy streets around this neighborhood..." Schwartz trailed off, and Ben muttered, "I get the picture."

"He doesn't act like he's scared of people, though, so I could be wrong. Maybe he was dumped," Schwartz offered, reaching out a hand to touch it.

The kitten tensed, its ears flattening against the side of its head. It spat and hissed at Schwartz so violently that Ben dropped the little terror to the shag carpet, but it didn't try to run, just continued to growl at Schwartz with narrowed eyes.

Schwartz reared back, glaring at the tiny animal. "Well, screw you too, fur ball."

"What do we do with it?" Ben asked.

Schwartz stared down at the kitten grimly. "The half-pint turd hurt my feelings, so my first inclination is the shelter, but they might put it down if they don't have room." Schwartz straightened up and pulled his phone from his back pocket. "I'll see if I can find a rescue. They probably aren't open on a Saturday, so you might be stuck with it a couple days."

No way was he going to be responsible for this animal all weekend. "They don't have after-hours numbers?"

"I'm looking. There's a bunch that have phone numbers but no hours posted."

Meow and Furever Cat Café popped into his subconscious. Even though Ben hadn't exactly hit it off with the woman this morning, she obviously loved cats, and they should at least be open this afternoon.

Unless she takes one look at me and sends me packing.

No, he couldn't imagine her turning a feline in need away, even if Ben was the one to bring it in. "Search for Meow and Furever Cat Café. It's right by work."

Schwartz's fingers flittered across the screen at supersonic speed. "Got it. And look at that, open until four. Wait, isn't this the place from the ad this morning?"

"Yeah," Ben muttered.

"Huh. I'd totally forgotten." He tapped one last time before Ben heard the loud ring of an outgoing call on speakerphone. Once. Twice... then:

"Hello. You've reached Meow and Furever Cat Café's after-hours message machine. If you've called during business hours, we are most likely assisting other customers. Please leave a detailed message after the tone and we will get back to you as soon as we can. If you would like to adopt..."

Schwartz ended the call, his gaze locked on the phone screen. "What do you say we just get in the car and drive it over there? They can't say no if they see it, right? As long as it acts all cute and friendly."

The kitten backed into Ben's leg as Schwartz took a step toward them, and the kitten arched its spine. Schwartz stilled and gave the kitten a rude gesture.

Ben shook his head at the ridiculous image of a grown

man squaring off with a pint-sized feline, but that was the only motion he made. The creature was riled up, and the last thing he wanted was to startle it and end up with a furry monster flying toward his face.

"There's an empty Amazon box in the living room. Why don't you grab it?"

"Sure." Schwartz waved his hand at the cat, addressing the hostile kitten: "This attitude? Not attractive."

"Stop harassing it!"

Schwartz paused, studying Ben's face. "Are you...scared of it?"

"No."

His friend—a loose term at the moment—quirked a brow. "You look a little pale, and you have a sweat streak on your temple."

"Will you just get the damn box?" Ben growled.

Schwartz left the room chuckling, closing the door behind him. The moment he was gone, the kitten turned slowly and proceeded to climb up Ben's pant leg toward him. The ears were no longer pinned back, but Ben still didn't trust it not to pounce at sensitive parts of his body. His eyes, for instance.

"Hey, yeah, no, why don't you stay on the carpet until he gets back?" The kitten balanced on his leg like a beam, putting one tiny paw in front of the other as it inched closer. Ben held a warding hand out to stop its approach, and the kitten butted its head against his palm, rubbing his body all the way down to its back and then turning around so it could use Ben's hand to stroke its other side.

Ben relaxed slightly until the kitten started lifting one

paw and then another while digging its claws into his jeans. The minute Schwartz came back in with the box, a switch flipped, and the kitten hopped around in that arched position. When Schwartz kept coming, the kitten made a spitting sound.

"What's he doing?" Ben whispered.

Schwartz stood a few feet back with the open box, watching the kitten warily. "He's staring at me like he wants to claw my eyes out with his back all arched up like—" Schwartz curled his back and turned his head to the side, giving Ben a visual he would have laughed at if needle-sharp claws weren't digging into his skin.

"I know what he looks like, but why is he doing that?"

"I think he doesn't like me, but it could be the box."

"How are we going to get him inside when he's all freaked out?" Ben asked.

Schwartz reached a hand out gingerly, and the kitten skittered across Ben's lap and up his chest. Ben fell backward with a yelp, hitting the back of his head hard against the wall as the kitten used his shoulder to launch himself away from Schwartz, landing on the carpet a few feet away in a crouched position.

Ben twisted to push himself onto his hands and knees, slowly climbing to his feet. The back of his head smarted, and he rubbed it, grumbling while Schwartz busted a gut. "Glad you think this is funny."

"Sorry, but watching you panic over an animal the size of a softball is too much," Schwartz wheezed.

"I've never been around cats before, and my natural instinct when something with sharp claws comes flying at my face is to get away." The kitten slinked across to the closed door, keeping one eye on Schwartz. "You've had cats before, right? Don't you know a special trick for calming them down?"

"All of my cats were sweet! They weren't possessed by a demon." Schwartz took a step toward the kitten again and it puffed up. "I think his eyes are even red, man."

Ben considered opening up all the doors and letting the kitten find its own way out, but as much as he didn't like cats, he couldn't imagine letting something so small fend for itself. At least if they took him to the café, he would be safe.

"All right, new plan." Ben kept his eye on the kitten, who was inching toward him with his entire focus on Schwartz. "Grab my sweatshirt from the living room and throw it to me. I'll wrap him in it so he can't scratch and hold him while you drive."

"Whatever you say, man." Schwartz walked briskly toward the door, and the kitten scrambled away, making a beeline for Ben. Before he could get out of its way, it sprang for the pants leg of his jeans and climbed up with little launches created by its needle-like claws digging into his denim-covered legs. Ben winced at the stinging digs and bent to pull the kitten off him, biting back his anger when he felt the tiny body trembling in his paws.

"Hey, you're fine," Ben muttered gruffly as he brought the kitten up to his eye level. "We're not going to hurt you, but can you lay off the claws? You're not a squirrel, and I'm not your tree."

The kitten's eyes drooped, and he released a pitiful meow.

Schwartz returned with the shirt, closing the door behind him. "Time to make a kitty burrito."

Ben noticed the kitten's ears drop back at the sound of Schwartz's voice and held a finger to his mouth with his free hand. "For whatever reason, he hates the sound of your voice, and I don't feel like getting torn up, so give me the shirt slowly and keep your mouth shut."

Schwartz lobbed the sweatshirt at him, and he caught it in midair, watching for any signs the cat would go Tasmanian devil on him. "All right, furry Freddy Krueger. I'm going to bundle you up in this, and you're going to be chill while we take a short drive. Deal?"

Ben slowly wrapped the kitten up in the shirt and cradled it against his chest. After several seconds of holding it like that, the kitten's eyes shut and a low crackle—like the sound of Rice Krispies in milk—emitted from the bundled feline.

"What is that sound?" Ben asked as he walked past Schwartz.

"He's purring." The kitten's eyes opened briefly to growl, but when his eyes locked on Ben again, he relaxed.

Schwartz opened the front door for Ben, giving the kitten a scowl. "Good luck getting adopted, Satan."

The kitten didn't even open his eyes when he hissed. Schwartz closed the door behind Ben, muttering something about being a "likable guy" as he jogged around Ben to get into the driver's seat. Ben held the kitten against his chest to grab the door handle, feeling it tense when Schwartz started the car.

"It's okay. You're fine." After he finished shutting the

door and getting his seat belt on, he reached down to stroke the kitten's forehead with his finger, smiling as that little purr started up again. His dad didn't like cats, so the only ones he'd ever been around were friends' pets, and he hadn't been very comfortable around them. They'd been a lot bigger, though.

Ben softly gave Schwartz instructions on where to go while the kitten continued to sleep. They drove past the front of the café, and there was no longer a line of people, which was good. Ben didn't really want an audience in case he had to deal with the woman from this morning.

Schwartz parked the car around back, and they climbed out, heading around the building. The kitten's eyes popped open when a car whizzed by, and Ben brought him back against his chest, cradling his charge close. They passed by the front window, where a rather large longhaired white cat was rolling onto its back. There were several people sitting at tables chatting, and Ben swallowed nervously as Schwartz grabbed the front door and held it open for him.

When they stepped inside, a gorgeous dark-skinned woman in butter yellow smiled warmly. "Welcome to Meow and Furever! What can I do for you?"

Ben wasn't at all surprised when Schwartz stepped in front of him and approached the counter with swagger. "Hey there. I'm Will Schwartz, and this is my friend, Ben. We were working on his house and found a kitten in his cooling and vent system."

The woman's eyes widened. "Oh, I see. Um, let me get my partner up here. She is in charge of intakes and... well, I'll be right back."

The woman disappeared, and Schwartz turned to him, mouthing the word *wow*. "I am so glad you suggested this place."

Ben rolled his eyes. Leave it to Schwartz to find someone to flirt with, even in a place like this. Although his friend was an amazing guy, Schwartz hadn't been serious about a woman since they met. Ben wasn't sure if that was by choice or because he had commitment issues.

When she returned a few moments later, the auburn-haired woman from this morning came into view with a sweet smile on her face.

Until her gaze met Ben's and her expression slipped.

"You."

Chapter Four

Matilda the Hun is a calico domestic shorthair who is prickly at first, but when she meets her human? She'll melt like warm honey.

HUMPHREY BOGART'S GRAVELLY VOICE echoed in Kara's mind as she silently paraphrased, *Of all the cat cafés in all the towns in all the world, he had to stumble into mine.*

Only there was no wistful nostalgia to the thought. The last thing she wanted was another heaping pile of unpleasant spooned onto her already achingly uncomfortable day. She'd managed to get through the morning without a complete breakdown as a steady stream of patrons had rolled through one after another for several hours. Now that the crowd had finally dispersed and they were down to mostly regulars hanging out in the social room, she'd thought her day was turning around.

Apparently, not so much.

The man from this morning stood just inside the door, clutching a wadded sweatshirt to his chest. He had a deer-in-the-headlights look, as though the last thing he'd wanted was to show up here, and it made her feel a little better about him. At least he wasn't completely oblivious to the way he'd stepped in it.

"You two know each other?" Charity asked.

"This is the man responsible for our good fortune this morning." She'd added a hefty dollop of sarcasm to her tone, but Charity brightened, ignoring the fact that, hours ago, she'd agreed that as a non–animal lover, this man couldn't be trusted.

"Oh!" Charity came around the counter, holding her hand out. "Thank you for picking Meow and Furever. It was a wonderful surprise to come in and see all of those people lined up."

Kara almost muttered "traitor," but Charity wasn't wrong. They'd made more in a few hours than they brought in most days. She'd needed to pop an antianxiety pill during the rush and take a decompression break when they got a lull in the crowd, but overall, it wasn't as bad as she'd thought it would be.

Still didn't mean she had to like the guy.

"Hi," he said, taking Charity's hand. "I am glad it worked out. Your partner wasn't thrilled with me this morning."

"Crowds make Kara nervous."

"Plus I never trust someone who doesn't like animals," Kara butted in, irked they were talking about her as though she wasn't there.

The guy cleared his throat, focusing his attention on her.

"I know we didn't get off on the right foot, but I found this guy in my house. I had no idea what to do for him and was hoping you could help me."

He unwrapped the kitten enough to show her a dirty face with gray-blue eyes. The precious creature released a pitiful meow when his gaze met hers, and Kara couldn't help smiling in return.

"Well, hello to you, cutie." Kara cut her gaze to Charity briefly. "You mind holding down the fort while I take these guys in the back and have a look-see?"

"Oh, I can stay up here and keep her company," the other man said eagerly.

Kara watched Charity for a signal that she wasn't comfortable with that, but her friend simply shrugged. "I'm good."

"Come with me, then," Kara said, heading for the back without waiting to see if he was following. She paused to hold the door for him and when he passed through, she waved her free hand toward the exam table. "You can set him there, but keep ahold of him. I need to grab something."

"Sure, and hey, thanks." He shot her a crooked grin made even more charming by the slightly imperfect placement of his left canine. Really, the guy deserved none of her animosity; he'd been paid to do a job and it had worked out well.

"Of course. I mean, who could resist a face like that?" she said, pointing to the kitten poking its head out of the sweatshirt so there would be no confusion on who she meant.

"If he didn't use me as a human climbing tree, I'd agree with you, but my skin is still burning from his pinpricks."

"Be sure to clean them with disinfectant when you get a chance. You don't want to get cat scratch fever."

He stiffened. "That's a real thing? I thought it was just a bad song from the seventies."

"It's both, but don't panic. I've been around cats all my life and never had it."

"That's comforting."

Kara backtracked to her office with a little laugh at his grumbling. She opened the bottom drawer in her desk, lifting the long, dusty black box she kept inside. She dropped it onto the desk surface and opened it, revealing her stethoscope.

When she touched it, a zing of familiarity zipped through her like she'd taken the hand of an old friend. She'd gone into shelter medicine to make a difference, but after several years, she'd come out with a heavier heart. With the café, she could save lives, and thanks to the dedicated fosters they'd recruited, they hadn't needed to turn any kitties away.

Of course, if they didn't see a serious increase in revenue soon, that wouldn't be the case.

If they could get the clinic going, Kara knew their luck would turn around, but that meant some heavy fundraising, and with the holidays fast approaching, there wasn't time to plan anything. And come the new year, it might be too late anyway.

She wrapped her stethoscope around the back of her neck and returned to where the man stood with the sweatshirt over his shoulder. The gray T-shirt he wore stretched over broad shoulders, and his muscular arms rested on either side of the kitten. She thought she saw him smiling fondly while the kitten attacked the string of his hoodie hanging down, but when he caught her watching him, he sobered.

Kara probably imagined it anyway.

"Let's get a look at this kid," she said, picking up the kitten.

"Thanks again for doing this. I'm Ben, by the way."

Kara looked up from the kitten, giving Ben a cursory glance. "And him?"

"I don't know. We just met."

Kara's lips twitched as she set the kitten on the table again. "Funny. I'm Kara."

"Yeah, your partner mentioned that."

"Charity."

"The baker. You're the brains."

Kara laughed. "I may have made up that part." She pointed to the otoscope hanging on the wall. "Will you hand me that and one of the cones out of the box next to it?"

She lifted the kitten's head and opened its mouth, checking the teeth and gums. "His color's good. And although he's on the thin side, he's not terribly underweight. Probably wasn't in your ducts long."

"Are you a veterinarian?" he asked.

"I am."

"So, does this double as an animal hospital?"

"Someday it will." *Hopefully*, she thought. "The plan is to turn this back area into a low-cost veterinary clinic, but until then, I do intake exams for the cats coming into the café," she said, using her stethoscope to listen to the kitten's heart. A rapid, steady thump sounded in her ears, and she smiled before removing the earpieces. "Excellent ticker, mis"—she checked the back end—"ter." When she pushed on his tummy, the kitten rolled into a ball and tried to grab her fingers. Kara laughed and tickled the soft underfur of his belly. "You wanna play, huh?"

Kara glanced up and caught Ben watching her thoughtfully. "What?"

"Nothing. You're good with him."

"Of course I am. He senses I'm a cat lover."

"He hates Schwartz, and he's a cat lover," Ben said.

"The guy who wanted to hang with Charity?" Kara asked, quirking a brow.

"Yeah, he hasn't met a woman he wouldn't flirt with."

"Only the pretty ones, though, right?"

"I guess I never thought about it. My father taught me every woman has her own unique beauty."

His words created a surprising warmth in her chest. "That is not a motto a lot of men have."

"A lot of men are idiots."

She swallowed as those arresting eyes swept over her face, as if he were mentally picking out all of her beautiful parts. Kara knew she wasn't conventionally pretty, not the way Charity was. Her nose sported a bump from the wrong end of a fist she'd encountered at fifteen, when she'd refused to return a neighbor boy's dog after he'd left him tied up outside in a thunderstorm. You could play connect the dots with her freckles, and while some men didn't mind the extra weight she carried on her middle and hips, she wasn't turning heads as she walked down the street. She'd been told too many times growing up that "the color black is slimming," but she didn't give a flying cupcake about that.

Colorful, fashionable clothes were her addiction, as anyone could tell by her mustard-yellow blouse with colorful falling leaves dropping across the bottom and stretchy blue jeans tucked into her boots. While her wardrobe may give off the impression she liked attention, she wasn't used to it. Especially not by strapping bearded men with—

The kitten nibbled on her fingers with sharp teeth, and she hissed. "Owie! You hungry or do I just taste good?"

"Probably both," Ben offered. "I didn't have anything to feed him."

"That's okay, I have lots of kitten food. You mentioned he wasn't a fan of Schwartz, but how is he with you?"

"Schwartz? I don't think I'm his type."

Kara rolled her eyes. "You know I was talking about this guy. He seems happy."

Ben lifted his hand, making a so-so motion. The kitten rushed across the table and rubbed against his fingers. "He thinks I'm pretty, at least."

Maybe there's hope for him after all. Kara strongly believed that there were two kinds of cat people, ones who were born loving cats and those that fell in love after meeting the right cat. Maybe Ben was the latter.

"Looks like he chose you. Good news is he seems healthy, just in desperate need of a bath. Let's get a weight on him while I fill a basin to give him a thorough washing." Kara turned to touch the scale's On button. "I'll give him a little food first before I clean him up. Then I'll deworm him, take some blood for a FeLV/FIV test—"

"What is that?"

"Two immunosuppressing diseases we test for in case he

is ever around other cats. And if he has fleas, he'll get some medication for that, too. He should be ready to go home with you in half an hour or so."

"Wait, home with me? Don't you want me to fill out some kind of paperwork?"

Kara's eyes narrowed as she pulled a small bowl from the cupboard and faced Ben. "Paperwork?"

"Yes, so you can take him into the rescue."

And there it was. The dash of warmth she'd felt for the guy was snuffed out. "Sorry, I thought you were asking for help with him because you didn't know what you were doing but you wanted to keep him."

"Oh, no." Ben chuckled, apparently missing her change in mood. "We definitely got our wires crossed. You are the only rescue I knew was open today."

"I see." She set the bowl in the sink and turned on the warm water to fill it up, maintaining eye contact with Ben. "You're not looking for help. You want to surrender him because you can't be bothered."

His eyes widened, and he stumbled over his words. "I mean...yeah, I can't...I'm doing a lot of construction on my house right now, and I don't...I've never had a cat before. It's not really a good time...for me."

"Can you set him on the scale for me?" she asked, mulling over his excuses as irritation set her teeth on edge.

"He really will be better off with you than me."

Kara held back a snort as she watched the kitten roll in his hands as if he thought the man was the best thing that ever happened to him. Kara sympathized with the kitten because she'd thought the same thing about Worthy. He had no idea the man who rescued him was getting ready to dump him. This guy thought he was some kind of hero because he found a kitten and brought it here? That was the bare minimum in human decency.

Ben set the tabby on the scale, and she logged the number on a loose sheet of paper she pulled from a drawer. "Kittens gain a pound a month, and even though he is underweight, I'd put him at not quite six weeks."

"What does that mean?" Ben asked.

"I'm saying I can give him his first vaccination, but he needs two in order to go into the social room and be available for adoption. And as you can see, I don't have any free cages back here."

"What about that one in the top?"

"I use it to transfer cats into when I clean cages." She glanced down at the kitten, who had hopped off the scale and was currently exploring the counter. Once he was of age, it wouldn't take long before someone adopted him. It was the older cats she struggled to find homes for. "I'm not saying I won't take him, but can you hang on to him today until I get his test results back? Once I know he's clean, I'll call around and see if I can find him a foster home."

"Like I said, my house isn't exactly kitten friendly. You really can't just find some place for him here?"

She shut off the water with a snap, her temper boiling over. "You found him in your home, but you take no responsibility for him? I'm surprised you didn't just shove him outside and wash your hands of him."

"I wouldn't do that," he said.

Kara shook her head as she crossed to the cat food cupboard

and pulled out a can of kitten food. "If you really wanted to help this little guy and give him a chance, you'd agree to hang on to him until we find a placement for him." She dumped the cat food on a plate and put it under the kitten's nose. He dived into it like he was starving, flattening his tiny paws into the golden gravy with abandon. "Instead, you want to make excuses on why this tiny creature is too much of an inconvenience for you while feeling like a good person because you... what? Brought him here? You want a medal for not being a jerk?" His mouth flopped open like a fish gasping for air, and she tapped her fingers off. "Every animal we have in this place costs us to medicate, feed, house. And you were right; we've been struggling to get people through the door. We're doing everything we can to save lives, but hey, you did your part, so you're good, right?"

He stared at her, the muscle in his left eye twitching. "Are you always this intense or is it me?"

"It could be you. Or maybe it's that I'm frustrated with my fellow humans." She shook her head. "I'll get you the paperwork."

"Wait." He caught her gently by the elbow, dropping it almost as soon as he touched her. "Say I agree to hang on to him until you find a placement. What would I need?"

Kara hesitated, afraid to hope. "Food. A litter box. Water. Toys. I can get all of that together for you. He'd do best in a small area, like a bathroom. They tend to be messy at this age."

"How messy?"

"Well, I mean..." She pointed at the kitten, who had food from his ears to speckles across his chest. "His entire face is brown. Imagine that, but now he's playing in the litter box, flinging poo about."

"I thought you were supposed to be selling me on the idea?"

"I'm not going to lie to you. This age is like a human toddler. They are into everything, putting anything in their mouth, and they have no fear. But it's only one kitten and not a whole litter. Big guy like you should be able to handle it."

"Your faith in me is overwhelming," he deadpanned.

"Does that mean you'll keep him?"

"Until you find someone to take him off my hands, yes. How could I not after all that?"

Kara bit back an apology, because it was the least he could do. "I'll get him cleaned up, medicated, and send you both on your way."

"I'll leave you my number so you can call when you find somewhere for him to go."

"Absolutely. Really, it won't be long at all."

Chapter Five

Peeta is a Siamese cross who loves bird-watching. Stare into his crystal-blue eyes and tell me you aren't falling for him!

BEN WALKED DOWN THE hallway of Kilburn Marketing, running a free hand over his face. It was late afternoon on Monday, and he still hadn't heard from Kara, with the exception of a voice message letting him know the kitten was negative for those diseases she tested for. He was ready to knock off for the day and head home, but was hesitant after the chaos he'd experienced yesterday.

When she'd said kittens were messy, she'd left out that they were destructive terrors.

Every time he opened the guest bathroom door, the little squirt burst out between Ben's feet and led him on a merry jaunt around the house. He'd swept and scrubbed the floor at least a half a dozen times because the creature couldn't seem to keep his food, his water, or his litter where it belonged, and he didn't even want to think of the noxious smell that permeated his house every time the kitten defecated.

He still couldn't believe he'd let Kara guilt him into hanging on to the animal, but it ended today. He was swinging by the café on his way home, and they were going to come to an understanding.

Ben checked his watch. Their online hours said they closed at 5:00 p.m., so if he left now, he could catch her before she left. Why he hadn't thought to get her number, instead of just giving her his, baffled him.

He grabbed his laptop bag and shut the door to his office with a click. With Thanksgiving on Thursday, they were only in the office until tomorrow, and Schwartz had everything set up for their next magazine feature. They still needed to put the finishing touches on the Choco Vino account, but they weren't set to pitch until next week.

"Hey, Ben! You got a second?" Roy Kilburn called from his office as Ben passed by. Backing up to his boss's doorway, he smiled despite the nervous leap of his heart. He was still the new guy at the company and needed to stay on his toes.

"Absolutely, sir." Ben walked into the office, clearing his throat. "Everything all right?"

"Please close the door."

This isn't good. He didn't think he'd dropped the ball on any of his accounts and racked his brain as he took each step closer to Roy's desk, his feet trudging like his shoes were made of cement. Roy was a good boss, but he'd seen him fire a guy who lost a client because he showed up to a presentation unprepared. The man was steel and completely unreadable.

"Have a seat." Ben took the chair he indicated, watching Roy's expression for any kind of tell. "Relax, Ben. I didn't call you in here because I'm disappointed." Roy leaned back in his office chair, his polo pulling tight over his slight beer belly. Roy was in his midforties with black hair pulled back in a sleek ponytail. Put him in a T-shirt and leather and he could model for a motorcycle club's advertisement. "You do good work, Ben."

His breath rushed out. "Oh man, you had me for a minute."

Roy's grin widened. "Yeah?"

"I thought you were firing me."

"Good," Roy said, with a jovial wink. "I want my employees hardworking, not going soft and complacent. I need innovative and creative people around me, making Kilburn the best on the West Coast. We're small potatoes now compared to LA or New York, but when companies think of us, I want them to think quality. Outside-the-box marketing and a good reliable team." Roy sat forward, leaning on his desk with his hairy forearms. "You're one of my best idea people. You're not afraid to put yourself out there, and I appreciate that. I know you only signed a six-month contract, but I'd like to talk to you about staying on when it's finished."

Ben hesitated. He'd moved to California as a change of pace. He hadn't expected to fall in love with the area or his job. His parents would hate it, but having these last few months of breathing room had been good for him, given him clarity. Boston was in his blood, but he could be happy here.

"I've definitely been considering it, sir."

"Excellent. I know there are still a couple of months left before you need to make a decision, but I really think you've got a future here, and to be frank, I'd hate to lose you."

Ben thought about the grueling hours at his firm in Boston, the late nights and weekends, pushing himself for a boss to barely remember his name. After years of feeling like he was running in place, it was nice to be moving forward. "I appreciate that."

Roy slapped his hands down on the desk. "That's all I needed to hear." He stood up and held his hand out to Ben, his signal that their conversation was over. "We'll talk more after the new year, but I am fully prepared to woo you."

"Woo me?"

"Win you by any means necessary. You like baseball?"

"Absolutely, but I should warn you, I'm a Red Sox fan."

Roy winced. "I'm a Giants fan, so, when they play against each other in the spring, we'll go to a game. Just try not to get me killed."

Ben laughed. "I'll do my best, but I can't promise anything. At least you aren't a Yankees fan, or we'd be having a whole other conversation."

"Glad it didn't work out that way." Roy waved his hand, sitting back down. "You can go home now."

"Thanks again." Ben left the office and took the stairs down the three flights, figuring it would be faster than the elevator. He reached the bottom step as his phone blared to life. He checked the caller ID and fought the overwhelming urge to press the Reject button. He slipped his earbuds into place and accepted his mother's call. "Hey, Ma, how are you?"

"Oh, so you *are* alive. I wondered, since I've been calling you for days."

"Yeah, I've been meaning to call you back, but it's wicked busy here."

"I know you've been avoiding me, Benjamin Michael Reese. I wasn't born yesterday."

Ben pushed out the front door of the building and turned down the sidewalk toward the cat café. "Mom, I can't talk long, but I'll call you later if you want to lecture me."

"No, I'm not taking the chance. I wanted to let you know we'll be coming out for Christmas since you can't be here for Thanksgiving."

"Who is *we*?"

"Your father and me. Birdy and her family. Brandon and possibly—"

"Don't say it, Ma. I love you dearly, but I don't want Boone anywhere near me, and I'm getting tired of you trying to force us to talk."

"How do you think this makes your father and me feel? Having our boys fight, when you've always been so close?"

"This isn't a fight, Ma. The man betrayed me, his brother. You don't come back from that."

"I know they hurt you, honey, but Boone assured me that nothing happened between them while you two were together."

Ben took a calming breath, counting backward from

ten. It didn't matter if they had or hadn't crossed a line physically while he was engaged to Amelia. The fact was that they'd lied to him for months. He wouldn't have cared that they'd hooked up years before he'd met Amelia if they'd been honest when he introduced them, but they kept it to themselves, even after they realized they had feelings for each other again.

But the absolute worst of it was that his brother hadn't had the guts to tell him any of it. Amelia had told him everything as she handed him back his ring. Nothing hits you square in the solar plexus like "I can't marry you because I'm in love with your brother."

"He's not welcome here, Ma, and that's it."

"I understand how you feel, but it's a bit more complicated than that."

"What do you mean?"

"Your brother took a new medical position... in Sacramento."

Ben pulled up short, his grip tightening on the cell phone. "What?"

"He starts in a few weeks. That is what I was trying to call you about. Your brother is flying out there tomorrow to look at houses, and he wants to see you."

Why here? He'd quit his job and left his family to move three thousand miles away, and his brother just happened to pick a position in a neighboring city?

"That's why you're coming out here for Christmas? Because he's moving here?"

"No, honey. We had planned to come out and surprise you before he made the announcement."

"Well, isn't that wonderful?" Ben laughed bitterly. "Of course she's coming too, right?"

"Yes, she's going since she's his wife. They eloped in Vegas last weekend."

Ben wasn't surprised. Seemed like any time his life started going in a promising direction, something came along to take the wind out of his sails. "I lose my fiancée, uproot my life to start over, and he gets everything he wants. Where is the karma in that?"

"I don't think it's about karma, sweetheart. You and Amelia weren't right for each other, and I know it hurts, but this leaves you open to finding the right girl."

"You know I love you, Ma, but this isn't the time for sunshine and rainbows and let's look on the bright side, all right? This state isn't big enough for the two of us, and you tell him I said so. I don't care what they promised him, he needs to find somewhere else to go, far, far away from me."

"Benjamin, be reasonable."

"You know, Ma, if you really think that they're the good guys in this scenario and that I'm being *unreasonable*, then maybe you all should just spend the holidays with the newlyweds and skip my place."

"You don't want to spend Christmas with your family?"

"Seems like if my family can't respect my feelings, I'm better off on my own."

Suddenly, his mother's voice was muffled, and he heard her say, "You talk some sense into him."

Damn, she was passing the phone off to his father.

"Ben?"

"Yeah, Pop?"

"You wanna explain to me why your mother looks like she's about to burst into tears?"

"I simply stated that if my feelings about Boone and Amelia can't be respected, then maybe the family shouldn't come see me for Christmas."

"Hang on," his dad said, and he heard muffled arguing, catching a few snippets of the conversation.

"Shouldn't make him—"

"Why you gotta push?"

"They're grown men who can work out their own issues."

Ben picked up speed again, checking his watch. "Pop, do you want to call me back when you two come to an agreement? Because I need to head into this shop before it closes."

"Yeah, I'll give you a call a little later, but do me a favor, all right? Think about the way you speak to your mother next time. As frustrated as you may be, she loves you and only wants peace between her children."

"Sure, Pop. Talk to you later. Love ya. Tell Ma for me."

"Love you, too. I will."

Ben ended the call just before he pulled the door to the café open. He stepped into the empty lobby and called out, "Hello?"

"Just a second." Several moments ticked by before Charity came from the back, her smile widening when she caught sight of him. "Hey, Mr. Marketing Guy."

"It's Ben. I was wondering if Kara was in?"

"She's not. Sorry."

"I was hoping to catch her before she left. I agreed to hang on to this kitten until she found an available foster home, but I haven't heard from her."

"Oh, shoot. You're the message she left for me." She pulled a sticky note out of her pocket with a sheepish smile. "Your name and number got a little water smudged, and I couldn't read it, but she said to hang tight. She's still got some feelers out."

"What does that mean?" he grumbled.

"Probably that everyone she called told her no, and she's scrambling. It's not easy to get foster homes, especially for kittens during the holidays. A lot of people travel, and that's one more mouth to feed. Two of our foster families dropped their cats off to us today because they won't be home this week, so we're overflowing at the moment."

"Can I get her number at least? I agreed to do this for a day, and it's been two. I tried to deal, but I am not cut out for this."

Charity made an expression that he read as *yikes*. "I can, but today may not be the right time to lay more bad news on her. She had some plumbing issues, and the guy she paid extra to come out on Saturday made things worse. That's why she isn't here today. Pretty sure she's trying to learn how to fix it via YouTube."

"That's perfect," he blurted.

Charity frowned. "Excuse me?"

"Sorry, I just meant that I know a thing or two about pipes."

"Really?"

"Yeah, my dad is a plumber. I spent a lot of summers shadowing him growing up."

She eyed him for a second or two before she snagged a

pen and a yellow Post-it note. "Under normal circumstances, I wouldn't do this, but you don't give me creepy stalker vibes." She blew on the small square piece of paper before handing it to him. "Give me five minutes to lock up, and you can follow me there."

Chapter Six

Finnick the Russian blue has led a life of adventure but is ready to settle down with the right family. Catnip cubes appreciated.

"SON OF A BISCUIT-EATING leprechaun!" Kara shouted at the top of her lungs as water rained down on her from the pipe above her head. She climbed down the ladder at breakneck speed, wiping at her eyes and face as soon as her feet hit the solid ground of her basement floor. She moved out of the way of the spurting water, ready to burst into tears.

Eight hundred dollars had gone from her hand to that charlatan of a plumber on Saturday, and he'd assured her the issue was taken care of. Kara even tested the pressure and everything seemed fine, until last night when her water stopped working. She started calling around again, but after several told her how much it would be, she'd thought maybe she could figure out the problem herself by watching

YouTube videos. She couldn't do worse than the other guy, right?

Despite the recent plumbing issues, she loved the three-bedroom, two-bath home. It was thirty years old, and while it was a fifteen-minute commute to work on the freeway, she appreciated the privacy of several acres of land. Her house perched on top of a hill, overlooking some of the valley that stretched below. And the rest of the house had been renovated with granite countertops, hardwood floors, and a large tile shower and claw-foot tub in the master bath. Even though it had taken nearly all of the money she'd received from her grandparents' estate, it was perfect.

Kara's phone skittered across the top of a clear tote, Charity's ringtone echoing through the dim space. Kara wiped her hands on the back of her jeans, the only article of clothing not completely soaked, and swiped the green phone to answer. "Hey, Char."

"Hi, babe. How goes the DIY situation?"

"Oh, you know. Awful. How was the café this afternoon?"

"Michelle and I had it handled, and there were no new intakes."

"Great. So, are you calling to tell me you're bringing dinner and maybe a bottle of wine over? Because I could sure use a glass."

"Actually, I've got something better. You know that note you left me for Ben? It got smudged, so I couldn't get ahold of him."

"Oh, man. That's okay. I'll call him and let him know I didn't abandon him. But how does that tie in with something better?"

"That's the thing. He swung by the café before I closed and asked if he could get your number. I told him about the trouble you were having, and he mentioned that he might be able to help, so... we're on our way over."

"Wait, what?" She shook her head to the side to get the water out of her ears, sure she misheard. "Ben is coming here?"

"Yeah, I guess I should have given you a heads-up sooner, but we'll be there in five."

"You're fired."

"I'm your partner."

"Then as my bestie."

"You can't get rid of me! I'm yours for life. Love you!" The call ended, and Kara stared at the screen for a moment before she rushed for the stairs. Her wet socks and shoes squished and squeaked along the wood planks as she ascended the steps. She burst through the basement door and tore down the hall to her living room, picking up discarded items as she went. Theo cracked one eye open when she pulled her royal blue bra out from under him on the couch, but otherwise he ignored her.

She threw all of the clothes she'd gathered up and tossed them into her room, slamming the door shut. One of her fosters, Finnick, stood at the end of the hallway, watching her antics, and when she ran right for him, he ducked low to the ground as she sailed over him.

"Sorry, Finnick!"

Kara skidded into the kitchen, staring in horror at the stacks of dishes from dinner, breakfast, and lunch, but there was nothing she could do without water. Her other foster,

Peeta, sat in the window, his ears twitching as he stared outside. Kara walked over and leaned in next to him, seeing Ben and Charity heading up the walkway.

"Lord love a duck. How bad do I look?" she asked the seal point Siamese, whose eyes narrowed and seemed to be giving her a once-over. The doorbell rang, and Kara groaned. "Too late to worry about that now."

Kara opened the door, her gaze shifting from Charity smiling sheepishly over Ben's broad shoulders to the man himself. He took up almost the entire doorway, towering over her.

"Hi. What are you doing here?"

"Charity mentioned you'd had issues with your plumbing. Figured I'd come over and see what I could do to help." His eyes darted up, lingering on her damp hair, and he cleared his throat. "I'm afraid to ask how it's going."

Kara narrowed her eyes at his joke. "I thought you were in marketing."

"I'm a man of many hats." He waved his hand toward her. "You mind if I come in and see what you've done?"

"I guess." She stepped back, letting him inside. "I tried to tighten something, and a pipe burst in the basement."

"I'll head down there and get it stopped. Which door?"

"First one past the kitchen. I'll be right behind you," Kara said, watching him head down the hallway and open the door. Once he disappeared from sight, she spun on Charity with her hands in the air. "What the fudge?"

"What? He showed up and offered to help! After that other guy screwed you over, I figure he can't do more damage than a novice like you." Charity smirked as she shut the door. "Besides, he's pretty cute. A little awkward, maybe, but then again, so are you."

"Do not play matchmaker with us. I barely know him, and what I do know is that we wouldn't be compatible in a million years, even if I were interested."

"The soaking wet woman doth protest too much."

"I don't care how pretty you try to say it. I'm telling you, with all the love in my heart, to butt out."

"All right. Do you want me to hang out until he leaves?"

"No, it's fine. I'm not scared of Ben. He's even less interested in me than I am in him."

Charity chuckled. "Girl, we are not the same. If I had a hot man working on my pipes, I'd be the one making a move."

"He thinks I'm a shrew."

"And whose fault is that?" Charity asked sweetly.

"You can go now."

Charity put her hand on the doorknob, leaning over to kiss Kara's cheek with a smack. "I love you."

"Love you, too."

Her friend ducked out the door, shutting it with a click behind her. Kara took a moment to wring her T-shirt out over the sink before heading back downstairs. She didn't hear any more running water, and as she cleared the final stair, Kara stopped to watch Ben work. He'd removed his short-sleeve button-down shirt and discarded it next to her grandfather's toolbox, which she'd left open on top of one of the totes. He stood on the ladder in a wet white T-shirt and pants with some kind of wrench in his hand. His arms were raised over his head, the muscles in his biceps and forearms tight as he twisted a fixture on the pipe, stopping the flow of the water.

Charity had a point about him being hot. The rugged beard mixed with the lumberjack shoulders was a complete contradiction to the slightly nerdy interior. He looked like he'd played defensive linebacker in high school and made quarterbacks wet themselves. The only reason she knew anything about football was because her grandfather loved it and used to school her on all the positions and stats. It was their thing, and she'd enjoyed every second of it, especially since she hadn't had him in her life very long.

Kara shook her head with a little smile. He'd have liked Ben. He was always complaining that modern men weren't worth the air they take in because they played video games instead of learning something useful. Fixing a leaky pipe was a skill he would have appreciated.

"Wow, you actually look like you know what you're doing up there," she said, stepping off the landing and crossing the room.

He paused his motions to glance at her. "Well, I had a better teacher than YouTube."

"*Har har.* Make fun of me all you want, but there are a lot of helpful videos on YouTube."

Ben snorted. "You checked your main shutoff valve first, right?"

"Yes, and the plumber that came out this weekend did as well. Not that it means anything."

"I'll do it, too, just to be sure, since he didn't fix the problem like he said he did."

"He said it was a clog in one of the pipes, and he just had to clean it out."

"All of this looks like original piping or close to it. My guess is you have a second clog somewhere, and he didn't bother to look."

"Great. How do you know so much about clogged pipes?"

"My dad's a plumber. I used to follow him around during the summers and he taught me a thing or two."

"You didn't want to follow in his footsteps?" she asked.

He climbed down the ladder with a grunt and set the tool back inside the box. "I would have, but he wanted me to have a college degree. Now, I'm glad he pushed me."

"What made you pick marketing? I've got to be honest, you don't come off like the smooth-talking type."

Ben's smile did crazy things to her heartbeat. "I guess I enjoy the structure and seeing all the puzzle pieces come together. Plus people usually like me."

"Do they?" she teased.

Ben pursed his lips. "People who aren't stubborn."

Kara hid a smile, pointing at the pipes. "So, what's the verdict?"

"I've got to check the rest of the pipes for clogs and grab some cleaner to remove the sediment, but if that doesn't work, you're looking at a full pipe replacement."

"That sounds scarily expensive."

"If I can replace just the compromised sections, it shouldn't be too bad, but depending on how many you have, it will be several hours of work."

"How much do you think for the sections?"

"I'll have a better idea when I get through inspecting the

pipes and pressure. Then if you're okay with it, I'll come back Wednesday. My boss closed the office so he could go out of town for the holiday and beat the traffic. I can come over early and get started. Is the café open?"

"Yes, but we're closing at two."

"Do you mind me being here when you're not? I'd like to come over in the morning and get started."

"I mean..." While Kara wanted to be here while he worked, she couldn't bail on the girls at the café again. "Yeah, that's fine."

"I'll probably drag Schwartz along to help. And by help, I mean he'll stand around holding things for me. Probably gripe and whine while asking if I'm done yet."

Kara giggled. "Sounds delightful."

"Oh, it will be a joy. You got some place you can hole up until I can get your water going again?"

"I can go over to Charity's. We're planning this whole Friendsgiving thing, so she'll be able to pin me down where I can't escape." She tucked a hair behind her ear. "I feel really bad letting you do this. If you don't want to waste your vacation working down here, I understand."

"Don't feel bad. I'm not doing this completely out of the goodness of my heart." His gaze settled on her, his tone low and gravelly. "You've got something I want."

Kara blinked at him, her mouth suddenly dry. "Wh-what?"

"I want you to get that food-slinging creature out of my bathroom."

It took Kara a second before her brain caught up, and she burst out laughing. "Oh, the kitten!"

"Yes, the one you said I'd only have for a few hours, and

I've had him for two days. Did I mention that I like my home clean and orderly? Right now, no matter how much I scrub it, my guest bathroom reeks like toxic gas and day-old tuna."

Kara covered her nose and mouth as if the mere mention of that smelly combo would conjure it. "That sounds awful. I tried finding someone, but all of my fosters are either at their limit or traveling. I know it's a lot to ask, but can you just hang on to him until next week?"

"Seriously? There is no one who can take him?"

"We had to do some major shifts to get enough cages for all the fosters coming in. I've got two of my own, plus Theo, and with all these issues with my plumbing, I can't take in another at the moment." She squeezed his arm, giving him her best pleading look. "Please, Ben. One more week and he'll be out of your hair."

"I've heard that before," he grumbled.

"I really appreciate you stepping up and coming here to help me out—you're slowly getting off my naughty list."

Ben rolled his eyes. "I know you're buttering me up so I'll agree to your terms, but Santa isn't too pleased with you, either."

"What if I sweeten the deal a bit?"

"I'm listening."

"How about free coffee and breakfast for every day you foster that kitten?"

"You can't afford to give away ten bucks a day."

"I told you, we're fine."

"Whatever you say."

Kara scowled. "You know there's this thing called tact,

right? You apply it so you don't come off like such a jerk when you speak?"

"Hey, I'm sorry. I guess I'm still wondering why you run a nonprofit café if you don't want people to come to it."

Kara's heart squeezed. "My reasons are personal."

"Personal feelings should be set aside if you want to run a successful business."

"Can we drop this and get back to my pipes, please?"

Ben stared at her for several ticks and Kara waited, afraid he would keep pushing, but finally, he shrugged. "You're right. It's none of my concern how you choose to run your business. I'll do this work on your plumbing and hold on to the kitten for a week."

"Thank you. Just let me know how much everything is and your labor costs and I'll get the money for you."

"No labor. You buy the supplies and get that kitten out of my guest bath, and I'll call us square."

Under normal circumstances, Kara would have argued and pushed to pay him for his time, but the dire circumstances of her savings account made her nod. "All right."

Ben closed up her toolbox and Kara's gaze kept straying to the expanse of white fabric clinging to his chest.

"You have email, right?" he asked suddenly.

Kara's eyes jerked up, but he was looking at the pipes and not her. Her cheeks burned at the thought of him catching her ogling him. "Yes, but I hardly use it. I prefer text."

"Then I'll text you the receipt and my Venmo after I grab the supplies."

Kara didn't mention she didn't use Venmo, only nodded. Charity could talk her through how to use it. "Oh, and if you happen to take any pictures of the kitten, that would be great for his future adoptive family."

"Is that your clever way of asking for proof-of-life pics?"

"What? No, I didn't think you would—"

"I'm kidding, Kara. You wouldn't ask me to keep him if you thought I'd ever hurt him, right?"

"Of course I wouldn't."

Ben slipped into his shirt, leaving it unbuttoned and hanging open. "I better get out of your hair before I tick you off again."

"Thank you. And I am sorry for jumping all over you the first time we met. I know you were just doing your job. I just hate social media."

"To tell you the truth, I'm not a big fan of it right now, either, but it's a necessity to reach people, unfortunately."

"I would think a guy like you would be on it every day, charming his many followers."

A shadow passed over his face. "You'd be wrong."

Chapter Seven

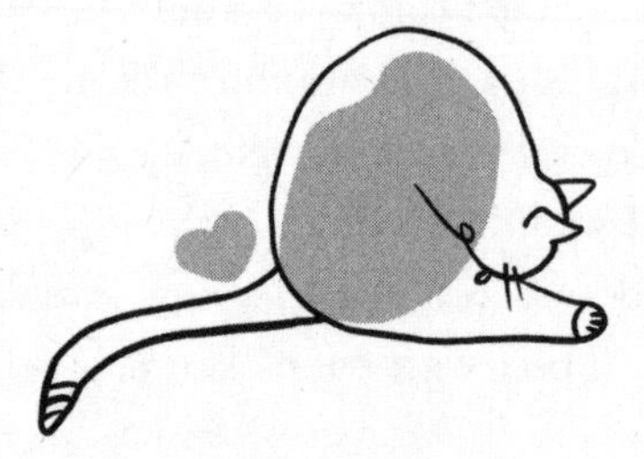

Luna the Bombay came to the café when her owner passed away, and although her fur may be dark, she'll light up your life.

"ALL I'M SAYING IS that pineapple on pizza is a sign of deep emotional trauma," Schwartz argued behind Ben as they stepped into Ben's house. Except for the black leather sofa set and entertainment center with a seventy-inch TV Ben had set up on Sunday, there was nothing else to the room yet. No pictures of family and friends on the wall. Since he didn't have any plans for Thanksgiving, he could get started on tearing out the carpet in the guest rooms and installing the wood floors in there.

And then the guest bathroom, if he could get that kitten out of it!

Ben opened the fridge and slipped the box of soda he was

carrying inside, quirking an eyebrow at his friend. "Where did you read that?"

"I think I saw it on TikTok."

"Oh yes, such a credible source of truth."

Schwartz placed the two boxes of pizza on the island and set the bag of plates, napkins, and cheesy breadsticks next to it. "Hey, it's weird, man. Pizza is meant to have meat and veggies, and even the latter is debatable. Not fruit."

"Good, because you can't have any of mine." Ben took a step toward the cupboard where his glasses were and pulled out two, setting them on the counter next to the boxes. "Do me a favor? Fill these with ice while I check on the creature."

"I'm surprised the demon hasn't overstayed his welcome."

Ben laughed. "Is this because he still hates you?"

"I don't care if that holy terror likes me or not. I'm thinking of you, my friend. Before you know it, he'll be tearing up your furniture, pooping in your closet, and jumping on your back when you're in bed with a woman and she'll never call you again."

"I thought you liked cats."

"I do, but not *that* one."

"Well, you don't have to worry, because as soon as Monday rolls around, he is gone. Not that your opinion on my life matters much."

"Ouch, that is cold! These hands helped you hang those cabinets, and you're saying that I mean nothing to you?"

"You mean a lot. Your opinion? Eh."

"Screw you twice, then." Schwartz tossed the top pizza box open with a satisfied sigh. "You mind if I get started? I'm starving!"

"Go for it, but there better be three breadsticks waiting for me."

"After you were rude to me? No promises."

"I mean it!" Ben hollered over his shoulder as he reached the bathroom. He turned the knob and an orange blur shot out of the room, turning back to rub against the side of his shoe.

Meow!

"What? You eat all your food already?"

The kitten hooked his claws into the sides of Ben's jeans and climbed up his leg. When he got to his thigh, Ben winced as the kitten's claws dug in, and he pulled him off. "Whoa, kid, you don't want to nick something important." Before he realized what he'd done, he cuddled the soft kitten against his chest, listening to the crackling purr as he stared in at the disaster he'd made. The food bowl was still nearly full, but his water looked like he'd thrown litter in it all day.

"You're messy—you know that, right?" Ben bent over, holding the kitten in one hand and grabbing the bowl in the other. The kitty squirmed out from under his palm and onto his shoulder, rubbing his head against his cheek. Ben walked out into the living room, and Schwartz looked up from his plate of meat lover's pizza long enough to snort.

"You're so whipped by that pu—"

"Keep talking and I'm going to make you drink this."

Ben passed by Schwartz close enough to show him the nasty water bowl.

"I was going to say putty-tat! I apologize!" Schwartz laughed, holding up his hands as if that would stop the water if Ben decided to throw it.

"As you should."

"Have you talked to Kara since you left her place yesterday?" Schwartz's question caught Ben off guard, and he spilled some of the water on his tile floor.

"Great." He pulled a few paper towels off the roll and mopped it up.

"That's a no then?"

"No, I haven't spoken to her except a question here or there about this guy and going to work on her pipes tomorrow. You're still coming with me, right?"

"Yeah, although I'm a little curious as to why we're working on her pipes when neither of us are plumbers or getting paid for it."

"Because I know enough about plumbing to fix it and you've got nothing to do."

"Yes, but I thought you couldn't stand this woman. Why are you going out of your way to help her?"

Ben considered Schwartz's question, because he'd been asking himself the same one. He didn't like that she'd already been taken advantage of by a guy she'd paid to fix her problem. If someone had pulled that with his sister, Birdy, he'd make them rectify the situation. He couldn't really say that he liked Kara, but he found her...entertaining. When she got irritated, her cheeks turned this pretty shade of pink and her eyes brightened like someone flipped a switch behind them, making them shine.

She was also stubborn, she liked to get her own way, and she could wear a man down with the sweetest smile he'd ever seen.

"Whoa, where did you go?"

Ben snapped to attention, realizing he hadn't answered him. "I just don't want to tick her off before she takes this thing off my hands."

"Yeah, you look like you're really anxious to get rid of it." That was all Schwartz said before he went back to eating, and Ben didn't add anything to the conversation. He cleaned up the water and grabbed a fresh can of food from the counter. He carried all of it back to the bathroom, the kitten continuing to ride on his shoulder like a fluffy parrot. When he squatted down to set the water on the floor, the kitten slowly dropped to the ground. Ben popped the top on the canned food and tapped it on the plate until the container was empty. The kitten dived into the round pâté face-first, his paws spread wide in the mush, and the small cat snorted like a pig as he devoured the food.

Ben released a low chuckle and pulled out his phone to take a quick video. The kitten didn't look up from his meal when Ben left the bathroom, closing the door behind him as he went back out into the living room, still laughing.

"What's so funny?"

"Do kittens usually snort when they eat?"

"I've never had one that did, but I've seen them in online videos. Why? Captain Evilfuzz do that?"

"Yeah, while shoving his face into his mush."

"I'm telling you, that thing is feral."

Ben shrugged and went about washing his hands. His stomach rumbled at the smell of his pizza, and after he dried his hands, he loaded his plate with cheese sticks and slices before joining Schwartz in the living room. "What are we going to play first?"

"How about *CoD*? It's a classic."

"Fine by me."

"Cool." Schwartz stood up from the couch with his empty plate in one hand and stretched. "I'm going to take a leak."

"Use my bathroom."

Ben bit into his pizza and tapped the Google app on his phone screen. He'd been thinking about Kara and the café since he left her place. Her aversion to marketing for personal reasons floored him, especially because there weren't any other cafés like it in the area. It should be hopping.

Ben typed the café's name into Google. Their website was barren, with a single page and mission statement. There were icons for Instagram and Facebook, but when he clicked those, they were as lackluster as the website. While many of the photos were aesthetically pleasing, there was nothing to set them apart from any other rescue. To get people's attention, you needed to give them a call to action, and all he was seeing was pretty foam lattes and cute cats... but what did they need? What could the public do to help them? These unanswered questions were the key to proper marketing.

But she doesn't want help.

Schwartz came out into the living room, and Ben held up his phone. "Look at this."

Schwartz took the phone from him, studying the screen. "What am I looking at?"

"The cat café's website."

"Oh, no. No, no, no. This is bad." Schwartz shook his head and passed the phone back. "They need a complete overhaul. Key words. Visuals. Branding."

Ben agreed, munching on his pizza as he went back

to Instagram, ignoring the pop-up that asked him to sign in. Ben knew the café was struggling, even if Kara denied it, and even if she was interested, they'd never be able to afford an in-depth marketing plan. The only way they would get any traction was a boost in traffic and clientele. Basically, they needed help but couldn't afford it, and Ben was afraid that if he offered their services for free, Kara may take it as him trying to be a white knight riding in to save her.

If only there were a way to help out the café without stepping out of bounds with Kara.

"You ready for me to destroy you?" Schwartz asked, holding a controller under his nose.

Ben took it sheepishly, setting it on the couch next to him. "Actually, I have a better way to spend our night."

Schwartz's gaze swung from his face to the phone, and his head shook back and forth rapidly. "Oh, no! I am off work and was promised pizza and video games. Besides, we need to circle back to why you want to help out some woman who a) didn't ask for your help, b) doesn't particularly like you, and c) isn't paying us?"

"Think of it as a pro bono project. I'll take it to them, and if they aren't interested in our advice, then I'll be the one taking all the heat."

"Pro bono projects get us brownie points with the boss. Are we telling him?"

"This is more of a secret pro bono project. Something to make us feel good, so we don't end up like Ebenezer Scrooge, standing in front of the ghost of Christmas past, looking at all the good we could have done but didn't."

"You do know I'm Jewish, right? Christmas ghosts don't scare me."

"Can you imagine the way Charity would look at you if you helped save the café?"

Several seconds ticked by before Schwartz sighed heavily, setting his controller aside. "This is the last time I let you trick me with promises of video games and pizza. You sit on a throne of lies and broken promises."

"I gave you pizza."

"Which is why I'm participating in this pity project. At least one of my needs has been met."

Ben grinned. "Is Charity the other reason you're helping out?"

Schwartz scowled. "Are we going to talk about girls or get this done?"

"Get this done. You wanna grab my laptop while I finish eating?" Ben asked.

"Where is your laptop?"

"In the spare bedroom."

"Sure, first you bamboozle me, and now I'm a gofer." Schwartz got up from the couch, paused where Ben could still see him, and hollered, "This thing is having a fit."

"You can let him out. I'm done eating."

"Greeeaaat." Schwartz turned the corner, and Ben heard the knob click. "Hello, Demon."

Ben laughed when the kitten answered with a high-pitched growl, a second before the small cat sped into the living room and rushed to Ben. He clawed his way up onto the couch next to him and rubbed against his outstretched hand.

When Schwartz came back into the room, Ben said, "Don't mind Schwartz, little man. Your aversion to him hurts his feelings."

Schwartz grumbled something Ben couldn't hear and sat down on the love seat, pulling Ben's laptop from the bag. "What are we thinking for their logo?"

"What about a plate with a cat curled on top? Maybe little steam swirls coming out the top?"

Schwartz burst out laughing. "You want it to look like they cooked the cat?"

"No, crap. Hmm...what about an espresso cup? The cat could be curled around it with little paw prints on the outside of the cup and steam lines above the cup?"

"Better," Schwartz said, tapping away at the keys.

"I think we should keep the font the same as their sign out front, but we need pictures of all the baked goods that they offer, maybe a full menu on their website—"

"What about a featured pet page?" Schwartz offered.

Ben snapped his finger and pointed it at Schwartz. "I like it. I also think they need to network and partner with local businesses for some cross-promotion. And Kara mentioned they eventually want to open a clinic in the back, which will need to have a separate page connected to the café. A Meet the Staff page with backgrounds..."

Schwartz tapped away as Ben talked, time speeding by as they spitballed ideas back and forth. It was well past eleven before they came up for air, and that was only because the kitten hopped up next to Schwartz, his tail twitching as he watched Schwartz's hands fly across the keyboard of the laptop.

"I'd stop moving. He's got you in his sights," Ben joked.

Schwartz held a hand out toward the kitten. "You ready to be friends now? You know I'm the one who convinced him to save you, right?"

The tiny cat pounced at his hand, wrapping his body around Schwartz as he attacked. Ben jumped up, ready to save his friend, but Schwartz's laughter stalled his rescue.

"Oh, you think you're tough, huh?" Schwartz set the laptop on the side table and went after him with his other hand, tipping the kitten onto his back and tickling his belly. "You're weak, son. I got you!"

Ben laughed as Schwartz gently shook the cat until the kitten finally escaped, only to turn around sideways and hop back toward Schwartz. Ben grabbed the laptop while they played and printed up their plan.

"Maybe you should adopt him now that the two of you are friends," Ben said as he returned to his seat.

"Nah, my apartment is barely big enough for me."

"How come you don't buy?"

"I like to keep my options open. You never know when I might decide to pack up and hightail it to the Bahamas or somewhere equally beautiful."

"Right," Ben laughed, leaning over to grab his phone when it beeped. He tapped his message app and stilled:

It's Boone. I know Ma told you I'm in town. Can we meet?

Ben's thumb hovered over the chat box as he stared down at the message.

"You okay? You've got a weird look on your face."

Ben pressed the Delete button harder than necessary and tossed his phone away. "Yeah, I'm good. You tired?"

"Not yet."

Ben grabbed the gaming controller with a smirk. "Because it's time I destroy you."

"In your dreams, Reese."

Chapter Eight

Smush is a fluffy Ragdoll cross looking for an adult-only home with plenty of toys, adoration, and a good stylist to tame his silky mane.

"I THINK HE'S QUIRKY."

Kara turned in the passenger seat, studying Charity's profile. Since Kara spent the night with her, they'd carpooled to work together. It was a little after two, and they were headed back to Kara's house to check on Ben and Schwartz, which was how the subject of Schwartz's "quirkiness" entered the conversation.

"Remind me, is quirky a good thing?"

Charity shrugged. "Kinda. I think he's funny. Seems like a nice guy."

"Oh no, the kiss of death for you," Kara razzed good-naturedly.

Charity snorted. "I don't always go for the bad boy."

"No, you're absolutely right. Tell me about your last date. The one you wore the yellow dress for? What was he straddling in his picture?"

"First of all, a motorcycle does not automatically make you a bad boy."

"No, but being on Tinder with a pregnant girlfriend at home does."

Charity grimaced. "I'm not arguing. He's a scumbag. I'm just saying it wasn't the motorcycle. Believe me, I'll never forget his girlfriend walking in to dinner and giving me a face full of red wine. Like I knew she existed."

"At least you learned to always background check, or at least social-media stalk, these clowns."

"Now you sound like my dad."

"He is a brilliant man."

"Yes, and if you give him the chance, he will tell you so."

"What is up with you? You've been especially snappy anytime I bring up your parents lately."

Charity groaned. "I know, I'm sorry. They're driving me absolutely insane. It was their choice to fly down to San Diego for Thanksgiving, and just because I don't want to tag along and meet their friend's eligible bachelor son, I'm this huge disappointment."

"You could have gone with them anyway. Just because your parents want to introduce you to someone doesn't mean you have to like him."

"It's a double-edged sword. If I do like him, then they win, but if I don't like him, I'm unreasonable and picky."

"Char, you are a woman in your thirties! When are you

going to stop acting like an angry teenager when it comes to your folks?"

Her friend shot her a side-eye glare. "You're losing bestie points. And you were five away from a free frozen yogurt."

Kara laughed. "Sorry, lovely. Sometimes I wish I had your problems is all."

"Ugh, and now I feel like a jerk."

Kara reached across and squeezed Charity's hand. "You're not. I just think it's nice having people that love you."

"I love you," Charity said softly.

"And I love you." Kara felt no real sadness at not having any family, because it was impossible to miss something she never really had. Her mother hadn't neglected her, but she wasn't the type to put Kara's needs first either. Her mother's string of boyfriends had taught Kara to like animals better than people, but only because the men were just as self-involved as her mother. Even when it was just the two of them, Kara usually felt alone.

It wasn't until she was fifteen that she got a brief glimpse of what it was like to have a family. Her father knew about her existence, but with the exception of one visit when she was two, he never came around. The money her sperm donor sent every month stopped, and when her mother called the lawyer to find out why, he informed her that Connor Ingalls had passed away, that his parents only recently became aware they had a grandchild, and that there would be no more support unless they were allowed to meet Kara. She hadn't even known she had grandparents until her mother left her on their doorstep a few weeks before Christmas like a UPS package. She remembered standing on the stoop of that grand house with her cat inside a carrier and a small suitcase, trembling with fear as the door swung open and a sweet-faced elderly woman opened the door. Kara held out the envelope her mother had given her and waited on weak knees as the woman read it.

To her utter shock, her grandmother cried out and dropped the letter. She was suddenly yanked into soft arms, the sweet smell of powder enveloping her, and her eardrum was blown out as the woman yelled, "Frank! Get out here! We got the best gift in the world!"

In Kara's opinion, it was the other way around. Frank and Ethel Ingalls were a bright spot in an otherwise mundane life. She'd never known her father, but it was hard to imagine the man was raised by such warm, loving people. They welcomed her into their home, allowing her to decorate her room, which was bigger than the whole single-wide she'd shared with her mom for fifteen years. They cultivated her love of animals, and when she graduated from high school with an acceptance letter to UC Davis, they were the reason she was able to attend.

She'd had her grandfather for seven years, and her grandmother had lived to see her graduate from veterinary school. They'd left her their estate and a trust, which included a collection of mutual funds she hadn't touched. She'd sold their house and used the money from its sale to buy her place, and what was left to live on while they tried to get the café up and running. With the exception of Charity and a few friends she'd made over the years, she had nobody else in the world, but Kara just accepted that as the way things were.

Maybe that's why she struggled so hard to connect with

someone, especially romantically. Worthy was the first man she'd ever let get close, and Kara suspected he was able to snow her so completely because she was lonely. There had been a few men before, here or there, but the relationships had always ended quickly. One of them mentioned she was exhausting to be around. Maybe he was right.

They pulled up the driveway to her house, the yellow exterior coming into view, but the cheery color did nothing to brighten her train of thought.

"Am I hard to love?" Kara asked as they parked next to Ben's car.

Charity swiveled in the seat. "What? Absolutely not! You are funny, smart, compassionate. The way your brain jumps from one subject to the next keeps me on my toes—"

"So, you're saying I'm quirky?" Kara joked in an attempt to stop Charity from humoring her. Kara didn't doubt her intelligence or compassion, but sometimes she wished personable and engaging could be used to describe her personality. She'd tried to loosen up around Charity's friends and even the customers at the café, but she often felt like a wooden puppet trying to be a real human.

Charity poked her arm. "Get out of my car, you nerd."

Kara did, grabbing her purse from the floorboard. She looked in the back, where Theo was curled up in his carrier. "Hey, T, you ready to go?"

He lifted his head slowly and stretched out his front arms behind the grated door.

"Yeah, sure, take your time, because we have all day." Kara reached into the back and picked up his crate, carrying Theo and her purse toward the house. "Do you think I'm crazy for leaving two men I don't know alone in my house all day?"

"I mean...people have done crazier things. Besides, I'm sure neither of them have a dangerous bone in their body."

"But are all their bones trustworthy?" Kara said, as Charity opened the door and waved her inside.

"You don't want me to respond to that."

Kara rolled her eyes. "You know what I mean."

"I was just trying to lighten the mood." Charity closed the front door with a soft *snift*. "It's quiet."

"A little too quiet." Kara set the crate and her purse down on the entry-room table, nervousness fluttering through her. She opened the cage door, and Theo jumped down to the floor, padding into the living room. "You don't think a pipe burst and they drowned, do you?"

"Doubtful, but not impossible. Let's go down there and—"

"Hey, you're here," Ben said, coming from the direction of her bedroom. Both women jumped with high-pitched screams, grabbing onto each other for balance.

"Where did you come from, stealthy?" Charity asked, breathlessly.

"Back bedroom."

Kara frowned, suspicion threading through her voice. "What were you doing in there?"

"Checking the water pressure. I wanted to make sure I didn't miss another blockage." He gave her a jaunty thumbs-up. "You're good, by the way."

"Oh, thank you." Kara's face burned, aware of his gaze on her. She didn't mean to sound so accusatory, but after Worthy and everything he did, she hadn't been around a lot of men, let alone let them in her house when she wasn't there. She'd never thought twice about allowing Worthy to use her computer or know all her passwords; she was going to marry him, after all.

Unfortunately, Kara learned from that mistake in the worst possible way.

Charity broke the silence with a clap of her hands. "I am so glad, because if we had to move Friendsgiving to my duplex, things were going to be cramped."

"You're having a Friendsgiving?" Schwartz's voice came from behind them, and they whirled around to find him taking a bite of a massive sandwich he'd either bought or brought with him.

"Yeah, tomorrow," Charity said, alternating her attention between the two men on either side of them. "Both of you are welcome to join us. Games start at two, and we'll probably eat around four."

Schwartz nodded his chin toward Ben. "We'll be there."

"Thought you had to go to your mom's?" Ben asked.

"They eat early. You can come with me to that, too. I'll just keep my sister away from you."

"His sister?" Kara cocked a brow, and Ben rolled his eyes.

"He's talking nonsense because tomorrow I'm not doing anything but installing flooring."

"By yourself?" Kara asked.

"On Thanksgiving?" Charity held a hand over her chest dramatically. "That's tragic."

"I'm doing a home remodel, and I only have time on nights and weekends. I've got the guest rooms and the bathroom to finish, and then I'm done."

"So, do that in the morning and knock off in time to come by for dinner," Charity said, her tone firm. "No one should be alone on Thanksgiving, right, Kara?"

Kara had a feeling Charity was up to something and barely refrained from scowling at her friend. "Of course. The more the merrier."

Schwartz walked around them to slap Ben on the shoulder. "I'll finish at my mom's and come by to grab you. I've never been to a Friendsgiving before."

"Sounds great. Thanks for the invite." Ben cleared his throat and waved his hand. "You want to test out the waters, so to speak?"

"Absolutely." She went into the kitchen first and turned on the kitchen faucet. The water streamed from the chrome neck without so much as a splutter, and she smiled happily. "Perfect."

"Let me show you some of the fixtures I replaced below. I was afraid I'd have to make a hole in the wall to check the pipes behind the shower, but luckily, everything seems to be running smoothly with the ones I already took care of."

"I appreciate not coming home to holes in my drywall," Kara laughed.

"We're going to stay up here and talk about Friendsgiving," Schwartz called as Kara followed Ben out of the kitchen.

"We are?" Charity said, archly.

"Um, please will you tell me more about Friendsgiving and what I can bring to help alleviate your burden?"

Kara snickered quietly as she reached for the basement

door. Charity never liked people to make decisions for her, even small ones.

"Nice save," Kara muttered.

Ben got there first and held it for her. "What was that?"

"Schwartz backtracking with Charity. I said *nice save*."

"Ah, yes, Schwartz can step in it sometimes, especially with women, but he's been great to me."

"He seems nice." Kara didn't add that he probably didn't have a snowball's chance in hell with Charity. While her best friend denied she had a type, with Charity, nice guys really did finish last.

Kara headed down first with him a half step behind her. When they reached the bottom of the stairs, Ben pointed to the exposed pipes. "I found three more sections besides the one your Saturday plumber fixed. You'll need to do regular treatments of drain opener to stop the mineral buildup, but other than that, this should get you by for a while until you can afford to fully replace it all."

Kara noted the shiny metal pieces standing out against the dingier piping and smiled at Ben warmly. "I can't thank you enough for doing this. I know I've put you through the wringer and you're probably regretting ever bumping into me on the street, but I really do appreciate it."

"It's not a problem. Honestly, I love this kind of thing. Especially when I know I'm helping out someone who's had a rough time. I hate people who take advantage of others."

His statement made her feel even guiltier about her earlier suspicions when he'd come out of her bedroom. Not that she thought everyone should have unwavering trust when you first met them, but she'd allowed her experience with Worthy to cloud her judgment so much, she didn't know if people were really acting shady or if she just expected them to be. Charity pointed out several examples of her chasing off a man because something he did reminded her of Worthy, but it was hard to allow anyone close after what she'd been through.

"I guess I'm not as smart as I let on, huh?" she joked, but to her surprise, Ben rested his hand on her shoulder and turned her to face him.

"Hey, having faith in humanity doesn't make you dumb. Their actions are on them, not you."

Kara swallowed, staring into his earnest expression and the temperature turned up to eleven with a dash of humidity. The heat of his palm burned through the thin cotton of her shirt to her skin, causing a layer of goose bumps to pop up along her arm.

"I... thanks. That's nice of you to say."

"It's the truth."

His eyes held her mesmerized in the dimness of her basement, and Kara's body swayed toward him involuntarily.

"Whoa, you okay?" he asked, catching her other shoulder.

"Oh, yeah, of course. Must be all the black mold down here. I got dizzy for a second." She pulled away from him and backed up, caught off guard when she bumped into a stack of totes, and Kara would have fallen over them if Ben hadn't grabbed her. Instead, she stumbled forward, landing face-first in his chest, his arm wrapped around her waist.

"Thanks," she mumbled against his T-shirt.

"No problem. You should move all these totes against the wall instead of leaving them about the room."

"I'll get right on that." Kara pulled her face away from his chest and stared at the smudge of foundation right in the center between his pecs. "I am so sorry." She ran her thumb over the spot, trying to wipe it off, but it only made it worse. "A little OxiClean and water will take that out, if you want to give it to me."

He caught her hand against his chest, stopping her motions. "It's just a T-shirt, Kara. I'll throw it in the wash when I get home."

"What's going on down here?" Schwartz stood at the bottom of the stairs next to Charity, both of them watching. Charity swung her arm in a sharp snap that caught Schwartz in the chest, and he yelped. "Ow! What was that for?"

"They were having a moment."

"No, we weren't!" Kara said quickly.

Ben didn't comment, but he dropped her hand, taking a step away from her.

"Okay, you could be right," Schwartz said, rubbing a hand across his chest. "I've been filling Charity in on our marketing plan for the café, and she's on board."

Kara looked from Charity to Schwartz and finally to Ben. "You made us a marketing plan?"

"Yeah. I know you said that you didn't need help, but we had a spare hour or two last night and came up with some easy changes we think can at least rev things up for the holidays."

"The folder's up on the counter if you want to look it over," Schwartz added. "We mapped out a twenty-five-day promotional event called Twenty-Five Days of Catmas, where each day you have something cool for your patrons. Maybe a free ornament, or on Christmas, because I'm sure you're closed, you drop a coupon on your website that can be used in the new year."

"They're pretty amazing, right?" Charity said.

She should be mad that he ignored her wishes and made a marketing plan after she'd told him they were fine.

Instead, Kara mused, "Amazing."

"You don't have to take any of our suggestions, but it's there if you need it." His warm brown eyes roamed over her face and Kara got that woozy feeling again in her legs. What the heck was going on with her?

"We appreciate the advice!" Charity called. "Don't we, Kara?"

"Yes," Kara ground out, her face burning.

Ben cleared his throat. "We should get out of your hair."

"I'm not in anyone's hair," Schwartz said.

Kara saw the disgruntled look Ben shot his friend before he met her eyes with a small smile. "I'll see you tomorrow."

"Yeah, see ya."

Ben mumbled a quiet goodbye to Charity before giving Schwartz a light shove up the stairs. When the two men disappeared, Charity stepped off the landing with her hands up. "What the heck was that? Why did you act like you were repulsed by him?"

"I didn't."

"You couldn't get away from him fast enough. The guy spent his day off helping you. That's when you pull him closer and offer to cook him dinner."

"Charity, he did it because I remind him of his sister."

"Ew, wait... what exactly did he say?"

"I can't quote it, but basically he hoped someone would do the same if anyone took advantage of his sister."

Charity popped her palm against Kara's forehead. "Not the same thing. Mark my words, my friend, men like *that* are few and far between. Don't be an insecure weirdo and miss all the signs."

"What signs?" Kara asked.

Charity grabbed Kara's cheeks, squeezing until Kara's mouth was puckered like a fish. "The signs that he likes you!"

"He does not," Kara mumbled through pursed lips.

Charity released her with a shake of her head. "I can't with you."

She turned and stomped up the stairs, leaving Kara alone in the basement with her thoughts. Charity was reading too much into Ben's actions, mistaking kindness for interest, but the fact of the matter was that Kara wasn't looking for anything. She had too much on her plate to add the complications of dating.

"Kara! Get your booty up here. We've got things to discuss!"

She climbed up the stairs and joined Charity in the kitchen, where her best friend was headfirst in Kara's fridge. Kara noticed the stack of mail on the table and leafed through it slowly. "You got my mail?"

"Yeah, I heard the postal carrier on the porch, so I just grabbed it from him."

A letter with familiar handwriting caught her eye, and her hands shook.

"Kara?" Charity called, her voice coming through like they were underwater. "What's wrong?"

The words stuck in her throat.

It's Worthy.

Chapter Nine

Tater is a buff domestic shorthair with a distinctive meow, who enjoys nature shows and lying in the windowsill on a sunny day.

KARA SAT AT HER kitchen table the morning of Thanksgiving, absentmindedly peeling potatoes as Charity and Tasha talked about which fork went on the outside of the place setting. Her gaze kept straying to the junk drawer on her left where she'd tossed Worthy's letter last night. Charity wanted to send it back to him, but Kara reminded her that he'd be out of prison soon anyway. If she sent it back, he might be tempted to seek her out to deliver whatever message was in the letter in person.

The last thing Kara wanted was to have Worthy show up at the café and for people to recognize him, to put two and two together and realize she was the Grinch's Bride. After everything went down two years ago, she'd thought about leaving the area, but Charity was here, and she was all Kara had in the whole world.

Besides, she'd expected Worthy to stay inside longer than twenty-four months. When she'd heard about the plea deal, Kara wanted to vomit.

She set the last peeled potato into the pot and took it to the sink to fill it up.

"Oh, Kara, thank you for doing that," Tasha exclaimed, waving long, artistically designed nails in the air. "I would have done it, but these cost almost as much as my car payment!"

Kara glanced down at her own short nails and back at Tasha's brown talons with jeweled tips. "No problem. I'm going to put these on to boil and then go take a shower. Are you okay with that, Char?"

"Of course. Are you going to put makeup on?"

Kara quirked a brow. "No more than usual. Why?"

"I was just thinking you could wear that green dress we got in San Fran and maybe some red lipstick. Make those babies pop."

"You do have great lips," Tasha offered.

Kara's eyes narrowed. "Charity...Is there something you want to explain?"

"I'm just saying, you might want to dress up a bit. There's a guy I want to introduce you to and—"

"You did not." Kara's gaze shifted between Charity's sheepish grin and Tasha's eye roll.

"I told you it wasn't going to work," Tasha said, shrugging when Kara looked at her. "I'm just saying, sweetie, you don't seem interested in men. If you're asexual, that's totally valid, but Adam is hmm-delicious, and I hate to see a fine man go to waste."

"Tasha, you have a man," Charity snapped.

"But I can still appreciate beauty when I see it."

"Kara, I only invited Adam because I thought the two of you have a lot in common. Adam's a lab technician at UC Davis, he has a cat named Spartan, and he is really shy at first."

"How did you meet him?" Kara asked.

"I saw him on one of the dating apps and contacted him after reading his profile."

"Wait, this guy thinks he's coming to meet you, but instead you're going to bait and switch with me?" Kara squeaked out.

"Of course not! I told him I had an amazing friend in the medical field I thought would be perfect for him, sent him your picture, and he said yes."

Kara's mind turned over too quickly, processing everything Charity said with abject horror. "So, you haven't even met him?"

"Do you really think I'd invite someone into your house I didn't know? We met for coffee and found out we have some mutual friends in common. I checked with them, and the consensus is he's a catch."

"Then why don't you date him?" Kara asked.

Charity sighed, wiping her hands on one of the kitchen towels hanging over the oven door. "Tasha, make sure nothing burns, okay? We'll be right back."

Kara let Charity take her arm and lead her into her bedroom. It was barely noon, so the only people in the house were the two of them and Tasha. Kara liked Charity's childhood friend but always felt like a mallard standing next to two swans. They accented their beauty with makeup, got their hair done often, and were always talking about skin care. Kara could barely dredge up the energy to keep her split ends trimmed.

Charity closed the bedroom door behind her and crossed her arms. "Is this about Worthy's letter?"

"What?"

"Is your aversion to meeting Adam because you're still spinning about that letter showing up from Worthy? Because you don't have to hold on to it like some kind of horror-movie object, waiting for someone to find it and unleash its evil. You can read it, see what he has to say, and chuck it or, better yet, burn it without reading as I suggested."

"It's not about Worthy. It's that this is an incredibly awkward way to meet someone, at a large gathering filled with a bunch of people I already feel weird around."

"What do you mean? You like Tasha and Rami, don't you?"

"I like all your friends, Char, but they are *your* friends. They already think I'm the strange, quiet girl who you adopted in college. I don't want to go out with someone you found for me. Did it ever occur to you that I'm happy alone?"

"I know you're used to being on your own, but you deserve someone amazing, babe, and hiding from the world isn't going to change that you fell for a jerk. I've fallen for dozens of toads dressed up like princes. It's time to get back on the horse."

"I don't like horses. You know that."

Charity snorted. "It's a figure of speech, and you know

it. You're really fine being without someone you could potentially spend your life with? I'm not sure Adam would be that for you, but you should try taking chances again. You don't need someone to complete you, but a date or two couldn't hurt, right?"

Kara wasn't sure how to answer that. Did she like being alone? No, but she was used to it. With the exception of the few months with Worthy, she'd been the girl who stayed home studying or reading most nights when other girls were out on dates. While she could count the number of guys who asked her out during college on one hand, it had never bothered her that she wasn't everyone's bag. Kara didn't need or want all the complications of dating. She'd rather find someone else who enjoyed staying in versus bar hopping on a Saturday night, who preferred ordering takeout to going into a crowded restaurant.

Worthy had played into all her likes. He'd even pretended to adore her cat, but sitting across from him with only a glass barrier between them, she'd finally caught a glimpse of the real Worthy.

"I can't understand why you don't believe me, Kara. I'm your fiancé."

"They showed me the evidence, Worthy. I'm not stupid."

"You sure about that?" he asked coldly, leaning closer to the glass.

"What is that supposed to mean?"

"I think it's about time we got our stories straight."

"What stories?"

"The one I'm going to tell my lawyer that will take you down with me."

"I didn't do anything!"

"Now, who is going to believe that?"

"Kara?"

She met Charity's gaze, wishing it was just the two of them today. But that wasn't healthy. Kara needed to branch out, meet new people. Not necessarily a guy, but actually make friends.

Opening herself up to those situations made Kara vulnerable to trusting the wrong person, and although the chances of her falling for a grifter-sociopath again were slim, they weren't completely out of the realm of possibility.

"I'll put on the dress, and I will let you introduce us, but not until after I take care of the cats at the café that need meds."

Charity clapped her hands gleefully before giving her a hug. "Yes. Thank you. It would have been terribly awkward if you said no."

"As opposed to the level of awkward now? I do find it ironic that you ditched your parents because they were trying to set you up, just so you could play matchmaker for me."

"They are doing it out of control, and I do it out of love and concern. That is the difference."

"If you say so."

"All right, I will let you shower," Charity said, releasing her.

"Thanks for respecting my privacy," she deadpanned.

"Oh, stop acting like you hate my meddling. You wouldn't know what to make of it if I stopped." Charity snapped her fingers and did an about-face. "Speaking of meddling, I know we talked about some of the marketing tips Ben and Schwartz gave us, but that Twenty-Five Days of Catmas really stuck with me. I thought we could expand on it, if you are willing."

Kara stopped pulling undergarments out of her drawer to study Charity's face. "Expand on it how?"

"Like, we do a new cat profile on Instagram every day starting December first. We could set the whole café up with holiday cheer and then plan a promotion every day like their proposal said. Maybe the first day, if they buy an hour with a kitty, they get a free cookie, or something. But we can sit down, fine-tune it, and make the plan work for us."

"Charity," Kara said, hating to put a damper on Charity's excitement, "even if we follow the plan, we need to be realistic. This might be our first and only holiday at the café."

"Which is why we should put everything we've got into this, like it's our last hurrah."

Kara slowly nodded. "Fine, we'll talk about it after we get through this Friendsgiving."

"Perfect. I'll leave you to it, and be sure to wear your good bra. It makes the girls look happy."

"Get out," Kara laughed, waiting until Charity left before she set her clothes aside and picked up the marketing plan. She'd glanced over it with Charity the night before, but hadn't been in the right frame of mind, especially after finding Worthy's letter. Charity wasn't wrong about the Catmas plan. Instead of rolling over and not trying, they should make this first Meow and Furever Christmas memorable.

When she flipped it open, the first thing she noticed was the logo of the kitten wrapped around the espresso cup. With color added to it, it would make an adorable sticker, something else they could add to their Twenty-Five Days of Catmas.

She looked over the next several papers, which included mock-ups of a reformatted website. When she'd made it, she'd done a simple template with nothing added to it. It would be easy enough to implement some of their suggestions with the website builder she used, adding a separate donation page along with a reminder at the bottom of every page and a newsletter sign-up. That would mean starting and maintaining a newsletter, but that was behind-the-scenes stuff that Kara was happy to do.

She skipped over the Meet the Staff page because there were only three people, and Kara did not want her face out there.

Here's the Grinch's Bride. Please donate to her rescue. Her boyfriend did it, really.

Kara glanced at her closet where the green dress hung, the tag hanging starkly from the armpit.

Getting through Friendsgiving, a marketing overhaul, and her ex-fiancé being released from prison? It was going to be a busy holiday season.

Chapter Ten

Snowflake is a white Turkish Angora cross with one blue eye and one gold, waiting for someone who likes a little variety in their life.

BEN FINISHED SETTING THE last strip of molding on the wall of his guest room, sitting back on his legs with a hefty sigh. With the exception of his guest bath, all the upgrades to the house were complete, and he could start bringing in furniture and really putting his finishing touches on it. Make it a home.

Only to turn around and sell it if his brother actually bought a house out here.

He'd received another text from Boone this morning, wishing him a happy Thanksgiving and asking him if he wanted to meet somewhere to talk. As if the half-dozen phone calls and text messages he'd ignored for the last several months weren't answer enough. Ben had no idea if his brother was being dense or crazy, but after their last explosive interaction, he struggled to imagine what Boone was thinking coming out here trying to extend an olive branch. Ben would light every one of them on fire and watch them burn with glee.

Maybe that was a little dramatic, but he was sick of his family acting as if what the two of them had done wasn't unforgivable. Love isn't the end-all and be-all. You don't destroy your relationship with your brother over someone you are attracted to. There are plenty of other women in the world, and the fact that Boone couldn't stay away from his fiancée said enough about his character. It didn't matter that they'd done him a favor by breaking his heart; at least he'd be more observant of signs his significant other was slipping away if he ever let anyone get that close again.

Kara's smiling face flashed through his mind, and his mouth went dry. For a moment yesterday, he'd had the same thought as Charity and Schwartz; they'd experienced a flash of something bordering on chemistry. But Kara's reaction to their friends' interruption was enough to determine that she hadn't felt the same zing when their hands met. It was for the best anyway. Ben didn't need to fall for anyone, especially with his living situation hanging precariously on the whim of his brother.

Ben climbed to his feet, stretching his arms above his head to loosen up his back muscles. He needed to find his phone and check the time. Schwartz told him he'd swing by around two thirty to get him, and he didn't want to make him wait.

He snatched it from the windowsill, checking the text messages.

Sorry, got caught up. Will leave here soon.

Schwartz sent that over half an hour ago. Ben tapped away a reply.

Hopping in the shower now. Just finished laying the floor. What do you think?

Ben snapped a picture of the room and attached it to the message. His phone beeped a few seconds later.

Looks great! No rush, I am still here. My uncle came in from the Bay Area an hour ago, and I didn't want to be rude.

At least he had some time to get cleaned up. He scrolled through the next few group texts from people wishing him and twenty others a Happy Thanksgiving. He had no idea why people thought mass messages were a good idea, but he hated it—the constant dinging, and most of the people within the texts he didn't even know.

He closed the messages and scanned his missed calls, noting two from his parents. He'd already wished them a happy Thanksgiving and hesitated to return the call, especially when he suspected his brother probably passed along the fact that Ben wasn't responding to his pitiful attempts to reconcile.

Despite his reservations, he couldn't bring himself to cut his parents off. Especially on a holiday when he'd usually be sitting around with them, eating his mom's Dutch apple pie with ice cream and teaching his nieces and nephews behaviors that would irritate his sister. Not being there created an ache in his heart, and part of him wished he'd gotten on a plane and headed back to Boston today.

Especially now that he knew Boone wasn't going to be there because he was too busy stalking Ben in California.

He tapped his mom's cell number and put the phone to his ear, waiting for it to ring. It barely got through one high-pitched tinkling before his mother's voice came over the line.

"There you are! What have you been doing?"

"I've been installing my floors."

"I still can't believe you'd rather stay there doing home improvements than be with your family."

"Interestingly enough, I was thinking about how much I miss you guys today and regretted not coming to celebrate with you," he said, ignoring his mother's guilt trip. While his family's habit of trying to sweep the seriousness of the situation with Boone and Amelia under the rug was grating, that didn't change how much he loved them.

"Aw, we missed you, too. I only had to make one apple pie with you and your brother gone."

"Well, hopefully, they have some at this Friendsgiving I'm going to. It won't taste as good as yours, though."

"Thank you, honey. That sounds like a lot of fun. Who are your friends?"

Ben didn't know exactly how to describe his relationship

with Kara, so he started with the easy answer. "My friend Schwartz, who I work with, is picking me up. He's the one who's been helping me remodel my house."

"And the rest of them?"

"There's Charity. She co-owns the cat café a few doors down from my work. She's a baker, and her pastries are delicious."

"Is she pretty?"

"Yeah, I mean, she is, but it's not like that."

"Anyone else?" she prodded, disappointment lingering in her tone. "I want to make sure you're not cutting yourself off from the world by holing up in that house like a holiday-hating hermit."

"I'm not. They invited me, and I said yes."

"But what about dating, honey? You need to keep your heart open to possibilities."

And there it was. His mother wanted him to find someone new because she thought it would make him more amenable to forgiving his brother. She wasn't asking about friends; she was looking for a potential girlfriend.

Unfortunately, she was about to be severely disappointed.

"The only other person I know who is going is Kara. She's Charity's partner."

"Oh, well, that's nice, I suppose. Maybe there will be some other single women there they can introduce you to."

Ben realized she thought Kara and Charity were a couple and quickly amended: "I meant they are business partners. Both of them are single, but again, not an option for me. I'm afraid it's just as you feared. I eat. I sleep. I work. Remodel. And that's about it. Oh, I did replace some of

Kara's plumbing this week. It was all gummed up, and this plumber she hired half-assed the job—"

"Did she pay you?"

"No, she didn't pay me. I told you, she's a friend."

"That's all? Your voice changes when you talk about her."

Leave it to his mother to think that. "No it doesn't, unless it's annoyance you're hearing. We started off fighting and have moved beyond that to simple bickering."

"Sounds like a match made in heaven," his mother deadpanned.

"I'm telling you, there is nothing there except a tentative mutual respect and the occasional snarky comment. She conned me into taking care of this kitten I found in my house until she gets it a foster home, but she's taking her sweet time doing it."

"*You* have a cat?"

"A temporary cat, but yes. She's a pain, I'm telling you."

"The cat? Or Kara?"

"Both, although the cat is a boy. In fact, I'm surprised I don't hear the little turd hollering. He hates being cooped up in the bathroom, and I shut him in there earlier while I was working with the saw." Ben left the guest room, and as he twisted the bathroom doorknob, he kept the phone braced against his ear with his free hand.

"What color is he?"

"Orange." He poked his head in. Ben's gaze swung to and fro, looking for a flash of apricot fur, but the bunched-up towel he'd laid on the floor was empty, and the kitten was nowhere to be found.

"Hey, kitty," he called, clicking his tongue. "That's weird."

"What's wrong?"

"He usually barges through the door when I come in." Ben lifted the towel and checked behind the shower curtain, his heartbeat picking up the pace. "Mom, I have to call you back."

"Ben, really quick, about your brother—"

"Mom, I really don't want to talk about him—ever—but that isn't why I need to go. I've got to find this kitten or I'm pretty sure Kara will kill me. Love you."

"Ben, wait—"

He hung up on whatever his mom was about to say and clicked his tongue. "Kitty." Ben squatted down, opening the cupboards and finding them empty. There were no holes in the wall, and the toilet seat was down, but he checked inside anyway. He stepped out of the bathroom, calling, "Kitty, where are you?"

How in the heck could he have escaped from the bathroom with the door closed? Ben got down on all fours, lifting up the couch and peering underneath. Nothing. Sitting back on his haunches, he texted Schwartz:

Hey, the kitten escaped and I can't find him. HELP!

He waited several ticks with no response and then climbed to his feet. Ben headed to the laundry room next, sweating bullets as he debated texting Kara. She may know where a kitten would go to hide, but he was afraid to admit he had no idea how it got loose.

Ben checked the kitchen cupboards next, opening them with one hand while he texted Kara with the other:

Hey, sorry we are running late. Schwartz is still at his family's dinner and I can't find the kitten. Any ideas where to look?

Unlike when he had texted Schwartz, his phone blared to life within a minute of sending that message.

"Hey, Kara."

"Hi. What happened?"

"I have no idea. I put him in the bathroom while I was laying my flooring because I was using a saw and didn't want him underfoot, but when I went to let him out, he was gone."

"Did you check the space behind the toilet?"

"Yeah, he wasn't there."

"Okay, don't panic. How big is the gap between the door and the floor of the bathroom?"

"I don't know. An inch or so."

"He could have squished himself under it."

Ben shut the cupboard in his hand with a snap. "You're kidding me."

"Nope. Cats are incredibly flexible and can get into and out of tight spaces. Check every closet and crevice, even if it looks impossible. You'd be surprised what they can squeeze into. I'll be there in a few."

"You don't have to come here. I'm sure I'll find him," he said, although Ben's body relaxed slightly knowing she'd drop everything to come help him.

The kitten. She's coming over to help find the kitten, and it has nothing to do with me.

"I have to grab some more wine and rolls, since one of the

other guests forgot to bring them. What's your address?" He rattled it off, and she repeated it back slowly before he heard a sharp tap, like she'd clicked the end of a pen against a paper pad. "I got it. Hang tight and I wouldn't worry too much. Kittens like to pop up in the most unexpected places."

"Thanks, Kara."

"See you soon," she said before the call ended. Ben continued searching the cupboards. Despite her encouraging words, he imagined the kitten stuck behind the cabinet where no one could reach him without power tools. The kitten could be scared or suffering from an injury.

He closed the last cupboard and walked into his bedroom. Ben rounded the bed and bent down to look beneath his nightstand when something on his pillow caught his eye.

Curled up in a little ball was the kitten, sound asleep, and Ben's breath released in a loud, relieved rush. It took everything in him not to pick up the little terror and shake him silly.

Ben pulled out his phone and dialed Kara. She picked up on the second ring.

"Did you find him?"

"I did, asleep in my bed."

"Aw, he wants to be near you."

"Yeah, I'm sure that's it and not my cotton sheets. I just wanted to let you know, so you didn't come all the way over here."

"Actually, I'm not that far, so if you want me to grab you, you can head back with me to Friendsgiving. Then you don't have to wait on Schwartz."

Ben hesitated for a beat. If he rode with her and Schwartz

didn't end up coming, he could always Uber home. That way she wouldn't have to leave the celebration with all of her friends.

"Thanks, that would be great. I'm going to hop in the shower, so you can let yourself in when you get here if I don't answer."

"See you soon."

Ben ended the call, shaking his head. He'd been sure Kara would lose it on him when she found out the kitten was missing, but she'd been totally chill. For how hyper she was when they'd first met, Kara had this soothing tone in stressful situations. Ben could see what made her a good veterinarian.

He stared down at the small creature who'd taken a few years off his life, clicking his tongue. "You're a tiny ball of chaos, you know that, right?"

The kitten didn't wake but rolled into a tighter ball at the sound of his voice, placing a small paw over his face.

Ben walked into his bathroom, chuckling softly. While he still wouldn't call himself a cat person, he could understand why someone might think cats are cute when they are little. He had no idea what to do to contain the escape artist until Monday. Maybe he'd pick Kara's brain for ideas when she arrived.

After he finished showering and got dressed, he walked out of the bedroom to see if Kara was there. He spotted her standing with her back to him talking to—

Ben pulled up short as he locked eyes with his brother Boone's blue ones.

"What the hell are you doing here?"

Chapter Eleven

Aslan is an orange tabby-Maine coon mix who enjoys the finer things in life, like organic catnip. Do you have room for this big guy in your home and heart?

"WHAT THE HELL ARE you doing here?"

Kara spun around at the sound of Ben's guttural tone, eyes widening. He was storming around the edge of the kitchen, his hair glistening wet from his shower and dark eyebrows snapped low over his eyes as he marched straight for them. With Charity's blind date candidate coming to dinner, Kara had jumped at the chance to go to the store for rolls and wine to clear her head. Faced with Ben's anger, she was seriously reconsidering her choice.

"Hi! I thought you said to come in?" Kara said.

"I did," Ben growled without looking her way, never breaking stride. "I'm talking to him."

Kara's gaze shifted between the two men, confused and

more than a little uncomfortable. Boone had come up behind her on the walkway and introduced himself as Ben's brother, holding out a pie Ben's mom made for him. She'd thought it was sweet and let Boone follow her into the house, but by the way Ben stood stiff, his fists clenched at his side, it didn't seem like the two of them were on "here to drop off a pie" kind of terms.

Kara sucked in a breath when he took a step in Boone's direction.

"Hello, brother." Boone's mild tone belied his sharp gaze and the way he straightened his shoulders. Whatever was going on between the two brothers, she was a little nervous one or both of them was going to throw a punch.

"I'll ask again. Why are you here in my house?"

"You wouldn't answer my texts, and Ma wanted me to bring you a pie." Boone motioned toward Kara, who had taken it from Ben's brother while they'd been talking. "Your favorite."

Ben's eyes flicked to the pie in her hand, the muscle in his jaw ticking like a clock. "Using Ma's baked goods isn't going to work, Boone. You've got nothing to say that I want to hear."

"Should I wait in the car?" Kara asked, her gaze shifting frantically between the two of them.

"Absolutely not, Kara," Boone said, flashing a bright smile at her. "Ben and I just have a lot to unpack still. You know how siblings can be."

Boone's voice might be pleasantly deep, but his patronizing tone rubbed her wrong. "Actually, I don't. I'm an only child."

"Ah, that has its challenges, too, I'm sure. See, Ben and I were inseparable as kids, really close. When I skipped a grade and ended up graduating from high school the same year as he did, we went to college in different states and only saw each other during breaks."

"She doesn't need to know our family history."

"I'm only trying to explain my position on why we had a falling out. It started way before this year, you just don't want to hear that version."

"You mean the made-up one you use to make yourself feel better?"

Boone cocked a dark brow at Ben, watching him with thin lips set in a grim line. "I mean that there are two sides to every story and it's about time you heard mine. The question is, do we discuss this outside, just the two of us, or in front of Kara?"

"The audacity you have, telling me that I somehow started all this. I've told you, Amelia, Ma, Pop, and everyone else in this family, we have nothing to talk about, so why do you keep trying to force me into a conversation I don't want to have?"

"It's because you're being an unreasonable pain in the—" Boone's gaze shot Kara's way, and he snapped his mouth closed, cutting off his curse. He seemed to take a minute to get control of himself and cleared his throat. "What's it going to be? Here or outside?"

"Neither. We're leaving. You can go to hell."

Kara sucked in a breath. "Ben..."

"He married my former fiancée and wasn't even man enough to face me himself. Instead, he sent her to give me my grandmother's ring back and tell me to my face that they were in love."

Her hand flew up, covering her mouth, as Boone roared, "She begged me not to go! She thought if it came from her, you'd be more understanding. I knew she was wrong, but..." Boone's pinched expression, obviously filled with regret, would have tugged at her heartstrings if she hadn't seen the hurt and betrayal in Ben's dark eyes. "I didn't want to hurt you, Ben. But how would it have made anyone happy for us to ignore how we felt?"

"If you'd come to me the moment I introduced you and told me you'd hooked up in college, I would have understood. Or when you realized that you two still shared a mutual attraction, fine. But you both dragged this on for months, lying to me. Treating me like a trusting idiot. Had you been honest at any point from that first meeting to the minute she placed that ring on my palm, I may have been able to forgive you, but not now. I had to move three thousand miles away just to find some peace, and now you want to come out here and take this from me, too?"

"I didn't take Amelia from you, Ben," Boone said softly. "We may have handled this badly, but that doesn't change the fact that she belongs with me and I love her, with all of my heart."

"What are you looking for? My blessing? Congratulations? If so, you traveled an awfully long way to be disappointed." Ben jerked his attention away from his brother and latched on to Kara. "Are you ready to go? Because I don't want to give him any more of my time."

Ben's words sunk like a stone in her stomach. This was

the reason he was here in California instead of on the East Coast with his family? At least when she'd left Alabama, and then lost her grandparents, moving here made sense because of Charity. For Ben, he'd had to completely start over and leave everything he'd ever known behind.

Kara couldn't say she blamed him for wanting to throw his brother out. She imagined that if she'd had a sister do the same to her, Kara would have cut her off, too.

"All right. Is the kitten put away?" she asked.

"He's still sleeping on my bed. I figured I'd leave him, especially since he'll probably just escape again."

"Then we should go," Kara said, stepping around Boone. "I need to stop at the store on the way back, though. There's one open downtown until three, so if we hurry, we may be able to make it."

"Sure, sounds good. You said something about wine, too, right?"

Boone seemed to get tired of being ignored by the two of them and threw up his hands. "What do you want from me? I've apologized for the way everything went down, but you two would have never worked out!" Kara glanced over her shoulder, getting a good look at Ben's strained facial features as he followed her out of the house, ignoring his brother as he kept going. "Breaking off the engagement was the best thing for everyone involved, and you should be happy—"

In a flurry of motion, Ben grabbed Boone by his jacket collar and dragged him over the threshold. He slammed him against the side of the house, and although Ben was only a few inches taller, he lifted his brother off his feet by nearly a foot.

"You don't get to tell me how grateful I should be. You know what I've felt? Stupid. Hurt. Humiliated. Wondering how I could have ever trusted you."

"Ben," Kara called softly.

He flinched, dropping Boone back onto his feet. Before he spoke again, he gripped the knob of the front door and closed it with a hard slam. "You know what I want? You to leave. Don't take the job in Sacramento."

"It's already done." Boone almost sounded sorry, but Kara had a hard time believing his sincerity. "I signed the contract yesterday."

Ben glared at him. "That's unfortunate."

He turned away from his brother, and to her surprise, Ben placed a hand on her lower back, gently guiding her down the walkway to the car.

"Come on, Ben! It wasn't like we planned it. You can't help who you fall in love with."

Ben took the pie from her with one hand and opened her door with another. Kara watched his face as he looked across the hood of her car at his brother, who hadn't moved from the front porch.

"Maybe not, but you didn't have to sleep with her the minute the ring was off. You didn't have to move her in with you two weeks later. And you definitely didn't have to come here for a job. Those are choices you made with only yourself in mind, and that, *brother*, is why I can't forgive you."

Kara climbed into the car, and he shut the door behind her. She couldn't make out Boone's response, but whatever he said had little effect on Ben's resolve. He got into the passenger side and shut the door, settling the pie in his lap.

"Are you okay?" she murmured.

"I just need a minute."

She could only imagine. Based on what she'd picked up from both sides of their conversation, his brother was a narcissist, and she didn't imagine his wife was much better. Not that it was her place to judge. And while she'd only known Ben for a week, he'd volunteered to help her on two separate occasions. That was reason enough to think Ben was a good guy who hadn't deserved what they'd done to him.

Kara pulled out onto the street, her gaze straying to the passenger seat. Ben had a hand over his eyes, his fingers rubbing his temples. He didn't look remotely ready to walk into a house full of strangers who may already be two glasses of wine deep with only an hors d'oeuvres board, and if she was being honest, she wasn't up to it yet, either.

"Feel like making a pit stop?"

Ben dropped his hand, turning her way. "Besides the store?"

"Yeah."

"What did you have in mind?"

"A little quiet time in my favorite spot."

"Sure. Sounds great."

Kara took a left at the next light and then a right through the residential streets until she found her way to the back alley behind the café.

"I should have known this is where you were taking me," he said without any heat.

She unbuckled her seat belt with a small smile. "I promise that we're not here because I have to administer medications. This is purely for your benefit."

"Right." He opened up his door and climbed out, but not before she saw the glimpse of a smile.

Kara opened the back door, and as they walked down the wide, dark hall, the lights flickered on, sensing their motions. She flipped the switch in the boarding area, and a chorus of meows greeted her when the lights came on overhead.

"Hi, guys!" She walked straight to Peanut's cage and opened the door, pulling the fat cat into her arms. Kara turned toward Ben, and his eyes widened as he got a good look at the big cat.

"Dang, what do you feed that thing?"

"Right now he's getting a measured amount of dry food that helps with weight loss." She set him on the table, scratching him under his chin. "He's already lost a couple pounds, but we're not about fat-shaming Peanut."

Ben coughed, but Kara heard the low rumble of a chuckle beneath. "I'm sorry. Did you say Peanut?"

"His owner named him, not me, but I think it's perfect for him." Kara picked Peanut up off the table and held him in her arms, pointing his face in Ben's direction. "Peanut, this is my friend Ben. He's had a bit of a rough day. Can you cheer him up?"

Peanut purred loudly, pressing and lifting his paws against her shoulder like he was kneading a lump of dough.

Ben reached out and scruffed the tabby's head, but when he tried to pull away, Peanut followed him, nearly tumbling out of Kara's arms.

"Oh, dang, son, don't fall," Ben laughed, rubbing the cat's ear and chin again. Kara's grin widened as she turned her head and watched Ben's formerly tense features soften. "Not everyone is trustworthy enough to catch you."

Kara swallowed hard at the melancholy in his voice. They'd both been through the relationship wringer, but unlike him, she could continue to cut every reminder of Worthy out of her life. For Ben, his family was one giant reminder.

"All right, Peanut, your job here is done. Back in your cage." She set him inside and locked the cage, pointing to a jar on the counter. "Will you pull a couple treats out of there for him while I wash my hands?"

"Sure," he said, lifting the jar lid.

Matilda growled when Kara passed by on her way to the sink. "Oh, you love me, and you know it."

"What's the cranky cat's name?" Ben asked, slipping a couple of small treats through the bars of Peanut's cage.

"Matilda. She comes off like a brat, but once you get her out of the cage and away from other cats, she's a sweetheart. Calicos tend to be adorable bundles of attitude."

"Why is that?"

"No idea. Maybe the patches of several colors make them extra peppery. All I know is she's going to be a hard one to adopt if I can't put her out where people can see her."

"Have you had a chance to go through my marketing plan yet?"

Kara hesitated, before she admitted, "I have."

"And? I'm assuming since you didn't bawl me out for overstepping, maybe you aren't as opposed to it as you may have thought?"

"Let's not get ahead of ourselves. It's good stuff, but figuring out how to do it all seems a bit daunting. I feel like we need four of us and fifty-two-hour days to apply the things that would work for us and still be able to sleep."

"That's why you need to delegate, and the great thing about social media is you can schedule posts." Ben came around next to her, leaning against the counter while she washed her hands. "Say you only have downtime on Sundays. Create all your images and posts and then schedule them for different times during the week. Or, if you have an employee who is a social-media whiz, make it part of their job to create and schedule the posts. It's okay not to do everything yourself, you know."

Kara narrowed her eyes at him while she dried her hands. "Are you trying to call me a control freak?"

"I mean, I'm trying *not* to call you one." He bumped her out of the way with his hip and went about washing his hands. Kara smiled in response to his teasing and sprayed the exam table with all-purpose cleaner and wiped it down.

"You may be right," she said, grabbing Aslan from his cage. The hefty longhaired orange tabby twisted until he could hang on to her shoulder while she carried him. "It probably stems from having a chaotic childhood. There were very few aspects of my life I had control over, so I like having things a certain way."

"I get that." Ben nodded toward Aslan. "What's up with this guy?"

"Antibiotics and pain meds. He had a dental cleaning yesterday, and they extracted quite a few teeth."

"Cat dentists? Next you're going to tell me that there's a proctologist that focuses on cats' butts."

"No specialists. Veterinarians do it all, including anal glands."

Ben made a face. "I don't even want to know what those are."

Kara laughed. "Will you hang on to him for me while I get his meds ready? He's a good boy, don't worry." She placed his antibiotic in a pill popper and greased it with canned cat food. "Hold him in front of you so he can't back up." Ben did what she asked, running his hands down either side of the cat's body. Aslan didn't even fight her as she opened his mouth and pressed the plunger. She rubbed his head with one hand, cooing to him. "Such a good boy."

Kara gave him his pain meds and put Aslan away. When she turned around, she caught Ben watching her closely, and her cheeks burned. "What?"

"I was thinking how lucky all these cats are to have you in their corner." Ben's hand came up, brushing against her temple, and her skin tingled all the way down the side of her neck to the small of her back.

"Thanks," she whispered.

"Thank you for bringing me. Were you trying to distract me?"

"That may have been my goal."

"I appreciate it." Ben moved so slowly that it seemed like time itself stood still. His mouth dropped down, but instead of touching his mouth to Kara's, his lips grazed her cheek so feather-lightly that she could have imagined it.

Kara turned her head slightly, her gaze meeting Ben's while his mouth hovered inches from hers.

"Kara..." Ben cradled her face in his palms, and her eyes fluttered closed.

Music shattered the moment like someone throwing a rock through a glass window. He dropped his hands from her face at the same moment her eyes flew open.

"It's probably Charity wondering where we are."

Ben shoved his hands in his pockets as though he was afraid to be close to her. "I can head down to the corner store and grab the rolls and wine." He took a step toward the door, but Kara protested.

"If you give me a minute, we can drive down there together."

"It's okay. I could use the walk."

He disappeared into the back, leaving Kara alone, the ringing of her phone and a swirling vortex of confusion twisting through her brain. Ben had been moments away from kissing her, and she'd stood there, waiting and willing despite everything she'd heard today. He was a broken-hearted guy who'd moved here as an escape plan. It was a bad idea getting attached to him, and an even worse one to cross the line. She'd avoided dating because she didn't want to be hurt again. Getting involved with a guy still hung up on his ex? That was like jumping in the water after seeing a dangerous tide sign.

Chapter Twelve

Buddy the Elf is a cream tabby Munchkin cross down from the North Pole and looking for a new home. Adopt him 'cause…he knows Santa.

I AM SUCH AN IDIOT.

Ben sat in the front seat of Kara's car as they pulled up to her house, parking next to a silver SUV. They hadn't said much during the drive over from the store, except a few comments about food and the weather. He'd almost called Schwartz to pick him up from the store and take him back to his house, but he didn't want to make an already awkward situation worse by having Kara think this was in any way her fault. She'd done something sweet to try and cheer him up, and he'd almost kissed her. This was all on him.

For a second, he'd thought she felt the same way, but the minute her phone rang, she'd put a mile's worth of distance between them.

Not that he could blame her. His brother painted him as a jealous, bitter ex who couldn't let go, but the thing about his relationship with Amelia was that he missed having someone to come home to, but he didn't miss *her*. It didn't give his brother a pass, but he wasn't wrong when he said that leaving was the best thing she could have done. When Ben came home from work after she'd moved all of her stuff out, he didn't miss her following him around with takeout menus, asking him what he wanted to eat. He didn't expect her to cook, but why was he always the one to pick dinner? It took him weeks to realize that while he was overcome with anger, hurt, and humiliation, the urge to win Amelia back never crossed his mind.

It didn't excuse the fact that his brother had several chances to be an honorable man, and instead he'd behaved like a coward. When pictures of them moving in together popped up on social media, with all of their friends—and some of his friends, too—congratulating them, he'd deleted every social media app from his phone. That and the distance helped, but there were times when he forgot for an instant, and his thumb still hovered over his brother's number, ready to call him and share whatever news had come his way.

That was the hardest part. Amelia was almost his family, but Boone was his blood, and they'd been more than brothers all their lives. They'd been friends. Had they drifted apart the last few years? Yes, they'd both been busy with work, but Boone acted like he should get a pass on his actions because he was in love.

Maybe Ben was a little jealous. No relationship ever made him ready to risk everything for a chance to be happy.

"I guess we should go in," Kara said, breaking into his thoughts. "Looks like Schwartz made it."

Ben followed her gaze through the windshield to the front porch where Schwartz stood with a few men, deep in conversation.

"Who is he talking to?"

"Matt and Rami. They run a little hole-in-the-wall in West Sac called Archer's Kitchen. They've been together fifteen years."

"How did you meet them?" he asked.

"Through Charity. She is the social butterfly. Rami was teaching a cooking class, and she attended. They hit it off, and he invited her over to have dinner and meet Matt, and they've been friends ever since."

"Was everyone here friends with Charity first?"

"Pretty much, unless we count you, but I can't exactly call us friends from the start, can I?"

Ben smiled sheepishly. "No, probably not, but I feel like we're getting there. Don't you?"

"At least I don't want to kick you in the shins, currently."

"There's always a possibility for later."

Kara laughed softly before sitting back in her seat, making no move to leave the confines of the car. "Most of the people here think I'm weird."

"They've said that to you?"

"Not to my face, but I've heard it mentioned. I am completely awkward when first meeting people. I jabber on about one topic, then boom, I hit you with something out of the blue. I'm sure I drive them crazy."

"Actually, that factoid about sociopaths? Incredibly

helpful. I've already detected three in my life, so I think your ability to converse in rapid zigzags is a talent everyone should possess."

"I have the book on my shelf inside if you want to read it."

"Does it come in audiobook? I'm not a fan of physical books."

Kara held her hand up with a snort. "Never mind, we're mortal enemies again."

"Because I'd rather listen than strain my eyes? It's still reading."

"Oh, it is not! I want the character to sound a certain way, and if I listen to someone's interpretation, it completely ruins the experience for me."

"That's too bad, because there are some amazing narrators that really suck you into the story."

"Okay, I will give you that the right narration is everything. Morgan Freeman could literally describe the taste of a stamp, and I would listen for hours. I love his voice."

Ben turned in his seat, watching her stare out at her house, and, without thinking, touched her arm. "Do you need a few more minutes of stalling before we go in?"

Kara stilled. "How did you know?"

"I've been there—when the thought of being around other people, even ones you love, sounds almost torturous."

"I wouldn't go that far, but I could use another minute or two." She leaned her head against the headrest, watching him. "I bet you've always been great with people, huh?"

"Until this year, I think so. I wasn't the golden boy my brother was, but I had a great group of friends. At least, I thought I did," he amended, thinking about the ones who drifted away when he'd split from Amelia.

"I never had anyone, really. A friend here or there, but most of them lived too far away for me to walk to their houses. Once we got into middle school, the kids started breaking off into cliques, and I tried a couple times to find my group, but I never quite fit."

"I'm sorry," he muttered.

"It's fine. I've pretty much resigned myself to being alone. Seems simpler that way."

Although Ben was fine on his own for now, he didn't want to remain that way forever. Eventually, he'd like to be able to trust again.

And while he liked Kara, it was obvious that they weren't meant to be anything more than...he didn't have a name for it, exactly, but despite the flickers of attraction he'd experienced, that didn't equate to the two of them being more than friends. She was socially awkward with an affinity for bringing home strays. He liked his life structured without surprises. Not exactly a match made to last.

"Tell me about the other people here?" he asked suddenly, realizing he'd been quiet too long. "Is there one in particular you're trying to avoid?"

"No. I mean, yes. Tasha. She and Charity have been friends since middle school, and she is overly nice."

"Wait...you don't want to see her because she's too nice?"

"No, it's...You're a guy, so you probably don't have this, but some girls will be so nice, you wonder if it's just a facade. Like, she's telling me she likes my sweater, when really, she hates it."

Ben looked down at her sweater with alternate stripes of brown, tan, white, and orange and a turkey on the front. The words "Gobble till you Wobble" circled the turkey, and Ben chuckled.

"Is that a laugh of disdain?" she grumbled.

"No, it's a laugh of 'I'm only noticing this funny sweater now.' I think it's great."

"Really? You aren't just being fake nice?"

"So what if I was? Everyone has their bits and pieces that make them unique and not a perfect carbon copy of someone else. Do you like the sweater?"

"Yes, I wouldn't have bought it if I didn't."

"Then who cares what that woman or anyone else says?"

"I love that you said that. I like who I am, but it's just hard always feeling like the odd duck out, you know?"

"I think I do." Ben stared out the windshield at the people gathered out front. "You know I almost canceled and said I couldn't come today."

"Why?"

"Because it's been a long time since I've socialized like this. I used to spend late nights going out for drinks with friends and clients, but after everything, I guess I closed myself off. I haven't been to a bar in almost six months, although I'm supposed to go out with Schwartz this weekend. Really, he's the only friend I've made since moving here."

"Why? You're a likable guy."

"Am I? I lost a lot of friends when Amelia and I broke up. People picked sides. I never asked them to, but they did, and I was on the short end of their decision. I guess I took that as a sign that I wasn't a good enough friend." Ben shook his head. "And maybe if I hadn't been so absent, I may have seen what was going on."

Kara released a heavy sigh. "I know what you're saying. A few years ago, I dated a man, and it turns out he was playing me the whole time. Because of his actions, I lost my job, and my reputation was in ruins. Needless to say, I haven't been looking forward to jumping back into the dating pool." She muttered something that sounded like "Although other people want to give me a push." But he couldn't be sure.

"What a sad pair we are. Sitting in the car lamenting our woes instead of being grateful for what we do have."

Kara turned to look at him, her cheek pressed against the headrest of her seat. "And what do we have to be thankful for?"

"The fact that we're alive? Neither one of us is currently maimed by some horrible holiday accident."

"Fine, I will give you that as a positive, but what else?"

"I have my home renovation and job, and you are saving the feline population. So we have purpose."

Kara's eyes sparkled as she sat forward. "We have working cars!"

"Now we're talking! And plumbing!"

"Pie," she said, pointing to his lap.

Ben held it away from her playfully. "It's staying in the car. I'm not sharing this with any of you."

"Wow, that's awfully selfish on a day of giving."

He grumbled. "Okay, you can have a small slice, but just you."

"You won't even share with Schwartz?" She laughed.

"No! You've never seen him eat. He may be skinny, but the man has a hollow leg and can pack it away."

"Me too, but my pie goes to my hips and thighs."

"Speaking of thighs, favorite part of the turkey?"

"I like breasts. You?"

"Dark meat is better."

Kara made a disgusted face. "In what universe?"

"See, now I'm grateful I don't have to share any of my delicious cuts of meat with your judgmental butt."

"I'm not judgy. I just think you're wrong. But I agree... more thick cuts of white meat for me. Slather a little cranberry sauce and stuffing tomorrow on a bun, and it makes the best leftover sandwiches."

Ben leaned forward, drawn to her bright smile and enthusiasm. "You might have to make me one, too, because I don't believe it's that good."

"Seriously? You've never enjoyed a Turkey Gobbler before?" He shook his head, and she took his shoulders, shaking him. "How have you survived this long?"

Man, she smelled good. Like honey and brown sugar. "Luck and grit?"

"Apparently." She stopped shaking him, but her hands continued to cup his shoulders, her gaze locked with his. "I do think that, sometimes, bad things happen so we can really appreciate the good in life."

Ben's smile widened. "Like berating a stranger, only to find out he has a wicked set of skills when your pipes burst?"

Kara rolled her eyes. "Are you ever going to let go of that?"

"It was last week!"

"Fine, fine! I am so sorry, Ben, for reading you the riot act when you were only trying to do your job."

Ben stroked a hand over his chin thoughtfully. "There is a hint of sarcasm and placating in your tone. Try it again, and this time say, 'My dear Ben, a master of all tools and'— Ow!" He laughed, bringing his hands up when she playfully smacked at his chest.

"I'm not calling you master in any way, shape, or form, you—" The driver's-side door flew open, and Charity leaned in, scowling.

"What are you two doing out here in the car?"

"Talking," Kara squeaked.

"Well, while you two are out here fogging up the windows, I am slaving away on the finishing touches for dinner and waiting on the rolls, and you"—she pointed at Kara—"need to get changed."

Ben grabbed the grocery totes from the back seat. "Sorry, we were talking about what we were grateful for."

Charity huffed at him, taking the bags before she put herself nose to nose with Kara. "Get your butt out of this car. Tasha is hovering over my shoulder, questioning everything, and I swear, if she touches my table settings one more time, I'm going to shove her in the oven like the witch from *Hansel and Gretel*."

"That's a bit aggressive, bestie."

"Cooking . . . by myself . . . " Charity ground out, "for twelve people . . . with little help . . . makes . . . me . . . aggressive."

"We are getting out now," Kara said, swinging her legs out and climbing to her feet. Before she closed the door, she shot Ben a little smirk. "You know what else I'm grateful for?"

"What?"

"The bottle of brandy in my room."

"Kara!" Charity called.

Kara shut the door of the car. Ben climbed out the other side, grinning. Was that her way of inviting him to partake in her secret stash? He closed the car door, following behind them.

Schwartz spotted him and rushed over. "Hey, what took you guys so long? I got that text that you would meet me here and then nothing for almost an hour."

"I had a surprise visit from my brother before we got on the road, and it shook me up a bit. Kara thought a pit stop while she medicated a couple of the cats would give me time to catch my breath."

"And the car make-out session?" Schwartz prodded.

"We weren't"—Ben glanced toward the car, which was still a little fogged up, and grimaced—"making out. We were in there talking."

"About what?"

"Why are you so nosy?"

"Because you're being touchy!"

"I'm not used to being interrogated by anyone other than my mother," Ben said, walking away from Schwartz and through the front door.

"I am just looking out for you," Schwartz said, following close behind on his heels.

"You're protecting me? From Kara?"

"Yes. I mean, no! I'm just saying, be cautious. I don't want anyone taking advantage of you, especially after what I heard."

"What exactly did you hear?"

Chapter Thirteen

Rosemary is a tabby and white longhaired kitty that wants to follow you everywhere, especially if it leads to a tasty snack and warm bed.

KARA CHANGED WITH LIGHTNING speed, fluffing her hair as she padded back down the hallway in simple flats. No way was she wobbling around her house in her only pair of heels. She was so out of practice, she'd probably roll an ankle and fall right through a wall.

Several muffled meows echoed behind her and Kara shook her head. Theo and her two foster cats wanted out of the bedroom, but with so many guests, Kara was concerned they'd accidentally get outside because someone didn't shut the front door behind them. Not so much Theo, but Peeta and Finnick were set to go into the social room next week.

She tugged at the tulip hemline of the dress. Both Charity and Tasha were wearing dresses suited to a night out, so she wouldn't look overdressed standing next to them, but the dress wasn't her. She'd loved it and bought it to wear out with Charity, but to Friendsgiving for a setup? And with Ben there?

Ben isn't interested in me. Kara knew that, just like she'd laid out all the reasons why they wouldn't work, even if either of them were ready. While Kara could tell someone where a bobby pin she'd picked up six months ago was located, there was no rhyme or reason to her organization, whereas if Kara walked into Ben's room, she suspected his clothes would be color coded.

Kara stopped at the edge of the hallway when she heard her name mentioned, her heart thundering.

"Did you know Kara used to run the fundraising department of a national charity?"

It sounded like they were in the living room and she ducked behind the partition, lingering in the small alcove to listen.

"So?" Ben asked.

"So, she got fired because her boyfriend gained access to thousands of people's private information and stole it, along with a ton of money the charity had raised."

Guilt seized her chest like a vice. Even though they'd been able to locate the money and Worthy returned it, he'd already sold the information he'd stolen online. Kara could only imagine how many people's lives were impacted by identity theft and fraud, something that haunted her.

"Why are you telling me this?"

"Because even though the cops said she wasn't involved, I think you should be cautious with her. I know your ex put you through the wringer, and I don't need to know the details, but I just...I want to make sure no one else hurts you."

Kara couldn't blame Schwartz for wanting to protect Ben, because she'd do the same for Charity. It didn't even matter who said something to Schwartz; the truth would have come out eventually if she kept hanging with Ben.

In her experience, once people knew the details about Worthy, they looked at her with a slightly guarded shadow across their faces. Charity told her more than once it was in her head, but she didn't believe it.

"I appreciate your concern, but no one is going to take advantage of me. Especially not Kara."

"What do you mean? I thought you liked her," Schwartz said.

"I do, but we're not compatible."

Kara was still reeling from the "especially not Kara," when his words sunk in. Compatible. It was something shelters told potential adopters when they didn't want them to take home a certain animal. *We just don't think your home is compatible with what the pet needs.*

She'd told herself that nothing was going to happen between them, but his casual confidence stung. When Kara's mother wasn't ignoring her, they were constantly butting heads. Her grandparents had been wonderful, but they'd only had her at home three years before she left for college. With the exception of Charity, she'd never really been compatible with anyone. Worthy definitely didn't count.

Kara heard the front door open and close, and the sound of footfalls across the linoleum echoed in the entryway.

"Schwartz, who is your friend?"

Kara recognized Matt's voice.

"Hey, I'm Ben."

"I'm Matt, and this is my husband, Rami."

"Kara!" Charity called from the kitchen and Kara jumped a foot in the air. "What are you doing?"

Kara crossed behind the partition into the kitchen, avoiding Charity's curious gaze. "Nothing, I was just..." She spotted the open bottle of wine on the counter and grabbed it. "I'm going to see if anyone wants more wine before we dive into games."

"Are you all right? You look a little green."

Kara shook her head, adding a bit more cheer to her voice. "I'm good, I swear. I'm off to offer the masses libation and herd them into the living room."

"Sounds like a plan." Charity gave her arm a squeeze. "Don't be nervous about Adam. You look amazing, and he is going to adore you." Charity let her arm go and opened the oven, pulling out two steaming Pyrex dishes. "I'll stick the last two casseroles into this oven and join you. And hey, thanks for hosting at your place. I know groups make you uncomfortable, but I hope you're having a little fun."

Oh, loads. Kara didn't have the heart to tell Charity that she felt like the odd man out on the best of occasions. She went to the café and came home. She didn't search out social events as a rule. Kara knew it wasn't healthy, but the worry someone would recognize her always lingered in the back of her mind like a finger poking her brain.

"It's a nice crowd," Kara said, escaping the kitchen in case Charity picked up on the emotional vortex currently spinning through her. She rounded the corner to find Ben, Schwartz, Rami, and Matt all standing in a semicircle, laughing.

"I appreciate you keeping this guy entertained," Ben said, smacking Schwartz on the back. "He's kind of like a puppy. You take your eyes off him for too long, and he wanders off and gets into trouble."

"I feel that," Rami said, his voice heavy with amusement. "Matt has no filter, and I can't tell you the number of times I've had to redirect a conversation before things got ugly."

The bottle nearly slipped out of her sweaty hands as she approached the men, keeping her eyes on Rami as she spoke up. "Hey, we're going to move into the living room and play games, but does anyone need a top-off?"

All four men turned toward her, four sets of eyes widening. She tucked her hair back behind her ear with a shaky hand, resisting the urge to check the front of her low-cut dress for a wardrobe malfunction. "Sorry, didn't mean to interrupt."

"I'm good," Rami said, giving her his friendliest smile. Of all of Charity's friends, Rami was her favorite because he seemed to get how uncomfortable she was and went out of his way to put her at ease.

Matt held out his half-full glass with a wink. "I'll take a splash or two more. I like that dress on you. Your sweater was cute, but this is stunning."

Kara's face warmed briefly before she cleared her throat. "Thank you." She turned her attention to Schwartz and Ben, noting that Ben hadn't lost his surprised expression. "How about you?"

"No, thanks," Schwartz said.

Ben finally spoke up. "You look great."

Her skin burned so hot that Kara thought she might melt, but Tasha made a timely entrance through the front door, calling, "Look who finally decided to show up!"

Kara saw Charity fly out of the kitchen with a smile, opening the door to greet the new arrivals. Five more people stepped inside with excited voices, talking at once. Kara recognized all of them except the tall guy with black hair.

That must be Adam.

"How do you know Charity?" Rami asked.

"Actually, I met Kara first," Ben said, drawing her attention back to the group of men. His brown eyes seemed glued to her lips, and her stomach flipped over. Was he looking at her red lipstick because he liked it? Or hated it?

"Really? Do you have a cat or something?" Matt asked, quirking a brow.

"I'm fostering a kitten, but we met before that. It's actually a funny story—"

"No it's not," she squeaked.

Ben's grin was breathtakingly wicked. "It kind of is."

"Based on Kara's expression, I definitely want to hear this!" Matt nudged her with his shoulder in a friendly gesture. "Kara's usually quiet as a shadow."

"Not when she's pissed off."

Kara wanted to sink into the floor. "It wasn't that bad."

"What did you do to her?" Rami asked.

"I told her I wasn't an animal person."

Rami released a low whistle. "How could you not like animals?"

Kara's mouth twitched a bit. "Thank you, Rami."

"I'd never been around them, honestly, but I found a kitten in the house I'm renovating, and Kara convinced me to foster it. I'll admit, the experience hasn't been the ninth circle of hell I imagined."

"Ah, another man done in by the p-word," Matt quipped, making Ben and Schwartz laugh.

Kara's jaw dropped while Rami groaned. "I can't take you anywhere."

"Kara, can I steal you for a moment?" Charity asked, coming up alongside her.

"Um, sure." Kara's gaze caught Ben's for a moment before Charity pulled her into the entryway. They passed by Tasha and several more of Charity's friends as they headed into the living room. Charity stopped in front of Adam, waving a hand between them.

"Kara, this is Adam. And this is the girl I've been telling you about."

"Hi." Adam held his hand out, flashing a straight white smile. He had thick black hair, cut into a short tousled style, and light blue eyes.

"Hey."

"I'm going to go get the game started while you get acquainted." Before Kara could open her mouth, Charity was backtracking into the living room.

"Does she do this often?" Adam asked.

"Organize awkward setups? Not for me."

"Then I'll consider myself a lucky guy," he said.

His smooth delivery twisted her stomach into knots. He didn't come across as the shy introvert that Charity described.

To her surprise, his face flushed red. "I'm sorry, that sounded cheesy. I'm nervous."

That might be true. Charity's advice from earlier fluttered through her mind, and she wanted to give him the benefit of the doubt. "I don't know if you'll feel fortunate once you get to know me. Charity tends to talk me up, but she sprinkles a little glitter on my personality."

"I'm sure she did the same with me, so maybe we forget this is a setup and pretend that we're just two people who happen to be at the same Friendsgiving, no pressure."

"I could probably do that."

"We're setting up teams," Tasha called from the living room.

"Guess that's our cue that the meet and greet is over," Kara laughed.

"After you." He waved his arm, and when she crossed the threshold of the living room with Adam at her back, Ben's gaze followed her as she crossed the room. She took the empty seat next to him instead of trying to sit on the floor in her dress. The outside of her thigh brushed against his. and for a second, she thought he might have pressed closer.

To her surprise, Adam settled on the arm of the couch next to her, reaching a hand across her to Ben. "Hi, I'm Adam."

"Ben," he said curtly, taking Adam's hand.

"Yikes, easy on the phalanges, big guy," Adam yelped, pulling from Ben's grasp with a shake. "I handle delicate equipment."

"Sorry, I was always taught to introduce myself with a firm handshake."

The tension between them hovered around Kara like a cloud, and she cast a glance at Ben, wondering what was going on in his head. Did he have a bad feeling about Adam? Maybe she'd ask if they got a moment alone.

"Kara, since you're the last in, you can go first. We split everyone into two teams, and we'll play until the timer in the kitchen goes off. Adam, you and Kara will be with me and everyone on this side of the throw pillow," Charity said, patting the single, square barrier next to her.

"What are we playing?" Adam asked.

"Heads Up."

"Prepare to go down," Schwartz taunted.

"I don't think so." Charity passed her the phone with a smirk. "You ready?"

Kara wasn't much of a game person, but in college, Heads Up was one she'd loved. Kara held the phone up to her forehead, returning Charity's smile. "Who am I?"

"Oh, oh! I could listen to you talk all day long!" Charity hollered.

"Plays a great bad guy?" Adam offered.

"On my hall-pass list!" Rami shouted, ignoring Matt's "Hey!"

"Idris Elba?" Kara laughed.

"You got it!" Tasha wrote the point down on the tablet, and Kara held the phone out to Ben.

"Your turn."

He gave her a curt nod and took the phone, his fingers brushing against hers. The short contact created a frisson of electricity, but he didn't even smile. Kara wondered why he'd gone from teasing her with the story of their first meeting to this kind of silent acknowledgment. Had Schwartz's information about her past sunk in? Was he considering whether or not she was really trustworthy?

A knot of insecurity settled in the pit of her stomach, and Kara wished she'd never overheard their conversation. She understood people having doubts about her integrity if they'd never met her, but Ben had spent time with her. Couldn't he tell Kara was a good person?

Ben put the phone to his forehead, and Kara bit her lip. Emma Stone.

"Played Steve Carell's daughter in *Crazy, Stupid, Love*," Tasha called out.

Ben stared at her blankly as they kept shouting hints. When the game timer on the phone dinged, his team groaned as he handed the phone to Charity.

Kara leaned over, lowering her voice. "Wow, Ben, you're bad at this."

"I'm not a game person." He turned his head, and their noses were nearly touching. "Kissing distance," as Charity called it, and Kara whipped away at the thought.

"Watch how it's done." Charity stood up, holding the phone to her forehead. Everyone, including Adam, yelled hints, and Kara joined in, laughing, "Main character on *Smash*!"

"Katharine McPhee!" Charity screamed.

Their team cheered, and Adam gave her a high five, holding his palm against hers a second too long. She caught Ben watching them and extracted her hand.

"All those in favor of splitting up those two"—Schwartz pointed at Charity and then Kara—"and banning them from ever being on a team together again, say aye."

The whole right side of the room chorused, "Aye."

"Fine, fine," Charity said. "I'll write down everyone's names and put them in a hat next time so it's fair."

Schwartz grinned. "I'll help you with that, so I make sure you're not marking the papers with some kind of secret code."

Charity rolled her eyes. "Whatever."

The kitchen timer went off, and Charity climbed to her feet. "Everyone, let's convene in the dining room for dinner."

"I'll help you," Kara said.

"No, Tasha can help me. You take everyone into the other room." She tilted her head toward Adam with a wink, and Kara would have glared at her friend, but Adam got up and held his hand out. "Here."

"Kara doesn't need assistance," Ben grumbled before standing up. The two men towered over her sitting position, and Kara frowned at Ben.

"I'm sure she doesn't. I was just being a gentleman."

Ben didn't say anything else, and Kara cleared her throat. "Normally, I'd agree I don't need any help, but in this dress, I appreciate it." She took Adam's outstretched hand and climbed to her feet.

"I like your dress," Adam said.

Kara was pretty sure she heard Ben snort, but he'd turned his back to her, so she couldn't be sure.

"Did I step in something?" Adam asked.

"What do you mean?"

"Is he your ex-boyfriend?"

"Ben? No, I hardly know him."

"Huh. He seems...protective of you."

Kara fought back a laugh. "He's probably protecting you from me. We didn't have the greatest first meeting."

"Well, if you say there's nothing there, then great." He placed his palm at the small of her back gently as they walked together to the dining room, and Kara couldn't help analyzing his touch. While his palm was warm through her dress, his touch didn't make her giddy with excitement or send tingles up her spine. Adam was attractive and seemed nice, but there didn't seem to be any...spark.

Of course, this was only their first meeting in a group of people, so it could be her nervousness. Maybe if they had a little one-on-one time, she'd feel differently.

Although I don't seem to have any issue sparking with Ben.

Why was she obsessing over Ben when, two hours ago, she was resigned to being strictly friends?

As the group crowded around the table, Charity set down a dish of ham and clapped her hands. "All right, find your seat. There should be a place card next to your glass with your name on it."

Kara found her name and narrowed her eyes. Charity had seated her between Ben and Adam. She glanced up at Charity, who was grinning, and irritation zipped through her.

I'm going to kill her, but first I need a new best friend to help me hide the body.

Chapter Fourteen

Loki lives up to his name by causing mischief wherever he goes. This tuxedo cat wants a home where he can hide around corners and pounce at your feet. Are you the playful partner he needs?

BEN GATHERED UP SEVERAL more dessert plates, stacking them on top of each other. He passed behind Kara, who was saying goodbye to Adam in the front doorway. The way the guy leaned into the one-arm hug she gave him set Ben's teeth on edge. The red-hot churning in his stomach watching her fawn all over Adam all night came back in full force, but there was no reason to be jealous of the two of them. He and Kara were friends, at best.

Except I'm attracted to her.

Even before she'd come up behind him in that curve-hugging green dress with her hair falling in waves around her shoulders that made him nearly swallow his tongue, he'd thought about her. Kissing her. Holding her. He was still picking up the pieces of his life, and he knew it would be wrong to cross the line with Kara, but it didn't change the fact he hated thinking about her with another guy. He'd almost kissed Kara in a moment of weakness, but he didn't want to use her to make himself feel better. And she deserved a guy who would shower her with attention.

Ben just didn't want a front-row seat for it.

He set the dishes next to the sink, where Schwartz and Charity were washing.

"How's it going in there?" Charity asked.

"Everyone's gone except that Adam guy, but he's halfway out the door."

"Oh, does it seem like they're vibing?"

Ben bit back a snarky comment and took several utensils from Schwartz. "I don't know. Where do these go?"

Charity nodded over her shoulder, her arms elbow deep in soapy water. "That drawer on the right. I really hope they hit it off. My girl deserves some happiness."

Ben didn't respond as he walked across the kitchen and pulled open the top drawer, but all he found was paper clips and pens, and sitting on top of a bunch of papers was an envelope with Kara's name on it from a Ferris Worthington.

Ben stared down at the address beneath. Federal Correctional Institution. A rush of unease settled in his stomach, the same sick feeling he'd had when Amelia told him about her and Boone. Was that her ex? Schwartz said the guy ruined her life. Why would she keep his letter instead of throwing it away?

"Did you find it?"

Ben cleared his throat. "No, I found a junk drawer."

"Sorry, the next one down," Charity called.

Ben closed the drawer and opened the one below it, depositing the silverware into the tray. He had just grabbed another handful of spatulas and spoons from Schwartz when Kara came into the kitchen, her cheeks rosy pink. His grip tightened on the plastic, his gaze dropping to her mouth to check for lipstick smudges, but her lips looked perfect.

Why am I obsessing over what Kara does with her romantic life?

It wasn't as though he'd been her date to Friendsgiving. Charity had been the one to extend the invite. She'd never given any indication she wanted anything more to do with him.

"Hey, there you are!" Charity grinned over her shoulder. "How do you like Adam?"

Kara's eyes darted his way before answering her friend. "I mean, he's nice. He was telling me about his lab work and his PhD. He's also been thinking about getting a playmate for his cat, so I suggested he come by and look at our adoptable kitties."

Of course the guy has a doctorate and a cat. He is perfect for her.

"Did he ask you out?" Charity asked.

"No, but we exchanged numbers."

Charity squealed, dancing in a circle with her hands above her head, and Schwartz hollered when she shook a handful of soap on him.

"Hey, now! You're getting me all wet."

"That's what she said," Charity laughed.

Schwartz grinned. "Well played."

"All right, I'm going to get changed out of this dress

and let my cats out." Kara caught Ben's eye with a little smile. "Don't leave before I get back. I've got good news for you."

Before he could respond, she'd ducked out of the room and disappeared down the hallway. After several more minutes of gofering dishes to their rightful place, Ben said, "I'm going to use the bathroom before we go if you two have this."

"We're fine," Charity said. "If Schwartz gets out of line, I'll pop him one."

"You should never threaten someone in front of witnesses."

Ben shook his head as he left the kitchen and headed to the bathroom. He did his business and washed his hands, the name Ferris Worthington haunting him.

He pulled out his phone and googled Ferris Worthington. It wasn't wrong to be curious. Dozens of news articles popped up, but he clicked the most recent one.

Hang On to Your Who-Pudding and Roast-Beast, the Grinch Is Coming!

Two years ago, authorities discovered a massive data breach occurred for people who donated to national organization Half-a-Million Lives and thousands of dollars were stolen. Ferris Worthington, the mastermind behind the crime, received only two years thanks to the plea deal his lawyer and the prosecuting attorney agreed upon. Mr. Worthington returned nearly eight hundred thousand dollars, and in a few weeks, he'll leave the prison system a free man.

His mind raced as he thought about what she'd said earlier, about being in a relationship that nearly destroyed everything and then Schwartz worrying about how involved she'd been in her ex-boyfriend's crimes. Why would the guy be writing her if they cut off all contact? Was he reaching out to ask for help? Was Kara hanging on to the letter because she was considering it?

No, Kara wouldn't hurt anyone. There must be another reason, but what? Did she still have feelings for the guy? Is that why she hasn't dated?

Ben opened the door, and when he stepped into the hallway, he plowed into Kara. His phone clattered out of his hand and onto the floor face down, and Ben fell back against the wall, Kara's body plastered against his.

She looked up into his face, her hazel eyes round. "I am so sorry! Are you all right?"

"Yeah," Ben murmured. The dim light of the entryway cast a shadow along the dark hallways, and he stared down at her face. She'd thrown her hair up, but small strands escaped to frame her face. "I think you need to install a stoplight at this intersection, or at least a yield sign."

Kara laughed. "I'll look into that."

Ben's gaze dropped to her full lips, no longer cherry red but her sweet, natural pink. "You washed your face."

"I hate the feel of makeup."

"I can't say I've ever experienced it." His heart kicked up when she licked her lips, following the gleam her tongue left behind. "Kara..."

"What?"

Ben didn't have a clue what to say. While Kara and Ben

didn't make sense on paper, he couldn't deny she was the first woman he'd been drawn to since he left Boston. Despite every argument with himself, every reason why he shouldn't, he dropped his mouth to hers. He waited for her to pull away and slap him, to tell him he was crazy, but when she parted her lips instead, Ben groaned, bringing his hand up to cradle the back of her head. She tasted like minty toothpaste with a hint of sweet beneath, and he deepened their connection, his arm slipping around her waist to hold her against him.

Schwartz and Charity's laughter drifted down the hallway, and Ben broke the kiss slowly, his mouth hovering over hers.

"What was that?" she whispered.

"I don't know. I just wanted to."

"But... you told Schwartz we aren't compatible."

Ben stilled. "How do you know that?"

"I overheard you talking about me earlier. I wasn't eavesdropping—okay, I was a little. But I heard my name, and it's almost impossible not to listen when people are talking about you."

"Kara," he said softly, "I'm not mad. I feel awful that you overheard us. Schwartz was worried about me and was being a good friend."

"I don't care about any of that because my past is a Google search away. It's earlier at the clinic and then now, kissing me. Why?"

Ben realized they were still plastered together and pushed off the wall, putting a few inches between them so he could think without her body flush against his. "You were there with Boone and me. I've got unresolved issues, Kara, and it's not fair to cross that line with anyone."

"But you just did. You kissed me."

"I know. It was a moment of weakness."

"Seriously?" She squatted down to pick up his phone. "I'm someone that you don't want to cross the line with, but you can't resist my charms? That makes no sense, and honestly..." Her voice trailed off, and he followed her gaze to his phone screen.

His search for Ferris Worthington was plastered across his phone.

"Kara, let me explain."

She handed it back without looking at him, but he caught the shaking of her hand.

"I guess you've got all the details now, huh?" she said, her voice choked up.

"There's a few things I'm fuzzy about, but it wasn't because I thought you were involved. I wanted to find out more about him, the kind of hold he might have on you."

"The hold he has? Absolutely none, but you won't find that on the net. I despise him and I regret being so stupid. But it's not something I like to talk about, so if you want to read all about how he completely fooled me, you have more googling to do."

Kara brushed past him, and he caught up to her in two steps, reaching out to gently take her arm. "Kara, stop."

She whirled on him, her hands flying as she spoke. "You know what, Ben, I get it. You have trust issues, and Schwartz was looking out for you, telling you about my past, but I've been trying to move on, and rehashing all the details of my last failed relationship isn't something I want to do."

"If you're trying to move on, why do you have a letter from him in your drawer?"

Kara's head swung up, her eyes narrowed. "You were snooping?"

"No. I pulled open a drawer to put the silverware away and saw the letter. I was curious what it was and googled his name."

"You saw an unopened letter in my drawer, and decided to find out what I was hiding? We aren't dating, so my mail is none of your business, and neither is my past. And while we're on the subject of bad behavior, what was with all those snarky comments directed at Adam?"

"What snarky comments?"

"'She doesn't need help,' for instance. He thought there was something going on with us and I assured him that there was absolutely nothing between you and me. Of course, I'd have to amend my earlier statement in light of that kiss, but at the time, there was no reason for you to be rude."

Seeing her with Adam and finding that letter had dredged up emotions he hadn't experienced since he'd found out about Amelia and Boone. "He was treating you like you are weak. You are the most independent woman I have ever met. You spent hours trying to learn how to do plumbing so you didn't have to rely on anyone else, and that guy acted like you couldn't take care of yourself!"

"So what? He was nice and cordial and at least we're *compatible.*"

"I wasn't trying to hurt your feelings, Kara—"

"You think that's what I'm worried about right now? If you think I'm a horrible person who would swindle people, then why are you still here? Why are you trying to dig up dirt on someone you aren't even interested in dating?"

"I wasn't trying to dig up dirt. I was trying to understand keeping a letter from someone you couldn't stand unless you wanted to forgive him."

"Why do you care?" Ben didn't answer right away, and Kara shook off his hand. "The good news I have for you? I found a foster home for the kitten. You can drop him off on Saturday close to closing, and I'll take him over to her place."

"That's . . . that's great." Emotions warred inside him at the news. He struggled for something to say, something to rationalize his behavior.

"I'm glad you're happy. Now you can have your house back, and you don't have to wonder why I do the things I do," she said, squaring her shoulders. "If you'll excuse me, I'm going to say goodnight to Charity and Schwartz and go to bed."

"Kara, can't we sort through this?"

"What is there to sort through, Ben? What Worthy did nearly destroyed me. Do you understand why I hate social media? Between the trolls and the media hounding me, I still struggle letting people get close. My entire life is out there for public consumption, but not all of it. Not my side." Kara let out a shaky breath. "I thought that the two of us were becoming friends."

"We were—are."

"You could have given me the benefit of the doubt, taken the time to let me open up, but you acted like every other person I've met since my world fell apart. You searched me out online to gather all the sordid details. I was hoping you were different. I guess I was wrong."

Kara walked away before he could come up with a plausible explanation, one that didn't make him sound like a confused idiot. He followed behind her into the kitchen, and from Charity and Schwartz's expressions, he figured they'd heard most of their argument.

"Come on, Schwartz, we should get out of their hair." He met Charity's hostile expression and politely added, "Thank you for dinner."

Schwartz nodded, turning to Kara and Charity. "Ladies, thank you for inviting us."

"You're welcome," Charity said, her gaze lingering on Kara, concern etched in the furrow between her eyebrows.

"Good night," Ben mumbled, pausing several seconds to see if Kara reached out, but she remained silent. He walked out of the kitchen swiftly and straight out the front door without waiting for his friend. Schwartz caught up to him at the bottom of the porch steps with a whistle.

"Well, that is not how I expected the night to end."

"I don't want to talk about it."

"I wouldn't either if I were in your shoes, but I think there are a few items we need to cover. First of all, why would you ask her about her ex if you aren't interested?"

Ben jerked open the passenger door and slid in without answering.

"If that's a stumper, how about this?" Schwartz asked as he climbed into the driver's side. "Were you being a jerk to Adam?"

"I don't know, Schwartz. Maybe. I didn't like the guy, all right?"

"Why?" Schwartz started the car and backed up. "He seemed like a perfectly amicable fellow."

"Oh yeah, swell guy. He couldn't keep his eyes off her chest."

"You sound jealous, my friend."

"Don't say that," he growled.

"What? It's an observation." Schwartz cleared his throat. "If it makes you feel better, I thought Charity was going to take my head off for asking about the whole Grinch thing."

"What did you say?"

"I just asked her if there was anything to what some of the media said about Kara being involved, and she flat out told me where to go. That if Kara were a criminal, they wouldn't be in business together."

Ben leaned his head back against the headrest. "I didn't think she was involved with his crimes, but I found an unopened letter from her ex in her kitchen drawer. Why would she keep that?"

"Evidence? Maybe he's harassing her? Whatever the reason, it brings me to my last inquiry..."

"What's that?"

"How are you going to fix this?"

Ben sighed. "I'm not. I'm going to drop the kitten off to her on Saturday and go back to my life."

"Too bad. I liked hanging with them."

I did too.

Chapter Fifteen

Calling all taco lovers! Taco Angus is a Scottish fold cross with gorgeous gray tabby markings. He's a beefy guy with folded ears; what's not to love?

KARA STOOD IN THE lobby of the café on Saturday afternoon, turning the artificial Christmas tree as she placed the LED lights over each green limb. Monday was the first of December, so they'd decided to get started on switching over to Christmas decor, especially since they were kicking off Twenty-Five Days of Catmas. It had been a busy day with Small Business Saturday foot traffic driving people inside for a cup of something warm before they moved on to another store, and they'd made sure to hand out the flyers they'd created yesterday while the café was closed.

"Whew, okay, this is the last of it!" Charity huffed as she carried several large tote bags through the doors. After they'd picked up the flyers from the printer, she'd dragged

Kara around to buy holiday stuff for the café and their homes. Kara suspected it was a thinly veiled attempt to distract Kara from Ben and what happened at Friendsgiving, but she appreciated that Charity didn't press her about it.

"Who is responsible for us going overboard on decorations?" Charity asked.

"That would be you. Do you know how much longer Michelle is going to be here? We're closing in fifteen, and she's usually gone by now."

"Not sure. I put her in charge of the adoptable cat posts for Instagram, so when she finishes those I guess."

Michelle was sitting on the floor of the social room, Christmas ornaments, garland, elf and Santa hats, and piles of other knickknacks surrounding her. She had her camera up to her eye, pointing it straight at Fluffernutter.

"That's great, but can you remind her that she can't leave any of that garland in there? Because if the cats eat certain things, they can get a blockage and—"

"Kara, breathe. She knows."

"I'm just saying," Kara grumbled, pulling a strand of red, green, and white beads from the tote at her feet with more force than was necessary and setting them aside.

"What the heck is with you today?" Charity stood up on her tiptoes and placed a length of shiny red garland on top of the supply shelf, fluffing it so some hung over the edge. "You're even more hyped than usual."

"I'm not. It's just . . . never mind." Her gaze flicked to the cat clock on the wall. Ben should be here any minute with the kitten, and she wasn't sure how it would go. While she knew Ben hadn't meant to stumble onto that letter, she wished he'd had more faith in her. That he hadn't been so hung up on the letter and why she'd kept it.

Especially when she still didn't have a good answer.

It was a bit like Schrödinger's cat. If she opened the letter, Kara would know for sure what Worthy wanted, but if she didn't, she could imagine that maybe it was a letter of apology that wished her well. It all boiled down to being scared to know, but she couldn't bring herself to destroy it without knowing.

My reasoning is even confusing me.

"What were you going to say?" Charity asked.

Kara sighed, tucking the end of the strand of lights behind another branch so it was accessible to plug the cat angel into. "I was thinking that I'm probably going to die alone, surrounded by cats, and when you finally remember that you haven't heard from me in a while, they will find my partially eaten body and say, 'Here lies Kara Ingalls. She was a lonely old bat who couldn't get her love life together.'"

"Good gravy, babe, that was morbid and disturbing."

"Well, it's also a pretty accurate prediction. Men are too baffling to me."

"What about Adam?"

"He hasn't texted."

Charity opened her mouth, but Michelle came out of the social room squealing. "Oh my god, this is the money shot!"

Kara and Charity both jerked her way, giving her nearly identical wide-eyed expressions.

"Michelle, honey," Charity said slowly, "I don't think that means what you think it does."

The way she said it hit Kara in the gut, reminding her of Ben's story about his mom and *The Princess Bride*.

"What?" Michelle cocked her head, her chin-length black hair perfectly curled under. "It just means perfect, right?"

Kara nodded, ignoring Charity's snorting laughter. "Yeah, let's go with that. What did you get?"

Michelle bounced over to Kara like a baby goat and pointed the viewer of the camera at her. "I really think the green of the wreath makes his fur pop, don't you?"

Kara studied the picture of Fluffernutter rolling on a buffalo plaid blanket. A large green wreath with red and white ornaments glued sporadically around the needles did make the cat's creamy white fur stand out, his eyes staring into the camera, wide, blue, and slightly crossed.

"It's adorable, Michelle." Kara patted her shoulder with a smile. "Thank you for lending us your talent. I know you've got finals coming up, so if this gets to be too much—"

"Are you kidding me? Oh, sorry," Michelle added, as if realizing she'd cut her boss off. "I just meant this semester is a cakewalk. I could sleep through half my exams and still pull As. Not that I would."

"Well, we appreciate you." They'd hired Michelle back in March before they opened, mostly because she was the only applicant, but she'd turned out to be the best choice. Michelle was a petite bundle of energy. The customers adored her foam art, and she was fluent in ASL because her older sister was born with hearing loss.

"I'll finish up taking pics of the cats in the social room and get them edited. Is there anything specific you want on each post?"

"I think it should be set up like a dating profile," Charity offered, setting a figurine of a cat playing with an ornament on the counter. "A clever tagline and then a background on their history but done in a way that makes them seem appealing."

"As the resident expert on dating apps, maybe you should handle that part," Kara teased.

Charity pointed her trigger finger at Kara, the red nail sparkling like Dorothy's ruby slippers. "I know you're being mean, but you aren't wrong."

"I'm not mean! Michelle, am I mean?" Kara asked, turning to their barista.

"I'm not getting involved. That's how a girl gets fired, and I have too many gifts left to buy."

"Left?" Charity cried. "I haven't even started shopping."

"I have a big family. I gotta space it out or my wallet catches fire."

Kara and Charity laughed while Michelle slipped the strap of the camera back around her neck. "I'm going to clean up, and then I'll head out. My roommate's brother is coming over to watch a movie with us, and I'm in charge of bringing home dinner." She bounced through the door and back into the other room, her muffled voice cooing to Robin Hood as she approached him.

Charity picked up a fat cat statue in a Santa suit, watching Kara lean over to grab the beads. "All right, now that it's us again, did you think about texting Adam?"

Kara didn't want to admit that she hadn't considered it. After Ben kissed her and everything imploded between them, going out with another guy was the last thing on her mind. Especially since Kara had never experienced another kiss that left an impression on her lips hours later. Every time she thought about his hands on her, and the way his mouth moved, her skin lit up like someone flicked a lighter and hovered it in all the right areas, creating a warm glow.

"Adam's nice, and I had fun talking to him, but I'm not sure we really . . . sparked."

"But you hardly spent enough time together to be able to know for sure."

"Then I'll wait for him to make a move. If he doesn't reach out, we know it wasn't meant to be."

"The modern woman goes after what she wants."

"Char, listen to me." Kara stopped hanging beads to face her bestie. "We've got a lot going on this month, and I'm going to put all of my energy into keeping the café's doors open. I don't want to think about men, especially since dating is another reminder that Worthy will be out of prison in two weeks, and I have no idea how that's going to affect me or our business. I'm stressed and could really use my bestie, and not a matchmaker right now. All right?"

Charity drew Kara into her arms and gave her a bear hug. "You're right. I've got to keep my focus. Que será, será."

Kara pulled away with a little smile. "At least I finally know how much we need to get the café into the black and finish the clinic."

"How much?"

"Roughly forty thousand."

Charity shook her head. "How in the heck are we going to come up with that in a month?"

"That's the total goal. We only need about six thousand to get the café in the black."

"Oh, is that all?" Charity grumbled.

"Hey, I'm trying to be the glass-half-full girl." Kara spotted Ben coming through the front window, her heart fluttering. "There he is."

"You want to go in the back and let me deal with him?" Charity asked.

"No, I'm fine. I don't need you to clean up my messes for me."

"You are my best friend, and it grounds my nutmeg that anyone would dare talk smack about your character."

"People are bound to have their doubts, Char. I appreciate you trying to protect me, but you can't police other people's thoughts and beliefs."

"But I can keep them away from you!"

Kara loved Charity in the unconditional, always-there-until-they-go-into-the-light-someday kinda way. But for someone who hated other people hovering and meddling in her life, she could be the biggest culprit of sticking her nose over the line.

Ben came through the door with a cat crate in hand, high-pitched, angry meows erupting from it. "He's not happy about being in here."

"It won't be for long. Charity is going to take him in a few minutes, right?"

"You sure?"

Kara knew that Charity didn't want to leave her alone with Ben, but Kara was afraid that Charity's overprotective nature would make an already awkward situation worse.

"It's fine."

Charity grabbed her purse from under the counter without any more arguments. She came around and held her hand out to Ben. "Do you want to say goodbye?"

Ben lifted the carrier up, peering into the cage. "I did back at the house, but I'll tell him again. Have a good life, kid. I hope you find a great home."

Kara's chest squeezed. While Ben sounded cheerful and optimistic, she'd been in his shoes too many times and saying goodbye was hard.

He passed the carrier to Charity, who headed to the door with it, waving at Kara. "I'll be back to help you finish decorating."

"I'll be here."

Charity walked out the door, leaving Ben and Kara alone. Well, except for Michelle in the social room, but she was completely absorbed with cleaning up.

Ben picked up one of the Twenty-Five Days of Catmas flyers, his eyes skimming over it. "Making them follow you on Instagram to find out what each daily deal is instead of having it listed on here is a great way to increase your social-media engagement."

"I know, I read your marketing report, remember?" She walked out from behind the counter and over to the front door. "I'm getting ready to lock up."

"Is there some kind of form I need?"

"No. You were acting as a foster home for Meow and Furever, so you wouldn't have to sign anything unless you wanted to adopt him, and since you didn't, we're square."

"Are we?" he asked softly.

Kara turned the lock with a heavy sigh. "What do you want me to say, Ben? I know you didn't mean to stumble onto that letter, but then you—"

Michelle stepped out of the social room and gave her a thumbs-up. Kara waved at her, and she headed out the back.

Alone again, he stared at her so earnestly. "Kara, I'm sorry."

Kara leaned back against the front door and folded her arms over her chest. "Go on."

"I should have forgotten about the letter the minute I saw it. I shouldn't have googled his name or invaded your privacy." He ran a hand through his hair, messing up his dark locks. "Amelia messed me up. Ask Schwartz—it took weeks for him to get past my defenses. And I wasn't attracted to him."

"But you are to me?"

"Yes, obviously, or I wouldn't have kissed you."

Her stomach flipped involuntarily and her hurt dimmed the slightest bit.

He cleared his throat. "With my brother moving to the area, I don't even know if I'll be staying in Roseville after my contract is up, but I was jealous of Adam, and I saw that letter and all those feelings took me back to my breakup. That isn't on you at all, I'm owning my screwup, but I feel like if I'm going down that rabbit hole with a girl I'm not even dating, I've got too many trust issues to be ready for anything serious."

"And you think I'm looking for something serious?" She laughed bitterly. "Ben, I haven't been with anyone since Worthy—"

"Wait, people actually call him *Worthy*?" He shook his head. "Sorry, but wow."

"Yeah, I've found his name pretty ironic the last two years, but my point is, I've got trust issues, too. All of our savings are tied into this café, and if it goes under, Charity and I won't be able to bring it back. I need to be here, not worrying about a relationship or whether or not it works."

"So where does that leave us?"

Kara shrugged. "I don't know. I like you. I'm attracted to you, but he gets out in less than two weeks. I have no idea how that is going to affect my life. You've read the articles, right? Did you see what they posted about me?"

"No, I didn't delve that deep."

"They were still tossing around conspiracy theories all over social media even after the police cleared me. His lax sentence is huge news, and what happens to the café if I'm tied to it? There is a reason it's been foam lattes and cats on Instagram. I'm so scared it's going to start again the minute he gets out, and I want to be able to walk away from this place before my connection to him destroys everything."

"If you're that worried about it, why not spin the narrative in your favor? I've got connections in the media, and I can help you write up an article about what happened, how false accusations ruined your life—"

"Ben, no. I don't trust them. All it takes is one reporter to edit out the right clip or word and I'm a villain all over again."

"Not all reporters are cut from the same cloth."

"I said no."

Ben held his hands up. "All right. No. What about forgiving me?"

"What if we make a deal? Since trust is an issue for both of us, maybe we'll concentrate on that. We'll hang out. No labels. No future promises. No expectations for anything except complete honesty and transparency. We'll be each other's healbound."

"Healbound?"

"Yeah. Not a rebound where it's all about sex and getting over the last person we were with, but two people who know they aren't right for each other, being there and supporting the other through a rough time."

"Like a friend?" Ben said, quirking a brow.

"Eh, that's a label. Besides, friends don't kiss."

Ben placed a hand on the door, leaning over her with a grin. "You saying you want to kiss me again?"

"I'm saying I want to keep the option on the table."

Chapter Sixteen

Evel Kitnievel will rocket his way straight to your heart with his bright green eyes! This furry daredevil would be the perfect TikTok star. All he needs is a great camerahuman.

MICHELLE BURST INTO THE back on Monday morning, making both Kara and Evel Kitnievel jump.

"We're gaining traction!"

Kara ran a hand over the tabby's stiff back, whispering soothingly. "It's okay, buddy. Michelle didn't mean to scare the poop out of us."

"Sorry, I got so excited I forgot you were doing intake exams, but guess what?" Without waiting for her to answer, Michelle held up her phone, showing off the picture of Fluffernutter she'd taken Saturday. "I posted this at seven this morning, and we're up to three hundred and two likes in three hours! That is more than we've ever gotten on any other post!"

"You dropped by just to tell us that? Don't you have class?"

"My professor canceled my first class because he stayed up too late last night playing video games."

"What? How old is he?"

"Close to thirty, I think. *Also*, I added the shortcut links to our bio and updated the website yesterday, and people have donated a hundred and fifty-seven dollars."

Kara shook her head. Although that was more than they'd previously received in one day, it was a drop in the bucket. "Will you put him back for me?"

"I'll have to include him in my Instagram pictures," Michelle said, taking Evel from her. "Maybe I could photoshop him into Santa's sleigh? Jumping the Foresthill Bridge?" She put him into his cage and closed the door on his raspy meow. "Something daredevily."

Kara finished writing her notes down in his chart with a laugh. "Whatever you want to do. The cat pics are your baby, and we bow to your expertise."

"Oh, I've got more ideas! I took enough to get us through to Saturday, and I'll take more pics then. That way we can showcase new kitties."

"Sounds great. How is Charity doing up there?"

"There were a couple of people in the lobby, but it wasn't bad. I'm going to post again about the free scone today only, and then later tonight, I'll post about tomorrow's Catmas deal."

"Good. I also ordered stickers, and they should be here Friday."

"Ah, I can't wait to see them. I love stickers!" Michelle's squeal hurt Kara's ears, but she just smiled through her wince. "All right, I am going to grab a soy latte and get out of here. I'll keep you updated. Later!"

"Bye," Kara called as Michelle disappeared through the door. She put the cat's chart up on the shelf and washed her hands, trying not to let pessimism overwhelm her. Rome wasn't built in a day, and like Michelle said, they were getting traction.

She pushed through the door and into the front, noting that Michelle's *few* was six people deep. Kara stepped behind the counter with Charity, happy it was one of their regulars at the front of the line. "Hi, Mrs. Wyatt. The usual?"

Mrs. Wyatt greeted her with a sweet smile, wire-framed spectacles perched on the bridge of her nose. A widow in her late fifties, Mrs. Wyatt had been coming in every day with her canvas laptop bag, tapping away at the keys while she sipped a vanilla latte or two. The cats loved crawling into her lap and sleeping because she'd stay for hours and never moved.

"Yes, Kara, I'll take my vanilla latte and two hours of visiting time." She set her purse down and pulled out her wallet. "How are you? I don't normally see you up here. Most of the time you're taking the cats back and cleaning up after the rest of us."

"Well, we've been busier lately, and I can't leave Char up here by herself. We have to take care of you so you can get a kitty in your lap."

"That's why I come here. My house is incredibly quiet since my husband died in March, and then I lost our cat, Whiskers, a few weeks later. It's nice to come in and get a little kitty love."

"I know I've told you before, but I am so sorry for your loss."

Mrs. Wyatt gave her a trembling smile. "I appreciate that, dear. I've been told the first holiday is always the hardest after losing your spouse, but thankfully, I have my children and grandchildren close by, so I won't get too lonely. I do miss having a companion, though."

"You should consider adoption when you're ready. We have so many awesome kitties." Kara handed her one of their flyers. "Today you get a free scone with an hour of kitty socializing. Do you want two?"

"Oh, goodness, no! I couldn't eat two of your big ole scones. But I'd love to take one."

"You got it." Kara rattled off her total and slipped on a glove to plate her pastry.

When she handed it to her, Mrs. Wyatt gave her two twenties. "Hang on to the extra for the cats."

"Thank you, Mrs. Wyatt. We'll bring your latte in to you."

"Sounds good." The older woman packed up her purse and hiked an old canvas messenger bag back over her shoulder.

"I can help the next person." A young couple stepped forward to order drinks, and Kara had nearly cleared the lobby when the door jingled and Wendy Kent stepped inside, holding a carrier.

Kara's heart sank when she heard the kitten's pitiful yowl. "Char, you got this?"

Charity saw Wendy and frowned. "Yeah, I'm good."

Kara walked from behind the counter and waved her hand. "Hey, Wendy, come on back, and let's talk."

Wendy followed wordlessly behind her, and Kara held her office door open. "What's going on?"

"I'm sorry, Kara, but I can't do this," Wendy said, her voice trembling.

"What do you mean?"

"This cat is destroying my house!"

"Wendy, he's a seven-week-old kitten. You know they're mischievous."

"I am telling you, I have been fostering cats for a long time, and this one—is evil!"

Kara looked through the cage door at his sweet face and swallowed back a laugh. "That seems a little extreme. What's he doing?"

"He crawled into the cabinet with my makeup bags and peed on them! I had to throw out hundreds of dollars' worth of brushes and sponges!"

"Wow, that is terrible."

"That's just the first thing. He's attacked Fluffy, and now every time she sees him, she screams and runs."

Kara didn't comment that the weirdly named Chihuahua was a jerk and probably deserved it. "Does Fluffy have any wounds?"

"A scratch on her nose, but nothing that needs to be looked at. But I had to sit on the floor so I could retrieve my father's remains from my Roomba!"

"Wait..." Kara's hand flew to her mouth. "He knocked over your father's urn?"

"Yes, and before I knew it, here comes Oscar sucking along!"

"I am... so sorry, Wendy," Kara said, pausing for composure.

She could not tick off one of her few foster homes, but she almost lost it at the imagery.

"I'm sorry to just drop by the café like this, but I need you to take him back. I cannot have this creature in my house."

"Wendy, please, it is an adjustment, but I'm sure things will get better."

"I adore you and Charity, Kara, but I will not keep this monster. I'm very sorry for the inconvenience, but I'm sure there is someone else out there who will appreciate his... high-spiritedness. It's just not me."

Kara grimaced. "All right, Wendy. It's no problem. I understand." Kara took the carrier and set it on the floor in the corner. "Let me walk you out."

"I know this is probably not what you want to hear, Kara, but I think I need to stop being a foster, at least through the holidays. We'll be traveling, and I thought taking in kittens would be fine with Fluffy, but this experience has exacerbated her anxiety, and I think it's best if we put a pin in this and let her recover."

"Of course." They walked back into the now-empty lobby, and Kara got the door for her. "I hope that Fluffy feels better, and I am so sorry for the trouble."

"Thank you. Please warn potential adopters about that kitten." Wendy shook her head. "He's not normal."

"I will definitely take your experience to heart."

"Happy holidays."

"You too, Wendy." Kara closed the door behind her and walked over to the counter, considering banging her head against it.

"What happened?" Charity asked.

"Ben's kitten really is possessed, according to Wendy Kent, and she no longer wants to foster."

"Wendy Kent is a crackpot. That last litter she brought back to us was traumatized by that demon she calls a dog."

Kara laughed. "Oh well. Guess I'll be adding one more foster cat to my roster. At least Peeta and Finnick are in the social room, so it's just Theo and me again."

"Maybe Ben would take him back?"

Kara snorted. "Really? He had the kitten for a week and couldn't wait to get rid of him."

"Well, we need to start searching for fosters outside the box. Maybe join a knitting circle and drop a few mentions of the rescue."

"I have been thinking about expanding my social circle."

"What's wrong with your current circle? I'm in it!"

"What's wrong is I don't have one. I have you and now Ben, so I have a social line."

"I get your point. What about a book club?"

"Pass. If I'm going to read, it is going to be what I want and not a club pick I have no interest in."

"Before you naysay me, hear me out. Bookin' It down the street has a book club every week. We could offer to let them use our social room. Schwartz and Ben's marketing plan mentioned cross-promotion, so what if we offer them the space on, say, Saturdays after we close? In return, maybe they sell us some cat-related books at a discount. We can set up a bookshelf against that wall, and you can make some new friends. Win-win."

"Why do I feel like you're pimping me out for marketing purposes?"

"Take one for the team, babe," Charity said with a wink.

Kara laughed. "Fine. I'll swing by Bookin' It and ask."

"Perfect." Charity leaned against the display case, watching her with a Cheshire-cat smile. "Since we're between customers, are you going to tell me next steps with Ben?"

"I don't know. You kind of busted in on our moment Saturday, and besides a few texts back and forth, we haven't made plans."

"And Adam's off the table, right?"

"Yes."

"Fine, I just wanted to make sure. What if you send Ben our Twenty-Five Days of Catmas list of promotions and see what he thinks? They aren't set in stone, so if he has a better idea, we can adjust. Besides, you could suggest a brainstorming dinner at your place. A little candlelight. Wine."

"I'm not forcing things with Ben. We already have an agreement to be each other's healbound, so I don't want to appear overeager."

"I'm sorry, you're his what?"

"It doesn't matter. You'll just laugh, and I've got this handled."

"Excuse me." A young guy who'd come in with his girlfriend poked his head out of the social room, a wide smile on his face. "Could we fill out an application for Finnick and Peeta?"

Kara smiled, ready to dance a jig. "Absolutely. We have an electronic application on our website, if you'd like to fill that out, or I can get you a paper one."

"We'll fill it out online. Do you have a link?"

Charity grabbed one of their business cards and passed it to him. "Here you go."

"Thanks."

When the door closed, Charity turned around with a quirked eyebrow. "I didn't know we had an electronic application."

"I created it when I was revamping it yesterday and figured, why not save a few trees? You just have to download the web-host app, and it will alert you to new applications."

"Well, look at you, embracing technology."

Kara rolled her eyes. "I've always respected technology. I just hate the media and online trolls."

"Have you read the letter yet?"

"And on that note, I'm going to set the kitten up in my office with a litter box and put together a couple of card-board carriers and adoption bags for the happy adopters."

"This avoidance isn't healthy, babe!"

"I never claimed it was!" Kara pushed through the door and into the back room, where she grabbed a small litter box and scooped a couple cups of litter into it. She walked back into the office and set the litter box down. When she opened up the cage, the kitty sprung out and rubbed against her leg.

"How could anyone think you are a terror?" She squatted down and slipped her phone from her pocket. Snapping a picture of the tiny cat, she texted it to Ben with the caption Guess who's back?

Your move, Ben.

Chapter Seventeen

Chaos is a young orange tabby kitten and is exactly the kind of trouble you're looking for. Watch out... he definitely lives up to his name!

BEN SAT AT HIS desk eating a pastrami sandwich and looking over visuals for the Choco Vino account they were presenting Thursday when his message notifications beeped. He picked up the phone and smiled when he saw Kara's name. He'd been thinking about her all day yesterday while he was ripping out the vanity in his guest bath but wasn't sure what to say. He clicked on the message and saw a picture of the kitten by her feet.

Guess who's back?

Ben smiled, an involuntary reaction to seeing the kitten's familiar face. He'd woken up several times Saturday and

Sunday night, searching for the kitten before he remembered he was gone. It was hard to admit, but he'd gotten used to the kitten greeting him when he came home, his cute snorts when he devoured his food, and the way he liked to curl up in Ben's hair on the top of his pillow.

How come he's with you?

His foster home didn't work out. There were a few instances involving a terrified Chihuahua, a knocked over urn, and a Roomba eating her father's ashes.

Ben laughed. And that was a hard pass for her?

I guess. So I'll take him home with me and bring him back when he's ready to be adopted.

Ben's phone rang, and his father's smiling face flashed across the screen. It was technically his lunch break, but he'd already spent some of it arguing with his mother about the scene with Boone on Thanksgiving, and he was so tired of saying the same thing over and over again.

He answered on the third ring anyway, clearing his throat. "Hey, Pop."

"Hello, son."

"That's a pretty serious tone for lunchtime on a Monday."

"I'm calling to tell you that you don't have to up and leave the area. Boone said Sacramento's a big city, and you probably won't run into each other."

"Pop, I'm serious about him staying away from me. He's

lucky I didn't break his jaw when he showed up at my house. I can't live less than a half an hour from him."

"He only came by because your mother told him to do whatever it took to make amends because she doesn't want her children fighting, especially during the holidays."

"And I get that, Pop, but why can't she see it from my side? I know what Ma wants, but this goes beyond Boone breaking my Lego structure when I was eight; he married my ex! How am I supposed to just be like, 'Oh, sure, water under the bridge, pass the eggnog?' "

"Look, I didn't speak to your uncle Rodney for years because he stole money from me, so I get it. If it wasn't for your mother, I wouldn't even be getting in the middle of this, but if it makes any difference, I do believe they truly love each other. I know that probably hurts to hear, but that's the reality of things."

"I'm not angry at him because they fell in love. I feel betrayed because they blindsided me and went public before the dust even settled. I mean, how come I didn't catch my fiancée and brother falling in love right in front of me?"

"I do not agree with the way they handled it, and if you want to cut them out forever, then that is on you. But your mother is worrying herself sick over Christmas and having to divide the day between the two of you because you can't be in the same room together. And before you tell me to skip our visit with you, I am not coming all the way out there and not seeing my son."

Ben sighed. "Pop, I'm running late for an appointment, so I'll think about what you said and give you a call tomorrow, okay?"

"All right, Ben. I love you."

"Love you, too."

Ben pressed the End button. He didn't want to hurt his parents and make the holidays a nightmare. It seemed like the easiest solution was to take himself out of the equation. Maybe he could convince Schwartz to go out of town with him. While Sacramento and Placer counties were large areas and the likelihood of running into his brother and new sister-in-law was low, it definitely wasn't a zero chance. If Boone moved to LA or even San Francisco, Ben could have handled it, but less than thirty miles? It hurt to think about, but he was seriously considering selling his house and relocating again.

His phone beeped again, and he checked the message. At least you could visit him at my place. If you wanted.

Ben smiled and tapped a response. That sounds great to me. How is Catmas going?

Our donations are up. The post of Fluffernutter has lots of likes.

I saw that! If you need any pointers, let me know.

Since you're offering, could I maybe pick your brain tonight? I'll cook you dinner.

I need to get my bathroom finished, but if you want to come help, we can talk and caulk at the same time.

I see what you did there. Okay. I need to get the kitten settled at my place, but I can come over after.

Or you could just bring him with you. I've still got all of his stuff.

Are you sure?

Sure. I'll grab dinner on my way home. How do you feel about tacos?

Love them.

Ben opened the door a few minutes before six, revealing Kara glaring darkly at him. "You."

"Whoa, déjà vu. I thought we moved past you being angry with me?"

She waved to the crate in her other hand. "This beast you created pooped in my tennis shoe!"

Ben coughed on a laugh, pressing his lips together. "How did he manage that?"

"Great aim?"

"No, I mean, weren't you wearing your shoes?"

"Yes, I was wearing my comfy shoes that have never touched the pavement until today so they don't scuff up the floors at the café. I leave the comfy shoes by the back door and swap them out when I come in. Then I drop the tennis shoes in my office so they are out of the way until I leave. I left him to play in my office with a litter box. I didn't see the pile inside until I picked them up, and my fingers squished all the way up to my knuckle—"

Ben held a hand up. "I get the visual." Ben squatted down to peer into the crate. "Were you a bad cat?"

The kitten meowed loudly, rubbing against the cage door. Ben took the crate from Kara and stood up. As soon as she stepped all the way inside and shut the door, Ben set the crate down and let the kitten out. The small orange cat sprang from the cage and immediately climbed up Ben's pant leg until he pulled him off and set him on his shoulders. He rubbed his cheek against Ben's, and Kara pursed her lips.

"He's pretending to be adorable, but he's plotting."

"I don't know about that. He's never pooped in my shoes."

"Good for you," she mocked, making a face.

"I think you're just hangry. Let's get a couple tacos in you, and you'll see that Chaos didn't mean it."

"Chaos?"

Ben grinned. "It's what I've been calling him in my head, and it seems to fit, considering the circumstances."

"You know, naming an animal is the first step in keeping it."

"Now, don't spoil my dinner. It's better than calling him pain in the—ow!" Chaos had bit his ear, and he reached up to get him off his shoulder. "No more perch for you."

"Please, you say that, but I bet he's back up there in no time. Admit it, you're kind of a softy."

Ben opened his mouth to argue, but he liked the way she smiled at him, as if his feelings for Chaos endeared him to her.

"Think what you want, but there will be no more biting

my ear tonight," he said, setting the kitten on the back of his couch.

Kara went to his sink and washed her hands. "How exactly do you want me to help you in the bathroom?"

"I need to seal my shower and the back of my sink. I could do it by myself, but since you wanted to spitball ideas, I thought you could keep me company while I work." Ben came up alongside her to wash his hands, too. "You want something to drink?"

"Sure."

Ben's shoulder brushed hers, and he could smell the sweet scent of honey as he leaned closer to her ear. "Thanks for coming." He handed her a paper towel, noting the blush on her cheeks. Was she nervous being here with him?

"I was happy to be invited. Now, wherefore art those tacos?"

"Microwave." Ben grabbed the bag and started pulling out containers. "I hope you like pork street tacos."

"I like any kind. Thanks." She took one of the containers and set it on the kitchen island, flipping it open with a sigh. "I'm starving. I brought a sandwich today, but it didn't stay with me long."

They stood in the kitchen and ate in silence through two tacos, but Kara closed her container on her final one. "I think I'll save this."

"Not me," Ben finished his food and tossed his container into the trash before wiping his face and hands on his napkin. "Should we reconvene to the bathroom?"

"After you."

He grabbed his work gloves off the step stool he'd set in the hallway. "You can sit here if you want."

"Was this actually supposed to be a seat for me or were you using this for something?"

"No, it's for you. I haven't gotten a kitchen table yet, so I don't have any chairs or stools to sit on. Although I might not bother doing that if I decide to move."

"Because of your brother?"

"Yeah. I'm thinking of taking off for Christmas so my family doesn't have to worry about splitting their time between us."

"Won't they be upset about not seeing you?"

Ben slipped his work gloves on with a shrug. "Maybe. I've told my ma and pop repeatedly that I wasn't ready to forgive my brother, and they keep pushing."

"I think that's what people that love you do. Charity is always 'trying to help.'" Kara used air quotes, but there was no malice in her voice. "I know she means well, so I don't fight her too much."

"If it were anything else, I'd let it go to make my parents happy, but not this." Ben picked up the caulking gun and bent over the sink.

"I always thought caulk was such a funny word."

Ben chuckled as he traced the edge of his sink carefully. "Because it sounds like something else?"

"Probably, but that wasn't where I was going."

"No?" he teased.

"I was just making conversation."

"Then I apologize for being inappropriate. It won't happen again."

"I thought we were going to be honest with each other?"

Ben's gaze jerked up to meet hers, but when he caught

the glimmer of laughter in her hazel eyes, he smiled. "You're right. It probably will."

"I thought as much."

"You want to give this a try?" he asked, holding the gun out to her.

"All right." She took the object, giving him a wink. "Is this just so you can wrap your arms around me from behind and show me how it's done?"

"Heck no, you're on your own."

Kara leaned over the sink, following his line. Without warning, she'd pressed her butt back against him.

Ben's hands went to her hips for balance as he stepped to the side, realizing immediately that was the wrong move when she stiffened. "Whoa, sorry, I was trying to get out of your way."

She spun around in horror, holding the gun out to him. "I'm sorry. I didn't mean to push into you like that."

"I'm probably shooting myself in the foot admitting this, but I'd be lying if I said I didn't enjoy it."

"Really?" She released the word like a breathy sigh, and his gaze dropped to her parted lips.

"I did, but if I don't scrape away some of this excess, it's going to dry funky."

Kara moved out of his way, and he used the caulking finisher to clean up the lines. When there was an even amount around the sink, he put the tool down.

"Is the kissing option still on the table?" he asked.

Kara wrapped her arms around his neck, her fingers playing across his nape. "Why don't you give it a try and find out?"

Chapter Eighteen

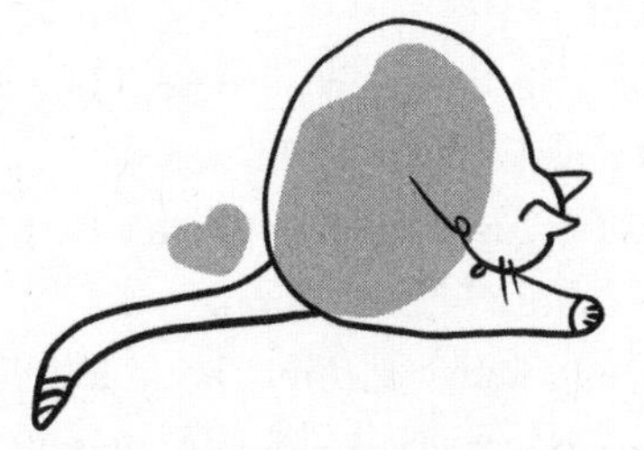

The Mad Catnipper wears a tuxedo and eye mask, his markings perfect for any true cat burglar. Give him the catnip or no one gets love!

KISSING HAD NEVER RANKED high on Kara's lists of enjoyable activities, but Ben's lips brushing across hers, his soft beard tickling her skin, sent delicious shivers down her spine. It was amazing how the meeting of mouths could send every nerve ending in her body into overdrive, and Kara couldn't help comparing this moment to all the kisses she'd shared before. Not a single one hit the same level of excitement, and it made her wonder if all the romantics were right. It had nothing to do with the act and more to do with the person.

Oh, don't think like that. This isn't a real relationship. It's a stepping stone, remember?

"Hmm, damn it." Ben broke away and looked down.

Kara followed his gaze to Chaos, who was hanging off the side of his pant leg, staring up at them. When he released a pitiful meow, Kara laughed, masking the disappointment of the lost moment.

"Do you think he did it on purpose?" Ben asked, his eyes twinkling as he picked him off his leg.

"I can't say for sure, but he couldn't have planned for a better time to stage a kisservention."

"Kisservention, huh? I think he could have waited a moment or two longer. I was enjoying myself."

Kara's cheeks warmed as she admitted, "Me too."

Ben held up Chaos so they were nose to nose. "You really are a demon." The kitten purred, batting at his face, and Ben tucked the small cat against his chest, letting him play with his fingers. "I've been thinking, Kara... he'll be able to go in the social room by New Year's, right?"

"He'll have his second shot right before Christmas so, theoretically, yes."

"You've got a lot going on with the café, and he's a handful. I don't have any knickknacks or breakables, and he's already comfortable at my place. Maybe I should just hang on to him until he's ready for his new family."

Kara cocked her head, considering. "I thought you couldn't wait to get rid of him?"

"Don't get me wrong, he's a pill, but I'm kind of used to having him around, so he doesn't bother me as much anymore. And I figure it will relieve some of your stress."

Kara pursed her lips. She had a feeling Ben's offer had more to do with missing Chaos than helping her, but she didn't call him out because he wasn't wrong. With everything going on, she'd appreciate not having a rambunctious kitten wreaking havoc around the house.

"If you're sure, Ben, I would really appreciate that."

"Then it's settled. Welcome back, man." Ben gave an attacking paw a high five, which turned into Chaos biting the side of his hand. "He probably wants dinner. I've still got a couple cans in the kitchen cupboard."

"I'll do it," she said, holding her hands out. "Gimme. That way you can finish your work. I've distracted you enough."

He passed Chaos into her waiting hands, leaning over to whisper in her ear, "I don't know about that. I could stand a little more distracting."

Kara pushed him away with a giggle. "Stop teasing me."

"Me? You're the one lingering." Before she could blink, he gave her a hard, fast kiss. "That should hold me."

Funny, I was thinking the opposite.

Kara left the bathroom with a wiggling Chaos, bemusement fogging up her brain. Hanging with Ben was fun, almost relaxing, and she couldn't figure out why she had been so scared to text him before. This no-pressure dating was fantastic, and Kara didn't understand why more people didn't try it.

She walked into the living room, eyeing the rows of cabinets above and below. "Which cupboard?"

"Above the microwave."

Kara opened the door, and the minute she pulled the can out, Chaos went crazy. Kara set the kitten down and opened the cupboard by the sink, looking for a saucer. She found a stack of paper plates and smiled. Ben was a definite bachelor, and this was obviously his pad.

She dumped the wet food on the plate and barely set the plate down before Chaos dived into it. "Hey, I fed you earlier. Don't pretend like you're starving."

The kitten's only response was to snort.

Kara washed her hands and returned to her step stool perch, watching Ben's bent-over frame as he worked on the tub.

"You need dishes."

Ben looked at her over his shoulder with a smirk. "I just finished my flooring. Give me a month or so to put my finishing touches on it." He paused to complete what he was doing and stood up, setting the caulk gun on the counter. "If I don't sell it, that is."

"You were serious about leaving? Or were you always planning on fixing it up and then flipping it?"

"No, I wanted to live in it, but with my brother and sister-in-law moving to the area, I may need to relocate. I hear Texas is nice."

"That is ridiculous! Just because they will be living here doesn't mean you have to interact with them. And you definitely shouldn't let them be the catalyst for another huge decision. You've already left your family and started over here. Forget them and live your life." She shook her head. "Besides, Texas is hot all the time. Also, I think you should invest in a dining room table, regardless of whether you are staying or not. Staging a house is a great selling point."

"I'm confused. Do you want me to stay or are you trying to get rid of me?"

"I'm playing devil's advocate. Just make sure you sit in the chairs and make sure they are comfortable. Charity bought this cute square table with modern chairs that kill your back after five minutes. Let's just say she buys her furniture for style, not comfort."

"I don't understand people who do that," Ben said. "My parents have had the same couch for twenty years because it is so comfortable, and my ma's convinced they just don't make 'em right anymore."

Kara laughed. "My grandmother had these floral couches that were pretty, but they were so stiff and hard. After a few years of living with them, my grandfather and I finally convinced her that she should get rid of them. Someone bought those awful couches for more than my monthly mortgage because they were antiques."

"The best couch I ever got was at a yard sale for my first apartment. I borrowed my parents' steamer and cleaned it all up." He squatted down with a sigh, scraping away the excess caulk. "I miss that couch."

"What happened to it?"

"My ex thought it was ugly," he grumbled.

"Well, your new setup is very modern bachelor. I was expecting neon beer signs and folding chairs before I came over the first time."

"I can't figure out if that is a backhanded compliment or still insulting."

"I mean, it's sleek. I prefer homey." Kara twisted her hands in her lap before she continued, "I know you say your brother moving here is a dealbreaker, but how has it been in Roseville for you?"

Ben stood up, gathering up the caulking gun and tools. His silence made her shift in her chair, and she almost apologized for being so nosy, but he finally said, "It's been great. My boss talked to me last week about extending my contract and sticking around, and I said I'd consider it. I love my house, and Schwartz is a great friend. With the exception of being so far away from my family, I could be really happy here."

"I know you think it would be better if you were gone, but wouldn't you like to spend time with them, even if it's just a few hours on Christmas Day?"

"I'd rather fly to them on New Year's and spend Christmas somewhere tropical."

Kara got up when he came toward her. "I guess that sounds nice."

"I'm going to clean this off outside, but you can follow me. What do you do for Christmas?"

Kara trailed behind him. "I spent last Christmas with Charity and her parents. I love her family, but she and her mom like to bicker, so it can be uncomfortable."

"Are you going back to Charity's for Christmas this year?"

"I don't know. She invited me to go to New York with them, but I was thinking about just spending it at home. She'll fight me on it, but it won't be my first Christmas on my own."

Ben opened the back door, waiting for her to step through before he closed it. He flipped a light switch, and a beautiful bulb light illuminated a wood-covered patio with textured cement flooring.

"This is gorgeous."

Ben looked up with a grin. "I added the lights, but the backyard is what sold me on the house. Someone loved this area once upon a time, and I wanted to bring it back to its glory."

"You have a green thumb?" she asked.

"A little, but I've been replacing the bushes with low-maintenance plants like small succulents that don't require a lot of water." He turned on the hose and went about scrubbing off the tool, while Kara took a turn around the large half circle, noticing the small rocks that surrounded it.

"I haven't done much with my yard, except for a few shrubs. I was thinking about creating a garden in the back next year, depending on how things go with the café."

"Why would the café affect whether or not you have a garden?"

"I guess it depends on how much time I have. If we can't make it work, I'll probably look for a full-time veterinarian position at a hospital in the area."

"Wouldn't that be easier?" He shook off the tool and set it and the caulking gun on top of the barbeque. "To work for someone else than run a rescue?"

"Maybe so, but most pets that are seen by a veterinarian have an owner to advocate for them. Displaced pets need as many of us to speak up for them as possible, and I know if I can get the café back on its feet, we can make a real difference in the community. My grandmother used to call me her little crusader because I got suspended for skipping my morning classes to take a cat I found on my way to school to the vet. When I got to school, I told them the truth about why I was late. It would have only been detention, but I mouthed off so they upped it to suspension."

"You, mouthed off? I couldn't imagine," Ben chuckled.

"I've always done what I felt was right, no matter what the consequences were, and my grandparents supported me, to a point. I had to write an apology, and my grandparents smoothed things over."

"That's great that you had them." Ben pulled up two patio chairs and waved his hand for her to sit. "It's not too cold. Wanna sit out here awhile?"

"Sure." She sat down. He'd put the chairs just outside the patio cover, so they could see the night sky, and Kara leaned her head back, looking up.

"You don't talk about your family much, do you?" he asked.

Kara shrugged, keeping her voice neutral. "It was just my mom and me, and I use the term *mom* loosely. She dumped me on my grandparents' doorstep and took off with some guy she'd met a few weeks before."

"That's really sad. Were your grandparents angry?"

"No," she said, her tone softening. "Living with them was the first time I ever felt the love of a real family. I had a real birthday with cake and presents, Christmas was beautiful and full of cheer. My grandmother used to host a Christmas Eve party for friends and neighbors, and the first year, I was so nervous, I hid up in my room for the first half of the party until my grandfather came and found me." She cleared her throat. "When they died, I used the sale of their house to buy my house here. I think they were afraid of my mom coming back and asking for money."

"Have you seen her?"

"Not since my grandfather died, and she showed up the day after the funeral. I met her at a diner in town, gave her a thousand dollars from my savings account, and told her not to come back."

Ben caught her hand in his. "Hey. I'm sorry."

"It's okay, really. I didn't know anything different."

Ben threaded his fingers with hers. "You could do that for the café."

"Do what?"

"Host a Christmas party. Invite the community for a special event. We can get donated items for a live auction. Tasty pastries from the café. The timeline would be tight, but I bet we could pull it together."

"You want to put together a major fundraiser in a little over two weeks? Are you crazy?"

Ben brought her hand up to his mouth and kissed it. "You're still doubting my marketing skills, but you're going to see. We're not just going to save the café, but we're going to get your clinic finished. Trust me."

Chapter Nineteen

Pawsome Sauce is a Lynx Point Siamese Manx who is described as "awesome but better." How can you say no to all that coolness?

"FOR CRYING OUT LOUD, will you stop smiling like that? It's creepy!"

Kara laughed as she opened Pawsome Sauce's cage and lifted the cat into her arms. "Do you hear Charity being mean to me, Paw? Get her." Kara held the petite cat toward Charity, but the cat simply hung there, purring, his nubby tail twitching with excitement.

"Do not try to distract me with that cross-eyed cutie. You ignored my texts for hours, and when you finally sent me a response, it was lips, heart eyes, and then melt emojis! Stop holding out and tell me what happened last night."

Kara's cheeks warmed, thinking that Charity wouldn't believe she'd spent several hours sitting under the stars with Ben, discussing fundraising and logistics for the rest of Twenty-Five Days of Catmas.

"We decided to run away together for Christmas," Kara joked, carrying Pawsome Sauce through the doors to the front with Charity hot on her heels.

"Wait, what?"

"I'm kidding."

"Oh, good. So you're still going to come with me and be a buffer between me and my mom?"

"No, thank you!" Kara stepped inside the social room and shook her head. It was Wednesday, and whatever Michelle was doing on Instagram had increased traffic tenfold. There was already a line of people outside, and they opened in twelve minutes.

Charity stood on the other side of the glass wall with her hands on her hips. "You're really not coming with me?"

"Absolutely not after last year." Kara set Pawsome Sauce on top of a cat scratcher shaped like a train, running a hand over his back. "You're going to get scooped up in no time, pretty boy." She caught Fluffernutter watching him from his sleigh bed in the window, and Kara blew him a kiss. "You too, Fluff."

Charity poked her head into the room. "Stop talking to the cats, so we can finish this conversation."

"The conversation is done. If I came home with you, I'd be on your mother's side."

Charity gasped. "You don't mean it."

"Oh, I absolutely do. You'll have so many blind dates, you won't have a free night until you're eighty."

"Why?"

"Because I think you need someone special to occupy your mind, so you'll stop worrying about me." Kara glanced around the room with a frown, looking for Robin Hood. He normally came out the minute he heard voices.

"Oh, honey, it wouldn't matter if you two got me a date with Charles Melton. I would still meddle in your life because I want you to be happy."

"I'm happy, except I can't find Robin Hood. Kitty, kitty."

Charity stepped inside, frowning. "He couldn't have gotten out, right?"

"No, of course not." Kara squatted down, checking inside the cat houses on the right side of the room, while Charity searched the ones on the left. When Kara peered inside the gingerbread house, Robin Hood lifted his head with a weak meow.

"I found him!" Kara reached inside and gently pulled him out, noticing right away that his back end was wet.

Charity hovered over her shoulder, her voice trembling, "What's wrong with him?"

"I don't know yet, Char." Kara picked him up and didn't need to ask Charity to open the door for her. She pushed into the back and placed Robin Hood on the exam table. Kara palpitated his bladder and felt the bulge, her mouth twisting grimly.

Charity hovered in the doorway, and Kara ordered, "Get me the paper towels on the counter."

Charity moved swiftly, handing her the roll, and Kara ripped off one, wiping his wet fur. "It's urine."

"It looks pink."

"He's most likely blocked, and this is just what's been

able to get through." Kara pulled up at the skin between his shoulder blades, noting it was slightly tacky. "I've got to knock him out and put a catheter in him."

"What do I do? We're supposed to open in a few minutes."

Kara took a deep breath and closed her eyes, centering her mind. Michelle had classes Monday and Wednesday mornings, so she couldn't come in.

"Okay, tell the crowd outside it will be half an hour due to an emergency, but give them each one of the free coffee cards in the drawer for the inconvenience. Then get back here because I need you to hold him for the sedative."

"Kara, I...I don't know if I can."

"You're all I've got, Char."

"Okay. I'll be right back," Charity said, her voice hoarse with emotion. She disappeared through the doors, and Kara stroked the cat's fur.

"I don't think you'll give me much trouble with how crappy you're feeling, but getting stuck with a needle is never fun." She rubbed his ears, clicking her tongue when he leaned into her pets. "I'm sorry I didn't know you were struggling, but I'm going to make you feel better."

The door pushed open, and Charity thrust a wide-eyed Ben into the room. "I found help."

"Whoa, I said I'd bag pastries!"

"I don't need you to help me handle the front. I want you to assist her so she can save my cat." Charity didn't even wait for another argument and disappeared back up front.

"Hi—shouldn't you be at work?" Kara asked.

"I volunteered to go on the coffee run and give the interns a break. I didn't know Charity had a cat."

"She technically doesn't, but she loves Robin Hood. Can you comfort him while I grab the stuff I need? He's in a lot of pain, so just run a hand over him gently."

"What's wrong with him?"

"His urethra is blocked, and he can't pee."

"Yowza. Sorry, kid."

Kara moved around the back, grabbing her supplies and the drugs from the locked cabinet. When she came back into the front area, she pulled several needles and tubes from the drawer next to the sink. "Are you squeamish about blood?"

"No, but you're not going to cut him open, are you?"

"Absolutely not, but I am going to draw some blood, and I didn't want you fainting."

"I'm good, but I should text Schwartz and tell him to cover for me."

Kara handed him a sterile drape. "Open this first and, when I lift him, slide it under to cover the table."

Ben nodded, and once Robin Hood was lying on the blue drape, Kara waited for Ben to finish with his phone. At least he'd be roped into helping on a catherization and not an abscess drainage. That might have been too much for him.

He slipped his phone into his pocket and came back to the table. "Okay, what next?"

"I need you to scruff his neck like this in case he decides he hates what I'm doing, and you're going to hold his leg like this and roll your thumb over the top so that vein stands out. Think you got it?"

Ben took her place and nearly perfectly followed her instructions. Kara wiped down the fur with alcohol and pulled off the needle cap with her other hand, shooting him a wink. "You're a natural."

"Yeah, right," he laughed, but she caught the nervous edge to the sound. Kara understood, because even though she'd done this hundreds of times in the past, there was always that flicker of adrenaline.

Kara finished her blood draw and dumped enough in each test tube. "Okay, now the fun part. This drug goes intramuscular, and he's lethargic now, but the liquid burns, so keep ahold of his scruff, and you're going to hold his back legs like this"—she demonstrated for him—"so he doesn't kick."

Ben took his legs and immediately pulled his hand back. "Why is he wet?"

"It's pee. Sorry, I should have warned you."

He took ahold of Robin Hood's legs again. "It will wash off."

Kara appreciated him sticking around, and frankly, he was all she had. She injected Robin Hood, and he cried out briefly before his body relaxed. Kara washed her hands and gloved up, nodding at Ben. "You might want to look away for this. Keep an eye on his breathing. It should be steady."

Kara applied eye ointment to protect his eyes from drying out and went to work inserting the catheter. She caught Ben peering back and watching what she was doing. Kara liked that he wasn't scared of this aspect of her job. Despite having no medical background with animals, he handled himself well. She couldn't help stealing glances at his face while she worked, and when she had the catheter stitched into place, she grabbed a sterile cup and squeezed his stomach to retrieve a sample.

"Let me get his cage ready, and then your job is done." Kara pulled off her gloves and touched his arm as she passed. "Thank you. I'm not going to get you fired, am I?"

"Nah, I'll tell them what happened. As long as I nail the Choco Vino account tomorrow, Roy will be happy."

"Choco Vino? Sounds delicious."

"It's rich, but good. Schwartz and I are pitching tomorrow."

"Are you nervous about the presentation?" Kara wanted Robin Hood in a middle cage so she could easily keep an eye on him and decided to move Wasabi into the bottom cage. She cleaned it, spreading a white towel along the floor of the cage while Ben responded.

"A little. An account like Choco Vino with a national brand will put Kilburn in the big leagues, and if I'm part of the team that does it, larger opportunities will open for me."

"That's great." Kara finished giving Robin Hood his subcutaneous fluids, lifted him off the exam table, and placed him in the cage, checking his gum color before she closed the door. "I'm going to warm up a disk for under his towel and clean up my mess, so if you want to get going, you can. But thank you. Really, you were fantastic, and if the whole marketing thing doesn't work out, you would make an excellent vet tech."

"Is he going to be okay?" Ben asked.

"He should be, but I'll need to get him to another clinic for an X-ray. I just don't have all the equipment I need. As long as the catheter doesn't block and he can pass the stone, he should make a full recovery."

"You're amazing at this."

"Inserting catheters?"

"Caring for animals. You're so calm and steady."

"When someone else's health and safety is on the line, it's almost like an out-of-body experience. I can see what needs to be done, and I do it. Emotional situations are trickier, which is why it's probably better that Charity didn't stay back here. It's terrible when you're watching an animal you love hurting and there is nothing you can do to fix it."

"I think you helped, and I know you don't want to hear it, but this is exactly the kind of thing the media needs to see and hear about you. If they got a glimpse of all the good you do behind the scenes, they would never believe you could—"

"Ben, please. I told you how I feel about it."

"Think about it again, okay?"

Kara sighed. "Fine. I'll consider it." She boosted herself up by her toes and kissed his cheek. "Now get out of here before you no longer have a job. And tell Charity there's no charge. You earned a hundred mochas this morning."

"I'm not going to do that, but it's nice to be appreciated." Ben winked at her before pushing into the front and out of sight.

Kara warmed up the disk and slipped it underneath the towel Robin Hood rested on. She covered him with another warm towel and rubbed him, happy the catheter seemed to be working. She pulled up a chair and sat next to his cage while she considered Ben's request. She'd dismissed it out of hand before, but Ben seemed adamant that it could help. And the whole point of what they were doing together was to rebuild trust for each other, but also the world.

An hour later, Robin Hood was up and sporting a cone of shame, since he'd already tried going for his back end. When Kara got cleaned up and walked up front, she was greeted by Charity, who watched her with worry.

"He's doing great. I figured I'd come up and check on you before I get back to him. He'll need to be transported to a hospital to get an X-ray, just to make sure he doesn't have any bigger crystals in there."

"Oh, I'm so glad. Thank you." Charity hugged her and stepped back behind the counter. "Who's next?"

A young guy with a nose ring and spiked blond hair stepped up and asked, "Are you Kara Ingalls?"

"No, I am," Kara said.

The guy held out an envelope to her with a nod, and when she took it, he said, "You've been served."

Chapter Twenty

Nutmeg is an Abyssinian mix who, like the spice, is always in your cupboards.

KARA CURLED UP ON the couch with Theo on top of her, kneading her legs through the blanket. It was almost 7:30 p.m., and she should get up and make dinner, but she wasn't hungry after eating her weight in hot cocoa and peppermint Hershey's Kisses. The tea on her side table had gone cold thirty minutes ago, and as she watched Jack Black get up and leave Kate Winslet at the counter alone to go chase his ex-girlfriend, Kara was half tempted to turn the movie off. Under normal circumstances she loved *The Holiday*, but watching an unrealistic happily ever after wasn't doing anything to brighten her spirits.

She heard someone messing with her front doorknob and

gritted her teeth, leaning back against the armrest to holler, "Go away!"

The front door opened and shut. "I will not." Charity's shoes tapped across the floor until she placed both hands on either side of Kara's head and leaned over. "How you feeling, babes?"

"You mean after discovering that things actually could be worse than the media coming for me all over again? I never want to leave this house."

Charity shook her head and disappeared from sight. Kara heard a drawer open and closed her eyes. "I don't want to read it."

"We're past that now. You need to read it, and then we're going to fight this stupid lawsuit—"

"How?" Kara murmured hoarsely, opening her eyes. "Even though the police cleared me, it is Ferris Worthington's word against mine that I wasn't involved, and obviously he has some kind of threadbare evidence he thinks he can hold over my head, or he wouldn't try. This is just going to cause negative attention to the café, and honestly, I don't know if I can take it."

"Babes, he's a narcissist. He's doing this to get to you because he thinks he can get away with it. We're going to prove him wrong." Charity shoved the letter into her hand. "Read it. You are a strong, independent, resilient woman who is not going to let this man control one more second of your life."

Kara involuntarily smiled as she ripped open the top with her finger. "You know you sounded exactly like your mother just now."

"Don't make me hurt you," Charity said, belying the threat by squeezing her knee. She sat on the edge of the couch while Kara unfolded the letter with trembling fingers.

Kara,

I have spent two years in here thinking about nothing else but seeing you. After everything we shared, where is your loyalty? You left me to twist, and now the piper's coming to collect.

I'm filing a suit against you for emotional distress. I thought I was taking all the responsibility for our crimes and we would be together when I got out, but not a single visit in two years?

If you want to avoid a lengthy legal battle, we can settle this between us for two hundred thousand. If not, I hope you're prepared for what comes next.

See you soon,
Worthy

Kara's breathing was short and ragged, her head swimming.

Charity took the letter and called Worthy an unflattering name before tossing it onto the coffee table. Then she took Kara by the shoulders, and Kara met her gaze, tears blurring her vision.

"Do you really think you did anything illegal?" Charity asked.

"If I hadn't left him alone—"

"You made a mistake, but you didn't commit a crime.

I don't care what he does, you are not giving him another ounce of your time and attention."

"I can't ignore him, Charity. He's suing me."

"What about some good PR? Worthy has a criminal record, and you do not! Any so-called damage to your reputation will be from idiots who don't do their research."

"I hope you're not suggesting I contact the media. They crucified me last time and they wrote about him with the off-color tone of *boys will be boys*!"

"Yes, the world can sometimes be more forgiving toward men than women, but the people who do the most damage are the only ones who can reverse it. Talk about how much pain he caused, but how you came out of it stronger, that you're happy to have this chance to put the past behind you and continue to make a difference for homeless cats, something you've always been passionate about."

"There's no guarantee some reporter won't manipulate what I say for clicks."

"What if we ask Ben to write some things for us and see if he has any trustworthy news outlets?"

"Absolutely not. He already brought this up to me, and I told him hard pass."

Charity put her hands up in the air. "It's the last time I suggest it, but I honestly believe you've let this entire experience with Worthy darken your opinion of people. Not everyone is evil, and some people care about the truth. We'll just concentrate on getting you a great lawyer and squashing this thing before it even gets before a judge."

"I have some mutual funds I can pull from if I need

money for a lawyer, but maybe it's time I step away from the café."

"Over my dead body, and frankly, I'm angry you'd even suggest it." Charity stood up, crossing her arms over her chest. "You're upset with social media and news outlets, but where is the fury for the man behind all your misery? Seriously, Kara, that turd got close to you and betrayed your trust, but you're blaming everyone else but him! You should sue him for emotional trauma, lost wages, and for extreme doucheness! Get mad!" Charity lifted up her foot and nudged her with it. "He proposed to you with a ring he bought with money from scamming someone else. Where is your indignation for them? For the people he victimized selling their information? You didn't do that, he did! Stealing from that charity almost cost animals' lives. Doesn't that tick you off?"

Worthy's twinkling blue eyes flashed through her mind as he told her about his banking job, how one day he was going to up and retire somewhere away from it all. She'd had no idea at the time he'd already stolen the donated funds from Half-a-Million Lives.

"He's extorting you because he knows he doesn't have a leg to stand on, and he's hoping you'll cave, that you'll try to make him go away, but you don't owe him a darn thing."

Kara flipped the blanket off her feet, her hands fisted at her sides. "You're right. I'm not letting that worm bully me anymore."

"That's the spirit. So what are you going to do about it?"

"I guess I'll need to get a lawyer and file a motion to dismiss."

Charity pulled out her phone. "Want me to call my dad and see if there's someone he recommends?"

"That would be great, thanks."

"Absolutely. I've got your back, and I'm not the only one. I think Ben's really into you."

Kara blushed. "I thought we were going to talk strategy, not boys!"

"Can't we do both?"

"He texted me a couple times, but I haven't responded."

"Why not?" Charity asked.

"Because I'm in my feels, and he doesn't need to be a part of that. We're having fun, and you know what happens when you start letting them see your anxiety attacks and mental breakdowns? It's no longer fun! I was incredibly impressed with his help the other morning with Robin Hood. Oh! What did the vet say when you dropped him off?"

"That he should be able to pass what they can see with no issues and that you did a beautiful job on his catheter."

Kara smiled. "Thanks for taking him."

"Honestly, his health is my responsibility."

"What do you mean?"

"You can consider this my official notice that I'm going to adopt him. Seeing him like that today made me physically ill, and I realized if something happened to him, I'd be devastated. So forget dating. Screw my landlord. I'll have my job, hopefully, my family, my friends, and my cat. The rest will work itself out."

"Really? You're giving up dating?"

"I deleted all of my apps earlier today."

"Wow."

"Yep. They never did anything for me anyway."

"Well, just so you know, if your landlord won't let you put down a pet deposit, you can always move in with me. I've got a guest room and no mortgage, so just utilities and groceries, and movie nights any time you want."

"I don't know. If you and Ben keep vibing, I'll end up being the third wheel."

"Nah, we'll bring Schwartz for you to hang with."

Charity snorted. "Oh, yay."

"What's wrong with Schwartz?"

"Nothing, but he's not my type."

"Maybe along with dating apps and toxic men, you should consider giving other guys a shot. Ones that are a little more down-to-earth."

"You think Schwartz is down-to-earth?" Charity scoffed.

"I don't know, but you don't have to date him. I'm just saying to maybe keep your options open."

"Fine. Speaking of new things, I do have some information that might cheer you up."

Kara sat back on the couch and pulled her blanket over her lap. "What's that?"

"Our donations were up to six hundred and twelve dollars this afternoon, and Dolores from Bookin' It came by to thank you for the cookies and the offer to use our social room and brought a huge box of feline-themed books as a token of appreciation."

Kara was glad she'd dropped by on Monday instead of putting it off. There was no way she'd have been up to talking to anyone today.

"Ben thinks we should have a big Christmas party with a silent auction during Twenty-Five Days of Catmas."

"How are we going to pull that off in a few weeks?"

"That's what I said, but apparently, he's got a plan. He suggested we start by asking local businesses for donations."

"What do you think?" Charity asked.

"Honestly, I'm willing to try anything at this point." Kara shot Charity a sharp look when she caught her smile. "There are exceptions of course."

"If we're going to do that, then it's best to ask in person. Harder for them to say no."

"For you maybe," Kara joked.

Charity frowned. "What does that mean?"

"That you're gorgeous, and people respond more positively to attractive people."

"I'm also a Black woman. Believe me, this world is not as evolved as people like to pretend. Sometimes it has less to do with beauty and more to do with the hate that blinds them."

Kara reached for Charity, taking her hand with a squeeze. "Hey, I'm sorry. That was incredibly privileged of me to say."

Charity nodded. "It's okay, bestie. I know your heart and that you don't think that way."

"I love you. And thank you for telling me. I would never want to say something insensitive and have you hold it in and not speak up."

"Do you know me at all? Never." Charity leaned over and picked up Kara's phone, passing it to her. "Now, let's get down to business and talk to-do lists."

Kara took the phone and saw the new message from Ben. She clicked on the text box, and there was an attached photo of Chaos sleeping in the crook of his neck.

Just two guys watching The Office before bed.

Never would she have imagined when they'd first met that Ben would be sending her proof-of-life pictures of a kitten he was fostering. She tapped back a heart-eyed emoji and went into her lists.

"All right, I'll take care of the ladies on Saturday for the book club. Then we need to make a list of all the businesses in the area and divide and conquer."

"You'll also have to ask Ben where he expects us to host this, and if he's got connections, to hook us up!"

"I'm sure you know more people in the area than him. You've lived here your whole life!"

"Fine, I'll call my dad now and kill two birds with one stone. Lawyer suggestions for you and possible party locations. You keep writing that list."

Kara shook her head, tapping away. Her phone beeped, and another message from Ben flashed across the top of her screen.

Do you want to go out Friday? I've heard there's this really cool place and I want to take you.

Sure, where is it?

I'd like to keep it a surprise. I promise it isn't something weird.

Maybe I'm into weird. What the heck made her say that? Before he got the wrong idea, she typed, I'm kidding. Friday sounds great. Maybe afterwards we could swing in somewhere and get me a tree?

Are you asking me to go with you so I can do all the heavy lifting?

Well, it's either you or the dude at the gas station down the road from my place.

I'm probably the safer bet. I'll grab you at six thirty.

Then takeout back at my place?

It's a date.

Despite their agreement not to label anything, her stomach fluttered.

Can't wait.

Chapter Twenty-One

Katy Purry is a Himalayan mix whose purrs start when you look at her. And at only five months old, she really is a teenage dream!

"WAIT, RUN THIS BY me again. You reclaimed custody of that tiny terror kitten?"

Ben glared at Schwartz as he exited out of the pitch video they'd made for the Choco Vino campaign, disappointment raging through him. The owner of the company and her assistant had sat through the entire presentation without cracking a smile. He'd thought their ideas were solid, but maybe he was off his game.

"The kitten is only staying until New Year's."

"And Kara? What's going on with you two?"

Ben snapped the laptop closed. "Can we get back to the presentation and what an epic failure it was?"

"What are you talking about? I thought it went well."

"How? They didn't even twitch when you showed them the commercial with all the drinks you could make with it and the foods that perfectly paired with the rich flavor. We missed the mark so hard, I doubt we're coming back from this."

Schwartz stilled, blinking at him. "Are we talking fired?"

"He fired Fitzgerald for blowing the Quartz Brandy campaign."

"Yeah, but Fitzgerald was an incompetent idiot, and we"—he waved his hand back and forth between them—"are awesome."

"I guess we'll find out in a few seconds," Ben said, nodding to Roy coming back around the corner, power walking back to the conference room entrance like his pants were on fire.

"Does he look angry? I can never tell," Schwartz asked.

Roy burst through the door, his round face tense. "You two! I thought I told you to bring your A game?"

"Sir, we're sorry. We thought—"

"Shut it, Schwartz," he snapped. "I don't want to hear anything from either one of you because you did"—his face split into a grin as he pointed at them with both hands—"exactly what I told you to do! They loved it!"

"They did?" Ben asked, completely thrown.

"Couldn't you tell?" Roy deadpanned, before he burst out laughing. "Of course you couldn't, because I didn't know the whole way down in the elevator until the assistant turned to me and said, 'Send over the contract. You're in.'"

Ben's breath *whooshed* out as Schwartz let out a loud whoop of excitement.

"You had us going, sir," Schwartz laughed.

"If it's ever bad news, I wouldn't even come back in here," Roy said. "We'd be having a different conversation in my office."

"That's good to know for the future," Ben said breathlessly.

"You." Roy wagged his fingers at them again. "You're going to get a hefty Christmas bonus for this one. This account is going to put Kilburn on the map, and I couldn't have done it without you!"

Roy left the room, and Schwartz jumped into Ben's arms, the two of them laughing and slapping each other on the back.

"Whew, I wonder how much he's going to give us?"

"I don't know, but we should celebrate. I've been thinking about Christmas and my family drama and was wondering if you'd be interested in going on a mini vacation with me? We'd be back the second of January."

"I mean . . . " Schwartz hesitated before giving Ben another hearty smack on the back. "Heck yes! What did you have in mind?"

"Somewhere warm and tropical?"

"Cruise!" Schwartz snapped his fingers. "We should book a singles cruise."

"With twenty-one days before Christmas?" Ben asked. "I doubt they have any spots left."

"They always have people back out at the last minute." Schwartz whipped out his phone with a grin. "What do you think?"

Ben shrugged. "See what you find."

While Schwartz tapped away at his phone screen, Ben

gathered up all their presentation props and carried them back to Schwartz's office.

Schwartz came through the door behind him, shaking his head. "Okay, maybe not a cruise, but what about a resort in Mexico?"

"Could be fun."

"Here we go. Round-trip flights out of Sacramento on Christmas Eve into Cancún. Nine nights at this resort, all-inclusive, is twelve hundred with tax." Schwartz punched him in the shoulder playfully after Ben dropped the stuff on his desk. "This is the best idea you've ever had."

"I hope so. Now I just need to tell my parents." Ben grimaced. "Will you book it, and I'll Venmo you? If it's a done deal, then they can't talk me out of it."

"I'm on it. Just remember, you are my wingman. No sitting on the sidelines for this trip. I'm not saying cheat on Kara, 'cause that's sketchy, but you can entertain a friend or two, right?"

Ben rolled his eyes but didn't bother correcting Schwartz about him and Kara being together. Despite their agreement not to label it, what they were doing sure felt like dating, and the more time he spent with her, the more their differences didn't seem so important.

"I'll do my best not to let you down, but I don't want to spend nine days partying."

"Don't be a dud! You can sleep when you're dead."

He wanted to relax on vacation, not chase girls. Maybe it was a mistake asking Schwartz. With someone else, he could just go and have a drink by the beach, listening to an audiobook while he napped in the sun.

His thoughts strayed to Kara's quiet Christmas at home reading and Theo curled up on her squishy gray couch. He'd never had a quiet holiday in his life, but it honestly didn't sound like such a bad prospect.

"Texted you the total. Now I'm going to go celebrate another night of Hanukkah with my family."

"Have fun. I'll see you tomorrow, and great job, partner."

"You too!"

Ben stepped out of Schwartz's office with a wave and headed back down to retrieve his belongings. He pulled out his phone and called his father. Better to rip off the Band-Aid now.

His father answered on the second ring. "Ben, how's it going?"

"It's good, Pop. We scored the Choco Vino account, so my boss is really happy with me."

"That doesn't surprise me. You've always been a hard worker."

"The thing is, we're getting a nice bonus for landing the account, and we decided to book a guys' vacation. We leave Christmas Eve and don't return until January second."

His father didn't respond for several seconds and finally cleared his throat. "I guess that saves us a stop while we're out there."

Guilt ripped through Ben. The last thing he wanted to do was hurt his parents, but this was better all around. He wouldn't bring down the festivities knowing they were heading to Boone's place after they were done visiting him, and they could spend more time exploring the area without feeling obligated to see him.

"I'm not trying to upset you guys, but after the year I've had, I need this trip. I hope you'll understand."

"I understand needing a relaxing vacation, but you couldn't have planned it any other time?"

"Yeah, I could have, but me being here just divides the family, and I don't want to do that to Ma, and I don't want to hear about it, to be honest."

"Are you going to tell her, or should I?"

"I can if you want to pass her the phone."

"She's not here now. I'll have her call you when she gets home."

"Thanks. I love you, Pop."

"I love you, too," he said, but Ben heard the disappointment in his father's voice. They said their goodbyes, and Ben made his way out of the building. He hated feeling like he was the villain in this story.

Ben found himself walking away from the parking garage where his car was and in the direction of Meow and Furever. He pushed the door into the café and waved at Charity.

"Hey, you," she called. "We need to talk."

"Uh-oh. Don't tell me I'm on your list, too."

"Depends. This whole Christmas party and auction was your idea, so I feel it's only necessary you jump into the planning with us."

Ben almost laughed aloud, relief rushing through him. "I'm happy to. Where is Kara?"

"She's in the back doing exams on a couple cats. Let me lock the front door, and we can walk back."

The front door opened behind him, and he turned to see

a short man with a shaved head and dark-framed glasses coming through the door.

"Sorry, we're closed. I just shut everything down," Charity said, coming around the counter.

"That's all right. I'm actually here to speak to Kara Ingalls."

Charity's lips thinned. "In regard to?"

"It's a personal matter." The guy straightened his shoulders as if he was ready to dig in his heels, so Ben flashed his good-guy grin.

"Hey, man, you might as well tell her because she won't let you near Kara until you do."

The door to the back pushed open, and Kara came through, her face breaking into a wide smile when she spotted Ben, and his heart sped up happily. Being around her really was doing wonders for his gloomy attitude.

"Hi, I didn't know you were here."

"I was about to bring him back when this guy barged in here asking to talk to you," Charity said.

Kara's smile dimmed, and she addressed the man warily. "I'm Kara Ingalls. How can I help you?"

"I'm Gerard Sutter with the *Metro Valley Post*, and I have a few questions about Ferris Worthington."

"I'm sorry," Kara said, her tone chilly. "I don't have anything to say."

Gerard frowned. "But weren't you engaged before he was arrested? And isn't he now suing you, claiming that you set him up to take the fall?"

"That jerk is a lying sack of scum," Charity snarled, pointing to the front door. "My friend didn't do anything, and the police proved that the first time around. The man is a narcissist, with a master's degree in manipulation, and only a fool would believe anything he says."

Ben heard Kara's choked sob before she turned and went through the door separating the café from the back area.

"Kara," Charity cried, going after her.

Ben turned to face the smaller man and watched his Adam's apple bob nervously.

"I...I didn't mean to upset anyone. I just wanted a new angle, and she's never talked to the press."

"Given your approach, I don't blame her." Ben escorted him out the door, pausing before he went back inside. "If you want to write something new, why don't you talk about the truth?"

"What's the truth?"

"Ferris Worthington used his relationship to gain access to sensitive information and accounts, destroying his fiancée's life and job with false accusations. She's come out of it stronger and is an essential beacon of hope in this community. The Meow and Furever Cat Café is hosting a Twenty-Five Days of Catmas to raise enough money to not only keep their doors open, but to offer a low-cost clinic to those who've fallen on hard times. That's what you should be writing about, not giving any more airtime to a criminal."

"And what is your relationship to Miss Ingalls?"

"I'm one of the foster homes the café uses when an animal needs more time before they enter the social room. I have the greatest respect for Miss Ingalls and her business partner, Miss Simmons, who makes the best cinnamon rolls I've ever had in my life. Really, you should check them out."

"Thank you, Mr...."

"I'm Ben Reese."

"I appreciate your time."

Ben nodded, closing the door on the man and locking it. He'd made sure to keep his answers formal and on topic, so that his words couldn't be twisted in case Gerard decided to run the story. He hoped the guy would at least do a few more hours of research, but reporters like him were the reason Kara was so against the media. He was looking for a sordid story that would make perfect clickbait. At least if he reported on the donations and the Catmas countdown, maybe it would boost the event.

Ben pushed through the door to the back room, but Charity was the only one on the other side, her mouth pinched. "She's in the bathroom."

"Is he really suing her?" Ben asked gruffly.

"She didn't tell you?"

"No." Ben didn't want to make a big deal out of this, but he wished Kara had told him about the lawsuit. They were still building trust between them, but he'd made it very clear he wanted to help.

"His crimes made national news for weeks, and during the trial, they hounded her. It was one of the largest security breaches in years, and a lot of people blamed her, even though she didn't do anything but think she was with a great guy." Charity hit the exam table with a growl. "Oh, I'd love to break his stupid face."

I'm right there with you.

"I know and you know that Kara would never jeopardize anything that helped animals. Were any of the news outlets sympathetic? Or interested in doing a human-interest story on her?"

Charity shook her head. "No. They either speculated about her guilt or ignored her."

"Back in Boston, we'd have to take on clients with troubled reputations and spin them to create a redemption campaign."

Charity puffed up indignantly. "Kara doesn't need redemption for anything!"

"Easy, Mama Bear, let me finish. No one except you had Kara's back, but what if we can get her story circulating, talking about how much she loves animals and the hurt she experienced, only to turn around and put everything she had into this café?" Ben grinned, getting fired up. "The world loves an underdog."

"Kara told you she didn't want a PR campaign," Charity said archly.

"Ah, she mentioned I asked, huh?"

"Yes, because I suggested it as well." Charity glanced at the back of the clinic and then met his gaze seriously. "She's so antimedia, she wouldn't even hear me out. If I wanted to help you set one up, what would you need from me?"

"Could you put together a background on Kara for me? Her childhood with her distant mom. Her grandparents and the short-lived joy she experienced with them. Her time as a veterinarian and why she stopped practicing to work at the nonprofit. Why cats?"

"Absolutely. But if this backfires, it was all you."

"I understand, but she doesn't deserve any of this, and I feel like the only way she is going to see that the world isn't out to get her is to let the good guys share her story. And if she won't give her blessing, it's better to ask for forgiveness than permission."

Chapter Twenty-Two

Meowise Gamgee is a loyal tabby that longs to travel to the ends of Middle Earth for you. He's a little nervous at first but warms up quickly.

THE CONVERSATION WITH HIS mother about his holiday plans had gone as well as could be expected. After his mother blasted him with every reason why he was being unreasonable, she broke down crying and handed the phone off to his father. Ben ended the phone call by telling them he loved them and he'd make plans to come out and see them after the holidays. His father told him they'd mail his gift. He could just imagine a box of coal showing up on his porch with a tag that read "World's Worst Son."

At least things with Kara were great. He didn't even realize until this last year that he'd jumped headfirst into all his relationships and always moved incredibly fast. He'd only been with Amelia a month before she moved in and six before he proposed, and every girlfriend before that had been similar, moving at the speed of light only to fizzle out within a year. With Kara, he enjoyed talking. The kissing was fantastic, but he didn't want to rush her into his bed. Or her bed. She understood him in a way no one else ever had, and part of that was their painful past relationships, but he thought it was more than that. She wore her empathy for others' pain on her sleeve, something that made her a wonderful veterinarian.

And an amazing partner.

His phone blared to life in his hand, and he recognized the East Coast number. Ben pressed the phone icon and put it to his ear. "Hey, Tony, I'm getting into my car, so there may be a lull as you switch to my Bluetooth."

"Yeah, no problem. I just wanted to tell you, the information you sent? Compelling stuff. Especially the parts about her being eviscerated by the media and found guilty in the public's opinion, while he gets a pass after two years? I'm furious on her behalf."

"Hang on, Tony," Ben called as he started his vehicle. When he heard the telltale click of the call connecting, he asked, "You there?"

"Yes. Anyway, I started reaching out to some friends of mine, and I think we can get a good spin going. I love the things her partner and employee had to say about her, but do you think she'd be open to an exclusive?"

Ben grimaced. "I don't think so. She's pretty antimedia of any kind."

"Understandable after what she's had to deal with. Leave it to me, my friend! I'll change her mind and prove we're not all clickbait demon hounds!"

"Thanks. I owe you."

"I'll collect soon."

Ben ended the call as he cruised through his neighborhood, studying the Christmas lights and displays as he passed. Charity had passed along a full history of achievements and hardships, along with testimonials from regulars at the café about Kara's dedication to helping animals. It would be a beautiful PR piece that he thought Kara would love, despite her aversion to being in the spotlight.

Another text came through, this time from his sister, Birdy, and he pressed the button on the screen to listen.

Ma and Pop canceled our trip to California. Boone backed out of the job and since you won't be there, no point. Just thought I'd let you know and I hope you have fun in Mexico. Not.

Ben frowned and tapped the phone icon. No matter how irritated she may be, he knew his sister would pick up. She thrived on being a buttinsky. He dialed Birdy's number, and she answered with a heavy sigh. "Hello?"

"Hey, Birdy. I got your message."

"Then why are you calling?"

"I'm calling because the last I heard, Boone already signed the contract and was out here looking at houses. I knew you would have all the facts."

"I do, but I'm peeved at you. Coming to California wasn't exactly a second honeymoon, but it would have been the first trip we've taken in years."

"I didn't cancel your trip. Blame Boone and Ma and Pop!"

"It's my pity party, and I'll blame who I want to," Birdy sang, a sign that she wasn't as angry as she played it.

"Can you be ticked off and still tell me what happened with Boone?"

There was a silent beat before she answered him. "Apparently, he decided to stay in Boston. When Ma and Pop told him you were considering putting your house on the market and leaving, he didn't want to mess up your life again and called the hospital to tell them he couldn't accept their offer."

"That makes him a martyr, I guess."

"Oh for cripes' sake, Ben. The man has been our brother for thirty-two years. He's not a monster."

"That statement could be debatable," Ben joked bitterly.

"He made some poor choices, but hasn't everyone? You're telling me you've never made a mistake?"

"I'm not beating this horse anymore, Birdy. All I'm saying is, now the guy can use this as some kind of evidence that he's tried to make things right between us and I'm the unreasonable one."

"Ben, I want you to listen and know that this comes from a place of love." He heard her inhale and exhale slowly before she snapped, "Get over it. She loved him, he loved her, now they're married, and going to have a baby!"

Ben almost missed the stop sign and slammed on his brakes, tires squealing.

"Ben! Are you okay?"

"Amelia is pregnant?" he asked, quietly.

"Yes. They found out a few days ago, and she doesn't want to leave her family or ours. So they're staying in Boston."

Ben slowly eased across the road and hopped on the highway headed toward Kara's.

"Ben? Are you still there?"

"Yeah, you just dropped another bomb in my lap, but I'm fine."

"I'm sorry, brother. I know you loved her, and it hurts to hear this—"

"Honestly, her leaving me turned into a blessing. I hated my job, my apartment. Out here, my boss respects me. My partner and I landed this national account, which is partly why we decided to take this trip—to celebrate. I finished remodeling my house, and you should see the before and after pictures. It's everything I ever wanted. And I'm going out tonight to look at Christmas lights with a friend."

"A girlfriend?" Her voice kicked up into a high-octave tease, and he glared at the screen. Things between them hadn't changed; even when they were kids, Birdy loved to mess with him.

"A woman who is my friend, yes."

"Is she cute?"

"She's attractive."

"Does Ma know?" Birdy asked.

"There's nothing to know. We're friends. You got wax in your ears or something?"

"You're such a jerk."

Ben grinned. "I love you, too, big sister."

"Have fun in Mexico for Christmas," she said, disgust oozing through the speakers like ectoplasm.

"Is that jealousy I hear in your voice?"

"Maybe a small bit, but only because I can't remember the last time Tom and I went on a vacation without the kids."

A twinge of guilt pinched his throat. "I'm sorry, sis. It just seemed easier to take myself out of the equation so no one would have to split their holiday."

"Well, now you'll still be all alone at a tropical resort while your family is here, celebrating and eating fabulous food without you."

"Dang, when did you master Ma's guilt-trippin' skills?"

"Since I became a mother. And you should call her. It certainly makes Boone look better that he's the one doing everything to keep her happy and you're being a mule."

"That's because he was wrong! How many times do I have to say it?"

"You can only play the poor-me game for so long, little brother, until all you are is a victim." She kept talking without giving him a chance for rebuttal. "Have fun tonight."

"Thanks," he grumbled, ending the call as he turned left into Kara's driveway, still spinning from Birdy's little announcement. He was going to be an uncle again, his little brother's first kid, and he was struggling with an array of emotions he couldn't seem to decipher. This was something he should be celebrating with them, and instead, they were so far estranged that, even if he wanted to mend fences, he didn't see any way back to where they were before.

Ben blew out a deep breath and climbed out of his car, thinking about Boone and Amelia. He couldn't seem to move beyond that, frozen in place, like he couldn't take a step toward Kara without figuring out how to handle his past. He'd been angry for so long about the way they'd handled their relationship, and maybe their decision not to move had nothing to do with him, but a small part of him, the piece of himself that knew his brother, thought it could have a little something to do with him. Perhaps they actually had been trying to do the right thing and let him have this fresh start. Why was this olive branch different from all the others?

Maybe because for the first time, he could look past his anger and put himself in his brother's shoes. Connecting with someone you couldn't get out of your mind and finding out they were engaged to your brother? He might not handle it the same way the two of them had, but meeting someone worth changing for? He could see not wanting to let that go.

Ben climbed the front porch steps and knocked on the door. Several moments passed before Kara opened the door, smiling widely.

"Hey."

"Hi." He leaned over, kissing her cheek. "You ready?"

"Yep, just need to grab my coat. Are you still okay taking me to get a tree after? I've got tie-down straps for my car."

"Don't worry about those. I can just leave the back of my SUV open, as long as you don't want a twelve-foot tree."

Kara laughed. "No, I think I'll stick to something I can reach without a stepladder."

"Then we're safe. Are you hungry now or do you want to go to your surprise first?"

"As long as it's a good surprise, let's go!"

"I hope it's a good one, but I guess we'll see." He'd seen pictures of Candy Cane Lane, and the neighborhood was amazing. He just hoped Kara thought so, too.

Ben took her coat and helped her into it. When she finished zipping it up, Ben reached out and entwined his fingers with hers.

"It's not labeling to hold your hand, is it?"

He caught the telltale flush in her cheeks as she shook her head. "I'm good with it."

Ben never expected Kara's hand to fit so perfectly with his as they strolled down the walkway to his car.

"How are things with your brother? Are you still abandoning ship?"

"I'm not selling the house, but I'm still going out of town for the holidays, even though it turns out I didn't need to."

"What do you mean?" she asked.

"My brother decided not to take the job in Sacramento, and since I'm leaving for Cancún, my family has canceled their California trip and are staying in Boston."

"How do you feel about that?"

She got to the passenger door before him and opened it. He hung over the outside of the door as she climbed in, considering his mixed emotions. "I'm not sure. I'm relieved that I won't accidentally bump into my brother because we're living in the same area, but then I know my family is disappointed. My older sister was looking forward to the trip, so now I'm the bad guy."

"Did he say why they aren't moving here?"

"I didn't talk to him." He shut her door and jogged around the front to climb into the driver's side. "My sister told me he wasn't moving because Amelia doesn't want to leave the families, since she's pregnant."

Kara's hand reached out for his. "Ben, I'm so sorry."

"Don't be. I'm borderline happy for them. I've been angry with them for so long, I didn't know how to not be furious, but I'm trying."

"Have you thought about canceling your Cancún trip and heading back to Boston to surprise them?"

"Nah, I've spent every holiday since I was born in the freezing cold, playing games with my very loud, very boisterous family. I think switching things up with something new could be fun. Plus, sunshine, sand, sweet drinks, and—"

"Schwartz?" she teased.

"Hey, Schwartz is good company."

"Do you think he has a thing for Charity?" Kara asked.

Ben shook his head as he turned around and headed down her driveway. "I can never tell with Schwartz. His girlfriends are short-lived."

"Charity likes to fix people or protect them, and she does not have any other modes. She has brief relationships, too, especially if they meet her parents."

"Why is that the catalyst?"

"Because if they like the guy, she immediately loses all attraction for him. I still haven't figured out why, and I've known her for fifteen years."

"Not gonna lie, that's a little strange."

"Yes, but when I tell her that, she gets defensive. We all have our little idiosyncrasies thanks to our parents, right? I'm emotionally neurotic, Charity is still rebelling in her thirties, and you..."

"Still struggle not to do whatever my mother tells me?"

Kara laughed. "Oh, that is not something a girl wants to hear!"

"I guess that's one thing Charity will want to fix about me, huh?"

"I'm not sure. Even though you say that you struggle not to do what your mom wants, you've put yourself in a few uncomfortable positions with your family standing your ground, so I think you're good. I'm supposed to give Charity a full report on tonight when I get home."

"Uh-oh. Should I be prepared for a clipboard to appear with a score sheet, like when you take your driver's test?"

"I'm fresh out of those, I'm afraid. I guess I'll just have to memorize every moment."

Chapter Twenty-Three

Meowdor may only have one eye, but it's a strong one! One glance into the Great Eye and you'll have no choice but to take him home to rule your kingdom.

KARA HOPPED OUT OF Ben's car with a coffee cup in one hand, smiling as he came around to meet her, his hand outstretched as if he couldn't wait to touch her again. They'd stopped for peppermint hot cocoa on the way, and it wasn't until they'd turned onto the street that Kara recognized where they were headed. Charity had dragged her around the extensively decorated Christmas street in college, but she hadn't been back since.

Kara's fingers laced with his, the warmth of his palm connecting with hers sending licks of heat up her arms and unfurling into her chest. A line of people rounded the corner ahead, shuffling forward at a snail's pace. When they reached the end, Kara took a sip of her cocoa, noticing that a toddler in a pink puffy jacket was staring at her cup with longing.

"This may be my new favorite holiday drink," Ben said, licking his lips.

"Hmm, I still prefer pumpkin everything, because fall is my favorite season, but this is good, too."

"I'd have pegged you for a summer girl."

"Nope. I hate to sweat. Autumn is the perfect season."

"I'm a winter guy. I miss the snow." Ben glanced up at the clear sky. "It doesn't feel like Christmas without it."

"I've only seen snow a couple times and I wasn't a fan," she said, smiling at the little girl. "Hi."

The toddler ducked behind her mom, peeking from around her leg.

"You like kids?" Ben asked.

"Yeah, I do. I didn't have the best role model for a mom, but I think I could figure it out. Lorelai Gilmore is my favorite TV mom."

"What show is she from?"

Kara's gaze swung his way, her eyes widening. "*Gilmore Girls*! You haven't watched it?"

"I've never been big on TV. Video games and movies are more my sweet spot."

"You play shooter games or something?"

"Yeah."

"I can't do those. They make me sick."

"Man, you don't like the snow, summer, or video games?"

Kara nudged him with her shoulder. "You don't like cats, real books, or TV. Such a weirdo."

"Eh, Chaos is growing on me, but I need to start wearing

something more than a T-shirt around the house, because when he climbs up on my shoulder, ouch!"

They moved a foot forward, but the crowd surrounding the house next to them was blocking most of the street. "I had a foster who liked to do that, but she was polydactyl and wanted to be lifted up where her food was. She was a bit of a prima donna."

"What's paradactyl mean?"

"Poly. It means extra toes."

Ben's eyes widened. "Is that normal?"

"It can happen with some breeds of cats as a recessive gene. As long as you keep the claws trimmed, you're fine, but sometimes they can grow back into the paw—"

"Yow, I get the picture. No need to describe any further," he said, shuddering.

"Funny, you weren't squeamish during Robin Hood's catheterization."

"I was in the moment, but I don't want to see open wounds and such."

"Are you a germophobe too?"

"A little bit."

"So if I get sick, don't ask you to take care of me?"

"I'll take care of you, but don't be surprised if I show up in a hazmat suit with gloves, and I push your food through a crack in the door while you stay six feet away."

Kara laughed. "I'm only teasing. I can take care of myself if I'm down and out. Besides, taking care of each other when we're sick is more of a boyfriend-girlfriend thing."

"And we're not labeling this," Ben said, his tone indiscernible.

"Exactly."

They crested the corner, and Kara let out an appreciative "Ooh," which Ben mirrored with his own "Cool." The first house they passed was set up to look like Whoville from *How the Grinch Stole Christmas*. They even had a large Mount Crumpit and blow-up Grinch staring down at the town. Thousands of lights sparkled on and off across the roof and fence with tiny strobes of color, and the little girl in front of them cried, "Look, Mom! There's Max."

Sure enough, a big brown dog sat next to his owner in the driveway wearing a red sweater with the name *Max* knitted on the back.

"I think it would be so fun to decorate like this," Kara gushed.

"Looks like a lot of work to me. I'm thinking about putting one of those projectors on the front of my house and calling it good."

"Ugh, really?"

"What? They are cool-looking, they save time, and they keep people off ladders. Do you know how many people fall while hanging Christmas lights?"

The little girl turned around and stared at Ben with wide-eyed horror.

"Ben," Kara choked, trying not to laugh, "you're scaring the children."

"Sorry." They got a good look at the next house with an *A Charlie Brown Christmas* theme, and Kara pointed. "I bet this is your favorite Christmas movie."

"Why?"

"Because you're kind of a downer."

"I am not. And actually, it's *Home Alone*."

"Really? It's so far-fetched, though."

"I don't watch movies for realism. I watch them to be entertained, and Joe Pesci flying backward off the steps is hysterical."

"I haven't watched it since I was a kid. I liked *The Santa Clause*. I used to dream about Santa being my dad and whisking me off to the North Pole."

Ben's chest tightened. "He wasn't around, huh?"

"No. He met me once, but I was too young to remember. Guess he liked being on his own. Maybe that's where I get it from."

"You really prefer being at home alone to being with people?"

She squeezed his hand with a smile. "Some people are okay."

They continued down the lane, and Ben's enjoyment was infectious. Kara found herself getting excited with him when they saw one display set up like a Christmas tree farm and another as a live nativity, with people inside the manger staying absolutely still. Except for baby Jesus, who appeared to just be a realistic-looking doll.

One of the three wise men broke into song, belting out the first verse of "We Three Kings," his voice coming out of the speakers set up in front of the manger. The other wise men jumped in on the chorus, and Kara paused a moment to listen.

"Do you like this song?" Ben asked.

"No, but I like their voices blending together. I wish I had the ability to sing."

"There's something we have in common. I can't carry a tune to save my life."

"Have you ever been caroling?" she asked suddenly.

"When I was a kid. Why?"

"I always thought it would be fun but never knew how to find a troupe."

Ben quirked a brow. "What kind of caroling are we talking about?"

"Where they dress up like they've walked right out of a Dickens novel and walk around the neighborhood spreading cheer."

"Or getting the cops called on them for trespassing."

"Where is the fun in that? Live dangerously, Ben."

"Have you met me? I'm a pretty boring guy."

"I wouldn't say that. I think you're fun." They were nearing the end of the street and Kara finished off her cocoa. "And this was great. Thank you for inviting me. The last date I went on was a Christmas party that got raided by the cops, so in my opinion, this is a major improvement."

This time, the parents of the little girl turned to look at her, curiosity on the father's face while the mother appeared annoyed. Ben shot them a wide grin. "Lovely night."

They turned abruptly and took a left, going the opposite direction from Kara and Ben. He shook his head. "Some people, am I right?"

"Well, I was talking a little loud to be heard over all the music playing. People can't help reacting when they hear something interesting. Have you ever seen those videos of the people on escalators who pretend to be saying scandalous things to someone on the phone? And you get to see the facial expressions and reactions of the people in front of and behind them? I think those are fantastic."

"I get not being able to help but overhear, but to actually turn around and be obvious about it? Mind ya bidness, Linda," Ben said in a high register.

Kara giggled. "How did you do that? Your voice is so deep."

"A lifetime spent mocking my older sister, Birdy, and her squeaky voice."

"Wait, your siblings are Birdy and Boone?"

"And Brandon."

"Why did your parents choose *B* names for all of you?"

"It's just something my mother's side of the family did. They're an odd lot."

"You realize you included your mother in that lump."

"Oh, she is." They stepped off the curb, and he opened the car door for her. When she got inside, he started to close the door, but she stopped him by calling his name. When he stuck his head back in the door, she reached up, putting her hands on his shoulders. Her lips pressed against his in a fast kiss.

Kara broke their contact and settled back into the car with a grin. "Okay, we can go now."

Ben's grin sent her heartbeat into overdrive as he cupped the back of her neck. "You think so, huh?"

He covered her mouth with his, and she hung on tight as Ben kissed her; she leaned forward, her lips melting against his.

When he finally pulled away, he gave her a soft kiss on her nose. "That's better."

Chapter Twenty-Four

Tiny Tim gets his name because of his short stature, but have you ever seen a Munchkin cross this cute? He'll bless his new family, and everyone he meets!

"YOU CALL THAT A TREE? That's more of a shrub."

Kara stepped back and smiled at her two-foot tree they'd stopped at Home Depot for. She'd also bought a bright red pot to put it into, instead of the plain black plastic tub it came in. "I think it's adorable. Theo has never paid any attention when I've had a tree, but in case I need to bring home any more foster cats, it's better to be safe. And I can plant it in the yard after the holidays, instead of tossing out a dead tree."

Ben sat on the couch, smirking. "As opposed to the tree Charlie Brown picked?"

Kara made a face. "Mock me all you want, but it's going to be so pretty when we're done. Okay, I'll grab the bags of tree trimmings from my bedroom."

"I think I'll sit here and watch."

"Um, no. You're not going to have a tree, so you need to be involved in this. It will put you in the holiday spirit." Kara tapped on her phone screen until Dean Martin's deep voice crooned over her Bluetooth speakers. "Perfect! Be right back."

Kara padded down the hallway, picking up the tote bags full of Christmas decorations and bringing them back into the living room, where she deposited them onto the couch.

"For a woman who didn't have many close relationships, you sure seem into Christmas."

Kara picked up a package of small red bows. "I love the emotions behind Christmas. The joy and giving. The magic. I didn't have that, not until I lived with my grandparents, but it wasn't about the gifts. It was the love they had for each other. For me." She removed the tape from the back and pulled off one of the miniature velvet bows. "Do you want to tie the first bow?"

Ben took the bow, and she watched him take the twist tie on the back and wrap it around a bottom branch. "My parents have tall ceilings in their living room, and my mom convinced my dad to buy this huge nine-foot fake tree at some warehouse store. It looks great once all the ornaments are on it."

"I didn't buy ornaments for this guy. Everything ties to his limbs."

Ben reached for another red bow, and she caught his smile out of the corner of her eye. "How do you know it's a guy?"

"I guess he just feels like one. Maybe I'll call him Chris Pine."

He chuckled. "You going to talk to him, too? I've heard some people have full conversations with their plants because they think it helps them grow."

"I've heard you talk to Chaos, and he can't talk back."

"I don't know what you're talking about."

"I'm sure you don't," Kara said, her voice shaking with laughter. She picked up some thin burlap ribbon and pulled off a strip. "We'll take this one around from top to bottom, tying it off a little farther back, and puff out the ribbon between the branches so it looks fuller."

"This is some really fancy tree trimming."

"It is, but that's only because I don't really have any ornaments for it. I do have one with a picture of each of my grandparents on it and a few paw prints of former pets, but it's too big for these branches."

"Sorry," Ben said, reaching around the back of the tree to tie another bow.

"Why are you sorry?"

"Because I'm being a downer about how you're doing Christmas. When we would do our tree, my mom put that really gaudy garland on it with all of the ornaments we've made or bought her throughout the years. She really loves these expensive glass ones and inherited a bunch of them from my grandmother. My father started getting her a new one every year after her mother died, and it's one of those really special things that's become a tradition."

"About your holiday escape plan..." she started.

"My plan?"

"Not seeing your family for Christmas."

"What about it?" he asked.

"I know I've questioned you about it, but I can tell how much you love your family by the way you talk about them, and this whole situation with your brother is stressing you out. No one should be stressed during the holidays."

Ben chuckled. "I thought everyone is stressed during the holidays?"

"Not me. Well, not for any of the regular reasons anyway. If getting out of Dodge helps you, I think your family will get over it."

"I appreciate your support, but I'm not so sure about my ma," he joked.

"I can't wait to hear all about it. I've lived in two states and haven't traveled anywhere else that I can remember. I'm too much of a homebody." Kara checked out their handiwork with a smile. "I bought all this stuff because Charity's tree last year was decorated this way, so I thought I'd give it a try because it was so lovely. I think this one will turn out the same." She reached into the bag with glee, pulling out a mini star she had found that lit up. "I even got a tree topper."

"Even an old Scrooge like me knows that goes on last."

"I know. I was just showing you."

They worked quietly for a few minutes with Kara's arms reaching under his to manipulate the ribbon the way she wanted. At one point, she bent down, and when she came up, she smacked his arm with the back of her head. She yelped as a jolt of pain set her teeth on edge.

"Hey there," he said. "You okay?"

"Yeah, but dang, what did I hit? Your elbow?"

"Just my arm."

"Well, you need to lay off the weights. That was like connecting with a metal pipe."

Ben chuckled as he pulled her against him, and when he pressed his warm mouth against her forehead, she sighed. "That isn't where it hurts."

"I thought this would be sexier than me kissing your hair."

Kara giggled. "You're probably right."

Ben leaned back, keeping his arms wrapped loosely around her waist, and she loved being this close to him.

"I think we got it," he murmured.

Kara nodded. "It looks good, right?"

"I'll Be Home for Christmas" streamed through the black square of her Bluetooth speaker and Kara hummed happily, swaying to the melody. "I love this song."

"Really? Isn't it kind of sad?"

"If you're listening to the lyrics, but it's the music that gets me."

Ben swayed with her, and she held on to his shoulders with a laugh.

"You never randomly dance in your living room?" he teased.

"Not usually. Charity used to try to get me to dance at parties, but I don't have any rhythm."

"Slow dancing is easy. It's just shuffling your feet in a circle and getting really close to your partner."

Kara's lips twitched with amusement. "Is that so?"

"Oh, absolutely."

Kara laid her cheek against his chest. "Like this?"

"That's perfect."

They continued dancing, and Kara only misstepped once

or twice, but Ben didn't complain. Never had Worthy or any other man she'd dated danced with her in or out of the house. This reminded her of those moments in romantic movies when the couple does something she couldn't imagine ever happening in real life, but being in his arms, surrounded by the scent of Ben's spicy cologne and his body, Kara thought she could stay in this moment, blocking out the world, the worry, the stress. She'd convinced herself that this was a healbound, a casual stopping point to prepare themselves for another relationship, because Ben was too different to ever really be a part of her future.

But the man she'd met that day on the street wasn't the same one Kara held. Or maybe Ben was, but that wasn't all there was to him. He was kind. Considerate. Selfless. He helped people, not because he expected anything in return, no matter his jokes about fixing her plumbing so she'd take Chaos. He did it because it was the right thing to do.

All of the reasons she'd tossed around in her head didn't seem as important as the feelings she'd developed for Ben. Kara missed him when he wasn't around because he didn't make her feel stupid or criminal. The way he talked about her, looked at her?

She felt strong, smart, and capable. Like a hero.

His hands flattened against her back, massaging the lower muscles, and Kara's heartbeat launched into a rapid tempo. Much faster than the slow melody of "Have Yourself a Merry Little Christmas," which played next. Kara looked up at him, her gaze drifting to his lips.

"What are you thinking?" he asked, tucking a strand of

hair behind her ear with one hand before returning it to her lower back.

"How good this feels."

Ben's grip on her body tightened, and when he leaned over, she stood on her tiptoes to meet him. The light brush of Ben's lips grazed hers, and Kara's mouth tingled. The second kiss was deeper, his mouth fully covering hers, and Kara held on tight until they stopped turning. Lost in each other, the melody filled the room around them with bells and horns, as if a professional composer picked the music for this moment and not a random playlist.

Kara slid her hands down his arms and laced her fingers with his, breaking the kiss to whisper, "Come with me."

Ben followed her without question, and her heart fluttered nervously as they crossed the threshold of her bedroom. Kara's eyes drifted over her bed before she turned around, her hand still in Ben's.

"Are you sure?" The way he asked, his tone rough with a mix of concern and pleading, lit a fire in her core.

She nodded, and instead of rushing her like she'd experienced in the past, clothes were discarded leisurely, with a sweetly pressed kiss across every inch of exposed skin. Faint music played from the other room as Kara's skin burned, breathy sighs slipping from her lips as she lost herself in Ben's lovemaking. He turned off the lights, and with every other sense heightened, she listened to him whisper how beautiful she was, how much he wanted her. And before she knew it, tears streamed along the sides of her face as she found her joy. It wasn't long after that he joined her, his hands tangled in her hair and his mouth hovering above hers, whispering her name. It was perfect.

Kara curled into the side of Ben's body, his arm around her waist. Ben's other hand held hers against his chest, which rose and fell in long, even breaths.

"I didn't expect that," Ben murmured.

Kara stiffened, a shock of panic ripping through her. "What do you mean?"

"Don't. Don't pull away from me. I only meant that I'd planned on waiting a bit longer before we ended up here."

Kara lifted her head, searching for his face in the dark, but the dim light from the living room didn't reach that far. "Waiting for what?"

"The right moment? I've dived headfirst into relationships in the past, and it didn't work out for me."

Kara squeezed his hand. "I don't regret it. Not one second."

She felt him shift and his lips found hers, giving her a soft kiss. "Me neither."

Kara settled back, listening to Ben's breathing grow heavy with sleep, her own eyelids drooping. One final thought floated through her mind before she drifted off.

I never want this to end.

Chapter Twenty-Five

Spicy Wasabi sure makes life interesting. This gray tabby will bring some real flavor to your life, and you'll wonder how you ever got on without him!

KARA HUMMED THE MELODY of "All I Want for Christmas Is You" as she put a few more cat Christmas ornaments in the red plaid basket on the display shelf in the corner. The doors didn't open for another twenty-five minutes, and the ornaments were the sixth day of Catmas surprise. Adopt or sponsor a cat and receive one of the beautiful red bulbs that read "Thank You for Saving Me" inside the shape of a cat's silhouette. She'd ordered them several weeks ago, but it was Charity's idea to give them away as a thank-you.

"You're cheerful this morning," Charity said.

Kara glanced over her shoulder at her friend, who was filling a few online orders they'd received, another new service option they'd included when they revamped the website.

"I told you. We had fun. It was nice to get out and see the lights."

"That's all? No kiss goodnight or anything?"

Kara's face burned as she thought about Ben waking her up this morning to kiss her goodbye, which turned into something else entirely. When he finally left to go feed Chaos, he promised to swing by later after the café closed.

Kara folded up the box of remaining ornaments and picked it up in her arms. "We did."

"And?"

"It was amazing, and I can't wait to do it again," Kara said, fighting a smile that won.

Charity beamed. "I'm happy for you, babe. You deserve it."

"Thank you. I'm happy for me, too," Kara laughed, carrying the box into the back, watching the cats in the social room. She didn't like to introduce new cats during the week because it didn't give them a lot of time to acclimate to the other kitties, but they'd had six adoptions this week and were down to four cats. She had no choice but to move a few up today.

Robin Hood yowled at her the minute she walked through the door from his corner cage, rubbing against the bars.

"I know you want out, big guy, but I gotta make sure you're still going pee." She needed to talk to Charity about whether she really wanted to adopt Robin Hood. His catheter was out, and with the antibiotics and special food, Kara was optimistic he wouldn't reblock, but he needed a place to go.

Michelle came in from the back and did a little dance when she saw Kara. "Guess what?"

"We're up to a thousand likes on a single photo?"

"Close, but no!" Michelle did a one-eighty and followed her into the side room. "Three families filled out the online adoption forms, and we had two animal sponsors for Peanut and Matilda this morning."

Kara set the box down, shaking her head. They'd always had available cats on the website, but having the Sponsor a Café Cat page was a wonderful addition, especially for cats who needed medication.

"That's awesome! I've been worried about both of them, especially since Matilda really needs to be an only cat." Kara knew Matilda would be difficult to place when she agreed to take her, but it wasn't the gorgeous calico's fault her owner had to move into assisted living and she hadn't been socialized.

"I'm going to take her pic this morning in one of the back rooms. Hopefully she cooperates."

"She loves those tuna treats, so take a bag of those in with you. I'm going to move a few cats up this morning before we open." Matilda meowed loud and long, and Kara felt sorry for the temperamental cat. "Actually, will you help me a minute?"

"Sure, what's up?"

"Can you set up a litter box and food and water in my office? She needs to get the heck out of that cage."

Michelle grinned, skipping to the cabinet where they kept the clean litter boxes. "I'm on it."

"Thanks. Hey, Matilda, how do you feel about being my office cat today?"

She butted her head against the cage with a little huff, as if to say, "Obviously."

Kara pulled a short cat tree from the storage room and put it in the corner of her office, attaching a sticky note to the outside that read, *Matilda's inside*. When everything was ready, she opened Matilda's cage, ignoring her hiss when she saw Wasabi's paw shoot out of the cage below.

"Hey, you agreed to this," she said, picking the cat up and carrying her into her office. Matilda really was all hiss and no scratch.

"Can you get the door behind me?" Kara called over her shoulder, and Michelle closed the door to her office once she was inside. Kara set Matilda on top of the cat tree, and the calico swung her head left and right rapidly, studying her surroundings.

"I'm going to shift the other kitties around, and then you and I are going to do some paperwork. Sound fair?" Matilda's butt lifted like an elevator as she stroked her back, and Kara heard the deep rumble of her purr. "Good. See you in a minute."

Kara left her office and went about moving cats, starting with Wasabi, who was a young bundle of energy. The gray tabby wasted no time exploring the social room once Kara set him down. Fluff watched her from his perch in the window as she brought in cat after cat. By the time she finished shifting them around, she had fifteen cats left in cages, sixteen including Matilda. And once the kittens in foster homes came in, these older cats would be overlooked again.

"Don't worry, guys. You're getting out of there soon." With the increased holiday foot traffic and the attention their Catmas pics were getting, Kara was optimistic.

She went into her office to change her shirt, and by the

time she walked up front, there were several people already seated and Charity and Michelle were serving a full lobby. A few weeks ago, Kara would have taken one look at the crowd and returned to the quiet of the back room, but she was trying to work through her aversion to people, especially after speaking over the phone with the lawyer Charity's father recommended. He pulled all the court documentation on Worthy's lawsuit against her and mentioned it was thin at best and he suspected it was more about intimidation than the suit itself. They were going to meet on Monday to go over her defense of the complaint, but she hadn't seen anything online about her yet.

"Kara," Charity called, and she pushed the meeting and Worthy's antics from her mind.

"Hey, how can I help?"

Charity pointed to two cups on the counter with foamy cat heads floating on the surface. "George and Lance Shoemaker are sitting in the corner. Would you mind taking these to them while I grab the next in line?"

"Absolutely."

"Also," Michelle called, "we approved their application for Meowdor and Meowise and they paid for their hour of social time online, so if they decide to proceed, then they just need the signature page and that discounted from their adoption fee."

"I've got it," Kara said with a smile. Kara picked up the cups, keeping steady hands as one of her regulars, Rochelle, grabbed the door for her.

"Thanks."

"No problem, Kara. Hey, where's Robin Hood?"

"He's in the back recovering from a procedure. At least your bear claw is safe."

Rochelle laughed. "I love that little thief and never mind sharing."

"You're a better person than me. I try to bite when he comes for my food."

Rochelle laughed, and Kara crossed the room to the two men cuddling Meowdor and Meowise against their chests.

"Here are your lattes." She set them down on the table. "I understand you are the Shoemakers?"

"Just our last name!" the tall, lanky guy said. "Definitely not by trade. I'm Lance."

"And I'm George. It's actually *his* last name, but mine is Butkis, and he refused to take it," the shorter man said, pushing his glasses up the bridge of his nose with one hand before going back to petting Meowdor.

"It's literally pronounced like 'butt kiss,' sweetie. I love you, but no."

Kara smothered her laugh. "Well, I'm Dr. Kara Ingalls. I oversee the daily care and medical needs of all the cats and am co-owner of the café."

"That is fantastic. We had no idea this place even existed until yesterday. I was scrolling through Instagram at adorable cat pics, because that is my happy place, and I saw this guy." Lance kissed the top of Meowise's head, who leaned into it with closed eyes. "We are huge Lord of the Rings fans and fell in love with Meowise and Meowdor's pictures first, and then once we saw their names, we knew it was fate!"

"Out of curiosity, do you know what happened to Meowdor's eye?" George asked.

"I don't. His eye was already healed when he was rescued. His foster mom had Meowise first and thought naming him Meowdor was fitting."

George nodded. "It is, but if you allow us to take them home, we'll probably change their names."

"Of course. I can get you the final forms when you're ready."

"Yay," Lance said, taking his cup. "Seriously, where do we sign?"

"I'll get you those and your welcome-home bags."

"Thank you."

"Thank you for giving them a home," Kara said, leaving the social room to get everything together and holding the door open for a family of four.

"They're definitely taking them?" Michelle asked.

"Yep. I'm going to get them a pen and have them finish the final paperwork and then make up welcome-home bags."

"Okay. That other family with the twins filled out an online application, too, but I think they want a younger cat."

"I think Wasabi would be perfect for them."

"We need an adoption bell or something," Charity said. "We ring it every time a cat finds a home."

"That's not a bad idea. I'll look for a cute one with cats online," Kara said, pushing into the back to get the Shoemakers' welcome-home bags together, including two cardboard carriers.

Her phone vibrated, and Kara pulled it from her pocket, staring at the unknown local number. Pressing the green phone icon, she placed it against her ear. "Hello?"

A robotic voice said, "This is the California Federal Correctional Institution. Inmate..."

"Ferris Worthington."

Kara hung up the phone, the world swimming. She stumbled into her office and sat with her back against the door, taking deep, even breaths.

Something rubbed against the side of her bent knees, and she lifted her head to find Matilda pushing her head against her pant leg, bending her ear back so it flipped inside out.

Kara choked on a laugh, fixing it for her. Tears spilled over her cheeks, and she wiped them with one hand as she stroked the calico's head with the other. Matilda crawled into her lap, kneading her chest.

People who say cats don't show empathy are so very wrong.

Kara stroked Matilda's soft fur for several minutes, taking deep breaths to calm her breathing. This cat had lost her person, been placed into a new environment filled with unknown smells and sounds. Matilda hadn't shut down despite all of the hardships she'd faced, yet here Kara was panicking because of a phone call. Intimidation tactic. That's what the lawyer had said.

Kara's eyes narrowed as she stared at the wall of animals she'd saved over the course of her career, the cards from grateful owners and pictures tacked in a giant collage like wallpaper. She'd survived her childhood with the help of her grandparents and turned her life around. Worthy's actions could have completely derailed her, but Charity's strength and support gave her the courage to take the chance on this café. She'd been so afraid of the media that she'd almost let the café fail. Why was she letting him have so much power?

You need to get mad. Charity's words echoed in her head,

something she'd told her dozens of times over the last two years. If Kara wanted him to stop coming after her, she was going to have to toughen up.

Her life was good, in spite of Worthy. He was a jerk, a thief, and she was done letting him haunt her.

Matilda gave her a gentle love bite, letting her know she wasn't petting her right, and Kara laughed. "I've got to start acting like you, huh? You go after what you want and don't take any crud."

Matilda purred in agreement, and Kara gave her one final love pat before setting her on the ground and getting to her feet.

No more hiding or letting other people protect her. It was time to show some teeth.

Chapter Twenty-Six

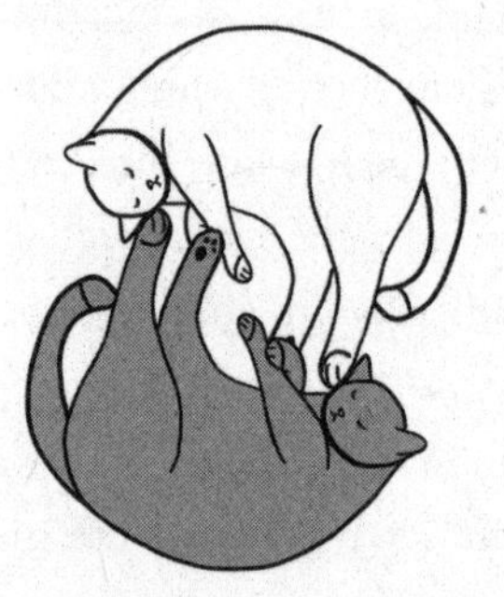

Comfort and Joy are bonded sisters seeking a home together, and their names perfectly describe these sweet, gentle souls looking for a lap to share.

BEN WALKED INTO FURRY THINGS on Saturday afternoon with a folder in hand. The large pet warehouse was locally owned and operated. Ben approached one of the employees in a bright blue vest. He planned on surprising Kara with several donations from community businesses for the Christmas party auction. He'd printed up donation agreements he'd made with Meow and Furever's logo on it and had managed to get seven of the ten businesses he'd visited so far to pledge something for the auction. He'd called this pet store to set up an appointment with the owner, and if their talk went well, he was hoping the arrangement would take the pressure off Kara and Charity for a while.

"Hi, I'm looking for Carol?"

The guy paused in scanning the shelf of toys he was working on and pulled his walkie-talkie off his belt, speaking in a monotone. "Carol, there's someone here for you."

"He can come back to my office," a distorted voice answered.

"Okay." The guy put the walkie-talkie back into its holster and said solemnly, "Follow me."

Ben trailed behind Personality-Plus Guy to the back of the store and through two heavy double doors. He stopped outside an open office door and held his arm out. "She's in there."

"Thanks." Ben stepped inside and held his hand out to the thin brunette in her early fifties behind the desk. "Hi, I'm Ben Reese, from Kilburn Marketing. We spoke on the phone."

"Yes, it's nice to meet you. I was surprised I hadn't heard of this café you mentioned. I thought I knew all the local shelters."

"It's a really cool place, and the food is fantastic." He pulled out one of Meow and Furever's business cards from his pocket. He'd taken a stack of them when he'd stopped in for coffee earlier in the week. "One of the owners is a veterinarian and provides all of the care for the cats."

"I would think that would be one of the biggest hardships for a rescue, finding veterinarians willing to do low-cost procedures or donate their time."

"Which brings me in, actually. They have this great space attached to the café they intended to turn into a clinic to help out low-income families with pets." Ben opened the folder and set several pages in front of her with pictures of the café, inside and out. "Unfortunately, they ran out of funding, and the clinic isn't complete. But if they received sponsored help and could finish, it would be newsworthy. Established local business backs cat café in opening a low-cost veterinary hospital for pet lovers. It's a worthy cause and a tax write-off."

Carol picked up the sheets of pictures, nodding. "I don't doubt it is, but it also sounds expensive."

Ben retrieved another sheet from his folder. "This is their donation goal. This amount is enough to care for twenty-five cats at a time, with medications and surgeries included, which would go down considerably if they could perform them in-house. This is what they need for the remaining equipment and supplies, but once they have that, these"—Ben set another page next to it—"are the profit margins on the clinic, which helps the community and keeps the café open to continue their good work without a huge need for donations every year. Because, like you said, when people are hurting and don't have anything extra to give, the non-profits suffer."

Carol met his gaze with a small smile. "You're good."

"It's my job to be this good. The café is hosting a Christmas party two weeks from today with a silent auction. We can plan a huge spotlight at the event where you hand over the check to them. You're competing with box stores on price points, and while they can afford to donate millions to national charities, you can give just a fraction of that and make a difference to people and animals in your own community. Besides, it's Christmas, and 'tis the season."

"I tell you what. Leave what you have, and I'll think about it."

"Absolutely." Ben picked up the rest of the papers on the desk and slipped them into the folder, handing it to her. "I'll make sure you get an invitation as well. It's going to be fun."

"I appreciate that." She handed him her card and shook his hand. "You let that café know they have a gem in you."

"I will." Ben paused in the doorway and pointed to the folder. "There is a donation agreement in the back of the folder, if you decide to go ahead."

"I appreciate that you're well prepared," she chuckled.

Ben left the store whistling, and once he climbed into his car, he went through his binder. Seven donation agreements for auction items and he had a few more stops to make before he stopped by the café. In case Furry Things didn't come through, he'd found several businesses that might. His goal was to get all of them on board and get Kara her clinic before the end of February, then have a special post-Valentine's weekend to celebrate.

Ben froze, realizing he was making plans for the future with Kara. Even if it was just a couple months away, it was the one thing they promised not to do. It was hard to pretend he wasn't developing feelings for her, though. She was funny. Sexy. She had the biggest heart.

He shook his head and started the car. He wasn't doing this. Ben was not going to press for more with Kara when she'd been very clear about what she wanted, and this was his MO—falling fast, before he really had a chance to know someone.

The important thing was making sure the café survived the holidays. Everything else could wait.

Kara watched the full social room, amazed that it was only three in the afternoon, because she was ready to crawl into bed. The café had experienced a steady stream of people since they'd opened the doors this morning, and so far, their four youngest cats had found homes. Luna went home with a lovely teenage girl and her single mom, and Smush was scooped up by a newly divorced branch manager whose ex-husband was allergic to cats. She'd had to run to the back after the morning rush and bring Tater, Buddy, and the dilute calico sisters, Comfort and Joy, into the social room. It was sweet to see them go home right after lunch with newlyweds who'd moved into their first house a few weeks ago and wanted to celebrate by adopting one cat but had fallen for two.

"Can you believe how crazy this is?" Charity asked.

"What? That the social room is still full and we close in an hour, or that we've had seven adoptions today?"

"A little bit of both. You want a peppermint mocha? I need a little pick-me-up."

"Yes, please, I feel like I'm going to drop," Kara laughed. "By the way, while the lobby is quiet, are you going to take Robin Hood home?"

Charity's face fell. "I asked my landlord about it, and he said no cats. I don't want to sneak him in and have him discover when I do move out that I had Robin Hood. He'd try to charge me through the nose for carpet."

"If that's the case, then why don't you move somewhere that allows cats, instead of renting from that landlord you hate and paying through the nose for a duplex where you share a wall with a couple who likes to have really loud activities?"

"Because I thought by now I'd be married and buying a place with my husband."

"And if you move to another rental, you won't have that?" Kara asked.

"No, Kara, I mean that I am going to be thirty-three in four months and eight days, and the longest relationship I've ever had is with you."

"Same, but Char, it's not like you don't have options. You could walk out onto the sidewalk, throw your hands up, and scream, 'I'm single and ready to mingle,' and there would be a line of men gathering in five seconds flat. You're the package. You're gorgeous, smart, talented, funny... okay, maybe more snarky than funny—"

"Ha ha."

"See? So much sarcasm. I think the biggest issue with your dating history is you either fall for the wrong man or won't give potential right ones the chance."

"I know," Charity said, covering her face with a groan. "I'm just in a mood. I agreed to let my mom set me up with one of her friend's sons. He's a sixth-grade science teacher, so good with kids. Hopefully. Educated. I Internet stalked him, so I know he's cute..."

"I'm waiting on the but," Kara said.

"But . . . I don't know. I hate setups."

Kara opened her mouth to remind Charity about ambushing her on Thanksgiving, but Charity held her finger up. "No, ma'am. We are not going to compare this to me inviting Adam to Friendsgiving. He's dating someone by the way, so you missed your shot."

"I'm happy for him. Now, back to the house situation. I'm going to bring this up again because the offer stands. If you want that cat and you hate your place, but you don't want to rent again, why don't you move in with me? The place is paid for, so we'll just split utilities and food. We know we can do it because we lasted four years in college and several more after that." Kara reached out and took her friend's hands in hers. "Plus, we could carpool some days and save on gas. Neither one of us is ready to move in with a significant other. Why not save a little money and gas? The best part is your roommate doesn't care if you adopt a cat!"

Charity finished up the drinks and put lids on them. She handed Kara her cup, a wide smile on her face. "I can't wait to get home and draft my notice letter. He's probably going to charge me for breaking my lease three months early, but I am over him."

"Do you want me to take Robin Hood home with me? No point in him staying here if he's already got a home. Then I can put him in the spare room and keep an eye on him."

"Yes, please. Thank you!"

"Of course. You'd do the same for me." Kara took a sip of the peppermint mocha, watching Charity over the rim, before she continued, "As far as the teacher goes, I think you should try it. You never know why someone crosses your path until suddenly, being with him makes you look at the world a little brighter and your problems don't seem so daunting."

"And we're done talking about me, hmm?" Charity joked.

Kara blushed. "Sorry, I was talking about you. I was just using my circumstance as an example of how the right guy can kind of sneak up on you."

"Hold up!" Charity nearly shouted, grabbing her shoulders. "I thought you weren't serious? You used that silly word—"

"Healbound?"

"Yes! But after one date, he's the right guy?"

"No, I mean. Maybe. I like him. The kind of like I've never felt before."

"Holy cannoli." Charity shook her head. "My mother always told me, when you know, you know."

"I thought I knew before, but this... is different."

Charity set her cup down and pulled Kara in for a hard hug. "I am so happy for you. Wait—" Charity jerked back fast, her mouth twisted in a grimace. "Does this mean we have to keep Schwartz?"

Kara laughed. "You know what I think?"

"What's that?"

"That you're making a lot of stink about Schwartz because you like him."

Charity turned away to lean her elbows on the display case, watching the front door. "And I think you've been drinking too much espresso and are hallucinating!"

"Come on. Schwartz can be a flirt, but do you really think he's that bad?" Kara prodded.

Charity shrugged. "I haven't thought that hard on the subject."

Kara didn't have a chance to call bull before a family of three came through the doors.

"Hi, we filled out an application online." The woman greeted them with a smile. "Do we have time to meet the cats?"

"Absolutely, let me look up your application," Charity said, grabbing the iPad from the locked drawer. "What is your last name?"

"Castillo. I'm Eva, this is my husband, Alonso, and our daughter, Sylvia."

Charity tapped the screen and looked up with a friendly smile. "I've got you."

Sylvia, a brunette with dark eyes and freckles, flashed them a gap-toothed grin. "We're going to pick out a new kitty because Cora went to heaven."

"Cora was my old cat," Eva said.

"Oh, I'm so sorry." Kara came around the counter and knelt down. "Do you know what kind of cat you want?"

"A nice one!"

"I think we're looking for a kitten so they can grow up together," Alonso added.

Kara climbed to her feet and addressed the parents. "We don't have any kittens at the moment because they're too young for the social room, but I'd be happy to show you pictures of them. They'll be available in January."

"Oh. We were hoping to bring it home as an early

Christmas present," Eva said, squatting in front of her daughter. "*Mi hija*, they don't have any little cats. Would you like to come back or should we go somewhere else?"

"Can't we just see the kitties?" Sylvia begged, her bottom lip trembling.

Her father spoke up. "Of course."

"And you know what? We're celebrating a Twenty-Five Days of Catmas event, and I'm going to let you have something extra special for coming in. Are you ready?"

Sylvia nodded, and Kara walked over to the shelf and grabbed one of the ornaments, handing it to the little girl. "When you find your perfect cat, you can hang this on your tree as a reminder of the amazing thing you did, giving them a forever home."

"Thank you!" She held it up by her finger, watching it spin in a circle. Her parents ordered two cappuccinos and a hot chocolate, carrying their drinks into the room. Several patrons passed them on the way out, but Kara watched Sylvia set her cup down, looking around the room. The little girl greeted Tater when she approached her, but it was fleeting attention.

Ben opened the front door, and Kara's stomach flipped at the warm expression on his face.

"How's it going in here?"

"Busy," Charity answered, "which is why I'm going to run to the back and use the bathroom while it's quiet."

Ben crossed the room and leaned on the display case, drawing so close she thought he might kiss her, but he stopped. "Hey."

"Hi. I was just watching this little girl. The parents

think she needs a kitten, but I am waiting for her to notice Loki. He's sleek, and he's only a few years old. Plus, he has a mustache."

"Every little girl wants a cat with a mustache," he teased.

"I think so. And when we grow up, we want a man with a beard."

"Do you?" He stroked his brown facial hair with a smirk. "Huh."

"Lost interest in the bearded guy already?"

"No, I just can't believe she noticed him." Sylvia had found Fluffernutter sleeping in the sleigh bed and ran her hand from the top of his head to his back. Suddenly, the fluffy white cat stood up and arched his back in a big stretch before he crawled up the little girl's chest. Sylvia picked Fluff up so his arms hugged her neck as she supported his rump with her hands, and Kara watched her young, heart-shaped face soften, recognizing that rush of love when an animal chooses you.

She turned to her parents, holding the cat who was almost as big as she was, and Kara heard her through the glass wall call out, "I found my cat!"

Ben chuckled. "I feel like she's going to tip over at any moment."

Kara smothered a laugh as she watched the child's parents look at each other, as if silently coming up with a plan to dissuade her, but Sylvia stubbornly shook her head when they tried to talk her out of it. Eva walked out of the social room, shaking her head. "I guess we are adopting today."

"I'll get your stuff together. Will you watch the front, Ben?"

"Yeah, of course."

Kara was so excited that she almost plowed into Charity in the hallway. "Whoa, where are you going, speed racer?"

"Fluff's going home!"

"What?" Charity squealed, and they threw their arms around each other. This was exactly what they needed, what Kara needed, to prove they could do this.

They could save Meow and Furever.

Chapter Twenty-Seven

Like his namesake, Eggnog is sweet with the hint of spice. Don't be surprised if he crawls under the covers and takes over half your bed. He likes to stretch out.

ON TUESDAY MORNING, BEN leaned back on a stack of pillows, watching Kara stare at her computer screen and tap away at the keys. She was wearing a loose tank top and yoga pants, her hair tossed up in a scrunchie. He'd taken a half-day for a dentist appointment, but it wasn't scheduled until nine, and he was enjoying watching her work.

"I sent out the newsletter to all fifty-seven of our subscribers, Michelle posted the information to Instagram, and I uploaded it to our website, and printed flyers that I started hanging around town yesterday. Is there anywhere else I can put this Christmas party invite or is that good?"

Ben sat up and scooted across the bed until he curled against her back, wrapping his arms around her. "You could have Michelle do a giveaway post. Anyone who shares the event to their Instagram story gets the chance to win a gift card to the café?"

"You and your giveaways," she grumbled, but he caught the small smile.

Ben curled his fingers and wiggled them against her side, laughing when her elbows flew back with a scream. "Ben, stop!"

"Don't be rude about giveaways, then. If the magazine hadn't done one, we might not have met."

Kara turned in his arms to look up at him. "And while that would have been a shame, it's rude of you to tickle me."

"It was my only recourse."

"Right." Theo raced into the room and around the bed, Chaos hot on his heels. The two of them flew up and scrambled across the bed and back out of the room.

"Hey, your monster is harassing my angel." Kara pointed.

"They're fine. Theo would have popped him by now if he wasn't having a blast."

Kara turned to look at him, her blue-light glasses sliding down her nose. "Oh, so you think you're a cat expert now, huh?" She leaned over and kissed his lips. "That's cute."

"You woke up on the feisty side of the bed." Ben set her laptop aside and flopped back on the bed, taking her with him.

"Ben!" She laughed. "I have a lot to do before work."

He tucked a strand of hair behind her ear. "Like what?"

"I have to procure at least fifteen more auction items, I still have over a dozen cats looking for a home, I have to come up with a deposit for the venue—"

"Which you aren't going to do in the fifteen minutes or so before you get in the shower."

Kara sighed, her eyes meeting his. "Fine, you're right. I'm trying to distract myself, I guess."

"Is this about him?"

Kara shrugged. "I mean, it doesn't help my stress. He tried calling me Saturday from prison, and I hung up on him."

Ben stiffened. "What did he say?"

"I hung up without accepting the call."

"Good. That turd doesn't deserve a second more of your time. I'd say I was surprised by his bal—" He cleared his throat. "Gumption, but after everything I've heard and read, I'm not." He kissed her softly, before asking, "What can I do?"

Kara cupped his cheek, and he loved the way she did that, her hazel eyes crinkling as she smiled at him sweetly. "Honestly, being here with you, talking? It helps. And you've done so much already. The marketing, finding the venue, collecting donations. You have your own stuff to deal with, and do not need to be taking on ours, especially when you aren't getting paid."

Ben frowned. "I know we're casual and everything, but I'm not charging you for anything. Ever."

"I didn't mean anything, except you made up that entire marketing plan, and I know what that is worth. You've done enough, and you should use your free time to relax."

"I like to have projects, which is how I relax, and I'm all out of those. My house is done—"

"You still don't have a kitchen table," she teased.

"Shush, you. I'm packed for my vacation, so that's off my plate."

"Already? You don't leave for over two weeks."

"I don't wait until the last minute."

"I don't either, or I sit around thinking about how there's something I forgot."

"I'm caught up at work, and I don't have any other friends but Schwartz. So use me."

Kara's hand slid back into his hair with a sultry grin. "Use you, huh? Can I use you for kisses?"

Ben responded by covering her mouth with his, giving her a deep, sweeping kiss. She kissed him back eagerly, their mouths playing together for several moments before he pulled away. "I'm thinking of calling my brother."

"That came out of left field." Kara's eyes widened. "What are you going to say?"

"I'm not sure yet. It's been on my mind for a few days."

"What made you change your mind?"

"Finding out they're expecting was a big factor. Everyone in my family, even my friends, told me that it was love, they were happy, but I thought it was going to fizzle out. I didn't want her back, but I wanted...I don't know, vindication? Then they got married, and now they're going to have a baby. My brother wouldn't roll the dice that way unless he wanted to have a kid." He flopped onto his back, taking her hand. "When Chaos left, my house was so quiet. My parents' home was always loud with all of us together, but my house didn't feel like a home. Which got me thinking about everything I'm going to miss if I don't at least try. And if I'm being honest, meeting you changed my perspective, too."

"How?" she whispered.

"Because until you, I didn't know what making someone

else happy could do. I look back on my relationships in the past, and I think—no, I own that I was selfish. I liked things my way, and I'll be honest, I still do." Ben's thumb glided over the back of her hand. "I've done more for you when we weren't even dating than I did for all of my past girlfriends combined. It makes me think about the friends I lost and how maybe it wasn't all them. I played a role."

"I dimly recall you offered to help me with my plumbing if I found a place for Chaos."

"Fine, I'll grant that was selfishly motivated, but I'm trying here." Ben rolled up onto his side and brought their entwined hands to his mouth, kissing the back of hers. "I just thought I'd tell you that this really has been a healing experience."

"I think so, too."

"Yeah? Tell me, how have I healed you?"

She wrinkled her nose. "Ugh, don't say it like that. It sounds cheesy. But if you must know, I made a decision about Worthy and the lawsuit. The lawyer filed the motion to contest it and dismiss, so we'll see what happens next. He thinks Worthy is trying to intimidate me so I'll give him money, because these lawsuits take years to resolve sometimes. The thing is, I couldn't pay him if I wanted to. I set up a small living stipend to be sent every month after I received my grandparents' trust, and the rest is tied up in this house, a few mutual accounts, and in the café. Before Worthy was arrested, I had money left over from the sale of their house in Alabama, so I'm wondering if he saw my bank statements or something. It's why I have the hardest time with people invading my privacy. Charity gets away with it, but when the media started digging into my life after what Worthy did, I lost it for a while." Kara turned on her side so he couldn't see the sheen in her eye as she continued. "But no matter what he throws at me, I'm going to fight. I'm not living my life if I'm afraid he's going to pop up like my own personal boogeyman and bring my worst media nightmares with him. I'm not opening the door to them, but I'm not afraid of their power anymore. If someone believes the worst of me, they didn't know me at all."

"Plus, Charity will eviscerate them."

Kara laughed. "Without a doubt, but I don't need her fighting my battles anymore. It's time I grew up." She stroked a hand over his beard with a sheepish smile. "Don't think I didn't notice that Chaos makes your house a home, by the way."

"I didn't say that."

"I read between the lines. You're becoming a cat person."

"Lies. I am a one-cat person. Chaos. No other cats."

"You don't like Theo?"

Ben paused, studying her face. What was she asking? Was it about liking Theo, or something more?

"Theo's chill. I can hang with him. Kara... about the casual nature of our relationship. Can we be casually exclusive?"

Kara flashed him her brightest smile. "I don't want anyone but you."

Ben pushed her back on the bed, kissing her with all the happiness spreading through him. He didn't want to jinx anything by asking for too much, but the more time they spent together, the less he saw their surface differences and noticed the character traits they shared at their core.

Kara's upbringing made her loyal to those who stuck around and were there for her. She was stubborn and guarded, like him, but with this big heart looking for someone to protect it.

Ben wanted to be the one to keep it safe.

Kara's phone alarm went off, and she pulled away from him, groaning. "I've got to get ready."

"I know." Ben rolled off her with a smile. "Although we could both play hooky and stay in bed."

"I wish I could, but I've got to get there early enough to help Charity box up the cookies for the ninth day of Catmas." Kara paused on the way to the bathroom, like she was listening for something. "Poor Robin Hood is having a fit being in that room."

"I guess you'll be sleeping over at my place once Charity moves in."

Kara laughed. "Oh god, I could just imagine her over breakfast. She'd be the little sister I never wanted, asking inappropriate questions to make you blush."

"I can take it."

"I will see you in a few minutes." She shut the bathroom door, and Ben lay there for a few minutes, mulling over their conversation and Kara's determination to take her life back. It was the same way he felt about his brother. He'd let his anger at Boone push him to make life-altering decisions, and while they'd worked out for the better, it was time to reconcile himself with his past. His bitterness had already strained his relationship with his family. He didn't want it to affect his future.

Ben grabbed his cell off the nightstand, tapping the app

store. He hovered over the Instagram app, and before he could second-guess himself, he tapped it to download.

It took several minutes, and he went through the process to re-sign up, scrolling through the suggested accounts. He saw his brother's name and clicked it. Amelia and Boone faced off holding a tiny onesie between them, the camera capturing the joyful way they looked at each other.

He followed his brother, his sister, and his youngest brother, Brandon, whose picture was of him biting into a huge sandwich with his eyes crossed.

While following Boone wasn't the same as having a long, deep conversation with him, it was a baby step in the right direction.

Ben went back to his empty profile and decided to start with a picture, looking through his gallery until he found one he'd sent to Kara of Chaos curled up in his hair. He clicked the bio box, but before he could type anything, his phone started ringing.

It was Boone.

Ben answered the phone by the second ring, clearing his throat before he mumbled, "Hello."

"Hi. Was that an accidental add while Insta stalking me? Or was that for real?"

"It was real."

"Wow. So I guess you saw our big news then."

"Birdy told me, actually. Congratulations."

"Thanks. It happened faster than we expected, but it was a blessing in disguise. It made it easier for me to turn down the job in California, which makes you happy, right?"

Ben shook his head, holding back his usual snarky retort.

"I'm not going to lie and say I wasn't relieved. I don't want to go through the rest of my life avoiding you, Boone, but that doesn't mean I want you here in my backyard at the moment."

"I get it. I guess a part of me was hoping that if I was that close, you'd have to forgive me."

"I'm getting there. That's all I can say for sure. Like it or not, you're my brother, and you've apologized for what went down. I know that beyond that, there really is nothing else you can do. I've got to come to terms with it."

"Thank you for saying that. I know I've been defensive and made things worse at times, but I really am sorry I hurt you, Ben. You're my brother, and I love you. Where do we go from here?"

"Take it a day at a time? Don't force it and maybe we can get back to a good place again?"

"I could do that. Hey, Ben?"

"Yeah?"

"Thanks for taking my call."

"I appreciate you making it. We'll talk again. And tell your wife I said congratulations on the baby."

"I will. Goodbye."

"Bye." Ben ended the call, shaking his head. There was no way he'd ever imagined forgiving his brother and sister-in-law. He'd been so caught up in his wounded pride, he'd wanted everyone else to be as miserable as he was, and when they weren't, it infuriated him. Now he had his own reasons for smiling, and he didn't want bitterness to poison it.

Or fear.

Kara came out of the bathroom in a robe, drying her hair with a towel. "You okay? I heard you talking to someone."

"Yeah, just working things out with my brother. Let the healing process begin."

"Do you feel any better?"

"I do. Hey, I know Thursday is going to be a rough one for you. Want to go to lunch with me? We'll hit that taco place next to the bookstore?"

To his surprise, Kara launched herself across the room to pounce on him, giving him a hard, fast kiss. "You're amazing, you know that?"

Ben grinned. "I mean, it's just tacos, but I'll take it."

Chapter Twenty-Eight

Scrooge McFluff is a black senior Persian cross who wants to give love on his terms, but once he opens up his thankful heart to you, it will be the best gift you ever receive.

KARA SAT IN HER office on Thursday, staring at a picture of Worthy in a designer suit, walking down the Roseville court steps while holding the hand of a statuesque blond. Beneath the picture, the news article read like a story of triumph, talking about how he'd spent his life going from one con to another and it took getting caught for him to turn his life around. Because of his mistake, he met the love of his life, who happened to be his defense attorney.

She slammed her phone down on the desk with a groan. How the heck could he do something so despicable and come out smelling like a rose?

There was a soft knock at her door, and she mumbled, "Come in."

Michelle poked her head inside with an apologetic smile on her face. "Sorry to interrupt, but can you cover the front? I gotta pee."

"Sure, I'll be right there." Kara got up from the desk, leaving her phone on top. Charity was delivering treats for several office Christmas parties around town, so it was just the two of them.

Kara greeted Mrs. Wyatt, who stood scanning the new bookshelf they'd set up with all the donated paperbacks Bookin' It sent over.

"Good afternoon, Mrs. Wyatt. How are you?"

"I'm very well, Kara. How are you?"

"Hanging in there."

"Well, that doesn't sound good. Do you read?"

"I do!"

"That's good. Reading can actually relieve stress. I was just admiring your selection of books. Mystery. Children's. Romance. That's a very eclectic shelf."

"But all featuring cats," Kara laughed. "So there is a method to our madness. The woman who owns the bookstore down the street, Bookin' It, offered to donate some cat titles to us, and her book club is going to meet here Saturdays after hours."

"I love it. I'm an avid bookworm myself. You know who you're missing, though?"

"Who?"

"Sabrina Wiley. She writes very sweet romances, and they almost always feature a furry companion on the cover."

Kara grabbed a pen and paper, writing down the name. "Do you have any titles you recommend?"

"It's a little late in the season for holiday books, but I believe she has a Valentine's Day one. Let me see." She pulled out her phone and swiped on the screen. "*Lovelorn at the Chocolate Factory*. It's about a plus-size chocolatier who falls for the man who opened up a rival candy shop down the way."

Kara chuckled. "How does that work out? I've seen *You've Got Mail*, and her shop had to close down for the two of them to get together."

"You'll just have to read it and find out," Mrs. Wyatt said with a wink. "Now, I'm going to want a peppermint mocha today."

"Changing it up on me, huh?"

"I've got a lot of typing to do, and I need the extra pep in these tired hands."

Kara filled up a silver pitcher with chocolate milk and went about steaming it. "What is it you do, Mrs. Wyatt, that's keeping you tapping away on those keys for hours on end?"

"I do a bit of this and that. Did you have many adoptions this week?"

"We had eight on Saturday and several more over the last few days, but chunky Peanut is still here."

"Oh, I do love Peanut," Mrs. Wyatt gushed.

"He is so sweet, but people tend to overlook the cats with weight problems. I don't know why. They make the best snugglers."

"That they do." Mrs. Wyatt placed a fifty-dollar bill on the counter and took the cup from Kara. "You keep the change, all right? I'll stay a couple hours and make sure I spread the pets to everyone."

"Thank you so much," Kara said, incredibly moved by the older woman's generosity.

"You're doing a wonderful thing, Kara, and I want to do my part to make sure you stick around. You order that book I told you about, all right?"

"I will. Thank you!" On days like today, when her anger simmered like a churning caldron in her gut, people like Mrs. Wyatt reminded her that not everyone was out for their own gain—that the majority of people weren't good or bad but trying to live their best life, and then there were extraordinary souls like Mrs. Wyatt who brought smiles and sunshine by being themselves.

Kara was in the process of washing the pitcher when Michelle came back to the front, tying her apron into place.

"Sorry, boss."

"You've got nothing to be sorry for. You're allowed to use the restroom."

"I know, but..." Michelle looked away, as if she was afraid to say more.

Kara sighed. "What did Charity say?"

"Just to be extra kind to you and don't leave you alone for too long."

Kara shook her head, loving her best friend while still wanting to strangle her. She was so worried Kara was going to have a nervous breakdown that Kara nearly had to shove her out the door to get her to do the deliveries.

Michelle leaned against the counter, staring out the front window. "It's kind of a dreary day, huh?"

In more ways than one.

Nope, she wasn't going to do this. It didn't matter that

Worthy was getting out. If reporters came looking for her, she'd ignore them instead of panicking. She was going to look at the glass half-full. The café was doing better, they had seven cats left to adopt out of their original twenty-five, and in thirty minutes, Ben would be there to take her to lunch. Life was good.

"You just gotta look at it from a different angle. While it might be raining outside, that means the land is getting lots of water, so hopefully our drought won't be bad this year."

"I guess," Michelle said. "Do you mind if I look at our Insta feed? I want to see how the cat posts are doing."

"Sure, but why don't you step out of sight to do it?"

"Are you sure you want to stay up here?"

Kara shook her head with a smile. "Don't you start. I'm the boss. Now scoot."

"Yes, ma'am," Michelle said with a cheeky grin, disappearing into the back.

Kara leaned on the glass counter, watching the rain fall outside. She'd walked around this week asking local businesses if they would be willing to donate items for the auction and six of them had signed the agreement page Ben printed for them. It was crazy how much he'd done to help them turn things around. The last time she'd checked the donation page on their website, they'd raised almost twenty-five hundred. Another sign that maybe social media wasn't always the evil entity she'd convinced herself it was.

Michelle burst up front from the back, holding her phone out. "Oh my god, will you look at this picture of Catnipper? It has twenty-three hundred likes and counting."

"How many?" Kara squeaked, leaning in. Sure enough,

the picture of the tuxedo cat had just ticked up a few more likes. The five-year-old feline was looking out of a cat-scratch fort in the shape of a gingerbread house, fluffy fake snow across the ground, and sporting a festive plaid bow tie collar. "That's amazing, Michelle."

"If they like this one, wait until they see Pawsome Sauce tomorrow!"

Kara chuckled. "You're really into this, huh?"

Michelle slipped her phone into her pocket with a shrug. "I like feeling useful. My parents were always on me to find a job that pays well or has benefits or relates to my future, but why can't I have a job that makes me happy? Coming here and getting to be creative, play with cats, and help find them homes? This is my joy."

Kara's eyes stung, and she discreetly wiped at the corners. "Well, we like having you here."

"Thanks."

The bell over the door jingled, and Charity rushed in like a whirlwind, shaking off her raincoat.

"Hey, Char. How did it go?" Kara asked.

"Fine, except my hair hates all this moisture." Charity's normally straight hair had tightened up into glistening curls. "I don't know why I bothered to straighten it this morning."

"Michelle has some good news," Kara said, nodding to their barista. "Why don't you tell her about it? I'll be right back."

Charity caught Kara's arm before she could escape, dark eyes heavy with concern. "How are you doing?"

"I'm wonderful. We have fantastic cats, amazing

customers, and I have the best partner and staff a woman could ask for."

Charity eyed her suspiciously, but Kara covered her hand, giving it a squeeze. "I am good."

Michelle pushed her phone into Charity's face, distracting her. "Look at how many likes we got."

"Holy crap, that's great. And look at that picture. So cute."

The bell jingled again, and Ben stepped inside, just the sight of him making it feel like sunshine indoors. "Hey, you're early."

"Yep, I'm hungry."

"Me too. Let me grab my coat. Is it still raining buckets?"

"Just a drizzle."

"Drizzle, my fanny," Charity said.

Kara laughed. "I'll get my umbrella, too."

"You don't believe me?" Ben called after her.

"You're from Boston. You probably have raindrops the size of cars," she responded, pushing into the back and opening her office door. Matilda lifted her head from where she was sleeping on Kara's office chair, and Kara clucked her tongue. "I gave you a perfectly good cat tree and you're going to take over my chair? I see how it is." Kara retrieved her stuff from the hook on the wall and leaned over to rub the calico's ears. "I can't keep you in here forever, lovely. Sitting in a windowless room all day is no life for a kitty."

Kara left the room and slipped into her coat as she returned to the front, her steps lighter as she hiked her purse over her shoulder. Spending time with Ben always put her in a better mood. "I'm ready."

To her surprise, Ben held out his hand. "In case it's slick out there, you better hold on tight."

Kara knew she was smiling like an idiot but didn't care. She let him lead her out, popping the umbrella open when they stepped outside.

"Are those cat ears on the top of that thing?"

"Yep, and it has whiskers." She swung it up over their heads with a grin. "Are you embarrassed to be seen with a woman who owns a cat umbrella?"

"Not at all," he said, taking it from her as they headed down the street hand in hand. "I'm actually thinking I should buy one because it would be a good look for me. Do they come in orange?"

"To match Chaos?" she laughed. "I'd have to look."

"Speaking of that crazy kid, I've been thinking. I don't want to bring him back to the café before New Year's."

"You don't?"

"No. Like I said the other day, my place doesn't feel right without him, so I think I'm going to have to adopt him."

"Ben!" Kara tugged on his hand, turning him toward her. "Oh my god!" Kara threw her arms around his waist, hugging him hard. He returned her embrace, the shelter of the umbrella disappearing as rain fell on them, but Kara was too happy to be bothered by the cold droplets.

"I didn't know you were going to be this happy or I'd have told you somewhere dry."

"Of course I'm ecstatic for him and you! When do you want to fill out the paperwork?"

"After lunch all right with you?"

"Absolutely." Kara hesitated for only a split second before she leaned up on her tiptoes and he met her halfway, kissing her on the street in the rain—like any moment now, swelling music would erupt in the background.

"Well, this is an interesting development."

Kara stiffened, recognizing the deep voice, and it definitely wasn't music to her ears.

Pulling away from Ben, her blood pounded in her ears. "Hello, Worthy."

Ferris Worthington stood a few feet away, his blond hair slicked back from his face. He wore a long, dark trench coat, and the woman next to him clung to his crooked arm, her gaze switching from Kara to Worthy.

"You shouldn't talk to her, Ferris."

"It's all right, darling, we're on a public street. And with two witnesses, she can't lie and say I threatened her."

Kara fought down the panic in her chest, Ben's arms dropping from her waist to take her hand. "Come on, Kara. You don't have to put up with this."

"Aw, you must be the new beau. She's sweet, isn't she?" Worthy's smile flashed like a baring of teeth, and it took her back to the story of *Little Red Riding Hood* and the big bad wolf. "I thought so, too, once upon a time."

"Ferris," his girlfriend said, her tone filled with nervous warning.

"You're going to want to stop talking to her," Ben said, taking a step toward Worthy, and it woke Kara out of her shock.

"Ben, stop." She tugged on his hand. "Let's just go eat."

"Ben!" Worthy put his hands together in a slow clap.

"I'm surprised to see you with her after the story I read, but thanks for speaking the truth. You're a good man."

"What are you talking about?" Ben snapped.

"You haven't seen it? Just google 'the truth behind the Grinch's Bride.' It's a very insightful piece." He nodded at Kara, his eyes bright with malice. "You two enjoy the rest of your day."

"I swear, Kara, I don't—"

"I know," she said, swallowing past the lump in her throat. "He's messing with me." Kara pulled out her phone and tapped on Google.

"What are you doing?"

"Seeing what he's done now. I have to document everything for my lawyer and the suit, so—" Kara's voice dropped when she found the article, her gaze scanning over it until she saw Ben's name. "Did you talk to a reporter about me?"

"No, I didn't."

Kara turned the phone around. "Because this says you did."

Chapter Twenty-Nine

With fur as white as snow, this Frosty won't melt when you bring him into your home, but he won't hear you call his name either. This special-needs kitty is looking for a calm, indoor home to keep him safe for Santa.

BEN STOOD ON THE sidewalk in the rain, staring at the article and his name in bold print.

> It's been two years since the world discovered the Grinch was real, and not only did he hate Christmas, but cats too! And while we're supposed to believe that—like the original hairy green guy—Ferris Worthington of Riverside, California, learned his lesson and is ready to embrace the true meaning of Christmas, some of us are having a hard time forgetting that he was responsible for one of the largest national data breaches we've seen in years. That thousands were stolen from a charity meant to save

the lives of shelter cats makes the crime even more despicable.

When Mr. Worthington was charged, he had a fiancée many believed was involved. Conspiracy theories flittered across Internet forums and blog posts for months, but the authorities cleared her of all wrongdoing. When she disappeared from the public eye, Mr. Worthington didn't wait long to replace her with his defense attorney, Rebecca Grayson. Thanks to her many motions and Mr. Worthington's return of the stolen donations in accordance with his plea deal, Mr. Worthington is a free man after less than two years.

But what ever happened to his Martha May Whovier?

Kara Ingalls was fired from Half-a-Million Lives after it was discovered that her fiancé used her computer to access the private information, but she didn't get very far. She is still in Roseville and is now the co-owner of Meow and Furever Cat Café, a nonprofit feline rescue that sells pastries and coffee drinks to patrons looking to spend a little time with adoptable kitties. Although Ms. Ingalls refused to comment, her associate Ben Reese told this reporter, "If you want to write something new, why don't you talk about the truth?"

But how can we know the whole truth until we hear from both sides? Mr. Worthington is suing Ms. Ingalls for emotional trauma and fraud, claiming in a statement through his lawyer that he believed that Ms. Ingalls would stand by him if he pleaded guilty. The police say Ms. Ingalls was the victim of a con man. Which is the truth?

"That son of a—"

"Please tell me that you did not give an interview in some misguided attempt to help me."

"No, when I walked him out of the café that day, I said that quote to him, but I wasn't giving an interview! I hoped he'd dig a little deeper and write it from an angle that would help you and the café."

"All this did"—she took the phone from his hand and shoved it into her purse—"was bring more speculation on me and now the café. How could you, Ben? I told you that I didn't want any involvement with the media. No good press!"

"Kara, I'll admit, I contacted a reporter friend of mine and sent him something I wrote up based on quotes from Charity, Michelle, and some of your customers, but it was only as a safety net. This was some jerk taking something I said out of context."

"Wait, you... you wrote a PR piece behind my back? And Charity helped you?"

"It wasn't going to run unless you agreed to it."

"But you lied to me, Ben! You went behind my back, disregarded my wishes, and pretended..." Kara shook her head, spinning on her boot heels. "I have to go."

"Kara, stop." He chased after her down the sidewalk, struggling to close her umbrella. Kara took a right down the alleyway before the café, and he caught her before she reached the back door. "I wasn't pretending anything. I'm sorry I didn't tell you about the article, but I swear, I was only trying to help."

"You were helping, Ben, without doing any of this. Being with you helped. Finally feeling like I'd found a guy I could trust was like an early Christmas present I got to open again and again." She shook her head, jerking her arm out of his grasp. "I know that you didn't mean to get quoted by that reporter. I get it, I've had it happen to me, but it's a symptom of the problem. You like to think you know what's best for me, but I have to decide that. Not you."

"I'm sorry, Kara. I knew how much you'd been hurt by how the media portrayed you, and I wanted to show you it could be different."

"Maybe I would have come to the conclusion that good PR was the right move. What would have happened then? You would have whipped out this magic article like, 'See! I knew you'd come around, so I went ahead and did it for you.' "

Ben's chest ached as tears fell from her shimmering hazel eyes.

"That doesn't work for me, Ben. Lying and manipulation is what got me here in the first place!"

"You are not comparing me with the man whose actions could have sent you to prison."

"No, but you know what they say about good intentions?" Kara let out a shaky breath. "I need time to process this. I don't know what to even say to you, how to look at you."

"Kara—"

She evaded his hands with a sob. "Don't touch me."

"Kara, I messed up not telling you, but I really thought

it would help. You changed your mind about social media and marketing for the clinic, and I hoped you'd decide to give this a go, too."

"But you told me about it. If you weren't going to run it without my go-ahead, then why talk about it? Guilty conscience?"

Ben scowled. "I think you're reaching. I told you because I didn't want you coming back to this out-of-context quote and thinking exactly what you're accusing me of now—manipulating you."

"Ben, the last man I let into my life betrayed my trust and blew up everything I worked for. You have trust issues because of your past relationship. If I'd gone out with a male friend and not told you about it because it wasn't a big deal to me, and you found out from someone else, how would you feel? Put yourself in my shoes, reverse the roles, and tell me again that what you've done is okay."

Ben rubbed his hand over his face, a lump of regret forming in the pit of his stomach. "I crossed a line. It won't happen again, but I wanted to make things better for you."

"I don't want you to fix me, Ben! I don't need you to make it all okay. I just wanted you to be the guy. My guy."

"I am yours, Kara. I know we said this would be casual fun, but I am your guy."

"Not anymore."

"What? Just like that? One chance, that's all I get. One mistake and everything we feel doesn't matter?"

"This thing between you and me was supposed to be about building trust, and we've lost that. No trust, no relationship."

She turned away, and the farther she got, the harder it was to breathe. "You're just scared!" he said, not quite shouting, but with a desperate edge that made him wince. "You'd rather be alone than work through this and be happy, because it's easier. Who does that? Who walks out on something good without fighting for it? I screwed up, Kara. I wanted to protect you and fix your problems because I care about you. I wanted to make you happy."

Kara turned with her hand on the door, tears streaming down her face. "Do I look happy?"

"No, you look sad and stubborn. Avoiding people doesn't make life better, Kara. It makes it lonely." He waved his hand toward the door. "You want to walk away from me, from us, go ahead. As people, we instinctively look for our group, for others that make life worthwhile. I thought I found that with you."

"Me too," she said, her voice soft and sad.

He took a step toward her, a shred of hope lingering. "Kara. Please."

For a moment, he thought she was going to step away from the door and come back to him—a slight sway, a tiny step. But she shook her head, twisting the doorknob. "Goodbye, Ben."

Ben replayed the last three weeks in his mind, thinking about what he would have done differently, but hindsight wouldn't help him now.

He stopped and leaned against the side of the building, fighting the urge to pound his fist against the concrete. When she'd asked him to put himself in her shoes, it clicked. He understood, but what he didn't understand was her finality. She was hurt, she needed time; he could respect that, but how could Kara say it was over like that?

Because she didn't love me the way I love her.

When did that happen? The first time they kissed? When she told him about her childhood? He couldn't pinpoint the moment he fell, but he knew without a doubt he was already gone, and the pain ripped through him like a knife.

He scrolled through his contacts, his vision blurring, and pressed the phone icon next to his father's number, waiting for him to answer.

"Hey, Ben. You all ready for your tropical Christmas vacation?"

"Uh, yeah, Dad. I think I am."

"What's wrong?"

"Honestly, Pop, I'm kind of messed up right now. I met this girl, and we weren't together very long, but I—I love her. I did something I knew she'd be angry about, and when I told her about it, she ended it." Ben's voice broke as he felt the emotions bubbled up and out in the form of tears. "I just don't know how to fix it."

"Without knowing all the details, son, I can't really give you advice; and besides, your mother's always been better at all the romance stuff, anyway. I'd screw up our anniversary if she didn't remind me every day leading up to it."

"It's a lot, Pop, and with Ma barely speaking to me, I think I just have this effect on women."

"Your mother's a fixer, son. Always has been. She fell in love with me for god knows why, 'cause I was the biggest fixer-upper in all of Boston. But when I got a problem I can't figure out, I ask her. And she's usually right on the money."

Kara had accused him of trying to fix her. Maybe the apple didn't fall far from the tree.

Ben cleared his throat. "Is she around?"

"Yeah, she's sitting right next to me with her big ears flapping, trying to hear every word you're saying. Ow! What, 'cause I called your ears big? I wasn't talking about their actual size, but the way they can hear everything. I'm handing off to her before I get myself hurt."

There was a short, muffled exchange before his mother's voice came over the line. "Ben? What's wrong, honey?"

"I'm looking for advice on how to fix things with a woman I've been seeing who isn't currently speaking to me."

"Oh, boy, what'd you do?"

Ben launched into everything, taking twenty minutes to chronicle from their first meeting to their blowup. Through it all, his mother only broke in twice to ask a question, which was unprecedented.

"So, that's it. Now I'm standing outside her work, thinking, 'what the heck do I do to convince her to forgive me?' "

"I can only tell you one thing. When I'm that angry at your father, I'm not in the forgiving mood until I decide I am, and no amount of apologizing on his part is gonna do the trick. You've done all that. The ball's in her court."

"And if she never throws the ball back?"

"Then she wasn't the right hoop for you."

Ben sighed, and his mother chuckled.

"I'm pouring my heart out to you, and you're laughing at my pain?"

"No, I'm just thinking, this is the first time you've ever called me with girl problems. She must be something special."

"I think so. When we met, we were both pretty much hiding and keeping people at bay. I mentioned we didn't really even like each other. Then we kept getting thrown together. She's a bundle of nerves most days, but then becomes this calming force in situations that rattle me. She makes me smile, so much my face hurts. I put all of our differences down on paper and think, there is no way this should work, but it does. At least, it did."

"I think it still could, if the two of you were really as happy as you say. Just give her some time. Enjoy your trip, and maybe not having you there will wake her up enough she'll get into the forgiving mood."

"Honestly, Ma, right now, I wish I was just coming home for Christmas. I miss you and Pop and everyone. Heck, I might even miss Boone a little bit."

"You know you're always welcome to come home, Ben. But you get that stubborn, mule-headed streak from your father. When he gets something in his head, nothing is gonna sway him from it. Yip! Don't pinch me there, you buffoon."

Ben listened to them bicker for several moments, closing his eyes as the familiar sound of home filled him with a sense of longing.

"Tell Pop I love him, all right?"

"I will, and Ben?"

"Yeah?"

"Your brother mentioned you talked. I just wanted you to know how proud I am of you for taking the high road."

"I know you are. Love you."

"I love you, too."

Chapter Thirty

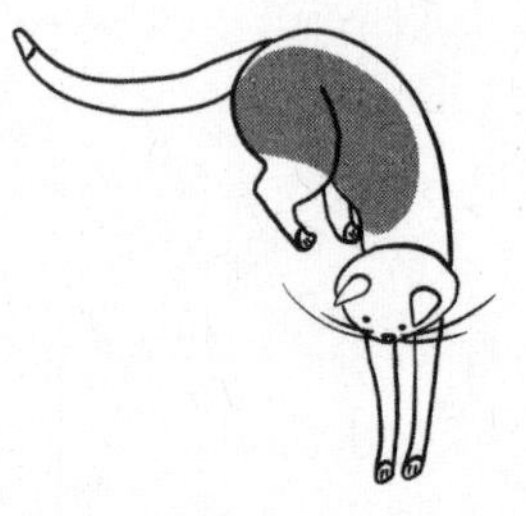

Missy Claws isn't going to take a back seat this Christmas. This adorable calico is ready to find her forever home with a family on the nice list!

FOUR DAYS AGO, KARA was living on cloud nine, and everything in her life seemed to be going in the right direction, until it took a sharp left off a cliff.

Kara was just happy that the news article hadn't affected the number of adopters coming in. They had five cats left of the original twenty-five, and while Kara tried to slowly introduce Matilda into the social room yesterday, she screamed in terror whenever another cat came near her. Kara moved her back to her office, but she deserved a home and her own person.

Charity was on her way back from the local shelter and should be there any minute. Kara had called them on Friday, asking if they had any social cats who continued to be overlooked, and they'd met with the director on Saturday afternoon right after closing and shown her around the café. While they'd put on a united front during business hours, they'd hardly spoken since she came back from her "not" lunch with Ben. Charity thought Kara was overreacting to the article, and Kara thought Charity was being obtuse. This was the longest time they'd ever gone without talking, and Kara hated it, but it wasn't right for Charity to brush off her feelings, especially regarding privacy.

The front door jingled, and Mrs. Wyatt walked through the door with six other adults and five children, filing into the lobby one after another. "Good afternoon, Kara! I brought my brood with me."

Kara brightened, giving the group a little wave. "Hi. Welcome to Meow and Furever. Are we doing a peppermint mocha today, Mrs. Wyatt?"

"Actually, I want an eggnog latte. I'm feeling festive. And whatever my children and grandchildren want."

"Mom, we can pay for our families," a man with salt-and-pepper hair said, carrying a little girl in his arms.

"Nonsense, it's my treat. Here, we'll write it down for you, if you have a pen and paper for me, Kara."

Kara handed her the paper and pen, which she passed to a thin woman with black hair while Kara tapped into the computer. "Do you want to stay or are you going to take it to go?"

"Oh, we're staying. I have been talking about your place for months, and I couldn't wait to get them all over here to see it. Do we pay for social time for everyone?"

Mrs. Wyatt started counting, and Kara laughed. "No, ma'am. It's per family, not person."

"So, four?" Mrs. Wyatt asked.

"Nope. You and your brood are all under one."

"I don't agree with that, but we'll discuss. Did you write down everyone's order, Christina?"

"I did, Mom."

"Then head inside and find us some seats and tell the kids to be quiet and kind."

The woman left the paper on the counter, and the adults ushered the kids inside.

"You don't have an age requirement for the children, do you?" Mrs. Wyatt asked.

"No, Mrs. Wyatt. As long as they are well-mannered and gentle."

"The youngest is four, but she's a love. I'm hoping that they might find a cat to bond with, but my eldest son thinks a dog would be better." Mrs. Wyatt shook her head. "Dogs are wonderful, but I'd take a cat over one any day of the week. Speaking of which—" Mrs. Wyatt set her purse on the counter and pulled out her wallet. "Is Peanut still here?"

"He is," Kara said, putting the long order into the computer.

"Well, I guess it's fate then."

"What's fate?"

"I told myself, if Peanut was here the next time I came in, I was going to go ahead and adopt him, so, when you get done typing that laundry list of drinks, I'd like an adoption application."

Kara stopped tapping, beaming. "Really?"

"Yes, but you finish what you're doing. Is it just you right now?"

"It is. We're down to five cats of our original twenty-five, so Charity went to pick up some kitties who have been at the shelter but haven't found a home yet."

"Oh, that's wonderful. I don't see five cats in the room, though."

"Matilda is actually in my office. Her owner had to be moved to assisted living, and she has been with us a little over a month. She is very sweet with people but doesn't like other cats."

"Oh, poor thing. If I wasn't in love with Peanut, I'd take her home."

"If I didn't have Theo and Robin Hood at home, I would, too. Okay, I think I have it. And because it's the fifteenth, you get 15 percent off as our Catmas special." Kara read off the total, and Mrs. Wyatt didn't blink and pulled out a hundred-dollar bill. "You keep the change for the cats. How is Robin Hood feeling?"

Kara almost protested the large tip, but Charity chose that moment to come in through the back. "Hi, Mrs. Wyatt. What are you talking about?"

"I was asking Kara about Robin Hood and how he was doing since she took him home."

"I'd like to know that, too," Charity said, putting a hand on the counter, one perfectly groomed eyebrow arched. "Since I haven't seen him in days."

Kara barely resisted glaring at Charity. "He's doing well on the food and finished his antibiotics, so I let him out of the spare room. Can you get Mrs. Wyatt an application while I start making drinks? She's adopting Peanut."

"Yay, Peanut!" Charity pulled an application out from

underneath and passed it across the counter. "We'll bring your drinks in as we get them done."

"Thank you very much, girls."

Kara and Charity worked silently filling the order until Kara couldn't stand it anymore. "How many cats did they send?"

"Six. I set them up in cages in the back and figured you could check them out before I moved them into the room with our cats."

"Good idea."

More silence. Charity and Kara took turns running the drinks and food to Mrs. Wyatt's table, and when they finished, Kara wiped down the counter while Charity did the dishes.

"I can't take this anymore," Charity exclaimed, slapping the dish towel on the counter. "I'm sorry I overstepped, okay, but this is my business, too. All of my money is tied up in this place, and if a man who went to school for marketing and loves *you* thought it would a good idea to have a PR statement on hand in case Worthy's release blew back on you, I'm going to listen. Because the cats in the café who depend on us should be worth more than your feelings."

Kara spun around, glaring at her best friend. "You're completely twisting this around to make me sound selfish and unreasonable and—" The full force of what Charity said hit her and she said, "Wait, you think he loves me?"

"That is what you took from that?" Charity made a rapid succession of frustrated hand gestures and finally groaned. "Kara, I don't think you're a selfish person, but I think your reaction to this *is* selfish! You're angry with us for overstepping, fine, but Michelle is fielding trolls on Instagram because you refuse to speak up. The PR statement was written to squash the crap you went through last time, and you are so hung up on the fact that we did it, you can't accept the fact that this isn't about you. That article could affect our business together. So, I reiterate, as your best friend, I am sorry for crossing your boundaries, but as your partner, get over it!"

Charity went back to doing the dishes while Kara's mouth hung open, completely out of her depth. She and Charity didn't fight often, and it was usually just silly bickering.

Before she could come up with something else to say, Mrs. Wyatt and her three adult children came back through the door, smiling brightly.

"I think we're going to need a few more adoption applications," Mrs. Wyatt said.

"That's great," Kara said, hoping they couldn't hear the wobbliness in her voice. "Who is adopting?"

"All of us," said the shortest of the siblings. "We are in love with the creamy cat with the black mask."

"Katy Purry? She is a love."

"My brother and sister are still deciding, but they need the adoption forms, too."

"We can speak for ourselves, Rachel," her brother scolded.

"But she's right. We do need forms." The taller sister laughed.

"And here's mine." Mrs. Wyatt handed her the two-page packet, and Kara set it to the side.

"This is wonderful. Here are those forms," Charity said, handing them the clipboards and pens. "You can fill them out in the social room if you want to sit down."

"And I'll head into the back and get some cardboard carriers and their goodies together."

"Thank you!"

Once the group filed back into the room with the cats, Kara left Charity to handle the front while she went to get the adoption bags together, thinking about what she'd said. She had no idea Michelle had been fielding trolls for days. She'd had tunnel vision, getting to work, doing her job, going home, taking care of the cats, and lying down to read. Mostly thrillers, no romance.

Maybe she had overreacted, and running into Worthy could have played a part in that. She was so thrown by seeing him. Despite everything Kara had told herself about being strong, she'd thought the world would spin off its axis right there. Kara didn't like Ben keeping secrets or Charity thinking she needed to take care of her. But she'd let her friend do it for so long that jumping all over her about it now probably made no sense.

Kara walked back up front with the four carriers and four adoption boxes, setting everything behind the counter. Charity finished her transaction with a couple of teenage girls, and when they left, Kara started to speak. "I thought about what you said. And I should have handled things better."

Charity sighed. "Kara, I love you, and I want to work this out, but not here. After work, we can sit down over a couple of lattes or scream our lungs out in the back room, but I can't keep getting interrupted trying to fix this. So why don't I handle the café while you go get this adoption paper signed?"

Charity handed her an online adoption form and the unsigned portion. *Ben Reese.*

Kara grimaced. "I've got to get the shelter cats checked out."

"After these guys leave, I can move them up, since we won't be mixing cats anyway. This is your deal with him, and you're the one who mixed business with pleasure. Get this finalized, and we will have officially adopted out twenty-four of our twenty-five cats."

"You suck," Kara grumbled, trudging toward the door.

"Oh, Kara?"

"What?"

"Do you know a Carol Lambert?" Charity asked.

"No. Why?"

"Because she dropped by an automatic litter box for the auction and—" Charity shrugged. "It doesn't matter."

"Did she say something else?"

"Nope. Hurry back."

Kara wanted to grill her for what she was holding back, but Charity was walking into the social room with the carriers, and Kara knew that if she didn't leave now, she might not go at all.

She stepped out onto the sidewalk, thankful that it wasn't raining today. The short walk to Kilburn Marketing left her slightly breathless, but that could have been her anxiety contributing to the band around her chest.

By the time she got off the elevator, her heart was pounding. She approached the reception desk and smiled at the woman behind the counter. "Hi, I'm here to speak to Ben Reese."

"Do you have an appointment?" she asked, her tone sweet.

"I don't. My name is Kara Ingalls, and I just have some paperwork for him."

"Okay, let me call down and make sure he's not in a meeting."

Kara stepped back with a nod, resisting the urge to cut and run.

"He's available. Follow me."

Kara trailed behind the short woman, watching her curly ponytail sway from side to side until she stopped in an open doorway and held her arm out. "Here we are."

"Thanks." Kara stepped inside and found Ben standing along the side of his desk, his expression blank.

"Thank you, Bethany," he said, his voice wrapping around her like a familiar blanket, and it hurt that last week she could have crossed the room and wrapped herself around him.

"Hi," she said.

"Hello. Bethany said you have something for me to sign?"

"Yes, the last page on Chaos's adoption papers." She took a few steps forward, holding them out to him. "It's just a formality, since you already told me you were adopting him, but we keep them for our records in case he is ever lost or animal control picks him up. Oh, you'll need to bring him in for his next shot and the microchip, and then his rabies. For the neuter, we've been working with a cat clinic in Folsom to get those done, so when he's around five months, we can set that up if our clinic isn't up and running and..." Her voice trailed off when she realized he'd signed the paper and was holding it out to her.

"I'll bring him in for his shots and the microchip before I leave for my vacation, but given the circumstances, I should probably find another veterinarian. Don't you think?"

Chapter Thirty-One

Blue Kitmas is a Russian blue cross whose stoic expression gives nothing away, but his deep, rumbling purr tells you exactly how he feels...happy and content.

BEN WATCHED KARA'S FACE fall, but what did she expect? She was the one who told him they were done. He wasn't even sure why she was here. He told Charity he would stop by sometime during his lunch to sign the papers, so why would she send Kara?

Stupid question. She was trying to get them to talk, but there wasn't anything to say. They had something; it didn't work out.

I just want to hold her.

Nope, he couldn't think like that anymore. She'd made it perfectly clear that he'd crossed a line, and he wasn't going to beg.

"Is there anything else?" he asked, needing her to go before all of his resolve went out the window.

"No, I guess not." She turned away, but before he could take a breath, Kara did a one-eighty. "Actually, I need to say something."

To his surprise, Kara closed his office door and set his application down on his chair, as if she needed her hands free for what she was about to say.

"Charity pointed out that what the two of you were doing wasn't just about me but for the good of the clinic, and I may have let my emotions cloud my judgment. I shouldn't have attacked you the way I did. I may not have liked the way you did it, but it turns out we—I might have to ask for that PR article."

"What?"

"It turns out that Michelle has been dealing with trolls on Instagram thanks to that article and Worthy's lawsuit, and no one wanted to say anything to me because Charity and I haven't really been talking since, you know, and I would at least like to read what you drafted."

Ben nodded slowly. "All right. I'll send you the article and the list of contacts who agreed to run it. You just need to email the go-ahead to Tony, and he will handle the rest."

"Thank you. Are you—I mean, do you know a woman named Carol? She dropped off an automatic litter box, and Charity was acting cagey about it."

Ben hoped his disappointment didn't show. Despite their current distance, Ben still wanted the café to succeed. Fine, he wanted Charity and Kara to succeed, too, and if Carol wasn't sponsoring them, did that mean the others would back out too?

It's not my business what happens. Kara had made it clear that she didn't want his interference, so he could just give her all the information on the article and wash his hands of it.

"I'm not sure who that is. I spoke to a lot of people when I was collecting donations."

"Thank you again for doing that. I know you're probably regretting wasting all that time—"

"Don't assume you know what I'm feeling." It came out harsher than he meant, and he tried again, calmly adding, "I want the café to succeed, so I did what I could to make it happen. I don't regret any of it."

Kara swallowed audibly. "I'm sorry. I feel like there's an elephant in the room we're not talking about, but I really wanted to tell you—"

Someone knocked on the door, and Ben nearly growled in frustration. He held up a finger and crossed the room to see who it was.

He opened the door, and Schwartz walked in without waiting, talking a mile a minute. "What, are you taking a nap in here or—oh." Schwartz stopped in his tracks and ran a hand over the top of his head. "I am so sorry. I'll come back."

"No, it's fine, Schwartz. I got the adoption papers signed, and you're going to email that other stuff, and we are good. All good. Have a great day and—yeah."

"Kara," Ben called, but she simply waved and left the room.

"I'm guessing I messed up."

"It's fine. Doesn't matter."

Schwartz put a hand on his shoulder. "I know it's a bum deal, dude. But it's her loss. You are a total catch."

"I appreciate the confidence boost, but it's not necessary."

"Hey, just so you know, I did like her."

"Me too." He was in love with her. It hurt to breathe knowing that he wouldn't listen to another crazy story with a shift in topic midway through. That he'd kissed her for the last time and would never know why her lips always tasted like strawberries, even when she wasn't wearing any lipstick or balm. How her infectious laughter could draw him out of the darkest thoughts.

A month shouldn't have been enough time to fall so hard, but he had.

"You could still go after her. It's not like you don't know where she works."

"I'm not running out of my place of work dramatically to chase a woman who doesn't want me. We gave it a go, and we're too damaged to make it work. I'm good being single, just like you."

"Oh no, dude, if I got a girlfriend, I'd drop you in a second."

"You're a jerk."

Schwartz grinned. "I can see you smiling. I was just trying to lighten the mood, my friend. You know you're stuck with me forever 'cause we're blood brothers."

"What? When did we cut our hands and shake?"

"What are you talking about? That's unsanitary. I mean we both cut ourselves while building the house, so we bonded over blood, sweat, and some tears, mostly mine."

"All right, did you come into my office for a reason or can I get back to work?"

"Oh yeah, the boss has your bonus for the Choco Vino account, and it is lit. I can pay off the credit card I used to book the trip and put money in the bank."

"Great, I'll check with him before I leave."

Schwartz put his hands up. "I get it, I will let you work. See you tonight?"

"Yep, you grab the pizza, and we'll meet at my place."

"Why do we always go to your house?" Schwartz asked.

"Because mine is closer and cleaner."

"Touché." Schwartz ducked out the door, leaving Ben alone. He crossed behind his desk and pulled up the information, including the article. He sent it to Kara's email and then pulled Carol's business card from his wallet.

Ben attached the article to the email and typed:

Good afternoon,

I hope you are doing well. I understand you decided not to sponsor Meow and Furever and generously donated an electronic litter box. Thank you. I admit I am disappointed by your decision, but you have to do what is best for your business.

I am attaching a spotlight article about one of the co-owners, Kara Ingalls. She is the veterinarian I was telling you about. I hope you enjoy it, as her background is fascinating.

Happy holidays,
Ben Reese

He got up from his desk and walked down to Roy's office. His boss was bent over paperwork on his desk, and Ben knocked twice on the open door, waiting to be invited in. Roy glanced up and smiled, getting to his feet. "Ah, Ben, you must be here for this." He picked up an envelope from a letter holder on his desk and held it out to him. "Congratulations."

"Thank you, sir." Ben opened the envelope and pulled the check out, glancing at the generous amount.

"What's wrong? Were you expecting more?" Roy joked.

"No, sir. Actually, with it being the holidays, I'd like to donate my bonus to a worthy cause at a charity event this weekend, but I don't want them to know it came from me. Would you be all right if I did it from Kilburn Marketing?"

"What kind of charity are you thinking?"

"It's for the Meow and Furever Cat Café down the street. They are trying to build a low-income veterinary hospital, but they ran out of funding to finish it."

Roy nodded. "Sounds like a worthy cause, and I like helping out a local business. What is this event?"

"It's a Christmas party at the community center this Saturday. They're having dinner and a silent auction. I can send you the link."

"Do that and Kilburn will match your bonus."

Ben's eyes widened. "Really, sir?"

"Absolutely. My children are huge animal lovers, and I could use another deduction this year, especially now that we're landing national campaigns."

"I'll send it right now." Ben left the office and forwarded

the invite with the ticket link to Roy's email. His bonus and Kilburn's match alone would be enough to keep their doors open.

And he couldn't even celebrate the good news with Kara.

Kara locked the front door and walked into the social room to sit across from Charity. The kitties from the shelter had settled in relatively quickly, and the remaining guests had enjoyed watching the transition as Peanut, Katy Purry, Catnipper, and Eggnog went to their new homes with the Wyatt crew and Charity brought up the others. The place had emptied out half an hour ago, and Kara let Matilda out of her office so she could at least walk around the back and not be cooped up in Kara's office.

"Are we ready to talk?" Charity asked.

"Yes, although I have a feeling we're both going to be ugly crying by the time we're finished."

Charity reached for Kara's hands, and she let her take them. "I am sorry that I didn't listen to you, but I hear you now. And I promise, if you forgive me, I will never—okay, I will be mindful of the fact that I am overstepping and do my best to curb the impulse to be nosy in the future. Can you please forgive me?"

Kara pursed her lip, staring at Charity long enough to make her squirm before pulling her in for a hug. "I forgive you. But I owe you an apology, too. I always worried about what would happen to the clinic if some reporter dredged up all these accusations again, and instead of taking your advice and Ben's, I dug in my heels. You both asked me multiple times about good PR, and instead of at least giving it a try, I stubbornly shut you out. We are partners, and I shouldn't have disregarded your opinion."

"Did you read the article?"

"Not yet. It's in my email."

"You should read it," Charity said, taking a sip of her coffee.

"I'm a little afraid it will make me feel worse."

"It might, but you're going to give the go-ahead to publish it, right?" Kara nodded, and Charity shrugged. "Seems like you should at least know what it's going to say."

"You've read it?"

"I have. It's great."

Kara pulled her phone out of her pocket and tapped her email, taking a deep breath as she started reading.

Overcoming the Not-So-Worthy

Kara Ingalls's humble beginnings didn't stop her from dreaming of breaking away from the confines of the single-wide in rural Alabama she'd shared with her absentee mother and saving lives one day—animal lives, in particular. Kara loved them all, dogs, birds, rodents, but her favorite of God's creatures was cats. After being taken in by her grandmother and grandfather at fifteen, Kara busied herself with working hard in school so she could attend UC Davis in California. With the help of her grandparents, she was able to not only spend four years in the Golden State, but also graduate summa cum laude before losing her grandfather. Sadly, her grandmother passed a few years later.

Kara finished veterinary school in Davis and relocated to Roseville, California, after taking her boards. Although she'd spent several years working in shelter medicine, it didn't take her long to realize she wanted to make a difference in an animal's life long before they ended up homeless. She took a job at Half-a-Million Lives, where she worked for a little over a year as the head of fund-raising. It was during this time that she met and fell for the charms of Ferris Worthington.

This one man would turn out to be Kara's downfall.

While most people may get a broken heart or a missing salad bowl from a bad relationship, Kara ended up in handcuffs, being questioned for hours. Her reputation in tatters, she was suddenly jobless and being doxed on Twitter by strangers assuming her guilt by association. Kara deleted all of her social media and went back to practicing veterinary medicine, hoping to put all of the ugliness behind her.

And she did, for a while.

Kara took the two years Mr. Worthington was in prison piecing together a new life for herself. Partnering with her college best friend, Charity Simmons, she opened a cat rescue in Roseville called Meow and Furever Cat Café in April of this year. If you haven't checked out their Instagram posts of adorable Christmas cats sporting some truly spectacular names, you can do that by clicking here.

Unfortunately, with the release of Mr. Worthington, some of the ugliness Kara experience returned, and although she doesn't do interviews with the media because of past experiences, several close friends and regular customers at Meow and Furever called Kara "an absolute delight, filled with infectious energy and a true love of animals."

Like a phoenix rising from the ashes, Kara took a truly devastating blow and said, "I will not give up. I've come too far to be stopped." Hers is an underdog story that can inspire everyone to push through the pain to achieve their goals and make a difference in the world...especially this holiday season.

Speaking of making a difference, if you would like to donate to Meow and Furever and help care for all the adoptable kitties in their care, please click here, and happy holidays.

Tony Ricci, the Voice of Boston

Kara wiped at her eyes and cheeks, a sob catching in the back of her throat.

"Are those happy tears?"

"Yes and no. The article is beautiful, but I don't know how an opinion piece is going to help."

"It couldn't hurt, right? Sometimes you've got to take a leap of faith and hope for the best. Besides, you've already got the local media outlets coming for you. Worst case scenario, you rile up the national ones, too."

Kara's eyes narrowed. "You just climbed out of the doghouse, bestie."

"And I don't want to go back in, but...friends also don't lie to each other. You're self-sabotaging."

"Because I'm afraid to post a puff piece?"

"No, with Ben."

Kara sighed. "He went behind my back after he knew how I felt."

"So did I. The only difference is, we have history. But Ben and I were in the same headspace, wanting to fight back against Worthy's dirty tactics and help the café succeed. Kara, Worthy used his relationship with you for evil. Ben tried using his connections to repair some of the damage Worthy did. You may not like the way he went about it, but let's not get it twisted. Everything that man did was for you. Why would you want to drag out this fight, blow it completely out of proportion? Don't let one man's brush color every other man you meet."

"I don't think Ben is anything like Worthy, but seeing Worthy on the street, mocking me and then acting like Ben betrayed me..."

"You let him get in your head. It took you two years to move on from that snake, and even then, you dragged your feet with Ben and then you ran away the second you two hit a bump. You need to decide what it is you want and go for it. Don't bounce around like a scared rabbit."

"I tried to tell Ben how sorry I was, but it was like I couldn't get the words out. He barely looked at me, Charity. I hurt him, and I don't know how to fix it."

Charity arched a brow. "Do you want advice, or are you going to tell me I'm nosy and need to respect boundaries?"

"Depends on if I like what you have to say," Kara joked.

"Fair enough." Charity squeezed her hand. "Speak from the heart. Be honest. And if he can't accept it, then at least you tried."

Chapter Thirty-Two

Bow Tie is a snazzy cat with two triangles of tabby markings on the white fur of his chest. He's good for a night on the couch or laser dancing in the kitchen. Your choice.

BEN CLIMBED OUT OF his car and grabbed the enlarged copy of the check from the back seat, studying the packed parking lot with triumph.

"I can't believe I let you talk me into this," Schwartz grumbled, adjusting the blue tie he was wearing.

"I just need you to present them the check and then you can Uber to whatever bar you're planning on hitting tonight."

"The way you're saying that makes me feel judged."

"Sorry, I'm a little on edge tonight." Ben had gotten a call from Tony letting him know that Kara had reached out to him and the article went live on Wednesday. She'd even allowed Tony to ask her questions, which he'd attached as a follow-up, and last Ben had checked, it had been picked up by BuzzFeed and a few large syndicates and achieved viral status yesterday thanks to thousands of shares on Instagram and Twitter.

Ben was happy that it worked out the way he'd hoped, but it hadn't changed a thing between him and Kara. He would have been satisfied with a simple text, but nothing, which actually told him a lot.

They crossed the parking lot, and Ben handed Schwartz the check before they got to the door and pulled the tickets he'd printed from his pocket. When it was their turn, Michelle beamed brightly when she saw him, but then her smile dimmed, as if she realized she wasn't supposed to be happy to see him.

"Good evening, Ben."

"Hey, Michelle. We have a check to present to Charity and Kara from Kilburn. Do you know what the schedule for tonight looks like?"

"I'm not sure, but I think the dinner is first and then the auction. Charity or Kara would be the one to ask."

"Thanks. Here are our tickets." He handed her the papers and led the way into the large ballroom. Ben searched the crowd, looking for a familiar head of auburn hair, but he spotted Charity first. "Here, we'll ask Charity so you can stop carrying that thing around."

"Thanks, because I'm afraid of hitting someone with it."

Ben chuckled, weaving through the crowd, when Charity turned their way in a red strapless cocktail dress and waved. "Hey, Ben. I'm glad you made it."

"Thanks. We've got a check from Kilburn we're supposed

to present to you guys later. Our boss got sick last minute or he would have done it himself."

"Yeah, follow me."

"You want to go with Charity and I'll get us a couple drinks?" Ben said.

"Sure, I'll take a beer."

"On it." Ben headed to the closest bar station, waiting in line behind two couples who appeared to be in their fifties. His gaze searched the crowd until he spotted Kara by one of the round tables, speaking to... Adam.

Jealousy was an ugly emotion, but as he watched Kara laughing at something the other man said, her long auburn hair falling around her shoulders in soft waves and her full figure wrapped in an off-the-shoulder green dress, his jaw clenched painfully. They didn't hit it off, so why was Adam here? Was he her date? Did she think Ben wouldn't come?

He stepped up and ordered two beers, unable to take his eyes off her as an older woman tapped Kara's shoulder and she turned to greet her with a hug. There was nothing awkward or anxious about Kara tonight as she stood with her shoulders straight, confident and poised, and it was another side he'd wished that he'd gotten to know.

"There you are," Schwartz said, taking the beer from him. He followed Ben's line of vision and whistled low. "Dang, Kara looks great."

Ben took another drink without saying anything.

"Man, why don't you stop scowling and turn on the charm?"

"She seems to be occupied."

Schwartz chuckled. "You're jealous."

"Yes, and I don't want to be."

"I get that. Just don't be a jerk about it. Once the two of you have a heart-to-heart, you'll both realize that not being together is crazy, and then you'll move forward stronger together."

"You're touchingly optimistic about my fictional relationship."

"Someone's gotta be, you grouchy pessimist." Schwartz snapped his fingers. "I know what we're doing. Follow me."

"Where are we going?"

"To get a seat at the good table."

Ben wasn't sure what Schwartz was going on about, but as they walked between the tables, he noticed the name cards placed at every setting. When they reached the tables closest to the stage, Schwartz grinned. "Ah ha. Let's see. Charity. Kara!" He picked up the name card, circling to the other side and swapping it out. "Now you're sitting next to each other."

"Who did you move?"

"Just me. I'll take one for the team to help you out."

"What do you have against Charity?"

"'She speaks poniards, and every word stabs.'"

"What?"

"It's from Shakespeare's *Much Ado About Nothing*. My mother used to make me perform in plays because she thought I was going to be the next Dustin Hoffman."

"You want to explain what you meant about Charity?"

"She's always got something snarky to say."

Kara and Charity walked up next to them, and Kara asked, "Who has something snarky to say?"

"A client we're working with," Schwartz spoke up quickly.

"Ah," Charity picked up the place card and shot Ben a sheepish smile. "Looks like they messed up the seating. I'm over here with Schwartz."

"Am I next to you?" Kara frowned.

"No."

Ben cleared his throat and held up a card. "Over here."

"Oh!" Kara's lips twitched. "Interesting."

"Definitely a coincidence," Ben murmured, losing himself in Kara's hazel eyes.

"Hey, Kara," Adam called, coming up behind her and wrapping his hand around her arm. "We're getting ready for the speeches, so I need you and Charity by the stage."

"Sure, we'll be right there."

Adam nodded toward Ben. "Hey, we met at Friendsgiving. Bill, right?"

"It's Ben," he said, wondering if Adam really forgot his name or if he was messing with him.

"Right, sorry. Okay, I'll see you ladies up there."

When Adam walked away, Kara smiled apologetically. "He's basically our MC tonight, so I better go. But I'll see you back here after."

"Yeah, sure."

Adam called over the speaker for everyone to sit down, and once they took their seats, he told a couple of jokes before calling Kara and Charity up onto the stage.

"Good evening," Charity said, holding the mic between the two of them. "I'm Charity Simmons, and this is Dr. Kara Ingalls, and we want to thank you for coming out here tonight and supporting Meow and Furever." The room broke into thunderous applause, and they both smiled. "There are so many people we need to thank because our night wouldn't be possible without them."

Charity passed the mic to Kara, and she took it with nervous laugh while Charity unfolded a piece of paper. "We didn't want to leave anyone out so we wrote them down. First, we want to thank Will Schwartz and Ben Reese from Kilburn Marketing for helping us put all of this together."

Ben's heart kicked up when Kara looked at him, and he started second-guessing his certainty that they were done. If Kara wanted to give things another try, was he willing to open himself up again?

One thing he knew for sure is, if he took another chance, no more casual. They were either all in or he was out.

Kara's feet were killing her, and they hadn't even gotten to the auction. When she made it back to her seat and sat down next to Ben, she groaned quietly. "I should have never let Charity convince me to wear heels."

"I don't know how you walk around in those, but I admire your sacrifice for fashion," he teased.

"Shut up." Her cheeks warmed when she realized what she had said. For a second or two, Kara forgot that this was the first time they'd talked in days. The fact that he'd wanted to sit next to her should mean that he wanted to talk.

"How is the food? I was watching them serve, and I just wanted to dive off stage and grab a plate."

"It's good, dig in."

Kara cut up her chicken and took a bite, humming appreciatively. "That is delicious."

"I was a little surprised to see Adam," Ben said.

"Why?"

"I didn't think you'd kept in touch with him."

"I didn't, but he shares some mutual friends with Charity, and when we were looking for an MC, he volunteered."

Kara thought she heard, "I bet," and she fought back a giddy smile. Leaning over, she lowered her voice. "I can't believe you're still jealous of Adam."

Ben jerked her way, and whatever he saw in her expression, it made him relax with a sheepish grin lighting up his face. "Can you blame me? We stopped seeing each other, and he pops back up."

"Are you saying you want to start seeing each other again?" she whispered, her stomach fluttering when his gaze strayed to her lips.

"I want to have this conversation with you, but I don't think this is the time or the place. But later?"

Kara blushed, nodding slowly. If Ben was ready to try, it might take some time, but they could get back to where they were before Worthy and the article.

She'd barely taken another bite when Adam was hailing Charity and her back to the stage so local businesses could present them with donations. Five people lined up on the right side of the stage with oversize checks, including Schwartz. When he presented the check, Kara's jaw nearly dropped. Between the five checks, they'd collected almost twenty-five thousand dollars.

It was a Catmas miracle.

After Kara climbed down the stairs, she went looking for Ben but got caught by Mrs. Wyatt and Dolores Olsen, the owner of Bookin' It.

"Who are you looking for, dear?"

"A friend of mine. He's tall with a beard. He's wearing a red tie."

"Oh, is this him?" Mrs. Wyatt pointed behind her, and Kara turned, spotting Ben as he broke through the crowd to stand next to her.

"Congratulations, this is quite a turnout," he said.

"You did a lot. Please thank your boss for the check. It was incredibly generous."

"I will."

"How did you two meet?" Mrs. Wyatt asked.

"The company I work for was in charge of their marketing."

"Oh, so it's business then?" Dolores was in her fifties, but she fluttered her eyes at Ben like she was a young woman.

"We're friends," Kara said, glancing at Ben for confirmation, but he was lost in his phone.

"If you'll excuse me, I better go find my associate, since I'm his ride home."

Ben turned away from her, and she mumbled a farewell, following Ben through the crowd. A couple of times she got caught by someone who wanted to say hi or tell her how much they loved the café, and panic clawed up the back of her throat as she lost sight of Ben.

When Kara burst out into the parking lot, Ben was already past the first row, and Kara hurried after him, calling his name. He paused by the hood of his car, waiting for her to get there.

"Why are you leaving?"

"I don't want to be your friend, Kara."

"I—I just said that because it's no one's business."

"Then how would you describe who I am to you? If Charity asked, what would you say?"

Kara's mouth opened and snapped closed until she blurted, "Man I was seeing? Who I want to date again."

"You mean go back to the casual, no-labels relationship where you don't even give me the benefit of the doubt before you drop me?" Ben shook his head. "I'll pass."

"What do you want then? I don't know what you want me to say."

"Kara, if you don't know, then we are not in the same place."

"Don't play games, Ben! I'm sorry for what happened, but if this is some kind of punishment or revenge to hurt me—"

Ben cupped her cheeks, startling her with the intensity in his expression. "If you think that I could do that, then why did you chase me out here?"

"I don't think you're like Worthy. I just don't understand. I thought you wanted to try again."

"I don't want to try, Kara. Trying implies you might fail." Ben leaned his forehead against hers and murmured, "Be with me."

"I—" Kara choked, that was the only word she could call it. She wanted to say yes, but a thousand thoughts jumbled together. They'd just had a major issue and needed to recover from that. They couldn't really go back to where they left off, and they definitely couldn't jump three steps forward, could they?

Ben dropped his hands from her face. "I guess I have my answer."

Chapter Thirty-Three

Fruitcake the tortoiseshell loves to be anywhere humans are. This speckled sweetheart may have a funny name, but your Christmas won't be complete without her!

KARA SCRUBBED DOWN TABLES in the social room while Matilda explored the currently empty area. Every once in a while, she would sniff a cat tree or scratcher and hiss, or her mouth would hang open as if she smelled something foul. Charity stepped out to deliver the last of the online orders for that day and the next. With only Matilda left, and Charity and Michelle going out of town for most of the holiday anyway, they'd decided to close down until the second of January. Kara had a sign for the door she planned to hang at the end of the day to let people know.

Kara sat down in one of the cozy chairs, and Matilda immediately made a beeline for her lap.

"Hey, beautiful. I guess I can bring you home with me

for the holidays and put you in the spare room if you get too stressed. But I don't want you to lose faith, okay? You're the final cat, but that means you're tough and amazing things are in store for you, I just know it."

Matilda purred, kneading her chest happily.

After the first delivery of shelter cats was adopted, the director had happily sent six more. Fruitcake was the last to go, with two women who had lost their older cat and were looking for a companion for their remaining three-year-old male cat. Of course, that ruled out Matilda since she didn't like other cats, but they'd fallen in love with Fruitcake's playful personality, and when they signed the adoption papers, they told Kara it was fate that they stopped in—that they were meant to be.

Meant to be. What did that even mean? You couldn't know for sure if the person you chose was your one and only.

Kara pulled out her phone and scrolled through the Instagram feed for the café, checking the tags to see if any adoptive families had posted new pics. Kara saw one from Ben Reese dated over a week ago and clicked on it out of curiosity. She didn't know he had Instagram.

It was a picture of Ben with his head on his pillow and Chaos tangled up in his hair. The caption read, I'm not a cat person, but I'm his person.

Kara's eyes stung with tears. She missed Ben so much that her heart broke thinking about the anguish in his eyes on Saturday. When he'd told her that he just wanted them to be together, her first instinct was to throw herself against him and say yes. Instead, her brain started playing through scenarios and shouting at her, *No, go slow! You've already had an issue. You're going to get attached and get your heart broken.* And a dozen other thoughts, so intense she couldn't think straight, and then he was gone.

Signing out of the café's Instagram, she clicked on the sign-up and entered in her personal information, her heart pounding as she hit submit. Kara selected a profile picture but stared at the blank little bio box and swallowed, typing, Love is about fear. You're scared to admit it. Terrified to lose it. And afraid you'll never find it again. She saved the changes to her profile and, before she could chicken out, liked and commented on his picture.

Kara heard the bell jingle faintly and sat up, waving at the thin brunette walking in the door. She set Matilda on top of one of the cat houses and got to her feet, hurrying out of the room. "Hello. Welcome to Meow and Furever. Sorry, I was just enjoying a little cuddle time with Matilda during the lull."

"Oh, you're fine. If I worked in a place like this, I'd have a hard time staying out of there, too. A cuddle from a cat can make everything better."

"That's how I feel," Kara said. "What can I get you?"

"Well, I've heard your pastries are delicious, so I'll take one of those cinnamon rolls and a cup of black coffee."

"Absolutely." Kara tapped her order into the computer, and after running the woman's debit card, washed her hands in the sink. "So, where did you hear about our pastries?"

"Ben Reese. He came to see me a few weeks ago about your café. Are you Kara?"

"I am." Kara dried her hands and poured a cup of coffee, setting it on the counter. "What did Ben come to see you about?"

"My name is Carol Lambert. I own Furry Things."

"The pet warehouse? Wait—" Kara picked up one of their cinnamon rolls and set it on a plate in front of her. "Did you donate an automatic litter box?"

"Yes, I did."

"That was so great of you! We actually had several people get into a bidding war over it. So, thank you."

"While I appreciate you saying that, I actually feel like I need to apologize."

"For what?"

"Ben was hoping I'd be a sponsor for the low-cost veterinary hospital you're building, but I'll admit that I declined because I read an article about you."

"Oh. That's all right. You don't know me, and I understand you wouldn't want to take a chance on someone you weren't sure you could trust."

"Thank you for being gracious. Then I saw the news this morning, and I felt terrible. Especially after Ben sent me that wonderful background piece on you, and I ignored it."

"Honestly, Carol, you didn't have to come in to apologize. I didn't know Ben did any of this. But what news story are you talking about?"

"That man they call the Grinch? I guess he drained his new girlfriend's bank account and tried to flee the country."

"Oh my god. How awful for her."

"Anyway, I saw that and wanted to deliver this." Carol pulled a red envelope from her purse.

"Thank you. Should I open it?"

"Absolutely."

Kara pulled open the tab on the envelope and removed a

beautiful Christmas card with a calico kitten playing with a sprig of holly. When she opened it, she found a folded check inside and caught her breath when she saw the amount. "Carol, thank you so much."

"You're very welcome. I hope between this and your Christmas party, you can finally finish your clinic."

"Actually, we can." Kara slipped the check back inside the card and into the drawer, locking it with her key. "Would you like to see the space and what we have planned?"

"Absolutely!"

Kara waved her back through the door, and when it opened up to the exam area, she said, "So, we have these cages for cats who are recovering from surgery or need to quarantine before we move them to the social room, exam table, supply cabinets to the left, and then down here..." Kara opened the sliding glass doors to the two rooms and flipped on the lights in each. "Right now, we're using them to store food and such, but this one will be surgery prep and recovery and the one across from it will be the surgery suite. This back area will be reception, and the bathroom is there, and this area will be closed off and separated to create two small exam rooms for nonemergency visits."

"So, they'll come in the front for the café and the back for the clinic?"

"Yes."

"I like it. I expect to be invited to the grand opening."

"Of course. I've thought about hosting a low-cost feline vaccine clinic on opening day. Let the community know we're here." Kara shut off the lights, and they walked back through the hallway and door to the lobby.

"You got all your cats adopted then?" Carol asked, picking up her coffee from the counter.

"All except Matilda. She doesn't like other cats, so we couldn't put her in the social room, and while her picture is on the website and I'd let people meet her, she can be intimidating."

"How so?"

"She didn't like being in the cage because she could hear and see the other cats, so she would hiss. But since I brought her into my office and let her explore more, she's great. I would have adopted her already, but with my cat and my soon-to-be roommate's cat, I don't think she'd be living her best life."

"I had my calico for twenty years, and while she loved me, she hid from everyone else, including my ex-husband, and we were together for ten years of her life."

"Aw, when did she pass?"

"Two years ago." Carol stared into the social room for several moments, and Kara got a wave of inspiration.

"Would you like to sit with her awhile? We can move your drink and pastry in there."

"Actually, I would."

Kara picked up her coffee and plate, and Carol got the door. "Where would you like to sit?"

"By the window, in that really big chair."

"You got it." Kara set her items on the side table. "Would you like a book or anything?"

"No, I'm fine, thank you." Carol made a cooing sound and Matilda's head swiveled her way, then she trotted across the room with her tail straight up in the air. She let out a chirping meow, and when she reached Carol's outstretched hand, she sniffed her fingers before rubbing against her. "She recognizes a cat person," Carol laughed.

"Or *her* person." Kara saw Charity come in through the back and continued, "I'll be back to check on you."

"We're fine," Carol said, patting her lap. Matilda wasted no time jumping up, and Kara left them alone to bond.

"Hey."

"Hi," Charity said, nodding toward the social room. "I recognize her."

"That's Carol. She owns Furry Things and donated the litter box for the auction."

"Oh."

"Did you know she wasn't going to donate money because of an article she read about me?"

"She only told me to let Ben know she didn't feel comfortable sponsoring the hospital build."

"Well, apparently she changed her mind after seeing a news story about Worthy taking off with his lawyer's money."

"What? I have to find this article." Charity whipped out her phone, tapping away. When she found what she was looking for, she read aloud: " 'The Grinch Who Stole Catmas Strikes Again! While Ferris Worthington may have spent two years in prison for one of the largest data breaches in years, the Grinchy Claus obviously didn't learn his lesson. Less than two weeks after his release, Mr. Worthington is believed to have drained not just his girlfriend's savings, but several of her high-profile clients' accounts, and stolen highly sensitive information as well. While the details are still emerging and the investigation ongoing, the FBI is now involved as they believe Mr. Worthington has left the country. This information comes after dozens of news outlets released a rather scathing article about Mr. Worthington's treatment of his former fiancée, whose life was destroyed in the wake of his previous crimes, despite being unaware of her fiancé's dark character. To read the article, click here.'"

Charity grunted in disgust. "If they don't catch him, I hope he ends up somewhere tropical and gets eaten by a shark."

Kara laughed. "Honestly, I don't care anymore. People know the truth, and I don't think his lawsuit against me is going to go anywhere after all that." Kara unlocked the drawer and showed her the card. "And thanks to Carol..."

Charity's eyes widened. "Kara, we did it! We more than did it! Between this and the money from the party and auction, minus expenses—"

"Not only are we keeping our doors open, but we can finish the clinic."

Charity threw her arms around Kara, quietly celebrating.

When they pulled apart, Charity put the card and check away, shaking her head. "We really need to do something nice for Ben. He did so much. Tracking down half the auction items, sponsors, donating his bonus—"

Kara's eyes widened when Charity clapped her hand over her mouth. "What did you say?"

"I wasn't supposed to say anything," Charity mumbled behind her hand.

Kara pulled Charity's hand down. "Tell me what you know."

Charity shrugged. "Schwartz told me the Kilburn check

happened because Ben told his boss he wanted to donate his bonus to the café from Kilburn Marketing so we wouldn't know it was from him. His boss matched his donation."

"I can't believe this." Kara shook her head. "He did so much, and I was so scared of letting him in that I took him for granted."

"Call the man and tell him that! Show up at his door, chase him to Mexico, but do something besides stand here boo-hooing because you messed up. Be Action Girl."

"Charity, he asked me to be with him, and I choked. There is no way he's going to forgive that."

"You know what it means to assume, right? You are human. You love him, don't you? I mean, I assume you love him because you were moping so hard this week I literally had to remind you to shower so you wouldn't scare away the patrons."

"Thanks," Kara grumbled.

"Don't mention it. That's what best friends do."

Kara pulled out her phone, staring at the screen. "What if he rejects the call?"

"Oh my goodness, girl, get some gumption! No, you know what, this is what we're doing." Charity started tapping away on her phone. "I'm going to get the flight information from Schwartz, and we're going to Mexico. Your girl is going to help you, so you don't overthink..." Charity paused with a sigh. "I'm overstepping again, aren't I?"

Kara grinned. "You are, but in this instance, I don't mind. I do have one question."

"What?"

"Why do you have Schwartz's number?"

"Hey, concentrate more on what you're going to say to Ben and less on me."

Kara shook her head, excitement bubbling in her chest as she went back into the social room to check on Carol. "How's it going in here?"

Carol smiled at her, Matilda asleep on her chest. "You know how it's going."

"I'm sorry?"

"You knew, putting me in the room with her, I wouldn't be able to resist taking her home."

"I mean, I hoped, but I couldn't know for sure."

"I do. Can I please get an adoption application? Your last cat is getting a home for Christmas."

Chapter Thirty-Four

Gizmo the sphynx cross can't wait to find a cat-savvy home that can give him regular baths to keep him healthy and happy—and maybe a red car bed for Christmas?

BEN HIKED HIS DUFFEL bag higher onto his shoulder as he walked through the airport with Schwartz, taking a drink from the Starbucks coffee cup in his hand. The taste of the peppermint in his mocha reminded him of Christmas lights with Kara, and he couldn't wait to get to a point where he no longer thought about her every other minute.

"Who is ready for eight glorious days in Mexico?"

"Me," Ben said, unenthusiastically.

"Yeah, no, that's the wrong tone. That is the same tone you had when you left the office holiday party early and missed Roy trying to moonwalk to 'Grandma Got Run Over by a Reindeer.' No appreciation for the epicness of the event."

"Sorry, man. I'll get with it."

"How was your cat when you dropped him off?"

"I didn't. I hired a house sitter instead. No sense in making Chaos stay in a cage for two weeks, and then I don't have to worry about my place."

"I swear, if there is such a thing as reincarnation, I'm coming back to life as your cat."

"I'd never adopt you."

"That was hurtful. You're still going to renew your contract in January, right?" Schwartz asked, settling into one of the empty terminal seats and tucking his own duffel under the seat in front of him.

"Yes, I talked to Roy."

"Good, because you're the best project partner and friend I've ever had, so if you were thinking about leaving, I'd make you take me with you."

"Like Renée Zellweger following Tom Cruise out of the building and starting their own sports agency?"

"What?" Schwartz asked.

"*Jerry Maguire*? 'Show me the money'?"

"I've heard that line but never seen the movie."

Ben rolled his eyes. "It's a great movie. Explain to me again why we had to be here so early?"

"Because I hate rushing. It stresses me out. Now we can sit back and relax, knowing there is no way we're missing this flight."

Only now Ben had more time to think about Kara and what she was doing. Did they make enough to finish construction on the clinic? It wasn't like Amelia, whose absence actually relieved his stress. Kara made his day better by existing, and living without her was more painful than if they'd never gotten started.

Every time he thought about how he'd stood there, asking her to be with him, expecting to plan a future together, and she choked, it ate him up inside.

Ben clicked on the café's Instagram and the most recent post was a series of pictures of Kara and Charity at the Christmas party, Michelle creating her foam art, empty cages, and...

Ben sat forward, staring at the woman in the picture, holding a calico cat in her arms. "Holy crap."

"What?" Schwartz asked, leaning over his shoulder.

"Nothing, I just recognized someone."

"Is that the café's feed?"

"Yes."

"Dude..."

"I'm just seeing if they made their goal. I'm not social stalking her."

"Whatever you say. I'm going to take a nap."

The final picture in the series was a close-up of a red ornament featuring the silhouette of a cat with script inside. *Thank you for saving me.* He scrolled down to the caption and clicked more.

> While we planned on being open this Christmas Eve, we have decided to take time from the twenty-fourth through the second of January to be with our families. But we've included the daily specials for Catmas Days 24 and 25 on our website, which can be redeemed anytime between the second and the fifteenth of January. Thank you

for making the first holiday season at Meow and Furever Cat Café such an amazing experience. We appreciate all of the generous sponsors who donated items for our auction and helped us raise money to open the Meow and Furever Clinic, which we hope to start construction on in January! To all the adoptive families who came out this year, we were able to find homes for not just our original café cats, but after partnering with our local shelter, twelve more kitties found their forever homes before Christmas. We couldn't be happier with this holiday miracle, and we plan to continue to serve our community delicious drinks and tasty treats and help homeless felines find their happily ever afters. Merry Catmas! —Meow and Furever Cat Café

Ben smiled and clicked the heart under the post. It felt like time to start fresh, and though the break from social media had been good for him, he missed seeing what was going on with his friends and family, especially with the distance between them.

Ben realized he had never finished his bio and typed something generic in the box. Then he scrolled through his notifications. Most of them were to let him know his family had followed him back, including Boone, but he had a new picture comment from Kara Ingalls yesterday.

I like your pic.

Ben clicked on her name, surprised she'd opened an account again after everything. He studied her profile picture of her face from the eyes up with Theo attacking her messy bun.

Then he read her bio: Love is about fear. You're scared to admit it. Terrified to lose it. And afraid you'll never find it again.

Ben's heart pounded as he reread her words. Was it a message for him? Or just a random quote she'd picked from Google?

Before he thought better of it, he called her number, but it went straight to voice mail. He ended the call, shaking his head. She was probably still sleeping. When the tone beeped, he left a voice mail. "Hey, it's Ben. I saw your Instagram and was... I don't know, but if you want to talk, call me back, and I'll listen."

A notification alert flashed across the top of his screen, and Ben clicked on the text message from his mom. It was a picture of the whole family at the ice-skating rink, bundled up for the cold and smiling wide.

> We went skating last night. The kids enjoyed it, but they missed their fun uncle. Really wish you were here.

Ben stared at the photo. He did too. He didn't want to disappoint Schwartz, but Mexico no longer sounded amazing. Ben didn't want to drink on the beach or play wingman for Schwartz when all he could think about was being with Kara. A resort in the sunshine didn't sound comforting to him. He wanted to be with his family, surrounded by love and the smell of his mom's cooking. That's what he needed, and he wished he hadn't let his anger and pride rule his decisions.

Ben turned to Schwartz and tapped his shoulder. "Schwartz, wake up."

"What?" He turned his head, peering with half-closed eyes. "What's up, buddy?"

"We gotta talk."

"Uh-oh. Why do you sound like you're about to break up with me?" Schwartz's eyes widened, and he sat up straight. "Dude, no. You are not bailing on me!"

"Schwartz, I want to spend Christmas with my family, and I know it sucks, but do you really want me tagging along, ruining the vibe? You want to go scouting girls and having fun. I'll bring you down."

"I can't go to Mexico alone, like some kind of creepy pervert!"

"Schwartz, please, man."

Schwartz took several moments before he released a low chuckle. "Fine. Go. Leave me and go to the cold streets of Boston. I'll think of you freezing your bits off while I'm sipping a margarita on the beach."

"You're sure?"

"Yeah, some chicks are into the loner type. I'll play up the mystery, and they'll be goners."

"Thanks, man." Ben gave him a one-armed hug and climbed to his feet, rushing back through the airport to get to the ticket counter. After what felt like an hour, he was called up to the front of the line. "Hi, can I get a ticket on your first flight out to Boston?"

"I told you we should have left earlier," Kara grumbled to Charity as they stood in line for security.

"You only need two hours at the airport. I swear, we're almost to the front."

Kara tapped her foot nervously, checking her phone. Service in the Sacramento airport was spotty thanks to her terrible cellular provider, and although she didn't have any missed calls, she had a new voice mail, but every time she tried to check it, the sound was garbled.

They finally reached the front, and after they removed their shoes and electronics, they passed through the machine with no issues. They'd each checked a bag at the main gate, and Kara had a backpack with her iPad, chargers, a book, and a pair of flip-flops for when they arrived. Right then, she had on capris and a T-shirt, and while she'd been freezing outside, she knew it would be warm on the plane.

"Do you think I'm making a mistake?" Kara asked for the millionth time. She'd been second-guessing herself ever since they bought the tickets last night.

"No! This is the moment he's going to realize you are so serious about him that you busted out the emergency credit card in order to go on this trip. But if it doesn't work out, you can always stay in my room. I'm thinking about turning my cell phone off so I don't have to pick up when my mom gets my voice mail telling her that I'm not going with them to New York."

"You didn't have to come with me," Kara laughed.

"You had me at Cancún, baby! And at least Schwartz will be there to annoy so I won't be a fourth wheel while you two are making up."

Kara bit her lip. "It's gate B12?"

"Yes."

"I don't see him, Char."

"Calm thyself. Oh, there's Schwartz. Come on."

"Wait, we're doing this now?" Kara squeaked.

"No time like the present!"

Kara followed behind Charity, who tapped Schwartz on the shoulder. He jumped, pulling his earbuds out while staring at them in wide-eyed shock. "What are you doing here?"

"She's here to profess her love for Ben, and I'm here because, Mexico. Duh." She sat down in the empty seat beside him.

"Where is Ben?" Kara asked.

"Uh, Ben left. He decided to change his plane ticket to Boston and go home to his family for Christmas."

"What?" Charity and Kara cried out in unison, drawing more than a few irritated stares.

"Yeah, he left about forty-five minutes ago."

"Do you know what flight? What airline? Anything?"

Schwartz stood up and pulled his phone from his pocket. "Hang on, let me see if I can get him on the phone."

"I'm going to check the flight board," Charity said.

Kara followed behind and pulled out her phone to type in gate numbers for all Boston flights.

Schwartz came up behind them with his stuff in hand and his phone to his ear. "He's not picking up."

"Dang it."

Kara looked over the flights again. "These two leave the soonest, so I'm going to start there."

"Do you want me to check some of the later flights?"

Charity asked, grabbing Schwartz by the shoulder. "Schwartz can take some, too, and we can split up. If we find him, we'll meet you back by the Starbucks in the food court."

"Wait, why am I in this? I just wanted to go to Cancún. It's not my problem my guy changed his flight last minute and you two came up with this terrible plan resulting in hijinks and chaos."

"Schwartz, I'm still going to Cancún, and if you don't help us, I will make your vacation very uncomfortable."

Schwartz and Charity stared each other down before he cleared his throat. "So, which flights am I checking?"

Kara let Charity handle Schwartz while she took off through the airport to find the flight gates. The first one was a bust, and the second the same. Her phone blared with Charity's ringtone, and she answered, "Hello?"

"Kara, I found him. Gate B21."

Kara swung her head around and went back the way she had come. "Has he seen you yet?"

"No—" *Crackle, crackle.*

"Charity? I'm on my way. Don't tell him I'm here yet."

"Okay, let me call Schwartz so he doesn't end up all the way at the other end of the airport."

Kara ended the call and counted off the gates in her head, her backpack flopping against her as she jogged, not because she thought he would disappear before she got there, but she didn't want to wait a second longer to tell him how she felt. That nagging fear was still there, yelling at her to turn back, to give up, but Kara needed to get her feelings off her chest.

Kara saw Charity and Schwartz standing in the middle of

the terminal, pointing. Kara saw the back of Ben's head and tried to catch her breath.

Charity was suddenly dabbing at her forehead with a napkin. "You're all sweaty."

"Yes, because I was jogging and I'm nervous as heck."

"If it helps, he loves you," Schwartz offered.

"It does." Kara brushed Charity's hand off her forehead and took a step in Ben's direction, one foot in front of the other. When she came around the row of seats and stopped next to him, he looked up, and his jaw dropped.

"Kara? What are you doing here?" Ben rose to his feet, setting his tablet to the side.

"So, I was supposed to be telling you I bought a ticket to Cancún to be with you, but Schwartz told us at the gate that you're going home to Boston instead."

"Us?" Ben turned, and Kara laughed when Charity and Schwartz waved. When he met her gaze again, his brown eyes were brighter, hopeful. "Why did you buy a ticket? You could have called."

"Because I didn't want to spend another minute without you. I know it's not fair to say, but it's true. When you asked if we could be together, I panicked because I'm not good at relationships and I was afraid that if I said yes again, I'd disappoint you. But I did that anyway, by being afraid, so I am standing here, terrified, trying not to have a full-on panic attack because I know this is highly presumptuous of me, but I love you. I want any and every label you can think of because I want to make you happy, as happy as you have tried to make me. And I took it for granted that you would be fine with something casual because you would move on eventually, and I'm going to stop talking because I think I'm not making sense anymore."

"Even when you talk in zigzag sequences, I understand you, Kara."

"Does that mean you can forgive me for being a stubborn jack—"

Ben didn't let her finish as his mouth covered hers, his hands cradling her face between them. He kissed her again and again with her hands hanging on to his waist. He broke away from her long enough to whisper, "I've missed you."

"I missed you," she gasped, wrapping her arms around his neck with a laugh. "It sucks that the whole goal of buying a ticket to Cancún was so we could be together and now you aren't going."

"Cancel your ticket and come to Boston with me."

"You want me to go home with you and meet your family?"

"You said you'd call yourself any label, right?" She nodded. "Then as my girlfriend, let's get your ticket changed."

She gazed up at him, her eyes shiny with tears. "I love you, Ben."

"I love you, too."

That was all she needed to hear.

Chapter Thirty-Five

Hope is this tiny tuxedo's name, and this ball of fluff can't wait to change your life. The question is, are you the one she's been waiting for?

THE UBER PULLED UP in front of his childhood home at a little after nine on Christmas morning. Ben had sent a text to his pop from the airport yesterday that there was a surprise Christmas gift coming and to keep his eyes open for it.

It had been hard to get out of bed, not just because he'd been loath to stop holding Kara, but also they hadn't arrived in Boston until almost one in the morning, thanks to a delay in Chicago. The only good thing about the long layover was that they could buy a few things to get them through until after Christmas, since neither one of them had packed for cold weather, and catch up on what happened while they weren't together. She'd filled him in on Carol coming in and apologizing, and he'd told her about officially staying at Kilburn.

Ben had booked a hotel as well, but by the time they arrived, they didn't do anything but curl up in each other's arms and fall asleep.

He kissed her cheek, trying to suppress a wicked grin. "You should press the button on that sweater when they answer the door."

"You're not funny, Ben! I can't believe I'm meeting your parents wearing this thing."

The sweater in question was the only thing in her size at one of the airport shops, an ugly green-and-red monstrosity that read "I'm a Tree-Rex," with Christmas tree lights weaving across the front and down the sleeves. A pair of black stretchy yoga pants completed the look.

Ben hadn't fared much better with a red Fair Isle sweater with a llama wearing sunglasses on the front, but he didn't care how goofy they were dressed. He was happy to be bringing his girl home for Christmas.

They climbed out of the car, and Ben took her hand, leading her up the steps, a red card with Boone's and Amelia's names on the front in his other hand. He hadn't bothered to shop for them earlier for obvious reasons, but he didn't want to show up empty-handed and have them think he was still holding a grudge. Before they reached the front door, it swung open, and a shriek of "Oh my goodness, it's Ben!" ripped through to the quiet street as his mother came bursting from the house as fast as she could.

"Hey, Ma." He caught her up with one arm, giving her a tight squeeze. "Merry Christmas."

"I can't believe you're here," she said, slapping his back a few times before pulling away, her gaze moving beyond him to Kara. "And who is this?"

"This is my girlfriend, Kara."

"Girlfriend, huh?" His mother practically pushed him out of the way to hug Kara, giving her a little rock back and forth. "I'm so glad to meet you. Come on in and meet everyone."

"We don't have bags, Ma. We got a hotel last night."

His mother plopped her hands on her hips. "Why would you pay for a hotel when we have a guest room you could have stayed in for free?"

"Because they probably got in too late and didn't want to disturb us," his father answered for him as he stepped over the threshold.

"Hey, Pop," Ben said, giving him a hug.

"This was nice of you to make the trip. Really makes Christmas special."

"Yeah, paid an arm and a leg for the tickets, but it was worth it to see Ma's face."

"And this is her, huh?"

Ben smiled as he watched his mother drag Kara into the house. "That's my girl."

"Glad you two were able to work things out."

"So am I."

They followed behind the two women, and Ben was surprised to find his nephews and nieces already there, playing on their tablets without looking up. His brother-in-law got up to greet him.

"Ben, good to see you."

"Thanks, Tom."

"Ben?" Birdy came racing into the room from the kitchen, squealing when she caught sight of him. She ran across the living room, nearly trampling her children to throw her arms around him.

Ben picked her up off her feet with a laugh. "Whoa, you trying to choke me or what?"

She smacked his arm, and he noticed her eyes were shiny with tears. "We didn't know you were coming or we wouldn't have opened your gifts last night."

"Are you kidding? I didn't even know we were coming until yesterday morning, so don't even worry about it. Did you like your gift?"

"Oh my goodness, yes! I was looking up that bed-and-breakfast you booked us for Valentine's Day, and it is so cute! Best brother ever!"

"Hey," the youngest, Brandon, hollered, poking his head out of the hallway. "I gave you that coupon book that included a free night of babysitting."

Birdy scoffed. "Last time I let you babysit, you let them watch *Killer Klowns from Outer Space*, and they had nightmares for weeks!"

"Hey, they liked it at the time!" Brandon came across the room and hugged him. "Heya, big brother."

"Hi." Ben returned the hug. "I'd introduce you to my girlfriend, but Ma's stolen her away."

"I was introducing her to Birdy," his mother snapped back from across the room.

Ben held up the card. "Is there somewhere I could put this? It's for Boone and Amelia."

"You could put it under the tree with the rest of the gifts. They should be here soon."

Ben nodded, sneaking around behind Kara so he could wrap his arms around her. As happy as he was to be home, seeing Boone and Amelia again had him on edge, and just having Kara near had a centering effect.

"So, Ben mentioned you're a veterinarian," his mother said.

"Yes, my friend and I run a nonprofit cat rescue. Ben helped us with a large fundraiser so we could also open a low-cost cat hospital there, and it was very successful."

"I've always wanted a cat, but my husband doesn't like them."

"Funny." Kara leaned her head back and gazed up at Ben, her eyes sparkling. "Ben didn't like them either when I first met him, but Chaos converted him."

"What's a chaos?" his father asked. Then he added, "Wait, are you keeping that kitten you found?"

"Yes. I hired a house sitter who is supposed to send me proof-of-life pics every day by noon." Kara giggled, and he kissed the top of her head. "Shush, you."

"This is not the same brother I remember," Birdy said, pointing a finger at Ben. "I told him I thought about getting a puppy for the kids, and he started naming off all the diseases they can transfer to humans. He hates animals."

"Oh, I have pictures that prove he loves his cat."

Ben snatched her phone and held it above his head. "None of that. Next thing you know, my mother will be busting out the baby pictures."

"We've already scheduled that for when you're distracted and after we have a couple of glasses of wine." His mother winked at Kara, and Ben shook his head. "I'm starting to regret coming home."

The front door opened behind them, and Ben turned with Kara still in his arms and watched his brother Boone coming through, packages stacked high in his arms.

"Brandon, give me a hand, would you? I can't see what I'm doing!"

Ben released Kara and stepped forward, taking the top five boxes from his brother. When Boone saw him, he startled. "Ben. I didn't know you were here."

"Boone. Merry Christmas."

"He surprised us," their father said, taking the remaining packages from Boone. "Where is your wife?"

"I'll go back out and get her. She had a little morning sickness on the way over and is still feeling woozy."

Ben and his father set the packages under the tree, and his pop nudged him. "You okay?"

"Yeah, I'm good." Ben climbed to his feet, and Kara shot him an encouraging smile when Boone came back inside, keeping a hold on his wife's arm.

"Sorry, everyone. Merry Christmas," Amelia called, her face white as a sheet. When she saw Ben, her bottom lip trembled a bit. "Hello, Ben."

"Hi, Amelia." Ben glanced at Kara, who crossed behind his mother to reach his side and take his hand.

Boone walked over to them and held out his hand to Ben. "Merry Christmas. Hello, Kara. Nice to see you again. How was your flight?"

"Hey, Boone. We made good time thanks to a hefty tail-wind, but we had a long layover," she said, pulling on the bottom of her sweater with her free hand. "Of course, that gave us time to get these festive sweaters."

Ben snorted.

"I feel like we're missing the joke."

"It's a long story, but neither of us knew we were coming to Boston until we got to the airport, and then all the luggage we had was packed for warm weather."

"I probably have some things you can borrow, Kara," Birdy offered.

"That's very nice, but I think we're going to find a mall tomorrow."

Amelia stepped up next to Boone, twisting her hands nervously in her blouse. "Hi, I'm Amelia."

"Kara. I've heard a lot about you."

"Oh, that's not good," Amelia replied with a high, nervous laugh.

"No, I just mean—dang." Kara shook her head with a sheepish smile. "I didn't mean to make it awkward."

"It was already awkward. You just didn't tiptoe around it," Ben teased her, trying to keep the tone light.

"We're really happy you're here, Ben. And Kara, too," Amelia said.

"Thanks."

Moments ticked by before Ben's mother clapped her hands. "Birdy, do you think we should bring out the cinnamon rolls and get started on presents?"

His nephews and nieces lifted their heads from their games at the mention of presents. As everyone made their way back into the kitchen, Kara squeezed his hand. "You good?"

"It's just weird, but I'm getting used to it."

"At least we can go back to the hotel tonight." Kara leaned up on her tiptoes, and he met her for a brief kiss. "And make up properly."

"Something to look forward to."

Kara sat on the floor between Ben's legs, watching his family laugh and razz each other as they opened gifts, the whole scene playing in slow motion. It was different than the other Christmas celebrations she'd been invited to. Her grandparents overdid it the first year she was with them, but after that, they each exchanged one gift. Charity's family was very proper and definitely wouldn't burst out laughing when the youngest boy opened up his prank kit and went straight for the whoopee cushion.

Kara silently took it in, a little overwhelmed, but Ben's consistent touch made her feel better about her own nervousness.

"Ma, that envelope is for Boone and Amelia," Ben called, his hand gently squeezing her shoulder, and she reached up to take his hand.

"Thank you, Ben," Boone said, taking the card from their mother. He pulled the card out, reading it silently, and when he opened it, his eyes widened. "Wow."

"What is it?" Amelia asked.

"He bought us a crib."

"I ordered it online, but if it's not your color or style, you can return it and buy what you want."

Amelia burst into tears, and Kara looked up at Ben to see how he was handling her reaction.

"Babe, why are you crying?" Boone asked.

"It's just so nice."

Boone looked over at Ben, nodding. "We really appreciate it. Thank you."

Suddenly, Ben climbed to his feet, and so did Boone. Kara leaned out of the way as the two men crossed the room and shared a back-slapping hug.

"You're welcome."

Kara noticed Birdy and Ben's mother both crying, and her heart squeezed.

"You know what I want for a belated Christmas present, George?" Ben's mother asked.

"What's that?"

"I want a kitten," she announced.

His father snorted. "Now that would be a Christmas miracle, me getting you a cat."

"I think once you get a cat, you realize what you've been missing," Kara said.

"Now, Kara, don't you come into this family and try to turn us into cat people," Ben's father said gently.

Kara blushed. "I...I just think, if your wife wants a cat, you should get her one."

"Hey, why are you being so nice to him?" Ben asked, coming back to his seat. "You railroaded me into taking Chaos."

Kara pinched his leg, mortified. "I did not railroad you. I simply stated you should help an overwhelmed system."

"I'm just saying, you and my mother should join forces

and bring my dad around. If you get a cat in this house before next Christmas, I'll shave my beard."

Kara caught Ben's mother's gaze, and they both grinned.

Ben's little brother burst out laughing. "Oh, you are so screwed, bro."

Chapter Thirty-Six

From our family to yours,
Thank you for making our first holiday season meowy and bright.
Merry Catmas,
Meow and Furever Cat Café

"I FEEL NAKED WITHOUT it," Ben said, rubbing his smooth chin.

Kara got out of the passenger side of the car and studied him, turning her head to the side. "To be honest, I miss it. How long does it take you to grow it back?"

"About a month to get it the way I want." Ben grabbed Chaos's carrier from the back, and the kitten yowled angrily. "Whoa, what happened to you? I come back, and you're acting like a spoiled brat. I don't know if we'll have Victoria watch you again."

"It's crazy how big he got in a week."

Their flight got in around four in the afternoon, and

they'd Ubered to Ben's house first to grab Chaos and Ben's car. Ben's family wanted them to stay through New Year's Day, but both Ben and Kara were ready to be home.

"I'm still shocked your dad asked me to help him surprise your mom with that kitten. I think he just wanted to see if you'd really shave your beard."

"Could be, but I think it was my fault. I talked up Chaos way too much and convinced him kittens were fun. Miracle is going to give him a run for his money."

"You didn't tell him about the flying poop then?"

Ben snapped his fingers. "I knew I forgot something."

Kara burst out laughing, popping the trunk to get her luggage.

"Kar, I'll come back for that."

"I can roll my dang suitcase up to my house."

"I still cannot believe my mother guilted us into staying with her the whole week and didn't even let us stay in the same room."

Kara climbed her porch steps ahead of him so she could unlock the door, her luggage banging against the ground. "Even if she'd said yes, I wouldn't have shared a room with you."

"Why not?"

"Because it was awkward enough with Boone and Amelia without having your family know we're...*progressing* in our relationship."

"Why did you say it like that?"

"That's the way your mother put it to me when she asked if we were moving in together."

"No, she didn't."

"Oh yes, she did."

"That's awful. I'm sorry."

"Ben, it's fine. I loved your mom and dad and everyone. Even Boone's growing on me, and I wasn't sure that would happen after our first meeting."

"It may sound weird, but being with you has helped me understand my brother better."

"How is that?"

Ben shrugged. "Not being with you was the most painful experience of my life. If that is what he felt, then I get the lengths he went to to stay with Amelia."

Kara turned the knob and pushed the door open for him to carry Chaos inside, protesting when he grabbed her bag as he passed. "Ben!"

"What? I can lift it with one arm." Ben headed down the hallway, disappearing out of sight.

"Show-off," she teased. "Theo? Robin Hood! I'm home."

Theo and Robin Hood bounded into the room.

Ben came back without the luggage and carrier, Chaos dogging his steps.

Kara headed into the kitchen, knowing there wasn't anything edible in her cupboards. She'd told Michelle and Rami, who switched off watching the cats, to finish off anything in the fridge. "I was thinking we could just have something delivered, but it will probably be crazy tonight with the New Year's Eve holiday."

"Are you hungry now?" he asked.

"No, but if we wait too long, we might not get in at all."

"I tell you what. I'm going to use the bathroom, and when I come back, we'll pick something out."

"Sounds good. I'm going to go through my mail and ignore all the bills until tomorrow."

"Solid logic." He kissed the side of her head and disappeared down the hall.

Kara sat down at the table, and Theo immediately jumped into her lap while Robin Hood hopped from the floor to the chair to the table to get some pets, too, stepping all over the pile of letters and packages stacked on the surface.

"I know it, you guys had this house all to yourselves. Was Rami nice to you?"

"You're talking to the cats again, babe," Ben said, squeezing her shoulder as he walked behind and pulled out the chair next to her to sit in.

"I can't help it." She picked up one of the packages, a heavy white FedEx box. Michelle must have swung by work and seen the attempted delivery tag, because it had her name on it but the café's address.

"What do you feel like? Italian? Chinese? Mexican?"

Kara pulled the tab open and unfolded the box. "What about Thai?"

"Noodles it is. An hour for delivery. That's not bad, right?" Ben looked up from the dining app on his phone.

"Not bad at all," Kara said, pulling the paper-wrapped package from the box.

"What is that?"

"I don't know." Kara removed a small envelope from the top of the package and slipped the card out. Her gaze traveled over the neat handwriting, her eyes widening.

"It's from Mrs. Wyatt. One of our regulars."

"What did she say?"

"'Kara, you once asked me what I was typing on my laptop in your café every day. This is it. Enclosed is my newest Sabrina Wiley manuscript. Yes, that author I recommended was a shameless plug for my own books. For months, I couldn't write a word, until I wandered into a little café on Main Street one sunny summer day and you greeted me with such warmth, inviting me into your world, and I fell in love with Meow and Furever. Thank you for giving me the inspiration to write another love story, and for my dear, sweet Peanut. He makes this old lady's heart a little less lonely. I donated a portion of my advance for this book to your café and hope you can do some good with it. All my love and regards, Sabrina Wiley, aka Mrs. Wyatt.'"

"Kara, why are you crying?"

She couldn't explain it, but as she tore off the paper, she discovered a bound manuscript with the title *The Cat Café on Main Street*. Under Sabrina Wiley's name was a curling signature.

"I just can't believe this."

"What? That you inspired a book?"

"Yes. I've never inspired anyone."

"That's not true."

She snorted. "I'm pretty sure it is."

"Kara, you inspired me to adopt Chaos."

"I bullied you, you mean."

"You bullied me into fostering him," he admitted, dodging her swipe at his arm. "But your relationship with Theo? The way you care for every cat in your care? That is what is inspiring." Ben leaned forward and kissed her. "Your heart is inspiring."

"I love you," she sniffled.

"I love you, too." He tapped his finger on the manuscript and said, "What do you say we finish ordering food, head into the living room with a glass of wine, and read your book?"

"I thought you only liked audiobooks," she teased.

"I do, that's why you're going to read it to me. And I hope you don't have one of those droning voices when you read or I'm going to pass out."

Kara stuck out her tongue at him before getting up to grab a bottle of wine and two glasses from the cupboard. She walked into her living room, flicked on the white lights in the window, and clicked the lamp on her side table. After pouring two half-glasses, she climbed up onto the couch, tucking her feet under her with the manuscript on her lap.

"All right, food is ordered, and I am ready." Ben sat down behind her, pulling Kara's back against his front.

"Ben?"

"Yeah."

"Did you donate money to the café?"

He stopped stroking her arm for a beat. "Charity told you?"

"Yes. Why were you keeping it a secret?"

"I don't know. I just figured it meant more if I didn't have to brag about it."

Kara tipped her head back with a smile. "Thank you."

"All right, stop making me blush, and let's hear this story."

"'The Cat Café on Main Street.'" She turned the page and cleared her throat. "'Kira Langley sat on the windowsill, watching the bustling crowds on Main Street hurry by, a large tabby curled in her lap...'" As Kara read the manuscript aloud, Robin Hood hopped up between her feet, while Theo and Chaos climbed up onto the back of the couch above them, watching the twinkling lights flicker as the afternoon sunlight dipped into night.

After finishing the first chapter, she looked up at Ben over her shoulder. "Are you falling asleep?"

"Nope, I'm just enjoying this moment."

Kara lifted her head to give him a long, slow kiss. "Happy New Year, my love."

"May we have many more together."

Acknowledgments

So many fantastic people went into the making of this book, but first and foremost, thank you to my amazing husband and two wonderful children for giving me the time and space I needed to finish *A Cat Café Christmas*. I don't know what I would do without you!

To my awesome agent, Sarah, for believing in me and working so hard behind the scenes every day. I appreciate you.

To my editor at Forever, Alex, who was so patient every step of the way. Thank you for all you did to make *Cat Café* shine.

Erica, my dear friend, thank you for reading this book and for all of your insights. They were truly invaluable, and I treasure you.

My sister from another mister, Tina, who is always there for me, even when her zoo is going crazy. I love you.

Miss Tara, thank you for entertaining me with your dizzying Marco Polos.

For my Lattes, who are constantly tagging me in funny videos, telling others about my books, and helping me share all my news, thank you so much for your support. I know you are all busy, and it is an honor to have you as part of my team.

I need to thank my TikTok family of amazing authors,

bloggers, and fantastic creators who entertain and inspire me every day. Love you!

For my talented and enthusiastic bookstagrammers, who have shown me so much love and kindness, I can't wait to see your Candy Cane stacks this year.

And last but not least, my awesome family, from my parents to my in-laws and siblings, my aunts, uncles, cousins, nieces, and nephews . . . although many miles separate us, I thank you from the bottom of my heart for being so happy for me and cheering me on. I love you.

About the Author

Codi Gary is the author of twenty-nine contemporary and paranormal romance titles including bestselling books *Things Good Girls Don't Do* and *Hot Winter Nights* under the name Codi Gary and the laugh-out-loud Mistletoe series under the pen name Codi Hall. She loves writing about flawed characters finding their happily-ever-afters because everyone, even imperfect people, deserves an HEA.

A Northern California native, she, her husband, and their two children now live in southern Idaho where she enjoys kayaking, unpredictable weather, and spending time with her family, including her array of adorable fur babies. When she isn't glued to her computer making characters smooch, you can find her posting sunsets and pet pics on Instagram, making incredibly cringy videos for TikTok, reading the next book on her never-ending TBR list, or knitting away while rewatching *Supernatural* for the thousandth time!

You can learn more at:
CodiGarysBooks.com
Twitter @CodiGary
Facebook.com/CodiGarysBooks
Instagram @AuthorCodiHallGary